ΗΕΛΙΟΓΡΑΠΗΙ

THE SKYLIGHT SERIES

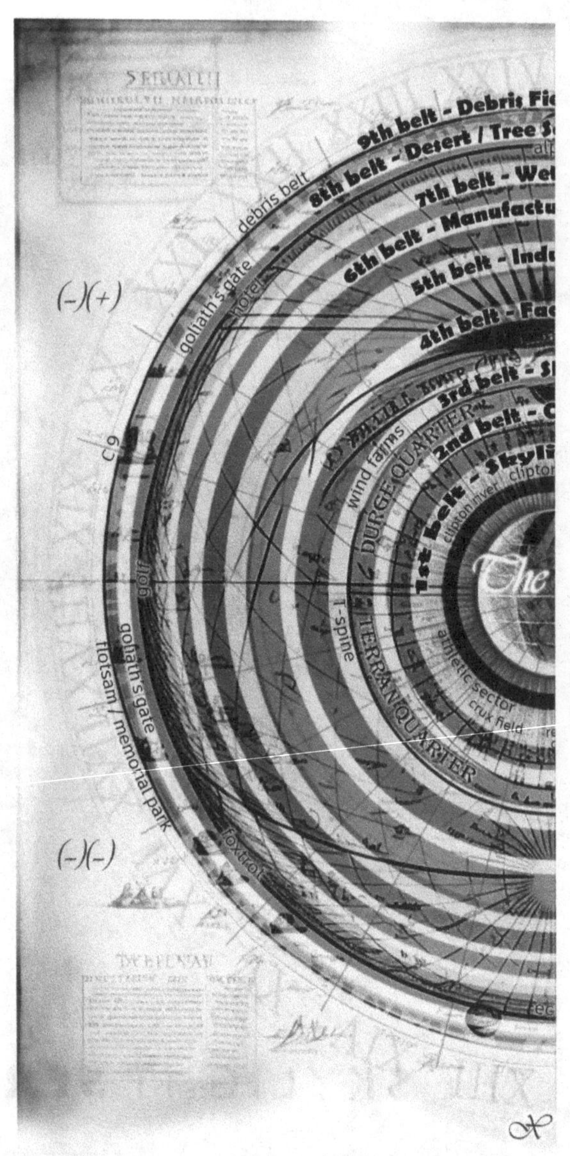
9th belt - Debris Fie
9th belt - Desert / Tree S
8th belt - Desert / Tree S
7th belt - Wet
6th belt - Manufactu
5th belt - Indu
4th belt - Fac
3rd belt - S
2nd belt - C
1st belt - Skyli
debris belt
goliath's gate
hotel
(-)(+)
c9
golf
goliath's gate
flotsam / memorial park
(-)(-)
foxtrot
wind farms
DURGE QUARTER
TERRAN QUARTER
T-spine
athletic sector
crux field
clipton river
clipton
The

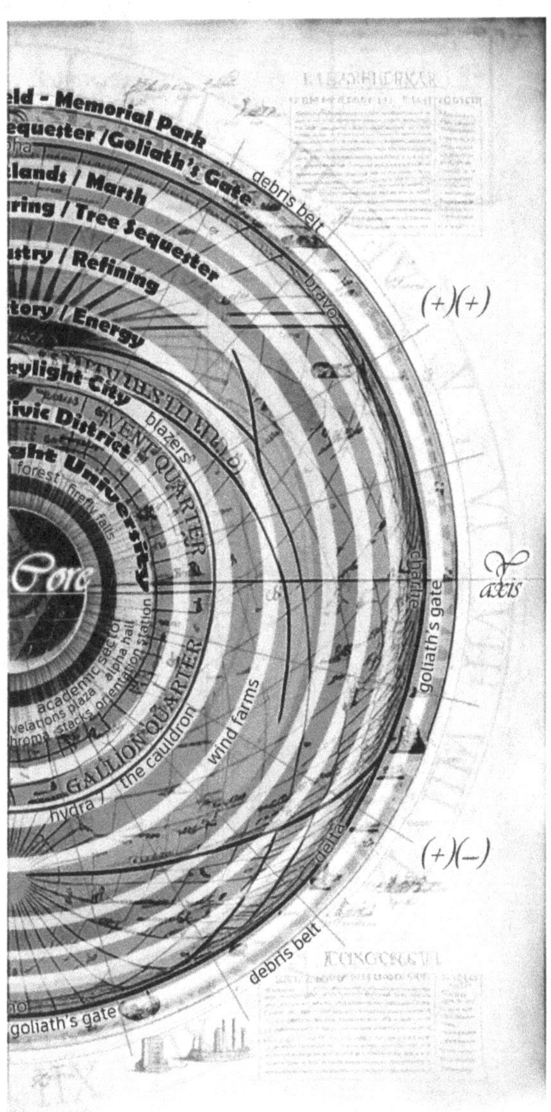
eld – Memorial Park
equester / Goliath's Gate
lands / Marsh
ring / Tree Sequester
stry / Refining
tory / Energy
kylight City
ivic District
ght University
forest
firefly falls
Core
alpha
debris belt
bravo
blazers
VENT QUARTER
academic sector
alpha hall
orientation station
velations plaza
stacks
hroma
GALLION QUARTER
the cauldron
wind farms
hydra
charlie
goliath's gate
delta
debris belt
goliath's gate
(+)(+)
(+)(–)
axis
axis

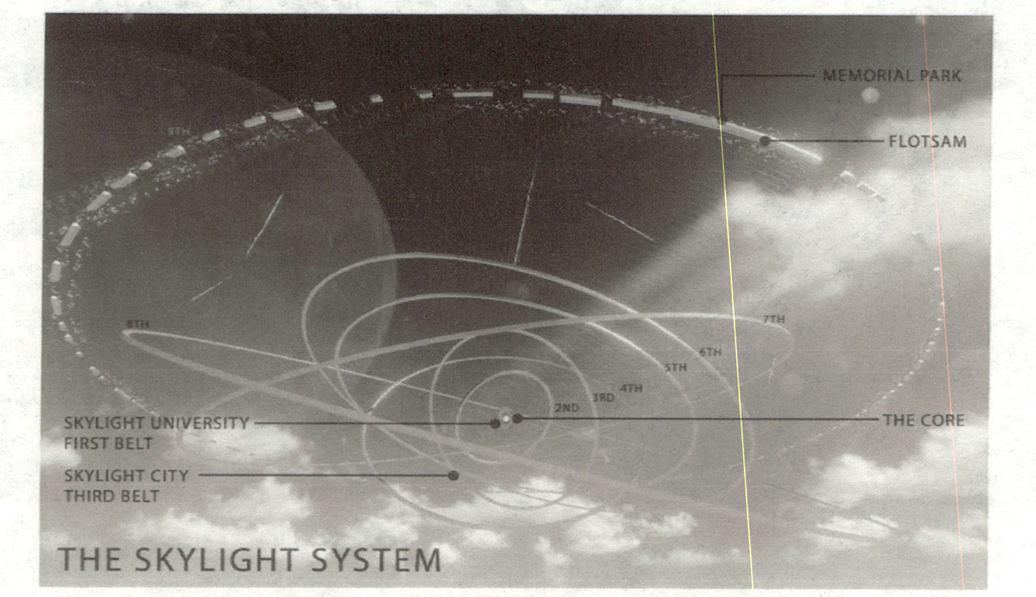
MEMORIAL PARK
FLOTSAM
9TH
8TH
7TH
6TH
5TH
4TH
3RD
2ND
SKYLIGHT UNIVERSITY
FIRST BELT
SKYLIGHT CITY
THIRD BELT
THE CORE
THE SKYLIGHT SYSTEM

SKYLIGHT UNIVERSITY

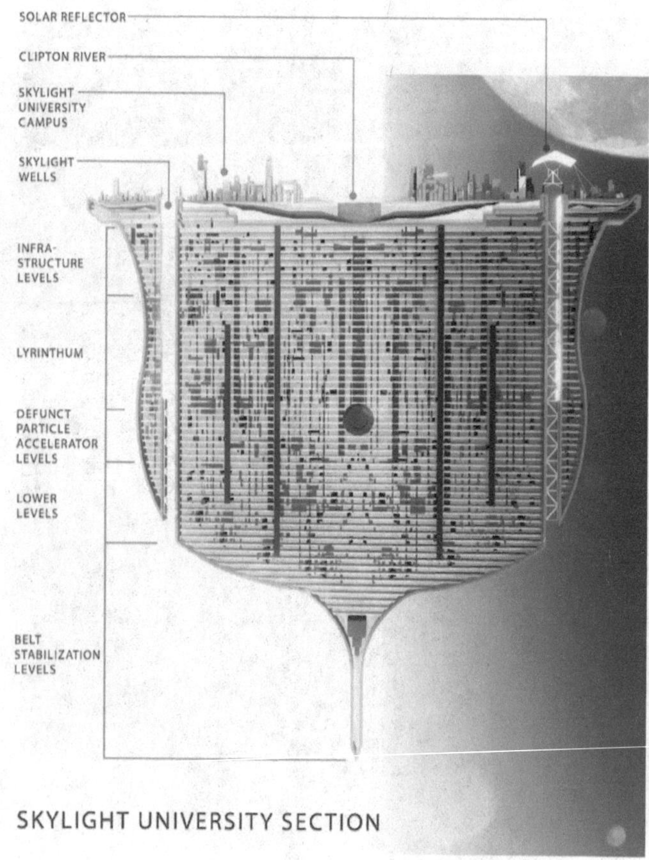

SKYLIGHT UNIVERSITY SECTION

ALBRIGHT
SHILOE
ANNAKA
TYBERIUS
BOOKER
HARRIET
DIJINN
TI-LEER
CORD
SOLAN
KAMBER
JET
VAIL
BRIT
BOFISTO
JOSHIA
SOJAHN
BO
HURSE
TETRA
MYRANDA
RENZIE
MOSSTROM
SYBOLD

UPPER
OBSERVATION
DECK
OUTER
SKIN
OUTER
DECKS
OBSERVATION
TUBE
INTERNAL
COGS
SURVEILLANCE
LEVEL

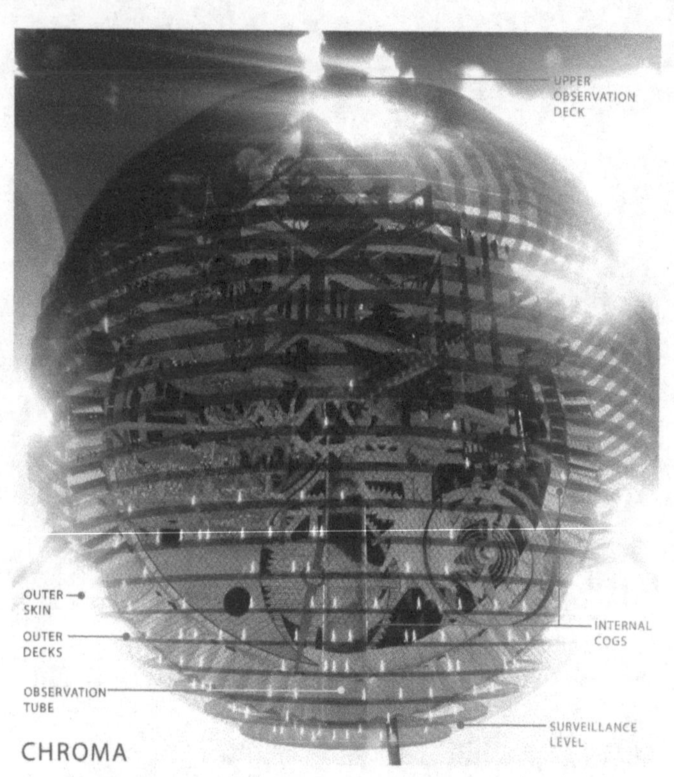

CHROMA

THE SKYLIGHT FALLOUT

BOOK TWO

OF

THE SKYLIGHT SERIES

www.theskylightseries.com

ISBN: 978-1-7363029-3-4

Edited by Caroline Barnhill

On the cover: Solan Alexander

***

THE SKYLIGHT SERIES

BOOK ONE: *THE PRISM EFFECT*

BOOK TWO: *THE SKYLIGHT FALLOUT*

BOOK THREE: *THE HELIOGRAPHI MEMOIRS*

BOOK FOUR: (FORTHCOMING)

BOOK FIVE: (FORTHCOMING)

THE
SKYLIGHT
FALLOUT

J WINT

"Every living being is an engine geared to the wheelwork of the universe. Though seemingly affected only by its immediate surroundings, the sphere of external influence extends to infinite distance."
—*Nikola Tesla*

For Ramsey

CONTENTS

CHAPTER 1

An Uneasy Handshake
Four Years Later

ΑΒΓΔΕΖΗΘΙΚΛ**Μ**
ΝΞΟΠΡΣΤΥΦΧΨΩ

J ET STROUD KNELT in the shadows.

He steadied his breathing and waited, trying to quiet the voices inside his head. A rat scampered by his foot, oblivious to Jet with his cloak drawn. He was nearly invisible, thanks to the cloak's ability to bend light around him. It was quiet down in the belly of the first belt, only the occasional sound of dripping water could be heard. The steel corridors smelled of dust mixed with an acrid scent. If it had a color, he imagined it would be a dull gray.

He waited for a long second and searched the area with his mind, lengthening out to feel for other nearby Heliographi. But he could only sense traces of ghostly voices, ethereal screams from other dimensions so common to this particular area. Somewhere behind him, cloaked and hidden, were DiJinn and Cord. But their thoughts were hidden from him. Any other Heliographi sneaking around down in Lyrinthum, a vast maze of tunnels deep below Skylight University, would be undetectable too. Whether it was Lucem or Atrum, he would sense no signs of either down here.

He continued, winding his way deeper into the bowels of Lyrinthum and darting between shadows. He had memorized most of the underground tunnel system now, after spending nearly four years wandering them since his days as a student. Still, he had to stop occasionally to regain his bearings.

He was approaching the rendezvous point, which was inside the Lyrinthum Particle Accelerator, at least what was left of it. The defunct atom smasher had been a real wonder, Cord had told him. During the early days of the university, planners used the interior of the belt for the accelerator's loop. Here, university scientists could smash particles together at the speed of light and gain knowledge about the origin of the universe. There was still enough juice left in the old equipment to create interference from other tracking devices. It was a perfect place to meet, considering the nature of his current business.

In years past, the old particle accelerator had been home to millions of experiments and trillions of atoms smashing into each other. The leftover residue from those explosions seemed to be transcribed onto the walls in a supernatural sort of way. He could almost see the remnants of those violent collisions with his eyes, and the walls seemed to glow in his vision. These halls felt haunted by the random voices he heard in his mind, whispering from the shadows. Solan had once mentioned the voices were haunted ghost particles—a gateway to other dimensions sought so desperately by scientists. *If they knew what inhabited those dimensions, they might not be so anxious to uncover it,* she had told him. *The human mind is not equipped to conceive what lies beyond our known dimensions.*

He had only discovered this area of Lyrinthum thanks to DiJinn. Apparently, she used this place for *sensitive* discussions from time to time. Jet was learning who the rulebreakers were in the Lucem. DiJinn and Cord seemed to be the two he could trust with this type of matter. Of course, Solan was trustworthy, as were all the other Lucem. But only DiJinn and Cord were crazy enough to help him with what he was about to do. They were the rebels, and DiJinn was always up for a bit of rule breaking. He had grown fond of her over the last several years and knew he could share certain things with her, just like with Cord. *Bending the rules a bit never hurt anyone,* Cord had said, and Jet couldn't agree more.

What he was doing bordered on insanity, maybe even conspiracy. Though he didn't know all of the rules yet, he was pretty sure that conspiring with the Atrum, their sworn enemy, probably wasn't on the ethics list. He might even be expelled from the Agency if caught. He wondered what the hell he hoped to accomplish here tonight.

He wiped sweat from his brow, not entirely from the humidity. From this depth, the air was thick and stagnant.

He slowed, finally recognizing the area he was in. He was close now.

He caught a flutter from his left, and a blurry mirage shot forward.

He had arrived.

Neither Jet nor the Atrum made a move, both assessing their surroundings. A long minute passed, and Jet finally lowered his hood, emerging from the shadows. Seconds later, the Atrum did the same. They faced each other, and Jet tried to probe his thoughts. The Atrum laughed and tapped his forehead.

In the next instant, someone grabbed Jet's arm and held him in a choke hold. The grip tightened but held steady.

"Tisk," the Atrum said. "Letting your guard down like that? Not what I expected from someone with your reputation. The Skylight Fallout, some say."

Jet couldn't see who was behind him, but he knew the Atrum standing before him. "I assumed we could trust each other," he said. "Apparently, our deal is off, Hurse?"

"We never had a deal to begin with." Hurse stepped forward into a moonlit shaft from the mechanical vent above. The lunar green moonlight shone down across Hurse's face, highlighting his short black hair and neatly trimmed beard. Shadow lines followed the curvature of his eye sockets and cheekbones, making him appear as a floating skull. His baritone accented voice filled the chamber in contrast to his relatively narrow frame and stature. His eyes shone brightly in a velvet-burgundy glow, burning intensely in the dim light. Like the other twenty-three Heliographi—each with their own unique color—there was no pupil or iris, just a vibrant illumination so disturbing that it frightened most people off.

"I could have you killed right now, as you stand there and I here," Hurse said.

"But you and I both know you don't want that," Jet replied, knowing this was just for show, and a bit of humor. "Besides," Jet continued. "I assumed you wouldn't come alone. So, neither did I."

DiJinn was on Hurse before he could turn. She kicked him in the thigh, then held him in the same headlock. She laughed, a bit too harshly in the cavernous tunnel. Jet could see she was enjoying herself; her thick accent was always more pronounced when she was having fun.

"Hanley Hurse," she said. "Always that little trick up your sleeve! I know you too well. And is that Miss Sojahn Quark I see? Goodness…aren't we quite the friendly group?"

Sojahn tightened her grip and looked at DiJinn. "Move on, Jinn. This doesn't concern you. You're out of place."

"Actually, this is just my place. We have unfinished business, if you'll recall."

A third Atrum shot from the shadows and leapt at DiJinn. But hiding nearby was Cord and he threw an elbow into its ribs. There was a howl, and Cord was on top of the shadow, pulling its hood off.

"This party just keeps getting better," he said. "Vail Hart, I believe."

Jet felt Sojahn's grip relax a bit, and it was just enough. He flipped around while she was distracted and bent her arm into his own elbow and forced her to her knee. A little move Solan had taught him—he'd have to thank her for that.

"That's enough!" Jet said. He let Sojahn go and shoved her toward Hurse. "It's not what we're here for, and we all know it."

DiJinn released Hurse and spun him around to face her. Her red hair shone in the light, her greenish glowing eyes flickering dangerously. Jet could see she was ready for a fight. There was more to her and Hurse, it appeared.

Hurse backed away and smiled at her with a wink.

Cord stood and lifted Vail with him and gave her a shove.

She gave him a long glance, "Mister brainiac himself…so arrogant. It's just a matter of time, Ledbetter. That pompous attitude will be your downfall someday, and I can't wait to see it."

The three Atrum stood on one side of the chamber as DiJinn, Cord and Jet waited on the other. Jet could sense Hurse probing his thoughts, trying to gain access. He shook his head. "Keep it here, Hurse."

"Is this everyone?" DiJinn asked, sounding annoyed. "Anymore of you skulkin' about in the shadows?"

Hurse stepped forward. "What is it you want, Stroud?"

"You know why I'm here," Jet replied.

Hurse waited silently.

"I know who your warden is," Jet continued. "She's a freshman by the name of Tetra Wride. She's your responsibility and you're sworn to protect her."

"As is Kamber Caster yours," Hurse said evenly, calmly. "Seems we are at an impasse."

"Which is why I'm here," Jet said.

"Are you suggesting a truce?" Hurse asked.

"Well, why not?" Jet lifted his hands and placed them on his hips. "Wouldn't that be easier for us both?"

"Ah…I see now. You believe we should just…trust each other? It's that simple, is it? Just like we've always done over the years?" Hurse mocked.

Jet didn't respond. He felt DiJinn tense behind him, ready to fight. He held out his hand for her to stand down.

"Centuries. No, millennia," Hurse continued, pacing. "We've been at this for a very long time, and you believe a truce will suddenly work? Well, I'll admit that is an interesting proposal. I suppose in return that the Lucem would also refrain from hostilities?"

"Toward just those two girls?" DiJinn asked.

"Who can say," Sojahn replied, glaring at DiJinn.

"Yes, we will," Jet said. "I will personally ensure that nothing happens to Tetra during that time. You have my word."

Jet watched Vail as Hurse spoke. She kept tapping the nape of her neck; three taps followed by two lines with her index finger, but it was barely perceptible. Jet tugged at her old locket that he still wore below his shirt. *Was she trying to tell him something?*

Hurse looked over his shoulder at Sojahn and Vail, then returned Jet's gaze. "If you value your warden's life, not a Lucem goes near Tetra, or the deal is off. I sense your concern, Stroud. You've risked a lot for this little meeting. Let's hope it pays off for you."

Hurse, Sojahn and Vail folded into their cloaks and vanished in a cloud of smoke, leaving Jet, Cord and DiJinn alone in the dark.

"That was fun. I doubt he'll stick to the agreement, though," DiJinn said and looked over at Jet and Cord. "I'll be on assignment tomorrow, escorting a shipment in the morning. If you need anything, call me."

"Jinn, wait," Jet said. "Solan will kill me if she finds out about this."

"No worries, lips are sealed," she replied. "Look, I understand why you want this, but you can't trust the Atrum, 'specially Hurse. 'Bout fifty years ago, Hurse, Quark, Ti-Leer and I were all school mates, like it was with you, Cord, Bo and Vail. Hurse got bullied, a lot more than the others. I don't blame him for hating those people. But that was a long time ago, and he's different now. Be careful, he's as devious as they come."

Cord waited until DiJinn had left and turned to face Jet. "Before you leave, I should tell you that I've made progress on Albright's code. I believe I've finally cracked it."

Jet stared at Cord in the dark corridor. Their glowing eyes lit the space between them. It was a bit of a shock, considering that Cord had been working on it for over four years now. "That's a big deal, Cord! Aren't you excited? Something else bothering you?"

"We can throw a party later, there's still work to be done. What I know is that the Skylight Fallout will trigger a clue during the Century Eclipse, one might refer to it as Albright's easter egg. I believe it's the key needed to locate the missing Heliographi Memoirs."

"How did you finally figure it out?"

Cord lowered his voice. "After the summit, we'll talk more."

Jet and Cord went their separate ways as they left Lyrinthum. Jet thought about what Cord had said and was anxious to hear more. But he was also just as curious about Vail. Had she sent him a signal, and if so, what did it mean? Should he tell the other Lucem about it? He knew he was playing with fire. These backchannels with the Atrum could backfire with his life as the consequence. He didn't relish the thought of any encounter without backup, and he wasn't sure how far DiJinn and Cord were willing to go.

But he had survived tougher odds by listening to that intuitive voice in his head. He was willing to take risks if he thought the outcome was worth it. And right now, his intuitive voice was urging him to figure out what Vail was trying to tell him.

He also wondered if he had done the right thing tonight by meeting Hurse. Had he unintentionally called attention to Kamber? Maybe she would have been better off without him butting in? Jet knew one thing for certain, though. It was his sworn duty to protect her until she could join the Lucem. Just like Solan had protected him when he was a student, it was now his turn to do the same for Kamber. He also knew that no matter what truce he struck with the Atrum, they would try to kill her as soon as the opportunity presented itself.

CHAPTER 2
Ambush

ΑΒΓΔΕΖ**Η**ΘΙΚΛΜ
ΝΞΟΠΡΣΤΥΦΧΨΩ

EARLY THE NEXT day, DiJinn and another Lucem named Ti-Leer sat next to a team of elite reconnaissance troops—more often referred to as *recon*—as their transport skiff bumped along between the eighth and ninth belts' air space. There was an excess of cloud cover, which was typical for the Skylight System. Thanks to the humidity that formed around each belt, water vapor gathered near the surface, and low-lying clouds regularly formed, which would sometimes build into thunderstorms, though rare. Today, the weather was fair with little more than gray curtains of mist, which occasionally refracted the sun into millions of tiny rainbows, often referred to as a prism effect by local citizens.

Their mission was to escort a shipment of refined rare-earth minerals to the eighth belt. Ti-Leer, whose alias was Professor Keoff, snoozed next to her. He was stout and portly from his excessive drinking habit. His thick brown hair fell across his eyes like a mop, covering most of his face. He and DiJinn were each other's warden and had been inducted into the Lucem together. He was like a brother to her, and they worked well as a team. But they also fought like siblings, and he wore on her nerves. Still, he had saved her life countless times, and she owed him a debt of gratitude.

She kicked at his short legs. "Oi! Wake up, Ti! How can you sleep through this noise?"

Ti-Leer scowled at her through his lime-green glowing eyes, turned in the opposite direction and went back to sleep.

DiJinn shook her head and looked back out the open bay door of the skiff. Over the last several months, the trade routes they often used had been attacked by marauders, and the Agency had called on the Lucem for aid.

Those supplies were needed for a top-secret project known as Goliath's Gate. It would replace the defunct particle accelerator located in Lyrinthum, buried below the university where they'd met the Atrum just yesterday. That accelerator's size had proven too small and been decommissioned nearly eighty years ago. The Skylight government now had a more ambitious plan with Goliath's Gate. The covert operation called for a much larger particle collider to be housed in the hull of the eighth belt. Its diameter was many times greater than the old collider and would allow for faster speeds and larger collisions. But the cost of the undertaking was tremendous. Furthermore, it required resources known as rare-earth minerals, which had to be mined and purified before delivery, a very expensive process.

Theoretically, Goliath's Gate would generate enough energy to smash atoms at high enough speeds to allow scientists to see things previously inconceivable. Now that it was nearly operational, it needed to be kept a secret, and protected. The materials used at its eight detectors were extremely valuable, and worth a fortune. The Agency's best troops, the elite recon, along with the Lucem as backup, were tasked to protect it. She didn't care about colliders, precious minerals or the Agency's agenda. It was all busy-body stuff for people like President Harok. The action and conflict surrounding the project... now *that* was enticing.

General Dane sat across from her. He had several new cuts along his face and neck. As long as she had known him, he was constantly banged up. He loved being in the thick of the action and would someday get himself killed, she suspected. But he was slick and had outfoxed death so many times, she often wondered if he might be a Lucem in disguise. Though she fought down the thought, she had a secret desire to know him better…much better.

"Ten minutes!" Dane barked to the group.

The recon troops were the top soldiers in the Agency. They'd been through some of the toughest training and survival courses, deadly in hand-to-hand combat and qualified with the latest weapons. She could rely on them but wouldn't need to. In fact, that's why she was there, in case the elite needed backup.

Outside the frigates' window, large chunks of metal debris could be seen in the distance. The ninth belt, or what was left of it, circled several kilometers outside the eighth belt's airspace.

As the line of frigates passed through the mist, a warning light blipped. Ti-Leer woke instantly and stood. "Breach!" he bellowed and pulled his hood over his head and disappeared. DiJinn swept her red ponytails under her hood and also disappeared. She felt their transport bank at a steep incline as it shot toward the back of the line of frigates. A missile-shaped skiff had maneuvered above the last frigate and latched onto its hull.

"They've cut through already," General Dane yelled and tapped his helmet's visor, and it slid closed.

Their transport hovered above the agency frigate. The bay door's bottom dropped out, and the recon troops, led by two mech units, surged down the zip lines. Dane ordered the rest of the recon through the bay door and followed. Ti-Leer and DiJinn leapt the twenty meters and landed deftly on the frigate's hull. Dane found the emergency access hatch, pressed in a code and the hatch spiraled open. The recon troops crashed through, rail guns locked and loaded.

Ti-Leer and DiJinn waited until the last troop disappeared, then leapt in, hoods drawn to avoid being seen.

What DiJinn witnessed inside the frigate was a blood bath.

It appeared the marauders had been prepared and picked off the majority of recon troops as soon as they hit the deck. A few of them had managed to find cover and returned fire. Both mech units lay mangled in a heap of steel. She could hardly believe it. The mech units were practically bulletproof.

How the hell could so many elite troops have been gunned down so easily?

She could only see a handful of marauders wearing a dilapidated patchwork of graphene armor and basic rail guns. Nothing fancy.

They have an Atrum! Ti-Leer said, projecting his thoughts to warn her.

She turned just in time to see the blurred motion of an Atrum. It sensed the presence of Ti-Leer and DiJinn and paused. DiJinn understood now. The dead recon troops were from the Atrum, not the marauders. She saw the faint symbol floating over the Atrum's left hand and clenched her fists. It was the symbol of a letter P.

It was Sojahn Quark.

There were fewer than a dozen recon left, led by Dane. He continued to bark orders at them as rounds pelted the reinforced graphene shields they hid behind. The rounds, powered by magnetically charged rail guns, whizzed by with deadly force. The heavy fire held the recon pinned as the marauders loaded the cargo onto their ship.

DiJinn dodged the rounds and moved closer to Sojahn. The Atrum saw her coming and stayed behind just long enough to make sure the shipment was loaded and shot up the opening and into the marauder's skiff. It disengaged before DiJinn could reach it.

Dane ordered the remaining troops back onto the recon skiff.

"Follow it," he said calmly.

The transport pilot closed the hatch and maneuvered behind the marauder's ship.

"It's damn quick!" DiJinn said. She could see they wouldn't be able to catch up to it.

"Are there any registration marks?" Ti-Leer asked.

Dane shook his head and wiped blood from a cut over his right eye. "Nothing. And I don't recognize that style of skiff. They're heading for the ninth belt wreckage. If they make it, we'll never find them in all that junk. Pilot, did you intercept any transmissions?"

"None, sir."

Then the marauder ship disappeared.

"They've cloaked," Ti-Leer said.

"Really?" DiJinn said with a hint of sarcasm and gave him a sidelong glance.

Dane hammered the console. "Harok's not gonna be happy about this!"

They slowed down and cruised into the debris belt. There was so much junk that the smaller bits sounded like a hailstorm raining down on the ship's hull.

"This is pointless, D.J.," Ti-Leer said. "Unless we can get a tracking device on one of them, those ships are too fast. The cloaking ability makes it unlikely we'll ever find out where they're taking the stolen cargo."

"Dane, what was in that cargo?" DiJinn asked.

"Refined rare-earth minerals. That's all these marauders ever take. Some of the other groups are after other precious metals, but the rare-earth is the most valuable to the Agency. It'll be impossible to complete Goliath's Gate without it."

"Why would marauders want it?" she asked. "And why the hell would the Atrum partner with these marauders?"

"No idea. The black market for rare-earth really isn't that lucrative. I've been tracking it, but none of the stolen rare-earth minerals ever come back on-line."

DiJinn listened to Dane halfheartedly. Inside, she was kicking herself for not taking point on the boarding crew. It was a shame that so many able-bodied soldiers had been taken out. But Sol had directed her to act as backup only. The elite recon always ran point, and Sol didn't want to interfere in their operations. But what had just happened wasn't a good look for the Lucem. She would find Sojahn and make her pay; that made her smile. Now, there was a score to settle, and she *needed* scores to settle.

On the flight back, Ti-Leer sat near the open side door of the skiff. DiJinn looked in on the hologram of Harok as Dane updated him on the raids. The skiff pilot followed close behind the other three skiffs full of recon troops. DiJinn looked away from the hologram. She felt something out of place and gave Ti-Leer a glance.

You feel it? she asked, projecting her thoughts forward to him.

Ti-Leer nodded.

The soldiers seated around them chatted quietly and seemed complacent.

"What is it? What's wrong?" Harok asked through the hologram.

"Dunno," DiJinn said. She was about to say something else when an explosion ripped through the cockpit and ejected the pilot and co-pilot violently. The skiff immediately went into a tailspin. DiJinn grabbed the harness nearby, and Ti-Leer did the same. A fighter skiff uncloaked and sped toward them.

The **Skylight Fallout**

The recon troops started to bail out. They strapped hover packs on, which allowed them limited mobility until they hit the ground. But there weren't enough packs to go around. Two recon soldiers were left. DiJinn grabbed one troop and Ti-Leer the other. Two mech units sat in their charging stations, and she tapped one to activate it. She shoved it out the side door and used her free arm to grab on to the mech unit's shoulder. Ti-Leer followed right behind her. The artificial intelligence on the mech unit took over, and its propulsion system fired up and slowed her fall about five meters above impact. The wrecked skiff plummeted just behind her. She hoisted the unconscious recon soldier over her shoulder and sprinted off just as the skiff's wreckage crashed down, leaving an impact crater in the forest floor. The shockwave from the explosion hit DiJinn in the back, knocking her to the ground.

She stood and checked herself for injuries, noting that her cloak had shielded her from the skiff's shrapnel. She immediately searched for Ti-Leer, who had landed nearby. His mech unit was split in half, not being able to completely slow their fall in time. The soldier next to him, Captain Thune, leaned against Ti-Leer for support.

"What just happened?" Thune asked.

"An assassination attempt," Ti-Leer said. "They were obviously gunning for us. Our skiff was the only one attacked."

"Yeah, I can see that," she replied. "The fighter skiff that hit us, what type was it?"

"A newer prototype. Jammer class, not cheap. Looks like they're putting the Agency's rare-earth to good use."

"It was cloaked when it hit us," she said. "Our pilots should've had shields up, right? That's standard protocol."

"Yes," Dane answered. "None of my troops are that unprepared."

Captain Thune sat down and pulled off her boot. Some blood covered her sock, and she winced. "Why were our shields down?"

"Because it was an inside job," Dane replied. "Those pilots knew what was coming. Probably bought off, families compensated. Come on. Let's regroup and get to that last station. I saw it a few klicks back."

The soldier DiJinn had saved woke, rolled over and threw up.

Dane used one of the handheld holopads to locate the other troops and launched a flare. Soon there were about ten soldiers surrounding them. About half of them had sustained some sort of injury. Dane led the way with Ti-Leer and DiJinn scouting ahead, cloaked and hidden in the underbrush. Captain Thune kept near the back of the line, limping badly but showing no signs of pain. They had fashioned two makeshift stretchers out of tree limbs for two of the seriously injured troops.

The **Skylight Fallout**

The group pushed through the thick brush as the sun continued to drop. Ti-Leer communicated with DiJinn through thoughts. He tried to convince her to push ahead and get back to the other Lucem with news about the ambush. The Agency was deeply compromised, considering what had just happened. Even the elite troops were being bought off.

But DiJinn wouldn't leave the troops in this state. She just hoped they didn't meet any more resistance…but that was wishful thinking.

DiJinn sensed movement ahead and paused. Camouflaged in the treetops were two snipers; they'd almost walked right into an ambush. She sent a message to Ti-Leer and hurried back to Dane.

She grabbed him by the shoulder and pulled him down to the ground as she uncloaked. She ran a finger across her throat and pointed to the trees ahead. The rest of the troops stopped and dropped instantly. Ti-Leer appeared beside them.

"Pair of snipers 'bout twenty meters ahead," she whispered.

"Can we skirt around them?" Dane asked.

"No need to," Ti-Leer said. "I can take them out."

"I'm 'fraid they're just a distraction," DiJinn said. "Something tells me there's more just beyond."

"I've called for extraction," Captain Thune whispered. "But there's no communication ping. Someone's taken us off-line."

DiJinn gave Ti-Leer a grim look. "They want us, not them. There's no reason these troops should pay the price."

"You want me to flush them out?" Ti-Leer asked.

"If you can take out those snipers, I'll draw the rest. Dane, it'll be clear behind us. Can you get 'em back to the crash site? There'll be search and rescue crews by soon."

"Should've stayed there to begin with," Thune said.

"We had no idea we were being cased, Thune," Dane said. "Okay, Jinn. Good luck."

Ti-Leer was already cloaked and moving to the treetops. DiJinn followed the recon troops just far enough to make sure they were okay, then she returned and watched for Ti-Leer's signal.

The signal wasn't difficult to spot when the second sniper hurled through the air and to the ground. DiJinn sprinted straight ahead, making as much commotion as possible. She saw about a dozen marauders and a few heavily modified mech units. The marauders didn't concern her too much, but the modified mech units were another story. They had an onboard targeting system and could see into different spectrums, making her cloaking ability useless. These mechs reminded her of the prototypes currently being developed by the Agency. They were becoming more advanced and deadlier with each new version.

She paused just long enough to give them a good look at her, then she sprinted off. The sound of the mech unit's propulsion system roared to life behind her.

I'll handle the mech units, she thought to Ti-Leer. *Pick off the remaining marauders; they'll be slower.*

She was quick but knew she couldn't outrun the flying mech units. A clearing ahead appeared, and she decided to make her stand there. The two mech units cut their thrusters and slammed to the ground. They were about three meters in height and made of reinforced graphene, which was a nearly indestructible material. Their heavy rail guns were mounted over one shoulder and spit out rounds as she moved between them. She flipped and leapt onto the back of one as rounds pelted it from the other mech unit. She focused her thoughts on the mounted rail gun and twisted it toward the mech unit's head. The slugs hammered the side of it and found a soft spot. The mech unit powered down and collapsed to the forest ground.

The second mech unit's system had to recalibrate, giving her enough time to roll under its thick legs. It lifted one and kicked at her, but it was slow and managed to stomp on the downed mech unit's head. She scaled up its leg and grasped one of its arms. Just then, Ti-Leer burst through the underbrush and grappled at its other arm. Together, they pulled, using their feet to gain leverage, and ripped its arms off.

Ti-Leer lifted the arm and thrust it through the downed mech, then turned to DiJinn. "This was no ordinary ambush, D.J. These marauders were gunning for someone specific."

"And I think I know who," DiJinn said. "That's what bothers me."

CHAPTER 3
The Summit

THE SUMMITS WERE annoying to Jet. He had been a part of the Agency for just four years but already found these meetings to be dreadfully cumbersome. Plus, it took precious time out of his training schedule. As far as he could tell, the other Lucem hated the summits too. Even Ti-Leer, who normally reveled in this sort of thing, would often doze off, his stubby frame slouched over with thick bifocals sliding down his nose. All the Lucem were required to use their alias at summits, and everywhere else outside of the Lucem quadrant, to help conceal their true identity.

Although everyone in the Agency knew they were really Heliographi, being forced to wear an alias seemed like an excessive precaution to Jet.

As Jet prepared for the summit that morning, he slipped on his ring and transformed into his alias; an assistant athletic director named Gunter Kepp. His guise was that of a well-built middle-aged man of average height and weight, which matched his own athletic frame. His broken nose—thanks to all the abuse he'd taken as a child—straightened, and his fair skin—from growing up in a cave system—darkened. His shoulder length black hair changed to an umber color with three-day old scruff around his chin to match. Most importantly, his turquoise glowing eyes had been changed to normal brown. This alias was, of course, a fictitious person created by the Agency, specifically to hide his real identity. For the next thirty or forty years, he would use this guise, and it would age over that time until he could be given another. The background for this alias had been pre-programed into the system to cover his tracks.

He had been given the athletic director assignment due to his forceful suggestion. He knew he would probably never play blaze again, but this would allow him to get closer to the sport he loved. It also got him closer to his old friend, Cutter Jade, who still played on the university blaze team as a senior. Together, they had played the sport as kids in the ARC district, where they'd first met.

Cutter had gone into a depressive nosedive after Jet's death, which had been fabricated and leaked to the media during his first year at the university. But he had grown more concerned about Cutter in the following years and wanted to keep a closer eye on him. Solan had allowed his assignment with one caveat: he was to have no contact with Cutter.

Jet hopped into his Agency skiff and set a course for the third belt and a place known as the Cauldron. He maneuvered his skiff between large chunks of debris and other leftover remnants of the ruined ninth belt. A mistake by the Skylight planners had left a portion of the belt outside the system's protective atmosphere, and a meteorite storm had destroyed it almost a century ago. Jet had often wondered if this oversite had been intentional, though.

Flight patterns in the Skylight System were pretty direct, although there were dedicated lanes to specific destinations. Jet guided his skiff into one of the thousands of lanes heading to Skylight City, which was the system's largest city and occupied the entire third belt. As he approached, traffic increased considerably with every manner of skiff imaginable.

The belts were each nearly two kilometers wide, and their cross-section reminded Jet of a great ship's hull; a wide top deck for buildings, forest and rivers, with hundreds of sublevels that housed the infrastructure needed to support it all.

When Jet arrived at Skylight City, he navigated his skiff around the belt, marveling again at its design. Massive solar sails redirected daylight into the skylight wells, and towering skyscrapers breached the low-lying mist. The sheer number of buildings packed onto the belt was mindboggling. Still, the planners had managed to carve out green space and parks for the citizens, following Albright's belief that nature should be at the center of the system.

The secret summits were located in an older industrial portion of the city, below an abandoned factory nicknamed the Cauldron. During every skylight eclipse at that location, which amounted to about every four weeks, this summit was held to discuss sensitive matters. The Skylight System's president, Jon Harok, who had recently been elected to a four-year term, would address the entire Agency. Usually in attendance was a select group of city officials and department heads, as well as the Lucem. When missions were doled out for elite recon teams, the Lucem were typically assigned to assist as backup.

Jet had gotten used to working with the elite soldiers and had even befriended a few. But missions could turn deadly, as he had witnessed just recently. His last operation had resulted in the first fatality under his watch, and it had shaken him up a bit. Solan assured him that all Lucem had experienced a fatality before. In fact, DiJinn and Ti-Leer had just yesterday lost more than a dozen troops in an ambush. Solan reminded him to stay alert. *For the safety of the other troops*, she had said. *So they can go home to their families at the end of the day.*

Jet docked his skiff in an underground hanger near the factory. He found his way to the correct corridor in a maze of equipment, defunct valves, and gauges. He eventually stepped into an antechamber and found Cord waiting for him.

Cord's alias looked much like an older version of himself. He was still tall and wiry, but his thick black hair and signature goatee were peppered with gray, and a pair of gold wire-rimmed glasses gave him a distinguished look. His olive-toned skin was the same, but his overall appearance was just different enough to hide his true identity. As Doctor Vinculum, Cord had access to all the resources he could ever need to continue his work.

"You're late," Cord said.

A procession of officers moved past them, and Jet and Cord fell in line at the tail end. They took a seat near the back and settled in as the crowd murmured in hushed tones around them.

The summit was held in a large chamber that reminded Jet of an oversized courtroom. It was too formal for his taste, and it felt out of place in the old factory setting. It was large enough to hold a thousand people, though a quarter of that usually showed for the summits. Jet scanned the room and located the other Lucem sprinkled around the space, all wearing their disguises. Solan and DiJinn sat next to the defense secretary. Jet looked for Tyberius, but he was missing. In fact, he'd been missing all week. Perhaps he was away on a mission, but it was odd that Solan hadn't mentioned it.

Jet leaned over to Cord. "You get your assignment yet?"

"The MathWorks lab again this year," Cord said. "Frankly, it's the best place for me, considering the complex work I'm doing."

Cord had been working on solving something he called *the splinter code*, a unique pattern in Albright's table. The painting called *The Verification* had been discovered by Solan over a decade ago when she had been a student at Skylight University. During that time, it had remained hidden in the stacks, a forgotten area of the library's basement. Within its ancient paint strokes, the painting held a mysterious mathematical language and hinted at prophesies, some of which Cord believed to be secrets about their ancient race, known as the Heliographi.

But was there more to it all? Cord seemed to think so and had tasked himself with continuing to solve it.

Shiloe Van Saint, the Lucem who had composed the work of art, might have more information, and Tyberius had been anxious to locate her. But unfortunately, Shiloe had been missing for almost a century now. Even

Christian Albright, their leader, had been unable to find her, and now he too had been missing for over a decade.

"What about you?" Cord asked. "Did you receive your assignment for the year?"

"I'm back at Crux Field again, except this year I've been promoted to an assistant athletic director. It puts me even closer to Cutter and Kamber, not to mention blaze."

President Harok took the podium and looked out at the crowd. He paused for effect and straightened his tie. His expensive dark suit matched his dark hair, which was feathered to one side. Harok's demeanor was confident and charismatic. He moved around the stage without hesitation; Jet could see he was comfortable and in his element. Harok's voice had a charming lilt to it—one reason he'd won his election, no doubt.

Jet was suddenly reminded of his first day at Skylight University almost four years ago. How that all seemed like a distant dream now. Since then, his death had been faked by the Agency, he had become a Heliographi, joined the Lucem and been labeled a skylight fallout.

Harok cleared his throat. "Thank you for attending, I'll get straight to the point. We have several items to discuss. First, as you are all aware, the Century Eclipse is approaching. It will take place on May 17th. The official event will be held at Revelations Plaza, which is ground zero for the eclipse, just as Albright had planned it. This once in a century occurrence will draw millions of tourists to the first belt. We are working on assignments, establishing a perimeter, surveillance teams, etcetera. We will take all precautions to ensure the safety of our citizens. I don't want any rumors spread from the Agency. All personnel are required to be on site or on call in case of an emergency. More to come on this as the time gets closer." Harok finished and nodded to his left. Solan stepped up to the podium.

Disguised in her alias, her dark hair was pinned to one side with a broach, and she wore a business blouse and skirt. Her age and frame were about the same; a young, athletic looking woman with dark skin, high cheeks, and a pencil-thin nose. Solan's alias as the powerful Senator Kiera required a formality that didn't suit her, but Tyberius had pressed her into accepting it. He had wanted her in a position of authority, and Jet wondered if perhaps he'd been prepping her for leadership in the Lucem. As a senator for the first district, she got plenty of practice at politics. But even after all that, Solan had never seemed to gravitate toward it, and Jet couldn't blame her.

"Lucem report and updates," she began. "I am assuming lead for Tyberius, who is currently out on assignment. We continue to search for Albright and Van Saint, but at this time, we have no leads on either. Secondly, our last known Heliographies are attending Skylight University this year—Tetra Wride, an Atrum, and Kamber Caster, a Lucem. Both are freshmen. We hope to leave Kamber at the university as long as possible but are aware that this is sometimes out of our control. We also continue to assist the elite recon troops on rare-earth deliveries. We understand the Goliath's Gate project is nearing completion, and raids on the rare-earth supplies have increased. We are looking into the source of those raids and hope to have something to report at the next summit. Whether it be drug lords, lone wolves or splinter cells, we'll get to the bottom of it." Solan looked over at Harok and nodded. "Finally, we are preparing for the eclipse. As always, the Lucem stand ready to assist in any way we can to protect Skylight's citizens."

As Solan turned to leave, someone in the crowd yelled out, "What about these rumors we've been hearing?"

Solan paused and looked at Harok. She walked back to the podium. "Could you be more specific, please?"

Jet noticed how out of place Solan seemed to be. Her cordial attitude and forced patience were traits counter to her true personality. He could tell by her body language that she hated it.

Another government official stood. "We've been hearing more about this Skylight Fallout. There's been talk about one of you, who is supposed to set off the next phase of something called the Prism Effect. What is this, and is it dangerous?"

A second official stood. "He's right. We've been intercepting all kinds of chatter about this Skylight Fallout person. What do you know and what's it all about?"

The assembly began to murmur and several more stood and pointed at Solan. "You Lucem should all leave at once. You're a danger to us and this Agency."

"It'll be the death of us," another man yelled out. "Demons! All of you cursed Heliographi! Go back to where you came from."

Harok looked at Solan and held up his hands as he walked back to the lectern. "Please. If you would all just settle down," he said. "Perhaps, Solan, it might be best if you let our young Mister Stroud speak to the assembly? I hear he might have direct knowledge about this Skylight Fallout person."

Jet snapped to attention, feeling awkward as everyone turned to look in his direction. He sat uncomfortably as everyone stared silently at him. He shrugged at Solan as if to say, *do something!*

Solan drew everyone's attention back to the stage as she spoke. "President Harok, I'll talk to Stroud myself, but if you have any further questions, direct them to me." She glared at Harok, and he took a step back. "Let me assure all of you that we are not a threat," she continued. "The Lucem are sworn to protect all of Skylight's citizens, regardless of who it is. That is our main objective. As for the Skylight Fallout, we are aware there are some rumors floating around. Many of them are conspiracy theories, but we are monitoring the situation. That's all I know at this time."

Jet watched Solan as she gripped the edge of the podium, her knuckles white and muscles tensed as if she was barely keeping her temper in check. Her normally stoic facade seemed to be on the verge of caving in.

The crowd of officials and dignitaries continued to grumble. There were still some angry shouts and a few threats hurled out, which Solan ignored. Jet wondered how these people could possibly place any blame or anger at them. The Lucem had protected civilians, soldiers, shipments and saved countless lives over the years. They had always answered the call, no matter what the price, and some Lucem had perished along the way.

Harok dismissed the assembly quickly as things looked to be getting out of hand. Solan stepped from the stage and walked directly down the main aisle and toward an exit.

"These people amaze me," she muttered at Cord and Jet as she walked past.

"The general assumption is a war is coming," Cord said and fell in beside her to beat the crowd of people exiting.

"I know what they assume," she said. "Just because there are supposed to be four phases to the Prism Effect, doesn't mean a war will follow."

"Still no idea who the Skylight Fallout is?" Jet asked.

"I suppose if you ask any of these *fine* folks, it's you," she said and pushed through a set of double doors and into a pre-function area where crowds were already gathering. Several officials glared in their direction.

Once they had cleared the area and were out of earshot, Solan stopped to look at them. "I know you're confused about this, Jet, but I don't have any leads right now. You'll be the first to know if I hear any information about the Skylight Fallout."

"By the way, I am currently working on several promising leads," Cord added.

"The splinter code?" Jet asked.

"Correct. I've been studying Albright's table in the Hall of Prisms. The splintered pattern intrigues me. I am beginning to wonder if it truly matches Van Saint's painting."

"Do you think there's a difference?" Solan asked. "I thought they were a perfect match?"

"I once believed that too. Now I'm not so sure."

"Keep at it." Solan straightened her tall frame and squared her shoulders. "I've been summoned by Harok. He wants to meet back at HQ in his office."

"Is it about the ambush?" Jet asked. "That's devastating news. How are Jinn and Ti-Leer?"

"They're both fine. They managed to save a lot of lives, but I'm sure Harok's getting pressured about the troops we lost."

"Well, good luck," Jet said.

"Something tells me I'm going to need it."

Jet waited until Solan was gone and turned to Cord. "What else do you know?"

Cord looked curiously at Jet in the secluded antechamber. "What are you referring to?"

"Apparently, you know more than you've let on," Jet continued. "What are you not telling me? You worried about this splinter code? Come on, let me in on this."

"What has Solan told you about the Skylight Fallout?" Cord asked.

"Well, she's told me about the legend, which is why the Atrum tried to murder me the night of the triclipse four years ago. You've heard the story, right? It'll be a Heliographi, one who's a Skylight University dropout, which pretty much includes all of us. I bet there's at least fifteen or more Heliographi who fall into that category."

Cord remained silent as he looked at Jet, as if considering something. "You're right. It's time I let you in on this. Meet me tomorrow at the stacks."

CHAPTER 4
Eviction Notice

ΑΒΓΔΕΖΗΘΙΚΛ**Κ**

ΝΞΟΠΡΣΤΥΦΧΨΩ

SOLAN STEPPED THROUGH a pair of heavy wooden doors and into President Harok's office back on the ninth belt. The interior was a traditional mix of wood trim, plush carpet, and period style furniture—way too posh for her taste. The stillness was palpable, and the sounds were muted from the thick carpet. Standing on either side of President Harok's ornate wooden desk were his two top generals, Yune and Dane.

General Yune's salt and pepper hair glistened with a light sheen of sweat, and his olive skin was flushed as if he had just finished a yelling contest. Dane's dark hair was cut high-and-tight. His wide shoulders and toned physique were apparent from years of running missions with his troops. Even as a general, Dane preferred joining the elite forces to maintain his edge, much to Harok's opposition.

Yune slammed his fist on Harok's desk. He slid a holopad out of his military fatigues and tossed it at Solan. A hologram displayed the elite soldiers who had been killed during the ambush. Solan closed her eyes and took a deep breath. "So. Straight to the point, Yune?"

"Your father would've never allowed this to happen on his watch. You have blood on your hands!" Yune said. "You Lucem think you're all above reproach. And these troops weren't the first to pay with their lives. President, we've let these Lucem go free for too long."

Dane held out his hands. "Yune, these people have saved countless lives and soldiers. What do you have to say about that?"

"Tell that to these soldiers' families!" Yune said, raising his voice. "Those were good troops, some of the finest."

"Yune, please calm down," Harok said. "Solan. I need a full recount if you don't mind."

Solan looked up at Harok and ignored Yune. "It was a typical run, according to DiJinn and Ti-Leer. They fought off the first raid but lost a lot of troops. The marauders got the refined rare-earth and cloaked heading into the ninth belt debris field. The group was heading home when a jammer class skiff ambushed them. Apparently, the recon pilots didn't have their shields up, and the skiff was shot down over the sixth belt. They were pinned by snipers, and DiJinn and Ti-Leer took them out. It was a well-planned ambush. Those pilots were bought off."

"Why would they specifically target the skiff your Lucem were on, I wonder?" Yune asked.

Solan remained silent. She already knew where this was going.

"Word on the street is that the true Skylight Fallout is a Lucem," Yune continued. "I hear it might even be the boy who just joined your group. Is it possible that the Atrum thought he might have been aboard our skiff during that ambush?"

"Yune, we don't know if that intel is accurate," Dane said. "It was intercepted, but we can't verify that."

"Jet Stroud *is* being targeted by the Atrum, plain and simple as that!" Yune said. "As long as the Lucem are here, they are endangering our troops and our missions. The raids have been bad enough. We're nearing completion of Goliath's Gate, but with all the rare-earth thefts, we'll never finish it. The Lucem have been helpful in those regards, I admit. But not at the expense of my troops!"

"Those were unfortunate losses," Harok said. "But the resources are just as important for this project. What do you propose, Yune?"

"We have the ability to protect against the raids without the Lucem. I have full confidence in my troops," Yune said. "The Lucem will bring those demon Atrum down upon us if they stay here. You've heard the grumbling, Harok. You know the troops are uncomfortable."

Harok nodded. "Yes, I've heard the grumbling. I know the troops are uneasy. Are you sure you can protect the shipments of rare-earth, though?"

"Yes, absolutely. It's what we've been trained to do."

"General Dane, what are your thoughts?" Harok asked and turned to face him.

Dane rubbed his chin. "I understand that many in the Agency have expressed frustration. But I've seen how valuable the Lucem are in action. I've worked with them successfully on multiple missions. Their support is valuable, whether the troops like it or not. Yes, we lost some good soldiers, but it's nothing compared to how many lives they've saved over the years."

"We can't control how our troops feel around them," Yune said. "The Lucem's presence has a negative effect on them. My vote is to disband our alliance."

Dane shook his head. "I disagree. And furthermore, I think you aren't seeing the full picture."

"My troops and their wellbeing are the only picture I need to see! If they can't focus on their tasks because of the Lucem's presence, then the Lucem must go."

Harok sat at his desk, fingers steepled in front of his face and eyes closed.

"I have to vote against that," Dane said.

"Well, you're in the minority, Dane. I have to side with my troops on this." Yune didn't look at Dane or Solan as he spoke, just focused his attention on Harok.

They waited to hear what Harok's decision would be. But Solan had known this moment was coming. She had already prepared for it, just in case it happened, and had moved many of the Lucem's belongings out over the last several months—just an intuitive voice that whispered to her on occasion. She had heeded it.

She wasn't oblivious to the grumbling troops. The uneasiness had always been there, but lately it seemed to be boiling over, and now it was about to burst. Of course, the Lucem made the troops uncomfortable; they made everyone uneasy, even after they'd been saved on a difficult mission. They still disliked the Lucem and would never accept them. It was an uneasy truce at best, and she had known it was only a matter of time. Her father had been able to hold the Agency at bay and appease them. But now that he was missing, relations between the Agency and Lucem were taking a nosedive. She just didn't have her father's skill as a politician, not that she ever cared to be in this position, dealing with people like Harok. Yet here she was, making tough decisions, and most likely the *wrong* decisions.

"President Harok." Solan stepped forward. "Let me save you the trouble. The Lucem will leave of our own accord. It's evident the time has come. It's unfortunate that it ends like this; our alliance goes back nearly a century. But if the majority of the Agency feels that we are a hindrance, then I won't continue to question it."

Harok sat forward abruptly to object. But then eased back in his seat and slowly nodded. Solan could have just read his thoughts, but she always refrained from doing such things unless necessary, as did all the other Lucem. It was something that Tyberius had impressed on her at an early age. It was immoral, in his opinion—everyone had a right to their own privacy. But she didn't have to read Harok's thoughts to see that he was grateful for not having to make the decision.

"I do have some conditions, though," Solan continued. "I hope we can work it out."

Yune started to disagree, but Harok held up a hand for silence. "Of course, Solan. Go ahead."

Solan crossed her arms. "We could still use the Agency's help with resources. We would prefer to maintain our alias and witness protection plans. There are some people we deem valuable to both the Lucem and the Agency."

Harok nodded. "What else?"

"We still have our oath to protect Skylight and its citizens. That goes back even before our alliance with the Agency. We will continue to protect them."

"Of course, as long as it doesn't interfere with our operations," Harok said. "I would assume no less."

Solan continued. "With the Century Eclipse coming up, we intend to be present regardless of what the Agency thinks. If there is any foul play, the Skylight citizens will need us."

Harok looked at General Yune and Dane. Neither said a word. Harok stood and started pacing behind his desk. "I accept all of your conditions, but I have a few of my own."

"I assumed you would," Solan said. "Let's hear it."

"The Agency may still need assistance from you. While I have the utmost faith in General Yune and his troops, we may call on the Lucem if the situation becomes dire. The Goliath's Gate project is the most important project to the Skylight System since its inception. It will eventually bring jobs, tax credits and additional research. But as you know, our resources are being plundered by these rogue marauders, splinter cells, and lone wolves. Drug overlords have established so-called territorial jurisdiction around our trade routes between the belts." Harok paused and looked at Solan. "Will the Lucem answer the call if Skylight needs you?"

Even though she wasn't the biggest fan of Harok, especially after his actions during the summit, she still had a responsibility to fulfill. "If these are your conditions, then yes," Solan replied. "The Lucem have always answered the call for Skylight, even at great cost to our own. Tyberius always honored that oath, and so will I."

"And, speaking of your father, where is he?"

Solan had known this question would come up but still wasn't sure how to respond. She didn't want to let on that Tyberius was missing in action. But it had been a few weeks now, and she knew Harok suspected something was amiss.

"I'll be honest with you. We don't know where he is." Solan looked Harok in the eyes as she spoke.

"What do you know?" Harok asked. His look of concern was barely detectable, but Solan noticed it.

"Only that he was on assignment on the third belt when he went silent," Solan said. "That's it. We've searched for him but have found no trace yet."

"Your father was a very resourceful man. I knew him well and have great respect for him. He'll be fine, wherever he is. If we can help in any way, please don't hesitate to call on us."

"Thank you, President," Solan said. "That means a lot to me."

"Where do you plan to relocate?" Harok asked, leaning against his desk.

Solan sighed. "I have a location lined up, but I prefer not to say. My apologies."

Harok chuckled. "You knew this was going to happen, I see."

"I have ears to the ground…all over the system. It's unfortunate that the troops cannot trust us, but I am accustomed to it, as are the other Lucem." She gave General Yune a long look, and he blinked and looked away from her glowing gaze.

"Solan. If you learn anything about the rare-earth raids, will you contact me?" Harok asked.

"Yes, of course we will," Solan said.

"Without the rare-earth minerals, we can't finish Goliath's Gate." Harok bent down and slid his top drawer open. He handed her a holopad. "This was recovered from one of the marauders."

Solan set the holopad down and switched it on. A red four-sided pyramid projected over the holopad, slowly spinning around. Solan gazed at the hologram. "That's a tetrahedron."

"Does it mean anything to you?" Harok asked.

She shook her head. "No, I've never seen this insignia before."

"Well, if you run across it, be careful."

Harok dismissed the two generals. Yune left without a word. Dane nodded to Solan and shook her hand. "Thank you, Solan. I will personally miss your presence."

Harok shut the door behind them and faced Solan. "Before you leave, I have one more question."

Solan stood near the door and faced him. "You want to know who the Skylight Fallout is, I'm guessing?"

"It would help if I knew more about this person. I've been hearing a lot of rumors that the next phase of the Prism Effect is to be set in motion by this special Heliographi. It's had a lot of the people in the Agency on edge."

"We know as much as you right now, President."

"Is it true that Jet Stroud is rumored to be the one?"

"Again, we have no knowledge of who it will be or when it will occur. In fact, we don't even know what the second phase is supposed to trigger."

Harok rubbed his chin. "Doesn't it seem odd that Albright wouldn't have shared some of this information with you? And doesn't it seem odd that the one person who might know more has just recently turned up missing?"

"You think that my father has knowledge of this?"

"Seems like a logical assumption, doesn't it?" Harok said. "So, I ask you again, where is Tyberius Alexander?"

Solan shook her head. "President. I've already told you… I don't know. Why would I lie to you?"

"That's a really good question," Harok said and held the door open for her. "It would be a shame if information about the Lucem were to leak. Your alias would be compromised, as would those of the other people you protect and care about."

Solan stared at Harok, slightly agitated. "I hope that's not a threat, President. The Lucem know plenty of the Agency's secrets too. That door swings both ways."

M

Jet quickly made his way back to the ninth belt and waited for Solan to leave Harok's office. He hid in a dark corner of the office quadrant, cloaked and invisible. He had followed her, thanks to that same intuitive voice that had guided him as a student. Though that influence had sometimes been Solan, much of the time it was the other voice, and it had become clearer over the last four years.

Some ten minutes later, Solan stood at Harok's door, where they engaged in a tense discussion. Solan turned abruptly and marched off as Harok watched, then he checked his watch and left. Jet stood still as Solan passed by him, then he darted off after Harok.

That same intuitive voice had whispered to him, *why was Harok so intent on singling him out during the summit?* Jet had to know more, and he wouldn't figure it out just sitting on his hands or twiddling his thumbs. His inquisitive nature would get him into trouble, but hopefully not today.

Harok moved down several levels and into a secure section of the office suite. He badged his way through several areas, with cameras, heat sensors and motion monitors. But thanks to the technology in his cloak, Jet didn't have to concern himself with any of that.

Soon, Harok entered a conference room. Armed guards stood at attention as he entered, and Jet slipped in just behind him. Harok immediately turned and locked the doors, punched some credentials into a keypad and secured the room. He sat at the large conference table; its glossy wood coat and plush chairs gave the room a high-end feel. Jet assumed this was where very important meetings took place…or very dark conversations.

Harok dialed a number on a specialized holopad. A large hologram displayed over the table. On the other end sat a person in dark silhouette. The person's face and age were impossible to discern, and their voice was distorted.

"Harok. You're calling back sooner than I thought you would."

"I've been considering a few things we discussed last time," Harok replied. "I'm hoping we can rehash those items."

"Certainly. I hope you are prepared for a serious negotiation this time, though. I don't have time to dance."

Harok steepled his fingers. "Let's go over the agreement again, if that's okay?"

"Simple. You require funding for Goliath's Gate, a great deal of it, which I will provide. I also hear that a large rare-earth shipment was recently stolen by marauders, and you require assistance to bolster your elite troops. I am willing to provide additional mercenaries to help prevent future raids."

"Yes, this is what I recall from our last discussion," Harok agreed. "Now, let's go over your demands again."

"First, I will remain anonymous until I choose to be announced. You alone know my true identity, but it must not be disclosed until I am ready. This is nonnegotiable, but you can simply refer to me as the Backer."

Harok nodded.

"Second, my drug operations must not be hindered by the Agency. You will steer clear of the ninth belt debris field, except for areas around Memorial Park."

"I can assure that we will not interfere," Harok said.

"Third. Albright's easter egg is mine."

Harok furrowed his brow. "The Agency has no knowledge of this artifact; therefore, we cannot guarantee that."

"All I require is your word that you will hand it over *if* you come into its possession *or* that you will not compete for it otherwise."

Harok ran his fingers through his dark hair, feathering it back. "Fine," he said. Jet noticed his slight hesitation and recognized it. Maybe it was his heightened senses, but he could tell that Harok wasn't being completely honest with this person called the Backer.

"And finally…we must eliminate Jet Stroud."

Harok had been staring at the table, but his head snapped up when he heard this. "That was not part of the deal last time!"

"Had you accepted our deal last time, then perhaps this wouldn't have been presented. But right now, this is the deal I'm offering."

Harok shoved the holopad in frustration. "What good does murdering a young Lucem accomplish?"

"He *is* the Skylight Fallout," the Backer said.

"So I've heard," Harok replied. "But according to the Lucem, no one is certain *who* the true Skylight Fallout is. From what I understand, the prophesy simply states that a university dropout, one who is a Heliographi, will usher in the second phase of the Prism Effect."

"I have my sources, and that is all you need to know."

Harok shook his head. "If you kill Stroud, then how can he trigger the second phase?"

"The Skylight Fallout's duty would fall to the next in line, which happens to be an Atrum named Vail. *If* Stroud manages to survive until the eclipse, then I will convince him to give me the information I desire."

Harok stood and paced the room. "The Atrum are involved in this now?"

"Perhaps, but that's really none of your concern, Harok."

"And what if he doesn't give you the information?"

"Then I would advise you to use caution on the day of the eclipse."

"What do you mean by that?" Harok stopped pacing.

"If I don't get the *information* I need, then no one will," the Backer said. "I will handle this part with or without your help, Harok."

"I don't know about this."

"If anything does happen, I will ensure that it all looks like an accident, so that you're not implicated," the Backer said, trying to reassure him.

Harok stared at the hologram, apparently still uncertain. "I don't relish the thought of going against the Lucem. They're not a group I want to cross."

"You still want to run for office next election, I assume?" the Backer asked. "Because I can be a powerful supporter or a dangerous foe. You decide."

Harok stuck his hands in his pockets, still considering.

"This will be the last time I make this offer," the backer said in a matter-of-fact tone. "Decide now."

Harok looked at the hologram, ran his fingers through his hair one last time and gave the Backer a devilish grin. "You have a deal."

M

Jet left the secret meeting and spent the rest of that morning in his quarters, deep in thought. He ran through a gambit of emotions, considering what he'd just heard.

The President of the Skylight System had just agreed to support an assassination attempt on his life.

He felt confused at first, but that feeling had slowly turned to anger, then uncertainty and finally to indifference. He had been threatened so many times throughout his life that he was somewhat used to it. But this was different…*much* different, and he didn't mean to take it lightly. He had some big decisions to make on what to do and who to tell.

Jet met Solan in her studio that afternoon, where he tried to push Harok's conversation to the back of his mind. Solan's quarters were large. Because she trained so frequently, there was an entire gym dedicated to her sessions. Training equipment and a sparring mat occupied the space. She had held regular training sessions for him ever since he'd joined the Lucem. But lately, he sensed her patience with him was dwindling. A lot of effort was being poured into his training, and Solan was a busy person. He was used to being adept at most things but struggled to grasp certain aspects of the training lessons. The physical portion and melee fighting, he was getting better at. But some of the psychic exercises were difficult, especially the meditation. His head swam with the amount of insight she had pushed on him over the last several years. It felt like she was downloading centuries of knowledge directly into his brain at times, and he had to stop their training occasionally just to steady himself. With Solan lately, there seemed to be an urgency when it came to his training. *I'm still responsible for you, until your warden is ready,* she reminded him.

When Solan trained, she didn't hold anything back, and today he sensed she had some aggression within. She had a long reach and powerful shoulders that drove her punches. Her kicks carried a little extra juice, and after an hour, Jet had to ask for a break. He flopped down on the mat, exhausted. Solan leaned against the wall and toweled some sweat from her brow.

"What's with you today?" Jet asked.

Solan dropped her water bottle and frowned. "Harok. He's been asking a lot of questions."

"About what?"

Solan crossed her arms and gave him a meaningful stare, as if she was on the verge of sharing something with him. But she shook her head and tossed a towel to him. "Nothing for you to be concerned about. Just focus on me right now."

"Solan," Jet said, standing to his feet. "Why are you asking me to watch over Kamber? I understand that she's my warden, but I just don't think I'm ready for this yet."

Solan started dancing around him, her fists up and ready to spar. "Everyone has their duties, and this one is yours."

Jet put up his fists and circled Solan. "What's wrong with me? Why am I struggling with this so much?"

"It's a mental block," she said and spun at him, landing a kick on his thigh. "We'll get there. Just focus on me right now."

Jet winced and brushed his hair out of his eyes, stepped back, then reengaged. "How did you handle it at first?"

"I never had any issues in my training," she said.

"Am I the only one who's ever struggled with this?"

"No. Jinn did, for years, before finally breaking through. She turned out fine, and you will too. Every Lucem has to find their own path through this."

Jet wondered why no one had mentioned this before. He made a mental note to approach Jinn and talk to her.

"I want to learn, Solan. I'm trying to understand all of this. But, I don't think I could forgive myself if someone is harmed because of me."

Solan feinted to her left, then jumped and kicked Jet. The ball of her foot connected with his sternum, and Jet dropped to the mat, trying to catch his breath. Solan leapt and brought her knee down toward his chest, and Jet was just able to roll and stand to his feet.

"Pay attention!" she snapped at him. Solan flew at Jet, and he backpedaled from the flurry of kicks and punches. Soon, he was off the mat and backed against the wall.

"Solan!" he yelled, trying to fend her off.

But she seemed to be in a trance, and he felt a moment of panic as she bore down on him. He managed to parry her blows until she struck the steel bulkhead of the wall and finally stopped. Solan let her head lean against the wall as Jet stood there, inches away from her, both breathing heavily.

"Lost you for a moment," he said. "Where'd you go?"

Solan pulled her fist from the wall and walked back toward the mat. Jet followed her at a distance and waited for her to say something.

"Have a seat," she said, finally turning to him and dropping to the mat with her legs crossed.

Jet sat down opposite her and waited.

They sat facing each other, their glowing eyes illuminating the space between them. His turquoise-colored eyes and her yellow-greenish ones mingled in the darkened studio.

"I'm sorry about that, Jet. There's a lot going on right now that I can't talk about. I shouldn't take it out on you."

"It's not because of me, I hope," Jet said.

"No, that's not it."

He sighed. "Good, I guess. You're under some stress. What can I do to help?"

"Nothing, at the moment…just continue your practice sessions. That'll give everyone some peace of mind. If you feel the need to talk to Jinn, then do so. Just remember, everyone has their own unique path to becoming a Lucem."

Jet toweled some sweat from his brow. "Listen, Solan. How is it that we've known each other for more than four years now, and I've never heard your story? Everyone struggles with something, yet you seem to have no weakness."

Solan's lip curled upward with the hint of a smile. "Oh, I have my faults. I just cover them well. It's mostly an exercise in controlling my emotions, as you can see."

"Well, you know about my flaws," Jet said. "Do you mind sharing yours?"

"Will it help?"

"I think so, at least, it might help my fragile ego, knowing that the great and powerful Solan isn't always perfect." He said this jokingly, but Solan didn't laugh or smile.

"Very well," she said and leaned back. "I was scared to death as a student at Skylight University. I had no idea what was happening to me, just like you and every other Heliographi who's experienced this. You saw the entries in my student journal. Toward the end, I was a shell of who I'd once been. I spent the first five years in the

Lucem learning, training, and picking up traits. I've run my share of missions, a lot of them with the elite recon. Outside of that, being a Lucem can be a lonely existence. There's a lot of stress, keeping an eye on Skylight's citizens. It's a thankless life; you shouldn't expect anything in return."

She pulled her knees up and leaned forward before continuing. "It was Ti-Leer who brought me into the Lucem and converted me."

"Ti-Leer?" Jet asked. "Isn't he Jinn's warden?"

"Yes, but my warden wasn't around at that time. He mentored me and helped me understand the ropes. He looks aloof, but Ti-Leer is dead serious when it comes to business. He was strict, probably because Tyberius was my father, and they expected great things from me. Maybe that explains my approach with you. If you are the Skylight Fallout, then you need to be prepared. Even if you aren't, I have a feeling that you'll play an important role."

"Speaking of wardens, do you expect me to bring Kamber into the Lucem?" Jet asked.

"Yes, when it is time. But we will hold out for the right moment."

Jet wasn't sure how excited he was about the conversion ritual with Kamber but pushed the thought away knowing he'd have to deal with it later. "Solan, can I ask you something?"

"Sure, but no promise that I'll answer it."

"This is more of a personal question."

She gave him an inquisitive look. "Alright, what is it?"

"When we met in the Hall of Prisms, the night I was converted four years ago, I asked your father about the dreams I'd been having. About the Serpent and the Prism."

Solan furrowed her brow and nodded. "I remember. What about it?"

"Well, I'm still having those dreams. I thought they might go away, after my fight with Sybold the night of the triclipse. Instead, they seem to be getting worse. Your father never really answered my questions about the dreams and what they meant. Why?"

"To be quite honest, he said nothing more to me that night," she replied. "He didn't seem to want to talk about it, and I didn't ask."

Jet watched Solan closely. He could tell she wasn't lying, but at the same time, she wasn't telling him everything she knew, either. "Alright, I believe you. But... can you tell me what you *do* know?"

"I know about the legend, some of it you've already heard. The Heliographi are beings from lore, an ancient race, though our origins are unknown. It is said that the Atrum are descendant from a serpent, or *wyrm*, as my father mentioned. The Lucem are beings of pure light and power, represented by the symbol of the prism."

"Yeah, I got that," Jet said. "I…I just thought there would be more to it."

Solan kicked at the floor and didn't look at him.

Jet crossed his arms. "Come on, Solan. If this involves me, I need to know."

She continued to look at her feet, as if considering. Then she finally looked up at him. "Yes, there is more to the legend."

Jet waited for her to continue. "And?" he asked.

"Albright…was fairly tightlipped about it with my father. However, since Tyberius *was* his second in command, Albright did share a few things. My father told me this a long time ago, before you and I met. He said the legend of the Serpent and the Prism represented a great battle, one that would happen soon."

"During the Century Eclipse?"

Solan slowly shook her head. "No, I don't think so. The timing isn't right. Remember, there are four phases to the Prism Effect. Only the first two phases have been set into motion. Whatever great war this is, my guess is that we still have time."

Jet held her gaze, then rubbed his chin. "Any idea how or why I'm involved in all of this? Why didn't your father just tell me himself?"

"My father believed that the legend seemed to center around you, in particular. I imagine he didn't want to place that much pressure on you just before your conversion. That's probably why he didn't say much.

Now that you've got four years under your belt, I don't have an issue sharing this with you."

Jet chuckled. "That doesn't make me feel much better."

"Just focus on your goals. That's what I do. It keeps my mind from wandering too far."

"Well, that's a bit of a problem, because I'm really not sure what my *goals* are at the moment. I mean, I know those can change over time. Not long ago, I thought I was meant to find a cure for E.M., and…well, that didn't happen the way I thought it would. I'm just trying to figure out what my purpose is here. I'm not very good at this, in case you haven't noticed."

"You'll be fine. Besides, you may not know your true goal or purpose until you're confronted with it. At the moment, you need to continue your practice in Vishmu and get better at it so you can watch over Kamber. The time may come when others' lives will depend on you. As for me, it's my family, my sister, the safety of the Lucem… that's what drives me forward. Even though I don't like being responsible for others, this is what I'm expected to do now. I don't consider myself a great leader, like my father. I struggle with it daily and worry that my decisions may cost other people if I'm wrong. I don't really enjoy it, and you may find that your calling is one you don't like either. But you will eventually rise to the challenge because people will be counting on you."

CHAPTER 5
An Old Acquaintance

ΑΒΓΔΕΖΗΘΙΚΛ**Μ**
ΝΞΟΠΡΣΤΥΦΧΨΩ

AFTER JET LEFT Solan's quarters, he wandered the halls of the Lucem wing. Their sector was vast and winding, with areas that were rarely frequented by most of the others. It was dusty and dark with the vestiges of damage still visible in the metal hull, which dated back to the Great Meteor Storm of 2188 A.D., nearly a century ago.

Jet thought about what he'd heard from Solan and Harok. He could hardly believe there was a bounty on his head, and if he hadn't listened to his intuitive voice, he would have never known. He was learning to heed that voice, and the more he did, the more it seemed to warn him in ways he didn't understand. But now, he had to decide who to tell about Harok's meeting. His biggest fear was being 'benched,' and perhaps that was his greatest weakness, too. If Solan found out and didn't think he could handle it, she would become an overprotective guardian, probably even bottle him up at headquarters, or place a curfew on him. He cringed at that. He'd rather take his chances out in the open than be caged. He had a lot to learn, true. But sitting on the sidelines was something he didn't think he could tolerate. His straight-forward nature and competitive fire just wouldn't allow him to let the others do all the work on his behalf. It was a risk, a huge risk, keeping this to himself, especially since he was struggling with his training. But he couldn't share this with Solan, at least not right now. But what about Cord, or DiJinn? Both were cut from the same fold of cloth, and he thought he might be able to confide in them. But he would also be placing Jinn in an awkward position. Solan was like a sister to her, and information of this magnitude needed to be reported. Jet thought he might be better off holding on to what he knew for the moment. He would probably share it with Cord, when the time felt right. He knew one thing for sure; he would not cower to this so-called 'Backer.' Of all the things he had been through so far, this might become his greatest challenge. The stakes were high, but maybe that's exactly what he needed to push him forward. With the Century Eclipse, a deadline loomed; he just had to survive till then…and work harder in his training.

Lost in thought, he stumbled into a remote area of the Lucem sector, a place the Lucem referred to as the Hall of Vital Records. It was a chamber deep in the Lucem wing that only they could access. He had discovered this area during his first year as a Lucem and found it mesmerizing. The old hall gave off a strange vibe, and Jet had known immediately it was a special place. He felt drawn to it in a way he couldn't explain. The mystical ambiance here was strong, unlike any other place he'd been to in the Skylight System. At times, it felt like the hall was calling to him, a ghostly voice that he heard in his dreams. When he meditated in the chamber that belonged to his own class of the M, he felt a stronger connection, like his abilities were supercharged.

The chamber was wide with high ceilings, and a skylight above filtered light into the space. Along the walls were old artifacts from ages past, and much of it hinted at their heritage. He would spend hours sometimes perusing the information about their lineage. Each portion of the chamber housed a special meditation room and encircled a large stone column. The steel hull juxtaposed with the ancient décor gave off a strange vibe, adding to the hall's mystical ambiance. Each of the twenty-four meditation rooms contained the lineage for a specific Heliographi, be it Lucem or Atrum.

At the stone threshold leading into each meditation chamber was a symbol. On the Atrum side was a fanged serpent, each one unique in size and shape. Carved into the stone threshold on the Lucem side was a jewel-like prism, each one faceted and also distinctively shaped.

Before he had been converted, Tyberius had explained that their ancient race dated back millennia, perhaps farther, no one knew. Each Heliographi had been given a name, represented by a symbol Albright had created, and it eventually became the Greek alphabet. Each of those twenty-four symbols was tied to a precise color on the spectrum. What was once a pure white light had been refracted into individual colors and affected all of the Heliographi's eyes. When a Heliographi died, their light chose a new soul, a persona that would reflect its fancy. A Heliographi's essence could not be destroyed, even though the physical form of the host could.

Although The Hall of Vital Records wouldn't let Jet track a Heliographi, he could feel their lifeforce. Recently, he had traced the lineage of his ancient symbol, the letter M, and every Lucem who had borne that symbol before him. What he found was shocking. Those prior Lucem were very similar to him in nature, almost like a long-lost brother, and they were always male. He had also discovered that the man just before him had died in action, working alongside Agency troops during a raid. If he focused enough, he could almost hear this particular Lucem's voice speaking to him. Unfortunately, this man's death in service to Skylight was a grim reminder that even a powerful Lucem wasn't immune to death.

When Jet got back to his living quarters, he quickly shed his alias and slipped into his cloak. The material was interwoven in a way that helped it bend light when the hood was drawn and made the user practically invisible to the untrained eye. He always kept it around, though it wasn't the comfiest of clothing, thanks to the reinforced graphene fibers. But the comfort level was a small sacrifice considering the level of protection the graphene provided.

His living quarters were sparse, since he spent little time there, and much more quaint than Solan's. A bed next to a small, round window lined one wall, and a desk with a lamp and a rug for meditation lined the opposite wall.

As a Lucem, it was critical to put meditation time in every day. It wasn't required, according to Solan, if you wanted to get rolled up during the next fight. That translated to, *you'd better do it.* Cord was an overachiever, whereas Jet struggled to understand the psychic aspect of meditation. Though he preferred the more physical part of training, he understood the importance of both.

He dropped the light levels and crossed his legs as he sat on the old rug. He slowed his breathing and then let his thoughts run wild. He released his inner light, and it took off. At times like this, he was simply along for the ride. Solan had attributed meditation sessions to *letting the kids out for recess.* The inner light of the Heliographi needed time to run free and recharge.

The things he saw during meditation were fringe, inconceivable and otherworldly. He didn't even know how to put it into words. He had front row seats to some of the strangest things a human's mind could possibly witness… nor should they. His being could barely contain the experience, which was one reason why he had to continue the sessions. It was practice, in a sense. It reinforced his mind, made it more capable of holding more knowledge. It expanded his psyche.

His inner light galloped across the cosmos, running from galaxy to galaxy. Distance didn't seem to matter. He could see when other Heliographi were meditating too. Different colored lights—streaks of blues, greens, and reds—all running, playing, and interacting together. It was a beautiful sight to behold, and his soul could barely contain the euphoria.

When he reined his light back in, it usually took half an hour just to come back into his being. His mind had to have time to decompress back to the physical world. Sometimes, when this transition occurred, thoughts, solutions and epiphanies would come to him. And that's when it hit him.

He knew what Vail's signal to him had meant.

His holopad buzzed, and DiJinn's face appeared.

"Hey, sleepy head. Better get yourself up to the Hall, pronto."

"What's the rush?" he asked, rolling onto his elbow.

"Just get your tail up here," DiJinn said and snapped the connection closed.

M

The entire group of remaining Lucem all sat in their individual chairs, waiting and silent when Jet arrived. The Hall of Prisms was their primary meeting place and had been for nearly a century. The ancient table dominated the rotunda room. Its circular shape was checked and cracked along the edges, reminiscent of some massive, felled tree trunk. In front of each of the twenty-four chairs was their individual Greek symbol, etched into the wooden table. Although no one sat on the left half of the table, which was the Atrum side, not every chair was occupied on the right side either. Christian Albright, Shiloe Van Saint and now Tyberius Alexander were all missing. The final Lucem was Kamber Caster, Jet's warden. Her chair sat empty next to his.

Jet sat down at his chair behind the symbol of the letter M. Two chairs over sat Solan, then Cord, Ti-Leer, DiJinn, Harriet, Booker then Annaka.

"What's the rush?" Jet asked as he settled in. "Where's Tyberius, by the way?"

"That's one of the reasons why I called this meeting," Solan said. "Might as well get this all out in the open. I didn't want to raise any alarm with the Agency, but they know now."

"Has something happened to him?" Booker asked. His normal alias was Coach Plannar. In reality, Booker was much the same in physical appearance and attitude. He was a behemoth and spoke in a booming voice. His dark hair was turning gray at the temples, and a long scar ran along the side of his face.

"We don't know," Solan said. "We lost contact with him several weeks ago. I can't even detect his presence anymore."

"He can take care of himself, Sol," DiJinn said.

"I'm aware!" Solan snapped, then shook her head and took a deep breath to steady herself. She held out a hand. "I'm sorry, Jinn. I don't mean to take this out on you or anyone else."

"It's okay," DiJinn said. She walked over and placed a hand on Solan's shoulder and gave it a squeeze. "We know you're in a rough spot."

"Solan," Jet said. "What can you tell us about him?"

"Just his location when we lost contact. The third belt, near Skylight City, Galleon Quarter."

"That's a fairly broad area," Ti-Leer said. "Any idea what he was doing?"

DiJinn glanced at Solan, who nodded. "He was looking for Albright. He had a lead and followed it, alone. He's always been heartbroken 'bout the night Albright was assassinated. You know he vowed to find him before the Atrum."

"You think the Atrum are behind his disappearance?" Ti-Leer asked.

"Maybe," Solan said. "But I need to know more. I don't want to place blame out of hand, even on the Atrum."

From what Jet knew about Tyberius, he was a very calculated and cautious man who was loyal to the Lucem and the Agency. He was kind and gentle, but dangerous when the situation called for it. To subdue him would take considerable force.

"Tyberius is my warden, Solan. What can I do to help?" Annaka asked in a thick accent and stood to walk around the table next to Solan. Her alias as President Starr at the university was still stuck in Jet's head from his time there as a student. Annaka's silver hair ran shoulder length with reddish highlights. Her skin was as tan as Solan's, but she was much shorter and bulkier. She gazed at Solan through her glowing orange eyes.

"At the moment, nothing, Annaka." Solan stood and pushed in her chair.

Once again, Jet could sense Solan's discomfort. He knew she preferred to work on the fringes and in the shadows, not being responsible for others. But like it or not, this was her duty for now. Tyberius was a natural leader, and Jet was betting Solan would rise to the occasion.

"I'm afraid our current standing with the Agency is about to change," Solan said. "We're moving out."

Everyone stood at that and began to talk.

"When the hell did this happen?" DiJinn asked.

"What do you mean we're moving out?" Jet said.

Booker stood and walked over to her. "What caused this, Solan?"

Solan held up her hands. "Everyone please, have a seat and let me explain."

Once the air had calmed, Solan continued. "You've all heard the grumbling from the Agency personnel just as much as I have. I knew this was coming, I just didn't expect it so soon. I've managed to get some of our items out already."

"Good thinking," Ti-Leer said. "One step ahead, just like your father."

"We have till noon tomorrow," Solan continued.

"That fast?" Jet asked. "We must have really upset someone."

"I don't think it was what Harok wanted, to be honest; he's not a git. He understands what this could mean for both of us. His general, Yune, was the one who insisted breaking ties with us. I tend to agree with him, to some extent."

"How can you say that?" Booker asked. "I know Yune. He's in it for the politics, regardless of what he says. Dane is the only one I trust around here."

"Whether we like it or not, we have an effect on these troops, and we must respect the Agency's wishes," Solan said. "They are uneasy around us. Perhaps our presence is detrimental to their focus."

"Not to mention the soldiers we lost on the raid yesterday," Ti-Leer added. "No doubt we got the blame for that?"

"Of course," DiJinn said. "Nothing new there! These people want us gone, fine. Let's see how they fare without our backup. The Atrum will eat them alive once word gets out."

"This isn't permanent yet," Solan said. "I agreed to leave with a few conditions, and Harok had some of his own."

"What were the conditions, if you don't mind?" Cord asked.

"His main request is that we remain available if he needs us. Obviously, Goliath's Gate is his main priority, and if these marauders get too aggressive and he starts losing more rare-earth, he will call on us. My guess is that will happen sooner rather than later."

"Did he have any information on who the raids are being conducted by?" Booker asked. "We know the Atrum are involved, but who are these marauders?"

Solan took out the holopad Harok had given her and slid it over. "He only had this to give."

They gathered around and looked at the hologram of the blood red tetrahedron. The four-sided pyramid floated, orbiting slowly over the table as they looked on.

"I have plenty of access at the university, but I've never seen that insignia before," Annaka said.

"The tetrahedron is symbolic of inner balance," Cord said.

"What's that supposed to mean?" DiJinn asked.

Cord shrugged. "I have no conclusion at this point. I just didn't expect to see something like this associated with a group of marauders," Cord said. "Perhaps there is more to this outfit than appears?"

Solan put the holopad back in her cloak. "We can't worry about it right now. Let's focus on relocating. Harok allowed us to maintain our assignments, our individual aliases, and the witness protection plan. Have your personal belongings ready to load by tomorrow; we're moving back to Skylight University."

❙

Cord stayed behind after their meeting that day and sat alone, lost in thought. He stared at Albright's table, studying its splintered pattern for what seemed like the thousandth time. It had been over a century since the

Prism Effect had taken place. By using Albright's own blood, Van Saint had created the painting called *The Plan*. She was murdered by Sybold as her final brushstroke fell. Albright's table ruptured at that same instant—creating what Cord now referred to as *the splinter code*—and the Prism Effect moved into its first phase.

The fragmented pattern from the table was almost an exact match to the painting's bloody pattern. Yet there was one very subtle variation he had recently observed. A particular section of its pattern was missing when he compared it to the painting; *fascinating*. While there was more to the overall riddle, two things were prevalent in his mind. First, the value he had discovered previously varied from the value he got from the table… by one digit. Secondly, the quadratic formula accompanied those values.

Almost four years prior, he had calculated a number of 2,412,630 from Van Saint's painting called *The Plan*. Until recently, he had no inkling what that number represented. However, the number he calculated from the table was 2,412,631. Albright and Van Saint didn't agree. There seemed to be two answers. In the world of algebra, the quadratic formula was unique because it sometimes provided two solutions. Again, fascinating.

He understood why so many people felt that Jet was the Fallout; the way the splintered area engaged his symbol on the table was unique, compared to everyone else's symbol. In reality, this could mean anything, though, and he wasn't buying all that Skylight Fallout hype just yet.

Outside of the small variance in numbers—a.k.a. the splinter code—the table and the painting's pattern were in lockstep with each other and matched exactly. This trivial variation in the number seemed to apply *only* to the Skylight Fallout.

However…there was more to the splinter code, something hidden between Van Saint's three paintings. It was a prophesy, one that he'd been struggling to accept.

The Skylight Fallout must die to fulfill their duty.

If the Fallout was Jet, then he was destined to die…at least, that's what the prophesy seemed to proclaim; intriguing. But legends and prophesies didn't sit well with him. He wanted to believe that a person determined their own destiny, and facts meant more to him than prophesies. The biggest question he was faced with now was how much he should share with Jet. But before he said anything, he needed to know more. He needed to see the painting called *The Plan* one more time.

However, since becoming a Lucem, he had seen things he couldn't explain; his world and what he once knew had been turned upside down. In reality—even though he was reluctant to admit it—he *knew* Van Saint's prophesy regarding the Skylight Fallout's death would be fulfilled. But…could it be changed? Could destiny be rechanneled or altered? Perhaps that's what the quadratic formula really represented? Or, perhaps, that's why Albright and Van Saint's solution differed, *even if it was by just…one…digit.*

Cord left the Hall of Prisms and went down to his studio quarters. Inside was a large training room and a rug for meditation. When he was troubled, this was where he spent his time. He trained hard, rarely needing a break, and when he was away on assignment, he felt his inner balance was off kilter.

Training was like medicine to him. He didn't understand why a Heliographi wouldn't want to spend as much time as possible doing it. Jet could be great… *really great.* Instead, he seemed reluctant to train and meditate. Cord thought he knew why, though. Jet was used to being adept at most things, probably from playing the sport of blaze throughout his life. He had been good at blaze, perhaps one of the best. Yet, so far, he hadn't quite gotten the hang of Vishmu, an ancient psychic art the Heliographi used. However, Vishmu wasn't based just on physical ability, which was probably why Jet struggled. Still, Cord had shown Jet a few tricks in hopes it would ignite his desire for training. He felt confident that eventually, Jet would catch on, and when he did, he would be a dangerous adversary. Jet's drive to succeed rivaled his own, and he had great respect for him. But, until Jet was more capable, Cord felt honor bound to watch over him as much as he could.

Cord turned his focus toward a small red ball sitting on a wooden stool. What Cord was working on was considered the very fringe of Vishmu. No one that he knew had the ability to do what he was getting close to achieving. Telekinesis.

As he sat cross-legged on the mat, he placed the tattered book of Vishmu in front of him. The language in it was archaic and difficult to comprehend, even for him. Its diagrams, charts and math were interwoven into a language that few, save Heliographi, could grasp.

Cord closed his eyes.

He focused on the red ball and projected waves from his mind. Like billions of subatomic frequencies at the quantum level, they radiated out from his inner being, building energy and vibration until the ball shifted ever so slightly. It rolled a few times, slowly at first. Then it tumbled to the floor.

|

An hour later, Cord left the Agency headquarters. He calculated there was just enough time to make the trip over to the Skylight Museum of Art. He engaged the skiff's cloaking device out of habit as he left the hanger.

Skylight City was cloaked in mist with enormous skyscrapers breaching the gray clouds. Multicolored glassy facades glinted in the brief flashes of sunlight. The traffic was a mess, as usual, with most of the skiff lanes being jam packed. He docked his skiff at the Agency hanger, grateful for the privacy, and pulled his cloak over his street clothes. The T-Spine, a mass transit system that suspended from a charged rail just above the street, was a quick way around the city. But Cord preferred avoiding people, even when wearing his alias, and made the trek to the museum on foot.

The Lucem's cloak had many tantalizing features. The one he enjoyed the most was its ability to scramble security systems. He moved seamlessly through the museum without notice, since no alarms could detect his presence. The painting was located near the back of the building.

Once there, he stood in front of it and simply stared. No matter how many times he had seen it, the painting always fascinated him. He was not one to gush over art or get lost in its meaning. He was an analytical person and knew he didn't possess an ounce of artistic ability. Before all of this, he never understood why some people collected art and spent so much money on it. But Van Saint's work seemed to take him places. It aroused something in his soul he couldn't describe. His hands would sweat, and his heartbeat increased. Often, he felt like he stood on the edge of a precipice with no control. It was disturbing in so many ways...and exhilarating.

The painting called *The Realization* was suspended in a clear vandal-proof case. The large painting depicted a barren landscape, perhaps the great plains of Northern America where Shiloe Van Saint had been raised. A storm cloud in the distance flashed behind a lone flower in the foreground. It bent in the wind, its petals being stripped away and littering the field beyond in a myriad of colors. Only one black and white petal clung to the flower. Cord loved the foreboding nature of the painting; it was right up his alley.

He refocused on the paint strokes until the holographic Roman numerals appeared. All twenty-four of them created a complete circle, twelve on the right side and twelve on the left side. He made a few mental notes and confirmed it was just as he remembered it. All he required now was one last viewing of the painting in Lybra's gallery called *The Plan*. But getting in there would be problematic.

A movement to his left drew his attention.

He immediately recognized the shape as another Heliographi, cloaked and hidden. Its movement caused light to bend around its shape, and only the trained eyes of a Heliographi could see it. Even then, he barely noticed. It seemed to be observing the painting, but was it a Lucem or an Atrum?

The other Heliographi didn't notice him as he waited. After several minutes, it sped swiftly toward the exit and Cord followed at a safe distance. He trailed it onto the main street, careful not to bump anyone. It didn't take long for him to sense that it was an Atrum.

But he was confused as to why an Atrum would show interest in Van Saint's painting.

He continued to follow it through dark alleyways and back corridors before sensing it was aware of his presence. The pursuit turned down another dark alley until the Atrum was no longer visible. Cord suddenly realized that a trap had been set and stopped just shy of entering a nook. He crouched in the shadows, scanning the area, then sprang to a suspended metal landing on the side of a building and waited.

He finally spotted the Atrum. It stood still, blurry in the faint light and about five meters to his left. It didn't take long for the Atrum to realize it had been figured out. Cord now had to decide if he should engage the Atrum or let it go. Solan had made him and Jet swear not to engage the Atrum if they encountered any, but…

That just seemed boring.

He leapt the five meters and landed directly on top of it. The surprise attack gave him an instant advantage, and he put the Atrum in a headlock. He had a good grip on it as they both tumbled to the ground. It rolled and clawed at his arm, rage and hatred emanating from it. He pulled tight and put enough pressure on its throat to hear it gasp for air. But he didn't want it unconscious, yet.

"Lower your hood," he whispered. Of course, he could've simply done it himself, but making this Atrum do it instead just felt more satisfying. He was having too much fun.

"No!" the Atrum replied.

He put a bit more pressure on its throat. Any more and he would crush its windpipe.

Another gasp, and then finally a tap on the arm. Cord relaxed his grip slightly, and the Atrum lowered its hood, materializing to reveal greenish-blue hair and glowing eyes. Cord let go of it in shock.

Vail glared at him, causing him to take a step back. He lowered his hood and watched her gaze go wide.

"Ledbetter?" Vail muttered in surprise.

In that instant of distraction, he was quick enough to catch a glimpse of her thoughts. The confusion, rage, and hatred he sensed shocked him. He hadn't known Vail that well during their time at Skylight University as classmates, but what he witnessed in her now was not the same person, not by a long shot. Though she looked much the same on the outside, Vail was nearly unrecognizable to him. He felt an instant of pity for her. Though he had suffered through the same ridicule during his time at Skylight University, he didn't like seeing how it affected her. His moment of empathy caught him by surprise.

"What?" she hissed. "Are you shocked, brainiac?"

"Perhaps I could ask you the same," Cord replied, regaining his calm composure.

"Back off, Cord. We have no business with each other."

"Oh, I beg to differ," Cord replied and lifted one corner of his mouth in a relaxed smile, the last word tapering off in his smooth drawl. "I'm in no rush to uncover your secrets, Vail. You should reconsider your position. You are good…but you cannot beat me."

"You're so arrogant, Ledbetter," she said. "I see nothing has changed with you."

"But you have," Cord replied. "What have they done to you?"

"I'd tell you to mind your own business again, but I know you won't. Even you couldn't comprehend what is happening with the Atrum right now."

"Do you really want to be a part of that?" Cord asked. "We were certainly not the best of friends, and I admit I didn't care much for you. But I never wanted this to happen. Let me help you and Bo."

She let out a laugh that sounded more like a cackle and shook her head. "Are you trying to save me? And Bo too? I'm impressed. Looking after someone other than yourself now. I should be the one asking what's happened to *you*?"

"Why were you at the museum tonight?" Cord asked, ignoring her sarcasm. He knew she would reject his offer to help; the images he had just witnessed in her thoughts told him everything he needed to know. He couldn't save her; she was well beyond that now.

"Say hello to Stroud and his girl, Kamber, for me. I'm sure I'll see him soon." She pulled her hood over her eyes and vanished.

CHAPTER 6
The Splinter Code

ΑΒΓΔΕΖΗΘΙΚΛ**Μ**
ΝΞΟΠΡΣΤΥΦΧΨΩ

THE NEXT MORNING, Jet changed into his athletic coaching gear and stuffed his cloak into a backpack, prepared for the first day of the semester. He held up an old ring and looked at its patinaed surface. It was a plain looking ring with a faded copper hue and had been issued to him when he'd joined the Lucem. But to a Heliographi's eyes, there were hidden details normal people couldn't see. The top of it shone with a color that matched his glowing eyes, and a faint symbol shaped like the letter M floated above it. It had several capabilities, but the most important one was his alias as Gunter Kepp, assistant athletic director for the blaze team. He covered its hologram to avoid being noticed by other Heliographi and walked to the hangers.

The Agency had assigned him a unique skiff, normally reserved for the elite recon. It had several countermeasures built in, and a cloaking system. Needless to say, he hadn't objected when they'd offered it to him.

When he arrived at Skylight University, he docked his skiff in an area designated for staff. The walkways were crowded with students heading to class as Jet navigated through the campus in no real hurry. It felt good to walk the campus again, to see the excited students rushing to class and hear the buzz in the air. The stark white stone buildings on campus all seemed to follow a consistent architectural style with heavy columns at the front entry and rooflines that cantilevered out like a feather.

He walked into the library and down to the basement level. An area near the back had a gate and a sign that read 'Off Limits.' He walked past it toward a wooden bookcase, checked to make sure he was alone, then slid open a false panel to reveal a worn brass handle. The bookcase swung open, and a stone staircase beckoned to him.

Down in the basement, Cord sat in an old wing-backed chair behind a claw-and-ball table that appeared to be as old as the university. Several large candles lit the space with dried wax clumped on the stone floor, and a breeze hummed through the space and threatened to extinguish the candle's flame. He stood in a vast barrel-vaulted chamber with millions of old books on stacks of metal racks. Jet hadn't visited the basement since his freshman term about four years ago. He and his classmates at the time had nicknamed the place *the stacks* and had held their secret meetings here. It brought back a flood of memories, not all of them pleasant.

Cord multitasked through numerous equations with spidery fingers tapping the air. He glanced at Jet but didn't stop working. "You're late, again."

Jet stood opposite the hologram and looked at Cord through its haze. "Nice to see you too. What's on your mind?"

"An insurmountable thirst for knowledge," Cord joked.

"Well, you should try to relax, you'll live longer," Jet replied, and Cord cracked a smile. It had become an inside joke between them. Now that they were both Heliographi, their life expectancy was off the charts. They would no longer age, but they were still flesh and bone and could be killed, if they weren't cautious.

"I talked to Solan and DiJinn, by the way. They're really concerned about Tyberius. What do you think?"

Cord finally stopped working and sat back. "My guess is that Solan will start searching for him soon, but

I don't imagine she'll want a committee when she does. I don't believe her plans will include us."

"Rumor is that Tyberius disappeared while looking for Albright near Skylight City."

"That's the rumor," Cord replied and crossed his arms, waited for a few seconds. "Shall we dispense with the small talk, Jet? I sense you're concerned about something else."

Jet settled in and studied Cord, who he considered his closest friend. Even though Cutter was alive and well, he hadn't talked to him in nearly four years, though Jet had secretly been watching over him. Cord had filled that void, and together they had shared their concerns, triumphs and fears since leaving Skylight University.

"I'm just wondering if I'm cut out for this," Jet said. "Maybe comparing everything to blaze is the problem. I understood how that worked, I was good at it. But this is so different. I've been at it nearly four years now, and I'm not getting much better. Solan's even losing patience with me lately."

"Remain steady," Cord said. "Your drive is unrivaled, and I have great respect for your intuition; I suspect everything will come together soon."

"That's easy for you to say, Cord. You're already one of the top Lucem. I'm just trying to find my purpose here."

"Yet you already have one. Kamber and Cutter require your assistance."

"But that's the problem! I'm struggling to understand Vishmu and the training, along with all of this Lucem business. How can I possibly protect them? I witnessed the strength of the Atrum that night of the triclipse—I was powerless against Sybold. Now I'm supposed to be responsible for myself *and* two others?"

"Focus on Solan when you train. She's one of the most accomplished Lucem we have. The odds are favorable you will succeed."

"But when will it all click?" Jet asked. "I'm afraid I'm running out of time, I don't want Kamber, or Cutter, or anyone else to suffer because I stink at this. I think any other Lucem would be a better choice to look after Kamber right now, don't you think?"

"You're not as awful as you think, not as good as you should be, but not as awful."

Jet grinned and looked at Cord, then shook his head, amused at Cord's bedside manner. His attempt at consoling Jet, though well intended, had missed the mark. Jet gave up and changed the topic. "Well, what do you think about our agreement with Hurse? I'm wondering if it was the right thing to do."

"Again, I would strongly caution you against trusting any of the Atrum. You should consider a backup plan."

"What type of backup plan?" Jet asked.

"One might refer to it as leverage. In the unfortunate event that something happened to Kamber and Hurse is behind it, what can you use against him as collateral? Bend the rules, bend them till they break. What you think is unethical, I think is a counter option."

"You're saying that harming his warden should be considered?" Jet asked, giving him a sidelong glance.

"I'm saying, how far will you go to protect Kamber?"

Jet shook his head. "I don't know, but I'm pretty sure murder isn't on my list."

"Murder doesn't have to be on the table. Just the illusion that it is."

"I'm not kidding around, Cord. She's the last of the Lucem. We need her."

"I am well aware," Cord replied. "Tell me, when you played blaze, were there times when you tried to guess your opponent's moves?"

"Yeah, all the time," Jet said.

"Think of it in terms of blaze and put yourself on the Atrum's menial level. That's how you will defeat them."

"Cord," Jet said, trying not to sound frustrated. "Can you just tell me what you'd do about Hurse?"

"Hurse is a nuisance. I would have eliminated him already. That's the most logical approach."

"Really? You would have killed him?"

Cord shrugged. "Perhaps."

"Sounds a bit dark, even by your standards. You feelin' okay?"

Cord shrugged his narrow shoulders. "I feel fantastic," he said dryly, but cracked a crooked smile at Jet. "I believe you know what to do. Just remember that Hurse, like all the Atrum, are demented, devious and devilish. You can quote me on that."

"Which makes me wonder why Hurse didn't kill me when he had the chance. He could've done it several times already. So why hasn't he?"

Cord gave Jet a serious look. "That would start a war they aren't ready for yet. They are waiting for something."

Jet stared at Cord, considering, then shook his head. "I don't know. I feel there's more to it. I just haven't figured it out yet. Maybe he's laying down a smoke screen to redirect our attention? DiJinn said he was the most devious of all the Atrum, and that's saying something."

Cord rubbed his goatee. "That sounds more accurate. Whatever the Atrum are hiding, expect it to rear its head soon."

"Right. I'll think about it. I need something up my sleeve."

"I believe that would be wise," Cord said.

Jet understood what Cord was saying. He had to get on Hurse's level. The Atrum didn't fight fair, so he needed to do the same, even if he didn't like it. But Kamber's safety was vital to the Lucem.

Jet stood and stretched. "Cord, I'm on the verge of letting Kamber in on all this. She deserves to know what's happening, don't you think?"

"I predict Solan will never allow that."

"I'm not planning to tell her about it."

"That's fair," Cord said. "I suppose I'd want to know too. What transpired four years ago with Sybold was a close call. I'm not going to dictate what you should do, but I would recommend that you consider the outcome carefully before you proceed."

"Understood." Jet turned his thoughts to the splinter code. He was about to ask when Cord spoke up.

"Yes, of course…the splinter code."

Jet had let his guard down for just a split second, but it was long enough for Cord to reach in and grab his thoughts. Most Lucem couldn't do it that quickly, but Cord had rocketed through training. He was more than a mathematical genius—he was a prodigy in Vishmu.

"I'm working on a few tantalizing theories," Cord said. "Unfortunately, I only have access to two of the paintings. I'm a bit uncertain about my conclusion as of now."

"I thought you had the one at Lybra's estate memorized?"

"Going off memory has brought me a long way. However, there are a few disparities in what I recall now. Albright's table in the Hall of Prisms has assisted me in fulfilling those disparities, to some degree. However, there is a slight variation between the table and the painting that I wish to verify."

"Are you saying you want back into Lybra's gallery?"

"Yes," Cord said. "That's what I should have just said."

Jet smirked. "From what I remember, she only let us in because we were students with E.M."

"Correct. And you happen to know a student with E.M."

"You want me to use Kamber to get us into Lybra's gallery? I haven't even met her yet."

"You're an athletic director for the finest athletic program in college sports," Cord said. "Sounds like you might have some influence, no?"

"Using a student as leverage like that, though…it makes me nervous."

"I understand that Kamber is quite the talented runner. Might you convince her to talk to the coach, perhaps see if she would permit a field trip?"

"Coach Minnett," Jet said and nodded. He could see where Cord was headed. "I'm sure a call from the newest athletic director might apply a little pressure on her, combined with a request from one of her top runners. That just might work."

Cord nodded agreement. "Then we simply accompany Kamber and gain access back into Lybra's gallery."

"Still, I don't know," Jet sighed. "We'd have to keep this to ourselves. Solan probably wouldn't go for it. She'd be furious if she found out we used Kamber for something like this."

"I understand your concern. But I'm on the verge of unearthing a significant clue. I require one more viewing of the painting. I suppose another option is letting ourselves in. It would be simple for us. I have Lybra's security layout memorized from our first trip, unless she's revised it, which is unlikely."

Jet shook his head. "I'd prefer to do this on the up-and-up first. It'll depend on whether I can work out a deal with Kamber's coach. If that fails, maybe then we can resort to more questionable tactics."

"I'll leave it in your capable hands, then."

Jet crossed his arms. "Can you share what this big idea is? Sounds like more than we originally thought."

"Follow me." Cord led the way over to the main rack of books and removed several of the tomes until a large painting was visible on the back wall. During his time as a freshman, they had located the final painting hidden here, but had left it undisturbed. The painting was an original by Van Saint and one of the three that held a prophesy of some sort. Its value was beyond measure, and only a handful of people knew that it still existed.

As Jet and Cord stared at the painting, the strange holographic landscape began to materialize, a mathematical language only a true Heliographi could see. According to Solan, Shiloe Van Saint and Christian Albright had coordinated to create the holograms within the thick brush strokes of the canvas.

"Ok," Jet said. "What's this big idea?"

"I believe that the three paintings, *The Realization*, *The Plan* and *The Verification*, are meant to work as one, and this 'so-called' prophesy is divided between them. It has been separated into thirds to maintain its secret. Furthermore, both Albright's table and Van Saint's painting, *The Plan*, are a map of the Skylight System. The numbers I've calculated in them represent coordinates."

"I'm not even gonna ask how you came to that conclusion," Jet chuckled.

"Well, perhaps you should buckle up, as they say, because I'm going to attempt to explain it to you. You need to understand this information in case something happens to me."

"That serious, huh?" Jet asked, leaning against a rack to get comfortable. "Is there a short version of it?"

"I'll attempt to simplify it for you. I've made multiple trips to view the first painting, which is owned by the Skylight government. As a matter of fact, I just returned. I bumped into an old friend, by the way."

"Really? Who?"

"I'll explain in just a minute. Let's discuss this first."

"Alright, but…why won't the table substitute for the painting at Lybra's gallery?"

"I've detected a subtle variation between the two. The splinter code in Albright's table is marginally unique from the painting's pattern."

Jet narrowed his eyes. "So…it's different?"

"Remember the number we found in Van Saint's painting four years ago?"

Jet laughed. "How could I forget? 2,412,630."

"There's more to it. That number was accompanied by the quadratic formula. It's a very basic algebraic formula with a plus-minus symbol in front of the root."

"I'm somewhat familiar with it," Jet said. "Go on."

"Then I assume you understand that it can have zero, one, or two solutions, and it's primarily used to plot points along the path of a parabola."

"I'm not sure I follow. A parabola is an elliptical path. Why would that be part of any of this?"

"Albright is a trickster," Cord said. "He loves to play games, and math is his medium. The quadratic formula fits into this whole riddle concept we've been pursuing since we were students four years ago. His equations were never meant to be solved, but rather to hide something—I know this now, so I always look at his work with this in mind. This quadratic formula was intentionally left blank."

"Well, back to the splinter code then. How is it different?"

"When I calculate the splintered coordinates in Albright's table, I get a slightly larger number of

2,412,631—one coordinate *greater* than Van Saint's painting."

Jet shrugged. "Considering how big the number is, sounds close enough to me."

"Nevertheless, it is two unique answers."

"So…two solutions?" Jet mused.

"The *possibility* of two solutions, just like the quadratic formula," Cord corrected him. "Perhaps Albright's conclusion varied from Van Saint's on purpose or perhaps they just didn't agree on the result. It's even possible that they didn't even *know* the outcome."

"Could there be two Skylight Fallouts instead?"

Cord rubbed his goatee. "I actually had not thought of that." He stood and walked back to the table. "I believe that the Fallout could be an Atrum or a Lucem. And, now that you've pointed it out, I suppose there could be one, two, or zero Fallouts. Who is destined to be a Fallout? Is it possible that the Fallout could change or alter their own fate? That's a lot to consider. Personally, I tend to believe that we determine our own destiny. Perhaps Van Saint and Albright disagreed on this fundamental principle and ended up with two distinct solutions? We may never know their true intentions."

Jet followed him. "My head is starting to hurt just thinking about all of this. What's your best conclusion?"

"Simply put; we have no clue who the Skylight Fallout will be."

"Then I wonder why so many people think it's me?"

"I believe that's due to the unique pattern that forms around your symbol. In both the painting and the table, the fracture pattern is different than all the other symbols. Then again, perhaps someone is simply spreading false information."

"Out of curiosity, does my symbol have anything to do with the splinter code?"

"No. The location of the splinter code on Albright's table is in a different area."

"I guess I never looked that closely at my symbol. But where's the location of the splinter code?"

"If we assume that the table represents a map of the system, then the splinter code is located at Revelations Plaza," Cord said. "The splinter code was the *only* coordinate in the tenth location from Albright. All Van Saint's coordinates in her painting were distributed between nine other locations. Revelations Plaza appears to be the epicenter of some special event."

"And this special event will take place on the same day as the Century Eclipse?"

"It certainly appears that way."

Jet looked at Cord's holopad on the table. "Are those numbers the coordinates?"

"They are. I calculated all 2,412,631 points using a three-dimensional Cartesian coordinate system—"

Jet stopped him. "Cartesian?"

"It's a grid system that uses an 'X' and a 'Y' axis to find coordinates, with a 'Z' axis for the third dimension." Cord pressed an area on his holopad display, and a three-dimensional map of the entire Skylight System projected over the table. The large orb-like hologram showed the nine belts and the Core. Nine clusters of coordinates populated the hologram, but at varying distances from the Core. There was one tiny blip located at Revelations Plaza on the first belt.

"Looks like these locations are all floating in space," Jet said.

"Because I haven't updated the time and dates yet." Cord took a moment and loaded some information. The belts adjusted inside the hologram and then aligned with the clusters of coordinates, one on each of the nine belts. "All the dates fall within a skylight eclipse as well," Cord said. "How fascinating is that?"

"Where did you get the dates and times from?"

"The other two paintings. The dates are from *The Verification*, and the times are from *The Realization*. Do you recall the twenty-four Roman numerals in *The Realization?* The first twelve represent the daylight hours, and thirteen through twenty-four represent the evening hours. It is the sun dial versus the moon dial. As I noted earlier, the riddle was divided between all three of Van Saint's paintings, and the rumor of the final painting being destroyed was spread to further prevent its discovery. Each painting was placed in a different location. As an additional safety measure, Albright included one additional coordinate in his table…the splinter code. One would not only have to crack the code in the paintings but know about the splinter code as well. That's quite an endeavor."

"So, we have everything we need?" Jet asked. "Does that mean we just show up at those times and locations?"

"I don't believe it works that way. As I mentioned to you earlier, there must be something we have to collect during the Century Eclipse, an easter egg or key left behind by Albright. The Skylight Fallout will trigger the second phase of the Prism Effect but will also reveal this clue. I believe that this clue will lead to the Heliographi Memoirs. Albright's memoirs are rumored to hold a great power and we cannot allow them to fall into the wrong hands." Cord hesitated for a split second, which caught Jet's attention.

"Something else to add?"

"No…that is all for now," Cord said. "At least until I view Lybra's painting again."

"What is it, Cord?" Jet said, pressing him. He could see there was more, and Cord's reluctance to share it concerned him. "Whatever it is, tell me. We've always trusted each other."

Cord stared at Jet for a long moment, then shook his head. "It's nothing."

"Alright," Jet said and shrugged. "If you say so. Now, let's hear about this old friend you met."

Cord stood and clapped his hands, as if moving on from whatever else was on his mind. "While I was at the museum, I saw an Atrum. It seemed to be studying the painting."

"Why would an Atrum be looking at *The Realization?*"

"I am uncertain. Regardless, I followed it, and it tried to ambush me. Three guesses who it was."

"Don't tell me it was Vail."

"Surprised me a bit as well. She was the last person I expected to see, especially there."

Jet rubbed his brow. "Did she say anything?"

"Well, I managed a glimpse of her thoughts. It was just a few seconds, but I didn't like what I saw."

"What did you see?"

Cord considered for a second, like he was trying to formulate his thoughts into words. "It was odd, maybe even fascinating, looking into her mind. It's not wise to get into an Atrum's head like that, I understand. But…it just didn't seem like her, at least the way I remember her. She was always defiant, perhaps bullish. But her attitude, her personality…her ideas were dark and angry. I saw rage. I dare say, evil…"

"Anything else?"

"She mentioned Kamber. She said she would see you soon."

Jet sat there in thought while Cord looked on silently. Last time he'd talked to Vail, she seemed confused. That night in the snowy courtyard when the Atrum converted her, he had felt her pain and uncertainty. That was the last time he'd seen her until recently. He tugged at the locket she'd dropped, something he rarely wore. His index finger traced it beneath his shirt, and he tapped it three times.

Jet finally straightened and glanced back at the painting. "Vail sent me a signal. She wants to meet me."

"When did this occur?"

"That night we met Hurse down at the old particle collider."

"Are you certain it was a signal? It seems odd that I didn't hear it as well."

"She didn't send it with her thoughts, it was morse code. I had to meditate to figure out the rest of it. But, it was definitely a signal; I just don't know what she wants."

"What would meditating accomplish?"

Jet looked at him with a bit of surprise. "I always meditate when I need answers, and sometimes, they come to me. Are you saying that doesn't work for you?"

"No." Cord looked at Jet and furrowed his brow. "Has this always been the case?"

"Yes, as long as I've been doing the meditations. Usually happens in that transition back to reality."

"That is *very* intriguing. I believe it is the first time I've heard of that particular trait in a Heliographi. This would seem to be a very rare gift."

"I just assumed it was normal."

"It most definitely isn't." Cord clapped him on the shoulder. "Be very cautious if you decide to meet Vail. She is not the same person she was in the past. Of course, you already know this."

"I can't resist an opportunity, and something tells me I need to do this," Jet said, but he was already having second thoughts.

CHAPTER 7
Solan's Reveal

ΑΒΓΔΕΖΗΘΙ**Κ**ΛΜ
ΝΞΟΠΡΣΤΥΦΧΨΩ

SOLAN WAITED UNTIL later that evening before she boarded her skiff. Even though it was her last night at Flotsam—their code name for the Agency's headquarters—she wanted to avoid any watchful eyes as she left for Skylight University. She believed there were several spies around the Agency, and she and Jinn had plans to set a trap and net them, but that would have to wait. Jinn was on an undercover drug run, and Solan had business at the university tonight.

The private faculty hanger at the university was mostly vacant. Solan pulled the hood of her cloak tight and disappeared. She found the nearest portal, which happened to be in the Clipton Woods, and hurried through Lyrinthum. Its dark musty corridors were quiet and vacant, just the way she liked it.

She followed a portion of the old, abandoned particle collider and eventually ended up near the science department. She hopped out of one of the building portals, which gave a brief flash, and hid beneath some underbrush.

Before long, a thin, dark-skinned lady walked by. She wore a shimmering blouse and a satchel over one shoulder that looked to have several holopads in it. Her younger sister, Sterllar, better known as Professor Sylvant by most, had always loved things that shimmered, like Solan's eyes.

Solan followed her back to the faculty hanger, hiding in the shadows of buildings and trees. She had been tailing her sister over the last month, mainly to verify her schedule, but also out of concern. Just last week, she had spotted an Atrum tailing her and grew alarmed by that. What in Skylight would an Atrum want with her sister? Murder? Kidnapping for leverage? Regardless, it was no longer safe.

Her sister always worked late, and tonight, Solan's instinct warned her to stay close and vigilant. She usually trusted her instinct, and it rarely let her down. She looked down at her hands. They shook with nervous anxiety— she could hardly believe it. After all the things she had faced in her life, this scared her more than anything. What she was about to do broke every code the Lucem upheld. Her father would be furious. But… her father wasn't here; he was in trouble. After tomorrow, though, the Lucem would no longer be under the Agency's umbrella, and that loosened up several restrictions. Still, she wondered for the tenth time that day if she was making the right decision for the Lucem, or for her own selfish reasons.

Solan kept her skiff cloaked as she followed her sister to the third belt and Skylight City. Sylvant docked at one of the large public hangers, and at this late hour, the facility was mostly vacant. She followed her sister, staying cloaked and keeping her eyes open for anything out of the ordinary. Soon, a blurry mirage appeared and followed. Solan fell in behind it, trying to subdue her anger. As much as she wanted to strike now, she had the advantage and wasn't ready to give it up. This Atrum was sloppy and had made several amateur mistakes. It was about to pay the price.

Sylvant hurried along the sparse streets of Skylight City, the clicking of her heels mixed with the occasional sound of music in the background from a local pub or restaurant. As she neared her apartment, she pulled an access badge from her purse and was about to swipe her door when the Atrum made its move. Solan bolted across the intersection and hit the Atrum, driving her shoulder under its chin. Caught off guard, it hit the building with a thud. Solan followed up with a head-butt and an elbow, and the stunned Atrum slumped to the ground, unconscious.

Sylvant froze from the commotion and backed against the door to her apartment building. Even though Solan and the Atrum were still cloaked, the loud noise hadn't gone unnoticed.

Solan took one more deep breath and stepped from the shadows as she lowered her hood, hoping her sister wouldn't keel over in disbelief. Sylvant took one look at Solan, let out a gasp and fainted.

Solan caught her sister before she hit the ground and laid her down gently. Then she turned to the Atrum and slid its hood down. She recognized the girl's red hair and chiseled features as one of the Atrum's newest members; a girl named Myranda Mason. Her inexperience could have cost her life—if Solan had been a bit angrier. Solan placed a hand on the girl's forehead and sent a thought. Myranda's eyes fluttered, and she woke.

Solan whispered to Myranda. "What do you think you're up to?"

Myranda took a second as the grogginess faded. "Just doing my job."

"Does that include murder?" Solan asked, straining to maintain her temper. "They send a child to do this? You're in over your head."

"Who said anything about murder?" Myranda said and wiped blood from a cut above her eye.

"So, kidnapping? For leverage I assume?"

"Maybe…maybe not," Myranda replied.

Solan thought about questioning her further but knew she would get no answers. Instead, she reached out and squeezed Myranda's collar bone tight enough to feel her tense. Solan felt a slight bit of rage course through her veins and for a split second relished the feeling, thought about squeezing the life out of this arrogant little Atrum, but purged the thought as Myranda went limp. Solan lifted Myranda's unconscious body and propped her up against the building, then slid her hood over Myranda's face, and she vanished.

Solan lifted her sister and carried her inside her apartment building, thankful for the late hour and lack of traffic in that area. The posh entry lobby was dimly lit with mood lighting, with some stylish lounge seating in one corner and a bank of vector accelerators to the opposite side. Solan carried her sister to a restroom and sat her down. She touched her forehead, and she sat up straight. Solan locked eyes with her as she stirred awake.

Sylvant rubbed her brow. "What is this? What's happening?"

"Just relax," Solan said, one hand on her sister's shoulder and the other held up in a plea to stay calm.

"Is this some sort of demented joke?" Sylvant asked and sat back, a look of shock and confusion on her face. "Explain this!"

"Easy, sis! I know this is confusing, but please just try to stay calm, and I'll explain—"

"Confusing?" Sylvant interrupted her and stood. "*Confusing!* It's been over a decade, and you suddenly pop back into my life, and you want me to stay calm?"

"Calm…down," Solan said firmly, looking around her and holding both hands out. She took a deep breath as Sylvant touched her forehead again and stood. She stumbled against the wall and tried to steady herself. Solan reached out and held her by the shoulders.

"You died. Now you're back…what's happening?"

Solan held her sister and stared into her eyes, then pulled her into an embrace and held her. Sylvant trembled and began to cry. The two sisters stood there for several minutes in the empty restroom. Solan gave her the time she needed and didn't care if someone walked in. Her sister was brave, in her own way, and had been through a lot. She deserved this moment.

Sylvant eventually pulled back and sniffled.

"I'm so sorry," Solan said. "This isn't your fault, and you shouldn't have to deal with all of this."

Sylvant knuckled away a tear and cracked a smile. "I missed you."

Solan smiled for what seemed like the first time in years. A ray of light shone inside her soul just hearing her sister's voice.

"This is going to need some serious explanation," Sylvant said, wiping her cheeks.

"We need to go someplace more private. Where's your apartment?"

Solan cloaked again, assuring her sister that she was still there, and followed Sylvant up to her apartment, which was on the eighty-second floor. Sylvant's apartment was efficient, with only one bedroom, a tiny kitchen and living room. Large windows provided a panoramic view of the city beyond, visible through occasional breaks in the clouds. Once inside, Solan uncloaked and stepped out to the balcony and waited there uneasily. Her reluctance to stay in one place too long was ingrained in her psyche, and she was already getting nervous. But a big part of her anxiety was because she'd broken her vow to the Lucem by talking to her sister. Hopefully she hadn't opened some pandora's box that she couldn't close now. From this point forward, she was responsible for her sister's safety.

Sylvant joined her on the balcony and stepped up next to Solan. She handed her a cup of tea and sat down, curling her feet under her legs, and cupping the mug with both hands. The tiny balcony was too cramped for Solan's liking, but she pushed the uneasy feeling down and leaned against the guardrail. She tried to calm herself and gazed at the sky. Stars twinkled at her, and she could see the faint outline of a few belts in the distance.

"Where should we begin?" Sylvant asked.

Solan took a deep breath. "I'm not sure, for the first time in a while. This is uncharted territory for me." Solan finally sat down. "I guess I should start by revealing who I really am. I'm part of an ancient order known as the Heliographi, and E.M. doesn't really exist, at least not in the way it's portrayed to the public."

"I can see that, and I'm glad that's the case," Sylvant said.

"The legend of E.M. has its purpose," Solan continued. "It's meant to protect our identity. After our deaths are faked, we're inducted into an order called the Lucem. We are, or were, I should say, part of a group called the Agency. We are sworn to protect the citizens of Skylight."

"But I take it that you're not supposed to be here?"

Solan shook her head. "No, what we're doing right now is forbidden."

Sylvant sat back, and alarm crossed her face.

Solan took a second to compose herself. "I'm not supposed to be here. I hope you can understand why I'm a bit nervous. I just need you to understand how serious this is. I vowed never to talk to you or discuss this with anyone. I'm involved in a dangerous business."

"I think I understand. I hope you don't face any punishment on my account."

"I'd face any punishment for you." Solan reached out and grasped her sister's thin shoulders and gave her a shake. "You give me hope, that's what sustains me sometimes. But lately, things have become so dim. I *needed* this."

Sylvant held Solan's hand and smiled. "Are you sure this is wise? Sounds like it's such a risk for you."

"You saw what happened down on the street. That thing is called an Atrum. They're like us but conduct themselves under a different set of ethics."

"Meaning…they aren't nice people, I take it?" Sylvant asked.

"That's a mild way of putting it. I think you've been on their radar for a while now, so I've been following you and noticed that one. Tonight, I think they were planning to kidnap you and hold you hostage to gain leverage over me and our group."

Sylvant looked at Solan with a shocked expression.

"Of course, when I figured it out, I couldn't allow it," Solan continued. "I just didn't believe they would go to that extent. Apparently, I've misjudged their mindset. Why they've chosen to do this now is a mystery."

"What does this all mean for me?"

"I'm afraid things are about to change for you," Solan said and reached out to hold her hand. "Tyberius would be furious with me if he knew I was doing this."

"Our father? Solan…we never got to talk after your final semester at Skylight."

"I know, and I'm sorry about that. For the record, Tyberius is our real father. He is also the leader of our group. I hope you get a chance to meet him someday."

"Why do I get the sense there's more to that story?"

Solan sighed. "Right now, he's missing, and I haven't seen him in weeks. But…I promise I'll find him."

"I have access to the university facilities, if I can help. But I imagine it's nothing compared to your intel."

"I don't want to bring you into harm's way," Solan said. "I'm here tonight because I knew you were in trouble, and I couldn't see you harmed. I also thought you deserved to know who your real father is."

"You're acting like something tragic has already happened to him."

"Don't worry," Solan said, wondering if she was reassuring herself more than her sister. "Our father can handle himself. He'll be fine."

They sat quietly for a moment until Sylvant cleared her throat. "Solan…you said that things are about to change for me. What did you mean?"

Solan held her gaze for a long moment, realizing now how reluctant she was to answer the question. "Danger follows us—it seems to follow all of the Lucem. The Atrum will use any advantage over us they can get. They will use you as leverage. Another Atrum will come for you, and I can't protect you like this."

Sylvant sat silently for a few seconds then looked at Solan. "This all sounds pretty serious. What are you asking of me?"

Solan stood and walked to the rail and leaned against it. "Obviously, I can't leave you here. The Atrum will be back, now that we know what they're trying to do."

"But Solan, I have a life. A great job. I'm not leaving all of that behind just because of this group, the Atrum—"

"You don't understand!" Solan interrupted, a bit harshly as she turned to face Sylvant and took a deep breath to calm herself. "They are dangerous, more than you realize. They won't hesitate to kill you."

"Then we go to the authorities. They can handle them."

"No, they can't. And besides, I don't trust the authorities, at least not right now."

"You're asking me to give everything up—"

Solan held up her hands, and Sylvant paused. "This is life and death now. I'm sorry, but things can't go back to the way they were before."

Sylvant looked down at her hands and wrung them together, then slowly nodded as if accepting what Solan had said. "Okay, Solan. But I need to understand what my options are. What are we talking about?"

Solan sat down next to her sister and took her hands. "I need you to come with me, now. Gather your things. You can't stay here any longer and certainly not tonight. That girl out there, she's already heading back, and she'll bring more Atrum with her. I can handle her and a few others, but if they all come back, I won't be able to fight them off."

Sylvant shook her head as Solan watched her and waited tensely for her answer. She knew her sister's stubbornness matched her own, and the last thing Solan wanted was to carry her out forcefully. But if that's what it came to, she was prepared to do just that.

After a moment, Sylvant nodded and squeezed Solan's hands. "Alright. I trust you. You know I do. Let me get my things."

They gathered up her belongings as quickly as possible. Solan hefted a few of her bags, and together, they left her apartment. Myranda was gone when they stepped out.

They boarded Solan's skiff and left. Solan cloaked the skiff immediately as they cruised into Skylight City's airspace.

Solan eased back, slightly relieved. "I'm so sorry about all of this."

Sylvant looked at her. "Let's hear my options."

"Alright. The Agency has what's known as a witness protection plan, of sorts. They have the ability to fake your death and give you a new alias."

"Like the one you use?"

"Yes. It's very similar to that. The Agency can handle the authorities and the press release. Usually, an accident or something will cover you. Then we'll discuss your reassignment."

"Reassignment? Like a job? So, I'm part of this Agency now?"

"Well, you have to earn your keep," Solan chided and nudged her sister. "All joking aside, this is serious. You'll be expected to work with us. Maybe as an informant, or eyes and ears on the ground. That's part of the program."

Sylvant smiled and shook her head. "Are you kidding? Me, a spy? I have no training or the stomach for such things. I'm not like you, Solan."

"Don't think of it like that," Solan said. "Your assignment will be something you can handle. And, whether you realize it or not, you're more capable than you think. There are many roles in the Agency. You won't be expected to do anything you can't handle. But you will be pushed."

Sylvant eased back in her seat and was staring out the skiff's window thoughtfully. "Can you give me an example at least?"

"What about going back to the university as a professor? Probably as a department head. We need surveillance at the university as much as anywhere else. There's a network of undercover professors there already, you would hardly believe the intricacies. You're already familiar with the university anyway, so it makes perfect sense. In fact, Jet is there as an athletic director. You two could have tea together."

Sylvant smiled and looked at her. Solan could see that she was at least considering it.

"I'm starting to like the sound of that," Sylvant said. "But do you have that authority?"

"I'm the head of the Lucem. Even though many people in the Agency don't like us, we have some pull," Solan said. "I'll make the arrangements. You'll have an alias, and you'll receive some basic training. And with the semester just getting started, it won't look suspicious. There are thousands of new professor positions filled every week."

Sylvant sat back and crossed her arms, as if she still had doubts. "Where are we going?" she asked.

"To our current headquarters. I want you to stay hidden when we get there, at least until I clear the way. My instincts tell me there may be a spy in the Agency."

Chunks of metallic debris welcomed them as they approached the ninth belt. Solan landed the skiff in a vacant hanger bay and hopped out. She signaled for Sylvant to wait. A few minutes passed before she returned. Together they walked as Solan explained the Agency and its operations to her.

"This is my apartment, at least for one more day. I only wish father was here to greet you, though he'd probably strangle me first."

"One more day? Are you moving out?"

"It's a long story. I want you to stay here for the time being. I'm not around much, but make yourself at home. I'll be back later. I have some reports to file and get your alias and assignment moving."

Solan's quarters were large with plenty of open space for her training. There was a study off to one side and a personal library stocked with old books she had taken from the stacks.

Sylvant dropped her coat on the sofa. "Did you steal those books from the university?"

Solan smiled. "I prefer the phrase long-term lease."

Solan handed Sylvant a small brooch. "Hold on to this. If you ever need me, all you have to do is activate it here." She pointed at a small button on the brooch. "It's a homing device, and I'll be able to find you anywhere in the system. But no communication outside of that. I'll answer more of your questions later. See you soon."

M

Jet met Cord in his studio on the way to a meeting Solan had called. It was their last day under the Agency's umbrella, and he wondered if the meeting had something to do with it. When he arrived at Cord's studio, Cord was still training from the previous day; Jet had never seen such devotion. Cord seemed to spend an unhealthy amount of time training and meditating.

"You need to take a break," Jet said. "You've been at it all night."

"Meditating *is* my break. If I fail, the Atrum might seize the advantage."

"Cord," Jet said and stopped him. "Hopefully, after all you told me yesterday, you don't think this all hinges on you."

"This is just what I tell myself for motivation."

"Are you sure?" Jet asked, taking a seat. "It almost sounds like you're not convinced of that. What is it that you're searching for? What's driving you?"

Cord turned and faced Jet and stared at him for a long second. "I have to be the best. I won't rest or take a break until I am. There'll be time for that when I'm dead," Cord paused again as Jet simply stared at him, not sure what to say.

"In all honesty, and don't take any offense to this, but I think you could learn a bit of humility."

Cord glanced over at him and shrugged. "I have no room for such emotions, Jet. Humility shows weakness."

"Humility has made me who I am today," Jet replied. "When I played blaze, I learned from other players by accepting the fact that I wasn't the best. When that happens, a whole new world opened up for me, and my learning increased exponentially."

"Are you suggesting that I'm arrogant?" Cord asked, but with no hint of humor. "If that's the case, you're beginning to sound like Vail."

"Hey, take it easy," Jet said, holding up his hands. "All I'm saying is that if you learn to open up to other emotions, you'll eventually understand more, and maybe become better than you already are."

Cord was silent for a moment. "Truth be known, it's not that I hate humility, I just don't understand it, and perhaps that frightens me. I've never really told you about my past, have I?"

"No, as a matter of fact, you haven't. I just assumed you didn't want to discuss it, like a lot of us don't. What does that have to do with anything?"

Cord pulled off his shirt and turned his back to Jet. Running vertically in crisscrossing patterns were hundreds of scars. The flesh had healed over the wounds many years ago, but the evidence was still there. Jet didn't speak and waited for Cord to say something.

"Get a good look," Cord said and finally slipped his shirt back on. "That is the type of motivation administered in my youth. As a euph, my father knew I would never mention it to anyone. And what if I did? Who would believe me? I would be dead before I turned twenty-four regardless, and my father knew this. I lied to you about my family; they were never supportive, my apologies for that. Much like you, I abhor sympathy; it is a weakness I will not allow in myself. Of course, you had blaze, Kamber has running…we *all* have some way to cope with our past, and studying was my *get away* from reality. That is where I feel the most relaxed. All that said, do not concern yourself with me. I can handle the late nights."

"Okay, fine. But you don't have to always be perfect, Cord. It's okay to miss on occasion. We all do."

"Not for me. Failure is not an option."

"So, what happens when you do fail? Because it will happen sooner or later. Trust me, I know. I've failed at blaze so many times that I should've given up. But sometimes failure can be your best coach."

Jet watched him for a moment longer, and a bit of sympathy hit him as he thought about what Cord must have endured…what they had *all* endured. Not just at the hands of their parents or guardians, but throughout their lives. Cord seemed to read his thoughts.

"I said, no sympathy. You've had a difficult life too. I once spoke to Cutter about your past. I know about the halfway home and what happened there. We are all survivors, are we not? Solan, DiJinn, Ti-Leer…even the Atrum share in our tragedy. Neither you nor I can afford sympathy, so let's do each other a favor and eliminate that feeling. We suffered in the past so we can move on, and that is how I prefer it."

They both sat silently for a moment longer, and then Jet stood. "Well, what do you think Solan wants with this meeting?"

"I never know with her," Cord said, straightening in his seat. "She keeps things close to her by design. I admire her approach. Tyberius is missing, we have an increase in Atrum activity, the Century Eclipse is approaching, and I sense there may be a spy in our midst. Perhaps vacating the Agency truly *is* the best tactic for now."

They made their way to the Lucem wing and walked into the Hall of Prisms.

Jet and Cord froze as soon as they entered through the doors. Across the table stood Solan and DiJinn. Next to Solan, seated in her father's chair, was Professor Sterllar Sylvant.

"What in Skylight is this about?" Jet asked.

"Professor Sylvant," Cord acknowledged.

Sylvant stood and smiled. "Nice to see you two as well." She walked over to them, and Jet gave her a hug.

Cord smiled his crooked smile at her. "Might I enquire what the *hell* is going on?" Cord asked.

"I thought this wasn't allowed, Solan," Jet said. "You told me—"

"I know what I said," Solan interrupted. "But my sister was ambushed last night by an Atrum at her apartment. She wouldn't be standing here right now if I hadn't been there. This was the only option I could think of. I can't protect her unless she becomes a part of the Agency."

"But…we're leaving the Agency, I thought?" Jet said.

"We're moving out, which might only be temporary," Solan corrected him. "Regardless, we are still working with the Agency. They've agreed to let us keep our assignments and the witness protection plan in place. That will allow my sister to have an alias and access to our protection."

"The Atrum tried to use Sylvant for leverage?" Cord asked. "Clever, actually."

Solan narrowed her eyes at him. "Clever, and devious."

"What about the rest of us?" Jet asked. "I think we have to assume that tactic will be used against other Lucem as well."

"Our agreement with the Atrum's been 'round for thousands of years, but this is one of the most aggressive tactics I've seen," DiJinn said. "Looks like this was the last straw, Sol. They just tried to kidnap your sister."

"I agree, things have changed," Solan said. "I didn't believe they would go this far either…I misjudged them."

"So…what about the rest of the Lucem and their families?" Jet continued.

"If we have evidence of a credible threat to other personal connections, then we'll bring them into the Agency as well," Solan said. "But we need to hear it. I don't want to start bringing in everyone we know over this."

"Isn't that a risk, though?" Jet said. "Shouldn't we be preemptive and not wait for it to happen?"

"For all we know, they might have been targeting my sister for something specific," Solan replied. "We can't tear people's lives apart on a whim. Now is the time for vigilance."

"But you could have said the same thing about Sylvant yesterday," Jet said.

"Sylvant's life will never be the same. She is sacrificing everything to be here. You went through the same thing. It's not an easy adjustment to make. We need to think long and hard before we tear people's lives apart by bringing them into this conflict."

Cord walked around the table. "I suggest we put ourselves on the Atrum's level. We need to think in terms of collateral."

"Are you suggesting we kidnap or kill people close to the Atrum?" Solan asked.

"No, not exactly. But we need to send the impression that we *are* willing to move to that extent. They need to understand that we are serious and there are lines they should not cross."

DiJinn stood from her chair. "Sylvant, welcome to our group. I'm glad you're here, we'll protect you and make sure you're prepared." DiJinn paused a moment before continuing, as if considering how to phrase her next sentence. "Sol, you've been really busy looking for your father, and now your sister's here. No disrespect, Sylvant, but Sol, we need you. There's a lot goin' on, and the Atrum are up to no good with these raids. The

Century Eclipse is just round the corner. Hell, we're down by four Lucem. We need to stay focused."

Solan leaned against the steel bulkhead with her arms crossed. "I agree with everything you just said, Jinn. Distractions are increasing daily, and we seem to be going in different directions. That's my fault. This has been one of the most uncertain times in my life. I didn't want to take the lead like this, but Tyberius made me promise, if he ever disappeared. I just never thought it would happen. He's the perfect fit for this role; he was the glue that held us all together. You know I'm not built like that; I prefer to work privately. I don't like being responsible for other people, but a promise is a promise, and I don't intend to back off." She walked around to stand next to Jinn and placed a hand on her shoulder. "I wanted to wait to tell everyone this, but I think now is the time. I've decided to suspend our support of the Goliath's Gate project, at least until we can assess what the Atrum are up to. We have too many things going on right now and not enough Lucem to cover it all."

"That won't make Harok very happy," DiJinn chuckled.

"I've already talked to Harok and his generals. He wasn't pleased. I'm sure it will have political repercussions. But right now, we need to focus on our own issues."

CHAPTER 8
Firefly Falls

ΑΒΓΔΕΖΗΘΙΚΛ**Μ**
ΝΞΟΠΡΣΤΥΦΧΨΩ

WITH THE LUCEM'S relocation to take place later that evening, it appeared they would all be spending more time at Skylight University. And, after talking to Cord, it made the most sense for Jet to be near the university anyway. He was one step closer to Kamber and Cutter. He was actually looking forward to the new location, not that he disliked being at the Agency, he just felt there would be more freedom, and he missed being at Skylight University.

Though Jet had managed to keep a close eye on Kamber from a distance, he decided to stop by the track facility and finally meet her in person. It was quiet, the track team still several hours away from practice, and maintenance crews roamed the field. The track stadium was impressive, though not nearly as impressive as Crux Field. The tiered seating utilized the same anti-gravitational technology and rose up and over the running track. It stopped just shy of connecting at the top to create an oculus to let daylight in.

Dressed in a light university gym jacket, sweats, and sneakers, he walked up the ramp and stood at mid field. Kamber was running laps. He sat down on the front row and waited. She seemed to be lost in her own world as she ran, reminding him of his days playing blaze, a feeling he sorely missed.

Eventually, Kamber stopped and checked her watch. Jet stood and applauded, catching her attention.

"Getting an early start, it would seem," Jet said as she jogged over. "Practice doesn't start for several more hours."

"Just getting loose," she said. "A bit of a warmup, really."

Kamber was average height with hair dyed green and purple at the tips with a few colored beads woven into her dreadlocks. Her eyes glowed in a bright greenish color, not much different than his own, and she had an olive-toned complexion like Cord's. Her build was slight, but she had powerful legs, and he could see she had been a runner for most of her life.

"How are the pre-season standings?"

"I'm currently in second, behind Tetra. She's a tough one."

"But you love the competition, though," Jet said with a smile. "I used to be in sports. I know the feeling."

She shrugged. "Of course, I can't deny it." Kamber pulled on her knee, stretching her legs. "You're Gunter Kepp, our new A.D., right? Coach Minnett mentioned your name. She also said something about a field trip?"

"A lady by the name of Lybra Howling owns a painting that a colleague of mine is doing some research on."

"Sounds interesting, but why me?"

"Well, I have to be honest, she only allows special students into her private gallery."

"Students like me and Tetra, you mean? Students with E.M."

"Well…yeah," Jet said with a slight hesitation. "It would be a huge favor if you could help out. And I hear it's a fabulous painting. Chance of a lifetime to see it in person."

Kamber tilted her head. "Mr. Kepp—"

"Please," Jet interrupted her. "Just Gunter will do."

"Gunter, sir. What I was going to say is that I've been having dreams about a painting. It's odd that you're asking me to do this, because I feel like I'm supposed to go see it."

"So…that's a *yes*?"

"Of course, we'd love to go."

Jet paused. "We?"

"Tetra and me. She's been having the same kind of dreams lately. We talked about it last week during preseason training. Of course, it made sense that she'd come along when Minnett mentioned your field trip."

"Well, Kamber, that's thoughtful, but Minnett has only approved for you to come along."

"Actually, she agreed Tetra could come along, if she wanted to."

Jet blinked a few times and wasn't sure what to say. Hurse had warned him about going near Tetra, and Jet really didn't care to, anyway. But Cord was desperate to get back into Lybra's gallery, and Jet wanted to avoid any breaking and entering. "Well, good. It's settled then," Jet said. "I'll make the arrangements and let you know when."

"Gunter, can I ask you something?"

"Sure," Jet said. He stepped onto the track, and they began to walk.

"Why are you being so kind, if you don't mind me asking? Everyone else has been pretty rude to me, to put it bluntly."

"Well, I used to know someone with E.M.. I saw how difficult it can be, and I promised to help if I ever had the chance. It seems like now is the time."

"Thank you. I could always use a little help."

"Tell me about yourself," Jet said. "Are you from around here?"

"I grew up on Skylight City, in the Durge Quarter, that's a slum area, in case you were wondering. It's not a pretty place. When I was about seven, I was adopted by a couple. They were odd balls…collectors, I called them. I was like an ornament, a thing of intrigue in their eyes. There was no love toward me, just a fascination for the bizarre, and I fit the bill. Both were scientists. They tried experiments, not the horrific kind you may have heard of. Just studies, more or less, trying to discover more about E.M."

"And…running helped you cope with it all, I take it?"

"Of course. Every chance I got, I was away from them and running."

They left the track facility and followed the cross-country trail as it wound out into the Clipton Forest. The sounds of the university noise faded as they walked along the dirt path, the sunlight filtered partially by the tree cover. Jet felt an odd sensation talking with Kamber, one he couldn't explain. He felt a kindred spirit being near her.

"I finally drew enough attention with my running. I was sent an invitation, and…who wouldn't want a chance to run track for Skylight University? Of course, I knew I'd face ridicule, no matter what school I went to."

"Do you have plans after graduation?"

"Gunter. I'm twenty-three years old," Kamber said. "You know about the legend of ephebus mortem. We all die before we turn twenty-four. I'll be dead before I graduate."

Jet paused for a step, then recovered. "You're twenty-three?" he asked.

"I know. I get that reaction a lot," she said.

"Well, how come you waited so long to do college?"

"It was tough getting cleared. I mean, I'm a euph. Not many people lining up to recruit me. The papers came through from Skylight suddenly one day. I was a bit surprised, of course."

"I'm shocked it took so long for people to notice. I read about your race times. You're an incredible runner."

She smiled at him. "Thanks. I assumed that's why Skylight finally reached out. But sometimes, I'm not sure. Anyway, I don't plan to waste a minute of the time I have left. Every second is precious. At least I get to spend my time here. The trees, lakes and campus are beautiful."

"I know. It's peaceful here, and I really enjoy the campus atmosphere. But…one question I wanted to ask. Are you frightened about the legend of E.M.?"

She looked sideways at him as they walked. "I get asked that a lot. I guess, I try not to think about it. I focus on running and school, of course. That's why I don't mind Tetra. Her pushing me takes my mind off a lot of things. She's annoying, but I'm glad she's here."

"But, you didn't answer my question," Jet continued.

She stopped and looked at him. "You're not like other professors and coaches. You're different. What is it about you?"

"You're avoiding my question," Jet said, crossing his arms, intent on hearing her out.

Kamber stood facing him on the dirt trail, then she tilted her head. "Do you hear that?" she turned and followed the noise down another trail, and Jet followed after her.

Soon she was jogging, then running. Jet struggled to keep pace with her until they finally burst into a clearing.

They stood at the edge of a ravine. The sound of a waterfall permeated the air around them. A light ahead punctured the tree mass and created a glow around the edge of the foliage. The tree canopy above them was so thick that barely any sunlight shone through it. Kamber continued forward, trotting down the ravine and through a curtain of trees and underbrush with Jet right behind her.

The path they had been jogging on ended at a rocky shore. The waterfall from the Clipton River plunged over a cliff some thirty meters above the lake. It cascaded down and shattered the silence on the rocks below. Lighting the entire glen were thousands of tiny fireflies—yellow and green iridescent points of light, dancing above the river and reflecting in the churning waters like a galaxy of stars. The underside of the tree canopy above lit up from the fireflies like a bonfire, and the dazzling greens and yellows created a dreamlike landscape from some far-off world.

"This is absolutely amazing," Kamber whispered in a distant voice.

"I've heard rumors about this place," Jet said. "I just never bothered to search for it. I honestly didn't think it existed."

"What is this place?"

"It's called Firefly Falls. I've heard others mention it, but just in passing."

She sat down on a rock and gazed at the waterfall. Jet sat down next to her, watching how her gaze lingered on the water. She pulled her knees up and hunched forward, resting her chin in her hands as she stared. He didn't say anything, enjoying the surroundings. It was breathtaking, mesmerizing and refreshing, and he lost track of time until his watch beeped, bringing him out of his trance.

"Kamber. We should head back." He stood and waited.

She looked up at him but didn't stand. "Gunter. Why are you really here?"

"I already told you. I wanted to help you because of your condition."

"I'm not blind," Kamber said bluntly. "I know you're not telling me everything. No disrespect, Gunter, but I've been around long enough to know when something's out of place, and right now, you're out of place. You're different."

Jet shrugged. "I'm not sure what you're talking about. I don't consider myself different."

He watched her and noticed how she didn't look him in the eyes. He already knew the answer to his question. He *knew* she felt just like he had as a student…she was afraid. *So why was he pushing her?*

"Well, to answer your question," he continued. "I'm simply here to help. That's all I can give you for now. I hope that's good enough."

"That's fair," she said. "Thank you. And, to answer your question…yes, *of course* I'm afraid. I'm terrified."

CHAPTER 9
Vail's Signal

ΑΒΓΔΕΖΗΘΙΚΛ<u>Μ</u>
ΝΞΟΠΡΣΤΥΦΧΨΩ

JET ESCORTED KAMBER back to the track facility and then made his way to his office at Crux Field, which was located near the top of the stadium. The interior decor was over-the-top with heavy wood trim and lavish finishes that reflected Skylight's rich blaze tradition. But in his opinion, it felt detached from the grit and sweat that the sport of blaze encompassed. He was grateful to even have an office, but he preferred to spend his time on the field and around the players and didn't stay long.

Being back on the field felt good, like home to him. Standing inside Crux Field still gave him butterflies, and he could almost hear the crowd's roar. The clear stasis field allowed him to see the seating below, and walking on it felt just like real turf. He had enjoyed his time playing blaze for Skylight, despite the short duration. His life on earth in the underground cavern system, known as the ARC district, had been a brutal existence. But learning the game of blaze had given him an escape, one he was thankful for. In many ways, it was responsible for his upbringing, as odd as it sounded, and he missed the sport desperately. He was living vicariously through the players now, but it was a distant cry from the exhilaration he got when he played blaze.

Booker, a.k.a., Coach Hemmond Plannar, waved to him from across the field. He trotted over to a group of players gathered at mid-field.

"Listen up! This here is Gunter Kepp." Booker clapped Jet on the back and grinned at him through his missing side tooth. "He's been promoted to an assistant athletic director, but I've asked him to help out with some of the coaching duties this year, so listen to him or off you go! Work 'em into shape." Booker shoved a blaze into Jet's arms and walked off.

Jet looked over the sea of players, and one stood out immediately. Cutter Jade, his old friend. The players stared at him and waited. Jet touched his ring, making sure his alias was in place, pulled his gaze from Cutter and clapped. "Follow me," he said and led the group to the sidelines. Jet was about to blow his whistle when he heard someone else do it. He looked over at a stocky man with a hooked nose. Korbin Daze.

Jet took a deep breath and shook his head. He searched the field for Booker and saw him with the blaze-out squad running wind sprints. Jet lifted his hands at Penn as if to say, *what are you thinking?*

In the last game of his short career, Jet and Daze had gotten into a fight. He had nearly killed Daze as a result. Unintentional as it was, Jet didn't know if it was a good idea to pair them together. He wasn't sure he could restrain himself for the entire year.

Throughout practice, Jet watched Cutter closely and noticed how off his timing seemed to be. He kept rushing the line and trying to force his way through it instead of waiting for an opening. He missed several blocks and seemed winded at times.

"Cutter," Jet whistled and paused the scrimmage. "What's the problem?"

Cutter pulled his helmet off and took a knee. He shook his head.

"You missing sleep?" Jet asked. "Having a reaction? Getting tired of the game?"

Cutter gave him a confused look. "No offense, A.D., but I don't think you understand blaze enough to coach me. You belong up there in your office."

"Really?" Jet asked and crossed his arms. "I bet I can outthrow, outthink and outscore you."

Cutter looked up at him and laughed, along with the rest of the team. "Is that a challenge?"

"If that's what it takes." Jet walked over, grabbed a blaze, and stood next to him.

Cutter stood and grabbed a blaze, twirling it on his fingertips. "What's the bet?"

"If I win, you take my advice," Jet said.

"And if you don't?" Cutter asked.

"Name your prize," Jet replied.

Cutter looked at Jet, his massive frame towering over him. Jet could see several new tattoos on his arms and was shocked to see one with his own initials and old uniform number.

"How about that cooler as the target?" Cutter nodded at a bright red cooler that sat on a chair about fifty yards away.

Jet considered for a second. "How about the one past that?"

Cutter looked down the field. "That's probably sixty yards away."

"Sixty-three, I'd guess."

Cutter shrugged. "Your call. If you can hit that from here, I'll take your advice for the rest of the season. But if you miss, you don't come down to this field again, at least not during the season."

"You really don't like me, do you?"

"A.D., you're a distraction here," Cutter said. "We don't need highbrows around. Down here, it's about respect for the game."

"You assume you know me, but you don't. You think because I dress a certain way or because I don't have a blaze pedigree, I shouldn't be on this field?"

"Just ask any of these players, they'd say the same thing."

"Well, maybe you should focus on what you're doing and not worry about others, because what I've seen out of you lately doesn't look like the Cutter I used to know."

Cutter tilted his head. "What did you say? I've never met you before in my life."

"I've seen you play before," Jet continued. "Just like everyone else here, and right now, you're slipping."

Jet turned without looking and threw the blaze. It zipped when it left his hand with a slight snap as his fingertip flipped the ball into a tight spiral. It soared up on an arch and stayed aloft for what seemed like minutes. Then it dropped right on top of the water cooler. The cooler exploded, its lid going in one direction and water splashing over the field. The other players stared at Jet in amazement.

"What the hell was that?" Cutter said and looked slowly back at Jet. "I've only seen one other player in my life make a throw like that."

"And who was that?"

"An old friend of mine."

"Well, maybe you ought to take his advice then?"

Cutter stood with his hands on his head and a confused look on his face. The other players remained silent.

"Alright, party's over," Jet said and clapped. "Hit the showers."

Jet walked toward the water cooler as Cutter followed behind.

"Where'd you say you learned to throw like that?" Cutter asked.

"I played blaze in a past life."

"Anyone who can throw the blaze like that is playing professional. You're not telling me everything. Who are you?"

"There's nothing to tell."

"Tell me who you are," Cutter persisted.

"Does it matter? I'm not even supposed to be here, right?"

"Look, you win. Apparently, you've got some advice for me. Let's hear it."

Jet knelt and picked up the cooler and placed it back on the chair, then turned to face Cutter. "Don't worry about it, Cutter. You want me gone? Fine. I won't come back." Jet wasn't sure how he'd work that out with Booker, but he would figure something out, if Cutter called his bluff.

"Hold on. I don't back out on a bet. You won that respect…you got it. So, you gonna give me that advice?"

Jet knew Cutter's situation and how hard life had been for him. His father had murdered his younger brother over a handicap. As a child, Cutter had fled to the streets and scratched a living until being accepted to Skylight. Then he had lost his best friends to E.M. four years ago. Cutter had as much reason as anyone to call it quits, but he hadn't. He'd found a way to survive through all his misfortune. But right now, he was struggling.

"Well, be honest with yourself, Cutter. Me being here isn't the problem."

"How would you know anything about my problems?"

Jet clapped Cutter on the shoulder. "Here's my free advice to you. Don't blame yourself for things you can't control. It's not always your fault—you don't have to take the blame for those who have moved on."

Cutter tilted his head. "Excuse me?"

"You're too hard on yourself. Let the past go. Drop that baggage of guilt and move on."

"I'm not sure I understand what you're talkin' about."

"Yes…you do, Cutter. You know exactly what I'm talking about."

"Have you been diggin' up dirt on me?"

Jet remained silent.

Cutter furrowed his brow, as if an inkling of recognition was finally awaking. "Who are you?"

"Think about it." Jet tossed the blaze to him. Cutter let it hit his chest pads and drop to the ground.

M

Jet awoke and sat up, sweat on his forehead and chest. In his dream, he was running to save someone…*someone familiar*. But his legs kept getting tangled in some sort of large metallic contraption. The faster he ran, the faster the contraption spun. All he had to do to free himself was speak a single word, but the letters wouldn't form in his mind. No matter how much he focused, the word he searched for remained distant and confusing to him. But try as he might, he couldn't say the word, and the person he was trying to save died. Although the vestiges of the dream were fleeting, he knew the word when he sat up.

It was Vishmu.

Unable to go back to sleep, he decided to pack up the rest of his personal belongings and prepare to move out of the Agency. He didn't have much to pack, mostly clothing and a few trinkets.

Solan was in the Hall of Prisms with the other Lucem and Sylvant, and she insisted they bring Albright's table with them. It was a chore to move, but they did it under the cover of night while the corridors were empty.

Their new base was located down in the bowels of Lyrinthum on the first belt, directly beneath the university. It was easy to get lost in the network of tunnels, which gave the Lucem all the cover they needed. An abandoned control sector for one of the collider's sensors would be their new base of operations, at least for the foreseeable future. Here, the old control quadrant was mostly defunct, with just enough power to run the makeshift headquarters. Most of the equipment and furniture had been abandoned; coffee cups and other clutter littered the space as if the previous operators had fled in a rush. Years of disuse had left a layer of dust on everything, and most of the gear was unusable. A glass window looked out onto the large detector beyond, the tubular tunnel that had once housed the collider's beam curved slightly downward and out of view. It was dark and gloomy with a musty smell.

As they all stood in the control room around Albright's table, Sylvant cleared her throat. "It sounds like you all have some very important work to do, but this new space doesn't seem adequate. What's with all the clutter and broken equipment? What happened here?" Sylvant swept a leftover coffee cup off the table and looked at the rubbish lying around.

"This is the old particle accelerator," Booker said. "It's no longer used."

"Yes, I can see that much," Sylvant said. "But why all the disarray? Looks like the former operators left in a hurry."

"If they could hear the same voices we do down here, then it's no surprise they left so quickly," DiJinn said. She sat in her chair with her boots kicked up on the table. She brought her heel down hard enough to wake Ti-Leer, who sat up and brushed his tousled hair out of his eyes. He muttered something in a foreign language about ale, then dropped his head back onto the table with a thud.

"Voices?" Sylvant asked. "What do you mean?"

"You'll hear them soon," DiJinn said. "If you stick 'round here long enough."

"I don't understand what that means…" Sylvant trailed off. "Is this place haunted? Where do the voices come from?"

"Other dimensions, some say," a Lucem named Harriet chimed in. She sat in her chair with her arms crossed. Of all the Lucem, Jet had talked to her the least. Harriet was reserved, spending most her time disguised as the university's head librarian. Her curly black hair and skin were as dark as her cloak, and her yellow glowing eyes shone like the summer sun. She seemed to be one of the older, more knowledgeable Lucem, with a background in medicine.

Ti-Leer woke again and immediately launched into conversation. "Old colliders like this one have smashed trillions of particles over the years, and that leftover residue is embedded in these walls. Ghostly remnants, neutrinos some say…perhaps a portal to other dimensions. At least, that's the accepted theory."

Sylvant looked around the dimly lit control room and hugged her arms. "Other dimensions? Solan, you never mentioned this to me. Seems like an important detail to disclose."

"This place is the best we can do for the moment," Solan said. "I'm sorry it's not a bit cozier."

"For the record, I like the voices," Ti-Leer said. "They talk to the other voices in my head, keep them company. Does no one else feel that way?"

DiJinn rolled her eyes and shook her head. She stood, pacing the room impatiently. "Cord. You've been workin' on a few theories. Anything to share?"

"I assume you are referring to the splinter code?" Cord asked.

"What else would I be talkin' about? You've mentioned it a few times," DiJinn said. "How 'bout you fill us in?"

Cord motioned to the table. "As you know, this table matches the painting called *The Plan*. When Van Saint was murdered, the table splintered into what you see now, and her painting matches the pattern almost exactly; it's quite fascinating. It has been a mystery for over a century. What I refer to as the splinter code is the splintered pattern in this table. But I have recently discovered a variation between it and Van Saint's painting, *The Plan*, though the difference is very subtle."

Cord crossed his arms and continued. "I've been constructing a three-dimensional model over the last year, based on a number we discovered in the painting, which was 2,412,630. What I realized was that number represents coordinates. When you input those millions of coordinates, you get nine distinct locations in the Skylight System. When you overlay the Roman numerals from the first painting, *The Realization*, you get nine different times of day or night, and when you overlay the information from the final painting, *The Verification*, you get nine specific dates."

"The table and the painting are maps of the Skylight System?" Harriet said. "That's genius."

"The Heliographi Memoirs," Sylvant said. "There were nine pages. Do you think that the nine missing memoirs could be hidden amongst the nine belts?"

"That is my assumption," Cord said.

"Tell me how the table is different," Solan said.

"Note this area here." Cord pointed out one small island of splinters near the center of the table. "This portion varies from the painting. It provides one additional coordinate for a total of 2,412,631…one greater than the painting."

"So, that itty-bitty thing is the splinter code?" DiJinn asked. "Looks like it's near the first belt."

"Revelations Plaza, to be exact," Cord said. "And the date and time align with the Century Eclipse. Albright hid the location of his memoirs between the three paintings and then separated them as another safeguard. This table may represent our legacy, origin, and heritage, but it's also the last clue he left us to go along with the holographic messages in the three paintings. The marriage of Van Saint's work to Albright's table reveals where we will find the first clue in this hunt for his memoirs. The Skylight Fallout will trigger this clue, and it's imperative we attain it first. If it's the key to finding the Heliographi Memoirs, that's a big deal. We can't let the memoirs fall into the wrong hands."

M

After the meeting, Jet quickly unpacked his belongings and snuck out of the control sector. Before he'd left, he had taken a closer look at his symbol on the table. As Cord had pointed out, the way the table had fractured around it did indeed appear different when compared to the other twenty-three symbols. His symbol, the letter M, was practically an island. The cracks in the table had nearly encircled it, and his symbol hung on by one tiny sliver of wood. He didn't want to admit it, but he *was* concerned. Did this really mean he was the Skylight Fallout though?

As he left Lyrinthum, he used a particular tunnel network that was becoming his favorite because it detoured through the Clipton Forest. It seemed to be the most remote and least used. Plus, the trees and vegetation provided good cover. Though he was mostly invisible, he still had to use caution.

He exited the portal and stole through the misty woods, using the sound of crickets as his guide. Tall evergreens pointed skyward, screening the bright moon and turquoise borealis. Soon he exited the forest and approached the literature department. He located the stone cloister, settled into the shadows and waited.

Nearly an hour later, something resembling smoke entered the dark cloister and moved to a spot near the opposite end of the colonnade. Jet crouched tensely, waiting to see what it would do next.

The shadow uncloaked, and Jet did the same.

He stepped forward and stopped in front of Vail. Her pale skin seemed to glow in the moonlight, her fair hair still dyed blue at the tips. She had more carelines around her lips, though. She was still beautiful, in her unruly way, but her presence felt dark and foreboding now. It had been nearly four years since she'd been converted by the Atrum, and in this very spot.

"Stroud," she acknowledged. "Didn't think you'd show up."

Jet held her gaze for a second. "This is where I recovered your locket…three dots, two dashes in morse code, I assumed 3 AM and it's been three days. Took me a second, but I got the message. Awfully brave of you. Also, very risky."

"You're so smart for figuring it out," Vail crooned in a mocking voice. It was the same cynical tone he remembered, but somehow darker, more sinister. Cord was right, the old Vail was long gone. But he wasn't giving up on her just yet.

"What did they do to you?" he finally asked.

She smiled. "You should ask what *didn't* they do to me. But I like to think that they set me free."

"Free? As if you weren't before?"

"You're so naïve, Stroud. You always were. No, I was never free…none of us were—you, Bo…even that idiot, Ledbetter. We were chained to our old existence of constant persecution. Those chains are gone now, and I intend to make the most of it."

"I don't know if I like the sound of that."

"You shouldn't."

"What are you planning?"

She crossed her arms. "Wouldn't you like to know?"

"Whatever it is, I'm not sure I can allow it."

"It's not up to you, Stroud. Besides, why would you try to stop us? All these people hate you, too. They laugh at you, mock you, fear you…and yet you protect them. I come for revenge. You should thank me."

"Vail. Do you remember the talk we had on Apex that day?"

She tilted her head as if trying to think through a cloud of confusion. Her pixie-like features contorted in the moonlight as she seemed to struggle with her emotions.

"You can't force people to believe in something. Taking your anger out on Skylight citizens won't change their opinion. Isn't it better to just let those feelings go?"

"I'm no longer trying to change people's opinion of me. I'm past that."

"Really? It doesn't sound like you are. Why not let those feelings go and move on? I think it's driving you. I sense the hate…it will eventually destroy you."

"Hate might destroy you, but it feeds me," she said, her voice sounding like a hiss as she spoke. "Don't try to get into my head, you wouldn't like what you see."

"What do you want, Vail? Why are we here at 3 AM?"

For the first time, Jet noticed her flinch. It was barely detectable, but he caught it. She was struggling to make a decision. "There is one person I would never harm, one who never judged me. But I can't protect this person, not from the others. They know him, Jet. And they want to use him for leverage against you. If they knew that I was here, sharing this with you… they'd tear me apart."

"It's Cutter, isn't it? When?"

"I can't tell you that. I can only give you this one warning. I don't want to see him harmed. Get him out. Keep him safe."

She seemed vulnerable in that instant—like the Vail of old—for just a split second.

"Do you still have feelings for Cutter?"

"I…I don't know what it is. I just couldn't bear to see him harmed, that's all."

Jet waited to see if there was more. "What about me, Vail? What about Cord? Do you want to see us harmed?"

"I will kill Ledbetter if I see him again."

Jet chuckled. "Didn't you just try that? Good luck."

"I owe him for that."

"What about me? Do you want to kill me? Here I am…this is your chance. Why not go for it?"

Vail bared her teeth and circled him. "I always liked you, Stroud. Don't tempt me. I might just take you up on that offer. I'm barely able to contain the rage inside me, it's overbearing. You can't understand how this being works."

"Being? What do you mean by that? Are you under some kind of control?"

"Don't try to understand us. You weren't meant to, just like we can't understand you. We are fundamentally different, down to our very essence. We will never be friends again. Our old life is gone forever."

"I don't believe that, Vail."

"Then you do so at your own risk. Don't say I didn't warn you. This is the last time we will leave on friendly terms. Next time will be a different story."

Jet took a deep breath. Whatever Vail had become, he was getting nowhere tonight. She was right; he couldn't comprehend what had happened to her, or worse yet, what she had become.

He unclasped her tarnished locket and tossed it to her. She caught it with one hand. "I'd hoped to give this back to you on better terms, but I guess your good deed of the day is done. I'll make good on Cutter and get him to safety."

Vail shook her head and tossed the locket back to him. "It's yours now. The person you once knew no longer exists. Keep it…for me. As a reminder of who I once was. One more thing, Stroud…be careful. There's a mark on you." Vail snapped her fingers and disappeared. The blur of her shadow swept out of the cloister and sped off into the night.

CHAPTER 10
Cutter's Nightmare

ΑΒΓΔΕΖΗΘΙΚΛ**Μ**
ΝΞΟΠΡΣΤΥΦΧΨΩ

JET SPRINTED ALONG the dirt trails of the Clipton Forest, back to the closest entry to Lyrinthum and then to the dorms. From the corner of his eye, something shot toward him. He had just enough time to turn and face it before being knocked to the ground. He hit a tree hard enough to shatter its trunk, and it toppled over him. He shoved the large tree trunk off his torso and rolled to his feet.

The shadow moved in, working through the heavy brush. "What do you think you're doing, Stroud?"

Jet faced the Atrum and uncloaked. It did the same, and Stephen Brit stared back at him. He was tall, reminding Jet of Daze in the way he carried himself. His confidence from playing blaze was evident. The man's light-colored hair was shoulder length and braided in long colorful strands that matched his brilliant blue glowing eyes.

"I saw what happened back there," Brit continued. "You must know by now that Vail isn't who she used to be. You need to accept that and move on."

"I still consider her my friend. I'm not willing to give her up that easily."

"She will kill you if it comes to that," Brit replied. "Trust me. She just gave you the only warning you'll get."

"Is that a threat, Brit?"

Brit smirked at the question. "You don't get it. We will kill you and any other Lucem that gets in our way. We had a truce once, but those days are gone. We are at war, whether the Lucem choose to accept that or not."

"A war that no one can win."

"That depends on who you ask. Either way, we will know very soon." He turned and was about to cloak but paused. "For the record, Stroud, I appreciate that you still think highly of Vail. But she's my warden and if you seek her out again, I'll kill you myself."

M

Jet stood at the doorway to Cutter's dorm room. He leaned in and listened but didn't hear any movement inside. It was nearing dawn, and he had to hurry. Now that the Lucem were no longer bound by the Agency's rules, things were different. He didn't feel so bad for what he was about to do. Although Solan would likely be furious with him, she'd done the same thing with Sylvant.

The locks around campus were no longer a hindrance, his Agency-issued holopad was designed to bypass most of them. Jet slipped into the apartment and paused. There was only one bedroom, and the door was ajar. Someone slept on the couch, and Jet moved in closer. Cutter was asleep on his back, one massive, tattooed arm draped across his forehead. In the bedroom sleeping on his bed was a girl…it was Plexus. Jet shook his head.

He walked over to the sofa and focused his thoughts. Cutter's eyes opened, and he sat up. He looked around his room, stood and walked into the bathroom and put on a T-shirt. Then he walked into the kitchen. Jet followed just behind him, still cloaked.

Cutter hit the brew button on the coffee maker and leaned against the counter as he waited.

Jet braced himself. He knew there was no going back and wondered again if he was doing the right thing. Everything was about to change for Cutter; he only hoped the shock wouldn't be too much for him to handle.

Jet lowered his hood just as Cutter brought his coffee mug to his lips.

Cutter let the mug drop to the floor, and it shattered the stillness.

Jet quickly held a finger to his lips and held his other hand out, pleading for silence.

Cutter simply stood there, his hand still holding an imaginary mug to his lips as he stared at Jet. From his bedroom, Plexus called out. "Cutter, you alright?"

"Yeah. I'm good. It's fine. Everything is fine."

Jet waited silently as Cutter continued to stare at him in disbelief. Jet motioned for him to step out to the balcony. Cutter followed and slid the door closed behind him.

"Is this a joke!" Cutter shouted.

Jet held up his hand again. "Wait, Cutter. Just wait a minute before you say anything, because I don't have much time, and neither do you."

"Is this really happening? Are you kidding me? I'm dreaming, right?"

"No. This is real, and I don't have time to explain. Right now, you're in danger. I need you to get dressed and meet me here." Jet handed him a holopad with a location pinned to it.

Cutter took it but didn't let his gaze leave Jet. "It's you…I can't believe it!" He put the holopad in his pocket and rushed over and grabbed Jet by the shoulders, practically lifting him off his feet. The smile on Cutter's face stretched ear to ear. Jet smiled back and clapped Cutter on the back.

"It's great to see you too, Cutter."

"Tell me how this is possible?"

"I will, I promise. But not now. I just need you to do what I ask. I'll tell you everything after that."

Cutter took out the holopad and looked at the location. He raised his eyebrows. "Okay…yeah."

"You need to hurry," Jet continued. "Just get dressed and go. Don't wait."

Cutter slid the patio door open and stepped inside. He turned to look back at Jet, but Jet was already gone.

Twenty minutes later, Cutter stood alone in the Clipton Forest, next to a shattered oak tree. Jet watched him from the shadows and waited to see if he'd been tailed by anyone. He reached out with his thoughts and probed the surrounding area. A few minutes passed, and Cutter started to look around.

Jet finally whistled to Cutter and slipped his hood down.

Cutter jogged over, and Jet grabbed him by the shirt and pulled him behind a tree.

"What the hell is going on?" Cutter asked.

"Just follow me and keep quiet."

Jet used his ring to open the portal in the ground. An area of dirt shifted, and the portal opened. Jet hopped inside and Cutter dropped in behind him. They moved quickly downward and along the tunnel system, stopping occasionally to listen.

Soon they neared the control room where the Lucem's new headquarters were located.

Jet slowed to a stop in a vast, tubular shaped chamber. It was dark with a bit of moonlight spilling in from a nearby skylight well. The sound of dripping water echoed in the background.

"This looks like something out of one of my nightmares," Cutter said and leaned against the steel bulkhead wall, arms crossed.

"Well, it's no dream. This is real, and it's serious."

"I need proof that this isn't some sort of hoax."

Jet walked over and stopped in front of Cutter, then slammed his fist into the riveted hull next to his head. The steel bulkhead crumpled like it was made of aluminum.

Cutter turned to examine the wall and nodded. "That'll do."

Jet shook his head and smiled at him. "Man, it's good to see you, Cutter." Jet laughed as he stared at his old friend. It was the first time he had felt happy since leaving the university. He slapped Cutter's shoulder.

"Yeah, it's good to see you too, Jet. But do you mind telling me what the hell this is about?"

Jet stood facing Cutter and gave him a serious look. "This might take a while, aren't you worried about Plexus?"

Cutter held out his hands and shrugged. "What can I say? We had a late movie night. Just friends."

"Right," Jet said with a smirk. "Anyway, as you can see, E.M. is not what people think it is. It's not a terminal illness, but something completely different. It's kind of hard to explain, but I'll try. I'm different than other people. Let's just call it a gift that lets me do things that don't seem possible."

"Bo, Vail, and Cord too, I take it?"

"Yes, and several others."

"What kind of special gifts?"

"Enhanced physical abilities and senses. We can read other people's thoughts. We know things before they happen sometimes. There's more, but I won't bore you with the details. All I can say is that I'm alive, and so are the others."

Cutter shifted. "What about Vail? Is she with you too?"

Jet took a deep breath. "Well, that's kind of the reason we're here."

Cutter waited and shrugged. "Come on, Jet. You brought me here. Let's talk. Is this something serious?"

"Well…kind of. Vail isn't like me or Cord. Some of us change, once we go through what's known as conversion. It's a process that must happen before we turn twenty-four. I'll just say that she isn't like she used to be."

"Are you telling me she's…a bad person now?" Cutter tilted his head as if trying to grasp what Jet was saying.

"To put it bluntly, yes. And Bo too."

Cutter held up his hands. "Hold on. I can't believe that about those two. I mean, they both had their moments, but don't we all? Hell, I've made bad decisions in the past, but that doesn't make me a bad person."

Jet thought how to phrase it. "It's not something they chose. It—whatever it is—chose us. We really didn't have a choice, according to Solan."

"Wait. Solan Alexander, as in Sylvant's sister? So, she's part of this too?"

"Well, yeah, she's not dead either. An organization known as the Agency helps fake our deaths and provides us with an alias."

Cutter shook his head. "This is a bundle of information I wasn't expecting when I woke up this morning."

"Well, you'd better hold on then," Jet said and chuckled. "Because it's about to get bumpy."

Cutter lowered his gaze. "You're kidding, right?"

"No, this is serious. You're in danger, Cutter."

"How much?"

"These people are known as the Atrum. The Lucem and the Atrum have been battling one another for a very long time. They are capable of anything, including kidnapping and murder."

Cutter crossed his arms and didn't seem fazed by what Jet said. But he could sense a stirring of concern in Cutter's thoughts.

"They will kill you, Cutter."

"Who told you this, Vail?"

"Yeah. Just a few hours ago, I met her, and she gave me the warning."

"And you believe her? Because I thought you just said she was part of this other group."

"She is, and yes, I absolutely believe her. She risked her life tonight to tell me this. They are specifically targeting you because you're a close friend of mine. Apparently, she still cares for you and doesn't want to see you harmed."

Cutter thought for a moment and heaved a sigh. "Why is all of this happening now? They've had four years to do this."

"Well, I think it has something to do with the upcoming Century Eclipse. Regardless, the way I see it right now, there's only one option for you. We need to bring you into our group. Sylvant was brought in just recently because the Atrum tried the same thing on her."

"Whoa, hold on a minute…what exactly would that mean for me?"

"I'm not gonna sugar coat it, you'd have to leave your old life behind. Just like Sylvant did and all the rest of us."

"You're askin' me to drop everything and start over?"

"I don't think we have a choice, Cutter. I can't really protect you here. I have other duties, and my main focus is on Kamber. Some of the other Lucem can help out, but they also have other responsibilities as well. Eventually, the Atrum would get to you and use you against me."

Cutter remained silent for a moment as he mulled it over. "Tell me more about this group…the Lucem. I need to understand what I'm getting myself into."

"The Lucem is a branch of the Agency, which is a secret government outfit. Basically, you'd be given an assignment and an alias. For example, Sylvant wanted to be back at Skylight University as a professor, so she's working undercover for us, or the Agency, I guess. We could get you back here as a coach maybe."

Cutter wasn't happy about the situation, and Jet could see his attitude was starting to reflect his frustration. Jet grew nervous he would decide not to go along. If that happened, Jet wasn't sure what he would do. He couldn't just let Cutter walk away, but he didn't have enough time available to commit to protecting him day and night either.

"I don't know 'bout this, Jet. It's a big ask. You…just showing up out of nowhere after being dead for the last four years, then asking me to kinda start my life over?"

"I know the feeling, Cutter. I went through the same thing not long ago."

"But you thought you were going to die anyway, so it's a bit different. I have a life."

That stung Jet, and he gave Cutter a meaningful look.

Cutter saw it and gripped Jet's shoulder. "Sorry. That came out wrong, I didn't mean it that way. I know you're just trying to help me."

"No. You're right. I hear what you're saying. I didn't have much to live for back then. But this is the best thing that could've happened to me. You've got a lot going for you right now. I understand the difference. But believe me, the Atrum will stop at nothing, and the authorities would be overmatched by them. Only the Lucem stand in their way. If you don't take this offer, you'll be dead in a week, that's my guess."

Cutter stood silently, considering. "Then give me that week. I'd like to wrap a few things up."

Jet breathed a sigh of relief. A week, he could handle. Losing his best friend a second time…that would be devastating. "I think we can work that in. I've got a lot to do, with the Century Eclipse coming up and keeping an eye on Kamber. But we can shadow you for a week."

"It's okay. I can take care of myself for a week."

"No, you can't! What's it going to take for you to realize that the Atrum will kill you? Your size and strength mean nothing to them."

Cutter held up his hands. "Hey, take it easy, Jet."

Jet shook his head. "You just need to understand how serious this is. My world is full of danger now; this isn't a joke."

"I guess I don't get it. Can these people also bend metal and crush rocks?" he said, half joking.

"Yes," Jet replied. "They absolutely can."

"Okay, I believe you. But the only way I'm going along with this is if you give me that week. That's my only term."

"Alright. I'll give you one week, and that's all. I can share it with Cord and a few of the other Lucem. Solan will be furious when she finds out, though."

"They'll eventually find out anyway, right?"

"Well, yeah. But technically, you're in right now, since I've already made contact with you. This is something we are forbidden to do. I'm bending the rules here, but since we're not under the Agency's umbrella right now, I don't feel so bad. I'll have to deal with Solan later."

Cutter crossed his arms. "Who is this Kamber girl you mentioned?"

"Well, she's one of us, a Lucem. She's still a student, though. We'll bring her into the group soon, but she's not quite ready. So, we have to wait for the right moment."

"But isn't she in danger? I mean, why not bring her in now, or at least warn her? Seems like a smart thing to do."

"I totally agree, and if it were up to me, I would. But Solan won't have it. That's why I have to keep a close eye on her."

"Just bend the rules a bit," Cutter said. "Sounds like you're already doing it, and there are a few others who don't mind."

"There are a few, namely Cord and DiJinn. I know they would back me up," Jet said and started thinking about it. He was stretched thin, but maybe Cutter could help him while he had the week to prepare. "Cutter. If I introduce you to Kamber, can you help keep an eye on her?"

"Absolutely," Cutter said.

"Good. She could probably use a friend anyway. By the way, I'm giving you a curfew."

"Hey! I don't think so."

"Sorry, Cutter. That's *my* only term."

Cutter shook his head. "This deal just keeps getting worse. What kind of curfew?"

"Simple. Just stick to large groups and absolutely no outdoor travel after dark. No walks, no dates out on the town. Got it?"

"Fine. It's just a week anyway."

"Cutter. I hate to break the news to you this way."

"Don't be sorry. I know you're just looking out for me. Besides, I should be the one apologizing. I should've never left you alone the way I did four years ago. You were right all along, and I doubted you. Won't happen again."

Jet smiled and clapped Cutter on the back and gave him a shove. "Nothing to apologize for, you fool. I was the one who pushed you away to begin with. Remember?"

"I remember. Just promise me you'll never do it again."

Jet shook Cutter's hand and gave him a smile. "You got it."

CHAPTER 11
Lybra Howling

ΑΒΓΔΕΖΗΘΙΚΛ<u>Μ</u>
ΝΞΟΠΡΣΤΥΦΧΨΩ

JET PLACED HIS focus back on Kamber. With the Lucem no longer providing oversight on the rare-earth deliveries, the responsibility fell to the Agency's elite recon soldiers. But he had heard rumors they were losing troops and resources at an alarming rate, and Solan had once again questioned her decision to suspend support to focus on their own matters. She felt it was only a matter of time before Harok called to plead for their help again, though. She had even considered shadowing the freighters, just to provide some assistance to the soldiers, though none of them had the time to spare. Jet hated to think about the troops facing the raids alone, especially knowing the Atrum were in the mix.

Jet had also notified Cord and DiJinn about Cutter. Between the three of them, they would take shifts keeping an eye on him. That, along with Cutter's agreement to stick to the curfew, helped Jet feel comfortable they could afford one week.

Jet met Cord at the Agency hanger atop of one of the taller ports on Skylight City around five o'clock. It was a blustery Wednesday afternoon, and the wind carried the hint of winter and a not-so-subtle promise of things to come. Thousands of citizens bustled about the port, hurrying home from work or school.

"I must admit, I'm surprised you were able to pull it off," Cord said.

"What? Getting back into Lybra's estate?"

"She does not admit faculty into her gallery. How did you manage it?"

"Persuasion," Jet said.

"With Vishmu? How deceptive of you. I'm impressed."

Jet shoved Cord. "I guess you're having an effect on me. Besides, Lybra had it coming."

They hopped on the T-Spine. The large people mover was nearly full, and Cord switched on the privacy screen. The charged rail sizzled, and the T-spine bolted off at a high rate.

"So, both girls agreed to go?" Cord asked.

"I don't think Tetra was too excited about it, even though Kamber said she was. Probably, she just didn't want to go alone."

"You know Hurse will want revenge. It's a risk, taking Tetra along. Hurse will be watching, and he won't be happy."

"I know, but it's the only way Kamber would've gone along. Besides, Hurse doesn't know our alias. For all he knows, we're just a couple of middle-aged professors."

"We don't know his either. And if you think he'll be fooled by an alias, you're mistaken. He'll know."

Blazers was exactly as Jet remembered it. The restaurant was jam packed with sports enthusiasts. There were famous athletes from the professional teams inside amongst the fans. Cutter was also there and sat in the middle of the restaurant with the rest of the blaze team. Several news crews surrounded him, trying to get an interview. Jet could see that he was making the most of his last week, which was fine, as long as he was in his dorm before nightfall.

In the corner sat Tetra and Kamber, with the rest of the track team ignoring them.

Jet and Cord stopped at Coach Minnett's table.

"How did it go today?" Jet asked.

She looked up at him. "As expected, Gunter. We start the season in first. Kamber crushed it, of course, as did Tetra. They're both friends and competitors and will be at each other's throats all season. They're over there," Minnett said, pointing toward a corner booth.

"Thanks again for this," Jet said. "I think seeing the painting will help them. I've heard it was actually composed by a lady who also had E.M."

"It's fine, Gunter," Minnett said. "Just have them back on campus before dark."

Kamber and Tetra sat across from each other in a booth, neither talking nor looking at one another. Both plates of food had barely been touched. Kamber had completely colored her hair since last time he had seen her. Green and purple accents shot all the way through now, and she had added some matching beads and braids. Tetra sat with arms crossed. She was about the same height as Kamber and also had the natural build of a sprinter. He wondered about her background and if she had faced similar struggles like the rest of them.

Jet held out his hand. "It's nice to meet you, Tetra. I've heard a lot about you through Kamber. I think you'll both appreciate the opportunity to see this work of art."

Tetra gave him an odd look but shook his hand. She stared at him for several seconds before clearing her throat. "It's…nice to meet you, too, Mister Kepp."

"Minnett tells me you both did a great job today," Jet continued.

"She's a bit upset at the moment," Kamber said.

"Yes, you beat me, Kamber. But only because I tripped on the home stretch. No need to rub it in."

"Sure, dear. If that helps your ego, of course."

Jet cleared his throat. "This here is Doctor Vinculum. He has an interest in the painting as well. Are we ready? Oh, before I forget, I wanted to give these to you both, compliments of the athletic department." Jet reached into his tweed blazer and handed a golden university lapel pin to each of them.

Kamber stood and pinned it to her T-shirt and grabbed her jacket. Tetra did the same and pinned it to her collar.

"Hopefully, this place we're going is more exciting," Tetra said.

"Just watch your manners," Cord said. "This lady is a bit uptight."

"To say the least," Jet chimed in.

They hailed a cab and made their way to the wealthy Vent Quarter of Skylight City. Middle-class condos gave way to posh homes and landscaping as they approached Lybra's estate.

Jet paid the taxi. "Let me do the talking, okay? Lybra will try and pry into your business. She is fascinated by students like you. Just try to ignore her and don't be alarmed if she comes across a little rude. If things get out of control, we'll handle it."

Cord rapped on the door several times before Lybra's butler answered. Jet remembered him by the name of Corsely. The old man cracked the door for them and skulked off.

They all moved into a tall rotunda. Jet watched Tetra and Kamber's expression as they looked at the paintings, slow fascination dawning on their faces.

"That painting, there," Kamber said.

"What about it," Jet asked, pretending like he didn't see anything special in it.

"You…can't see those holograms?" she asked.

Cord shook his head.

Tetra moved over to stand in front of it. "I see it, Kamber…but what does it mean?"

A lady cleared her throat from a balcony above, and they looked up to see Lybra. She looked the same as Jet remembered her; short, shriveled, and loud, but her eyes were still bright and piercing. She clutched the same metal cane in one arthritis-riddled hand and a cup of tea in the other. A multi-hued scarf was wrapped around her hunched shoulders as she hobbled down the stairs.

She stopped in front of Kamber and looked up at her. She turned her head to Tetra. "Goodness, look at you two. Future stars, aren't we? And the last of the euphs."

"That's a bit uncalled for, don't you think?" Tetra said.

Jet cleared his throat. "Miss Lybra. My name is Gunter Kepp, we talked earlier this week. This is Dr. Vinculum. We'll be accompanying these ladies—"

"I don't think so," Lybra interrupted him with a wave of her hand.

"But that was the agreement, I believe."

"I've reconsidered my decision. I won't allow it."

"I don't understand," Jet said. "Why the change?"

"This is my gallery, young man. My rules. And I say no."

"I appreciate that this is your gallery, and might I say it's a spectacular collection," Jet replied. "Are you sure you can't make an exception, just this once?"

"Flattery, is it? My…you are desperate."

"Miss Lybra," Cord said. "If we aren't allowed in, then we will have to take Kamber and Tetra with us. It'd be a shame if they were denied access, considering the painting's heritage. I know it would mean a great deal to them both."

Lybra looked at him intently, as if trying to place an old acquaintance from long ago. Jet could see her mind working and was reminded how sharp Lybra really was. She was no fool. But their alias was well established. "I'm going to allow it this one time. It will never happen again. I suppose that these two young ladies shouldn't be turned away. This painting is as much theirs as it is mine. Corsely! Come!"

Lybra turned and walked down the hallway.

"Not a word," Jet whispered to Kamber and Tetra.

Along the way, Lybra hummed to herself with the only interruption being a long coughing fit. Like before, the gallery was housed on the upper floor and occupied the entire footprint. Lybra bragged about a few of her more expensive paintings as they strolled through the gallery, stopping in front of the painting called *The Plan.*

Jet watched Kamber and Tetra's expression. Both stood in front of the large painting, staring up at it in wonder. The dominant feature, a large circular eye, was divided into twenty-four equal sections by the string-like cones and rods of the iris. An enormous number of mathematical equations seemed to vibrate and buzz into the foreground of the hologram that projected in front of them.

Jet nudged Cord. "You see what you need?" he whispered.

Cord simply nodded.

Lybra noticed the expression on Tetra and Kamber's face and waited a moment before breaking the silence. "My dear ladies," she said and stood between them and the painting, snapping a few times to get their attention. "Apparently you see something quite interesting. I've owned this painting for nearly half a century, and yet I still have no idea what secrets it holds. I've watched other euphs like yourself stare at it in awe. To this day, not a single one has talked about what they've seen. You two are the last of the euphs, there are no more known in existence. That means when you die, which could be soon, whatever secret this painting holds goes with you. You *must* tell me what you see. It is vital, I don't think you understand the importance."

Kamber looked at Tetra, who shrugged.

"We don't see anything," Kamber said, and Tetra nodded in agreement.

"This is simply not true," Lybra said, raising her voice. "Every time I let a euph in here, I get the same answer. I know it's a lie! But I'm not letting it go this time!"

Lybra raised her metal cane and struck Tetra across the face. Tetra fell to the ground and held a hand to her cheek in shock. Kamber moved forward and grasped the cane and pried it from Lybra's clutch. She tossed it across the room. "Are you mad?" Kamber said.

Lybra backed away and pressed a button on her bracelet.

Jet looked anxiously at Cord.

Tetra lay on the ground, and Kamber knelt to help her up.

"I'm not letting anyone leave this place until I hear what I want. So, you two had better rethink your answer."

"You just struck a student!" Jet roared and tried to remain calm. "That's a felony."

"I practically own the university and the authorities, young man," Lybra said. "You're in as much trouble as these two if you don't hush up!"

Four large security guards walked up the stairs and stood behind Lybra.

"Now. Let's start over, shall we?" she said.

"I was hoping this would happen," Cord said.

"You need any help?" Jet asked.

"No. This should be enjoyable."

"Wait," Kamber said. "I'll tell you what you want. Just don't hurt anyone."

"Keep quiet, Kamber," Jet said.

Cord stepped forward and stood in front of the two girls. Lybra started laughing until she was coughing. "One last chance, ladies. I'd hate to see these professors get roughed up."

"Enough talk," Cord said and moved past Lybra. He lifted the first guard with one hand and slammed him to the ground. Then he spun and hit the one next to him in the stomach. The guard dropped to a knee, and Cord slapped the back of his head in one smooth motion, knocking him unconscious. Cord stepped over them as the other two guards spread out and circled him. They rushed and Cord ducked, spun, and let them crash into each other. Before they could untangle, he grabbed both men by the neck and slammed their faces together. Both men fell to the ground, noses bloodied.

Lybra backed away and looked at Cord with wide eyes. "That's impossible. Who are you?"

"Just a couple of professors. I think we'll be leaving now."

Jet guided Kamber and Tetra toward the stairs. Cord faced Lybra as her guards started to stir.

"You know me," he whispered to her. "You do not want to cross me."

Lybra's eyes went wide as she stared up into Cord's eyes. She went white as he probed her thoughts, prying into her deepest fears.

"Understand now?" he asked.

Lybra nodded.

CHAPTER 12
A Call to Arms

ΑΒΓΔΕΖΗΘΙΚΛ**Μ**

ΝΞΟΠΡΣΤΥΦΧΨΩ

THE FOLLOWING MONDAY, Solan asked Jet to escort Sylvant to the university on her first full day of duty. He picked her up for tea on the third belt, to ease her nerves, then cloaked his skiff to the university. Solan had managed to push Sylvant's assignment through, bumping her up to the top of the witness protection plan. She had called in most of her favors to do it, though. She'd also managed to keep it quiet to avoid Harok's attention. Now that the Lucem had temporarily suspended their assistance of the Goliath's Gate project, Harok was furious. Any future favors from the Agency were likely dead-on-arrival. However, Solan didn't seem to care much, and Jet sensed she was simply trying to consolidate what little resources were left to them. They were getting down to bare bones.

We need to trust each other and be vigilant, she had told Jet that morning. *Avoid distraction. We're on our own now.*

"What's it like?"

Jet pulled his gaze from the console and looked at Sylvant. "Sorry. What was that?"

"I said, what's it like being…a Lucem? It's Lucem, right? Did I pronounce it right? Does it feel different in any way?"

Jet shook his head. "I guess I don't feel any different, at least not that I've noticed, except when I practice Vishmu. I can't really explain it, but I'm slowly learning new things, not as quickly as Solan would like, probably."

"Vishmu?"

"Oh, that's right. I keep forgetting you're almost as new to this as I am. Vishmu is an ancient art. It combines our training and meditation, the physical and mental aspect, which allows us to realize greater potential in our souls."

"Okay," Sylvant said slowly, her brow furrowed. "I'll take your word for it. I'm still in shock about this. I just wanted to apologize to you. You tried to tell me all along…and it was true after all. It doesn't make sense—scientifically, that is. None of this should be possible."

"Well, don't worry about it. I think it was best that you weren't around when all of that happened. That night of the triclipse was intense."

"Solan said that the leader of the Atrum tried to kill you that night."

"I was lucky. I hope it doesn't come down to the wire like that with Kamber."

"Is she the young lady at the university with E.M.?"

"Yes, she's one of them. There's another one named Tetra. Kamber is my warden, and I'm assigned to protect her. It'll be easier now that I'm on the first belt, and closer to her."

"Solan promised to explain more when she has time, whenever that is," Sylvant said and crossed her arms. "I suppose I'll never understand the depths of it entirely. A group opposed to you called the Atrum, that's been around for thousands of years. Vail, Bo…Myranda. All part of that group. This sounds like something straight out of a fairytale."

"More like a nightmare, Professor—"

"Please," Sylvant interrupted him. "Don't call me that, Jet. Not anymore."

Jet suddenly realized how difficult the last several days must have been for Sylvant. Her old life no longer existed, she had a new alias, she was part of a secret agency and, to top it all off, she was caught up in a dispute that dated back millennia. It brought back fresh memories of when he had first learned of the Agency.

He could have simply reached out and read her thoughts and understood her feelings at that moment. But that invasion of privacy was morally wrong, and he refused to go down that path unless he had good reason to do so. Solan and the other Lucem felt the same way. But he could see by her body language she was anxious.

"Sylvant," he said, and turned to look at her. "I know how difficult this must be for you. I'm sorry that it worked out this way. I know that doesn't mean much, but let me know if I can help."

"I'm just not sure what to expect. I had everything figured out in my former life…geez, it sounds so strange to say that. I'm so uncertain right now. This has happened so quickly."

"Well, you'll adapt. Once you get into your assignment, it's not that bad, actually."

"But all my old acquaintances and the things I've worked for over the years—that's all gone. It's like starting over."

"But you have your sister back in your life now," Jet said, trying to reassure her. "And I'll always be here, along with Cord. You can count on that. And, we'll find your father, I'm sure of it."

"I never thought I'd meet him. I'd always hoped that Solan was right, even though I never admitted it. I suddenly have a family again…it all feels so surreal."

"One thing I can tell you about your sister; when she sets her mind to something, there isn't much that can stop her. Finding your father is at the top of her list."

When they finally neared Skylight University air space, Jet turned to face her. "Did Solan explain how your alias works?"

Sylvant held out a brooch. When she pinned it to her hair, her facial features changed slightly, her hair lightened a shade, and her eye color turned dark blue. She was still herself, but different enough to avoid any comparisons.

"Just watch your p's and q's and you'll be fine," Jet said.

Sylvant reached out and grabbed his arm. "I'm afraid, Jet," Sylvant said. "I don't think I can make it here. I have no business in all this. Those Atrum…they aren't like you. How does Solan handle all of this?"

Jet looked down at her hand, caught slightly off-guard, and looked up to her. "I hear you. I'm still trying to understand this myself. Every day, I question my ability, which is something I'm not used to. But you're never alone. You can do this, Sylvant. You're an amazing person, and that trait seems to run in your family."

Sylvant sat back in her seat. "I don't know. I have my doubts."

"Happens to me a lot too. Just remember to be yourself."

They settled down in the Clipton Forest, and Jet hopped out with Sylvant. "I'll walk you to the edge, then you're on duty," he said with a grin.

It was a brisk morning, with some light dew clinging to the ground and the sun trying to pry through the gray curtains of mist. Jet walked next to Sylvant, dressed in his alias attire and his cloak tucked under his arm, enjoying the silence of the forest. Before long, he felt a buzzing sensation, and the intuitive voice began to scream at him. Perhaps it was a preemptive warning, he wasn't certain, but the words *CLOAK* came to him, and he turned immediately and grabbed Sylvant just as a loud clap echoed through the trees. He pulled her to the ground and rolled on top of her, shielding her body with his. He draped his cloak over them, and they vanished instantly. He scanned the tree line for what he knew now to be a sniper. All was silent for several seconds before a missile-shaped skiff rose from the underbrush. The jammer class skiff cloaked, nosed up, and shot skyward. The entire event had happened so quickly that he hadn't noticed the bullet hole through his shoulder had also penetrated Sylvant's stomach.

She was barely breathing, and blood caked her hands as she lay there in the mist, shivering. Jet waited a second longer before removing his cloak and examining her wound. The sniper had used a high-powered railgun, and the round had exited through Sylvant's lower back. Jet looked into her eyes. Tears flowed freely down her dark-skinned cheeks as he lifted her, and a gasp of pain tore from her lips. Jet carried her quickly to the nearest portal and knelt next to it, setting her down gently. He decided to reach out to her with his thoughts, realizing there wasn't enough time to get the help she needed.

When he made the connection, her pain was excruciating, and he could barely endure it. She was in a state of hysteria, her thoughts racing in her mind. He called to her, calming her. Then he absorbed her pain and took her mind in his. He knew now it wouldn't be long. If he left her to go for help, she would die in anguish. Besides, she was down to her last few breaths now. He could at least comfort her and ease her passing.

Jet set aside his own fear and spoke words of serenity using his thoughts as he waited for her to pass. Her final reflections were mainly focused on her sister, and how Solan would handle this. Even in death, Sylvant was concerned about how her sister might blame herself. A few more seconds passed as Jet continued to comfort her and ease her suffering. He witnessed the light in Sylvant's soul slowly fade as he sat next to her on the cold forest floor. The sounds of the forest surrounded them, and the shadows deepened as he lay slumped next to her and wept until the sun had set.

"How many troops have they lost?" DiJinn asked. She sat at her chair in her usual pose with her worn tactical boots kicked up on the table's edge.

Solan stood behind her own chair, rubbing her temples with her eyes closed. Something was bothering her and had been throughout that day. She had sent Jet out to escort her sister to her first day on duty. But it was late, and he should've returned with her hours ago.

Cord, Ti-Leer, DiJinn, Annaka, Harriet and Booker sat quietly, waiting to hear what she had to say. A bit of stray moonlight from a skylight well washed across the massive round table as Solan stood silently with her arms crossed and head bowed. They had just settled into one of the lower control rooms deep in the bowels of Lyrinthum, and the new surroundings were completely different than what she was used to at the Agency.

"More than fifty troops have been lost already, according to Harok," Solan replied and paced the room, still rubbing her forehead. "Too many lives are being lost over these minerals."

"You alright?" Ti-Leer asked Solan.

She waved him away. "I'm fine." She walked to the front and brought up a large three-dimensional map of the system. "This area here, you say?" she asked, giving DiJinn a glance.

"Yeah," DiJinn said. "But Harok said the jammer skiff cloaked goin' into the ninth belt debris field, just like last time. Hell, I want in on this assignment, Sol. I need to see if Sojahn—"

"Jinn, I know you want payback, but our role is to plant a tracking device. That's all Harok is asking for right now—that's our main objective, and we will answer the call one more time. I'm as curious as you are about the Atrum's involvement, but we've got our own problems, and I don't want to get drawn into this any more than necessary."

"Seems like too much of the system's resources are going into this collider, Goliath's Gate," Annaka said. She stood and brushed her gray hair from her eyes. "Solan, do we know everything there is to know about this project?"

"We've never inquired into their business, and they've always left us to ours," Solan said. "Tyberius was always adamant about separating our dealings. The less we know, the less likely we are to get dragged into political theater. That said, I'm not as textbook as my father. So, I've been asking around, but everyone in the Agency is pretty tightlipped, even my personal contacts. For now, we need to just do our duty. After things settle down, I intend to dig into it more."

"I just don't trust Harok," Annaka said. "I understand the collider and its importance, but the amount of money, resources and now lives being dumped into this is astronomical. I have full access to the budget on this project through the university. It's staggering to the point of nausea. I knew Harok when he was an assistant at the university, and I never trusted that man. He seems overly ambitious about this project. There's more to this whole thing."

"Again," Solan said. "Once things settle down, we can take a deeper dive into it."

"Back to the question of the rare-earth," Cord said, speaking up for the first time. "These elements have little use for most people—"

Solan shook her head and then slammed her fist down on the table hard enough to make it tremble. Everyone paused and looked at her in shock. The room remained silent for a few long seconds.

Solan took a deep breath and planted both hands on the table and leaned forward. "There is no sense in speculating. Let's just get a tracking device on one of their frigates." She switched the three-dimensional display off in frustration. "The Agency's next convoy is scheduled to leave tomorrow morning to Goliath's Gate. It'll be heading out early from the largest refinery on the fifth belt, and Harok wants two Lucem on that frigate. Cord, you and Jet are next in line. You're both far enough along to handle this assignment. If you see any Atrum, try not to engage them unless you have to."

"What about Kamber?" Cord asked.

"I'm assigning Ti-Leer and Booker to cover for Jet," Solan said. "Annaka and Harriet will continue their assignments. We may no longer be under the Agency's umbrella, but we still need to uphold our duties."

Everyone stood to leave, and Solan turned to DiJinn. "Come with me."

DiJinn walked over to Cord. "Keep your eyes peeled. Things are getting' wonky 'round here," she said and followed Solan out of the room.

Solan's makeshift office was large with an old dusty desk and chair in one corner with a couple of garish looking lounge sofas on the opposite side. She had too many things running through her head at the moment and cursed. She hated being in this position and thought for the twentieth time that day how much she would give to have her father back. But she knew better than letting her emotions out of control. She would have to do better. But her sister was still in the back of her mind. *Was she having regrets already?* Even though she knew bringing Sylvant in had been the logical choice, she couldn't help feeling a bit guilty about the other Lucem and their family members now. All that had been wearing at her nerves, along with a dozen other things. Seeing her sister again had refueled her desire to live, and she'd needed that little bump. Then again, her sister was in a whole new world of danger, and Solan had yet another person to be responsible for.

Solan waited for DiJinn and closed her office door behind her. She immediately turned and held her hands up. "I know what you're going to say, and you're right. I'm sorry."

"What's going on, Sol?" DiJinn said, taking a seat on the sofa. "You're not actin' like the girl I know and love."

"I'll talk to the others later and apologize. Right now, we have another issue to discuss."

"You wanna go after Tyberius? Just the two of us?"

"I don't trust anyone else right now."

"And by that, what do you mean?"

"Just that I'd rather keep this between the two of us—we need to move fast. We can't wait any longer for Tyberius to just magically reappear. It's been too long—something has definitely happened to him."

"What'll the others say when were both out?"

"We shouldn't be out long," Solan said. "Hopefully, we can find what we need without raising any suspicions."

DiJinn shrugged. "You know the others'll be furious if they find out you decided to take this on alone."

"That's why I've got you, Jinn," Solan said and clapped her on the shoulder. "The others need to stay focused on their own assignments."

"Where do we start?" DiJinn asked.

"The Galleon Quarter on Skylight City. That's the last place Tyberius was when we lost communication."

"That's a rough part of the city. An odd place for him."

"It is," Solan agreed. "But if Albright's there, then it makes sense. No one would think to look for him in an area like that."

Someone hammered at Solan's door, and it swung open. Booker's hulking form stood in the opening, his face white and fists balled. "You need to come with me. Now."

M

Jet sat in the control room at his chair with his head on the table. He held his hands folded in front of him, trying to keep from rubbing at the dried blood covering his fingers. On the table in front of him lay Sylvant's brooch, also covered in dried blood. When Solan came into the room, she stopped and stared at Jet, DiJinn right behind her.

"What the hell is this?" DiJinn snapped.

Everyone waited for Jet to speak, but he didn't. He simply stared at Solan. He didn't need to say a word as he looked into her glowing eyes. He opened his mind and reached out to her, sharing his thoughts. He revealed those final moments spent with Sylvant, making sure none of the other Lucem could see them. He felt her shock, then a fierce rage erupted inside her. The light of her soul blazed like a dying star, enveloping everything in oblivion. It was blinding and unbearable, and he snapped their psychic connection closed. Jet knew then that Sylvant's killer would pay dearly.

"Where is she?" Solan asked. She had managed to pull herself together, but Jet had seen how close she was to the edge. Solan was calm…for the moment.

Everyone left the control room together.

Jet had left Sylvant wrapped in his cloak just inside the forest portal. It was a solemn walk, everyone knowing what they would find at the end of the tunnel.

When they reached the portal, Jet lifted Sylvant's body and handed her to Solan. He took his blood-stained cloak and wrapped himself in it.

"Jet, you're wounded," Harriet said.

Jet ignored her. "I was walking her up to the forest edge. I sensed the sniper, but I was too slow to shield her. If I'd had my cloak on, I could've taken the round…it all happened so fast."

Solan stared at Jet as she held her sister's body, and for a split second, he thought she might rip his throat out. Everyone waited, their heads bowed.

"What else did you see?"

"The sniper left in a jammer class skiff, same one that ambushed Jinn and Ti-Leer…an ambush that was meant for me. I know about that, Solan…they were after me that day. The Atrum want me dead, it's obvious. Just let me go. I don't know what I'm doing anyway. I'm a danger to you all and everyone around—"

"That's enough!" Solan's voice echoed inside the portal. Jet noticed her hand shaking slightly, and she clenched her fists to steady it. "You will continue on, just like me! Just like the rest of us!"

Jet stood silently for a few seconds. He knew he could just leave on his own when no one was expecting it. He didn't need anyone's permission. But then Sylvant's death would be in vain. The thought of anyone else suffering on his behalf made him feel sick to his stomach. But abandoning the other Lucem and Cutter to the Atrum now seemed cowardly.

"I understand," Jet said.

"You and Cord will leave tomorrow and finish the Agency's mission. Everyone else will continue their duties, no questions."

"Sol," DiJinn said. "Let us help with Sylvant—"

"No, Jinn," Solan said in a low voice. "Please, not now. Leave me…I need time alone."

M

Tuesday dawned with Cord kicking at Jet's door. Jet rolled out of bed and made a quick call to Cutter to check in on him. He let Cutter know that Booker would be taking his spot. Then he dressed, grabbed his duffle bag, and walked with Cord to the hanger bay. They each took separate skiffs to the refinery on the fifth belt. Jet had plenty to ponder during his flight. His shoulder had already healed, but his heart and soul were wounded. What he had experienced with Sylvant would follow him for the rest of his life. He had witnessed plenty of heartache and suffering throughout his life; death was everywhere growing up in the ARC district. But never had he been so close to it before.

Was Sylvant dead because he'd kept quiet about the bounty on his head? Would things be different now if he'd brought the matter up to Solan and the other Lucem?

Sylvant had been a kind and caring person; she hadn't deserved to die like that. The simple fact that she would be alive had she not been near him stung the most. Solan had placed so much trust in him to protect her, and he had failed. If his intuitive voice had just warned him sooner, or if he had been more alert, had his cloak on, or reacted just a split second faster in shielding her... The thoughts ran circles in his head and gnawed at him, mocking his weakness. How long would Solan continue to place trust in him? When he had been a student toward the end of his time at the university, he'd hit rock bottom after losing his friends. But what he felt right now was so much worse. Solan's only sister, her most prized possession, was now dead. She'd held herself together for the sake of the Lucem, yet another responsibility of her leadership. Before, Solan might have flown into a rage and immediately started hunting Sylvant's killer. None of that changed how he felt at that moment, though. His confidence was as low as it had ever been, and his soul felt mortally wounded.

He *had* to work harder at becoming the Lucem Solan felt he could be, if for no other reason than to prevent anyone else from dying under his watch. If this wasn't the push he needed to become stronger, then nothing would do. In a sense, he had no choice—if he didn't figure out his mental block with Vishmu, he would probably die at the Century Eclipse. He wanted to find Sylvant's killer and bring them to justice, but exactly how would he manage that when he couldn't even protect the others around him? When he thought about his struggles with Vishmu, he felt like he did when he'd first started playing blaze…a rookie. Then something Cord had said the other day came to him. It was like a moment of clarity that made him sit forward in his seat. *Of course*, he thought. *It seemed so simple now.*

What if he approached his problem like a game of blaze?

At least he knew *how* to prepare for blaze. Just thinking about it made him feel excited for the first time in a long while. He felt the butterflies in his stomach, like he was sitting in front of his locker preparing before a game. Was it possible that he could break through just by associating Vishmu to blaze? Solan had told him that every Lucem finds their own path. Perhaps this was the path forward for him.

Once they arrived at the refinery, Jet took in its operations. It was a heavily guarded facility, and troops were stationed everywhere. No raids took place here, and he could quickly see why. The marauders were smart enough to wait until the refined minerals were en route to their destination, as it was a much easier target.

The refinement process for the rare-earth minerals looked complex, with designated areas set up for the raw ore to first be ground into a powder form. Then separated and cooled into its pure form.

An Agency transport waited for them nearby. It was large enough to carry twenty-four personnel—a pilot, co-pilot and twenty of the elite recon troops, led by General Dane. Jet had met Dane on a few occasions, but this would be Jet's first extended mission with him. Dane was a disciplined, well-rounded leader, from what he'd seen thus far, and his troops were loyal to him. Someone with Dane's rank would normally never see any type of action. But Dane led by example and loved being out in the field with his troops.

He barked at the recon troops to get in line where they checked their gear and weapons. Cord stood nearby, hooded and cloaked from view.

"You okay to do this?" Cord whispered, not bothering to lower his hood.

"Later, Cord. I'm not really in the mood to chat," Jet replied.

Dane walked over to Jet and nodded. "Where's the other Lucem?" Dane didn't look directly into Jet's eyes as he talked. Even here amongst the hardcore recon troops, they still didn't trust the Lucem and seemed disturbed by his glowing turquoise eyes.

"He's nearby," Jet replied. "We ready?"

Dane nodded. "Always." He whistled, and the troops boarded in two equal lines. They took their seats along benches that lined the edges of the tube-shaped cargo hold.

The cargo door slid shut, and they taxied around. Jet held the handle above, buckled in and took note of the troops. They were all relatively calm, a few joking in hushed tones, which Dane didn't seem to mind. But none of them looked his way, except for a few quick glances. Cord, still cloaked, had taken a seat next to Jet and sat quietly.

Jet leaned over to Dane. "Any thoughts on these raids?"

"Just what you've probably already heard. A group of marauders but no former knowledge of who they are. Intel shows they're interested in the rare-earth minerals, but only after they've been refined."

"Well. Our mission is to get a tracking device on one of their skiffs. We can provide backup if needed, but we'll respect your space. If we are attacked, the tracking device is our main priority. It's the only way we're gonna stop these raids and save future losses. That's coming directly from Harok."

Dane nodded. "I appreciate that. We can handle ourselves. Do what you need to do. Hopefully, nothing happens, and this'll just be a relaxing visit to the eighth belt."

But Jet had his doubts. Dane ran a tight crew, and Jet didn't want to insert Lucem into recon business. He could see the discomfort and distrust from the troops, even though Dane didn't seem to mind their presence.

Cord remained in a state of meditation as Jet tried to relax during their flight. Their transport ship was positioned roughly in the middle of the convoy of frigates, which would allow them the quickest access in case they were ambushed. Two fighter skiffs were positioned at the front and back of the convoy, something that had recently been added at Harok's orders. Of course, the frigates had their own assortment of defenses and counter measures. But with the Atrum lending their hand to the raids, there wasn't much that could be done, short of placing a Lucem on board each frigate—something that had already landed them in quite a bit of trouble with the Agency. Apparently, Harok was at his wits' end.

However, the convoy wasn't ambushed on the way to the eighth belt, and all seemed to be uncomfortably calm. There were eight main docking ports positioned equally around the eighth belt. They delivered the precious cargo to the sixth port, which had been nicknamed the Foxtrot detector. The construction of the collider had made progress up to that port, which represented about seventy-five percent completion. Each of the eight ports—which were spaced equally around the entire belt's circumference—housed something called a detector below it, with many smaller detectors in between. The massive detectors, as Cord had explained it, were devices used to map out and document the collision of particles at near light speed.

The topside of the belt had smaller towns and provinces nestled into the landscape. The mainstay appeared to be farming and livestock. But the geography included desert landscapes and hilly terrain in a few places. Jet recalled from his orientation day at the university years ago that supplies for construction and industry were sourced from this belt. Outside the Foxtrot detector, though, was a dense forest that appeared to be undisturbed by humans. No one would guess that a massive particle accelerator lie buried below the hull of the belt.

Jet noticed how thin the air was as they unloaded, making it slightly more difficult to breathe. It was like being in a higher altitude, and he assumed the system's protective atmosphere was thinning out the farther away from the core they were. The color of the sky was darker with the vestiges of space just kilometers above them.

"Recon. Let's double it up," Dane snapped. "I don't want these supplies sitting out." More faculty from inside showed up with mech lifts to handle the heavier pallets.

"Strange surroundings," Jet muttered to Cord.

"We're not far from being in outer space. Quite fascinating, actually."

Jet continued to scan the crews. There were hundreds of workers milling about, each with a color-coded uniform, which Jet assumed designated what department they worked in.

"Keep your eyes open. Something tells me this place is full of spies."

CHAPTER 13
The Tetrahedron

THE NEXT DAY, Solan insisted on taking separate skiffs. DiJinn didn't object as they cloaked their way to the third belt, maintaining radio silence the entire way. Solan had stayed out in the Clipton Forest the entire night before, finally building a pyre for her sister. The time alone, under the stars and amongst the trees with the aurora borealis casting its soothing light, had helped give her some temporary closure. The loss of her sister wouldn't soon wear off, and it had taken all her will to continue on. She hadn't spoken to the others about it yet and knew they would avoid the topic until she was ready to talk. What was devastating yesterday was quickly turning to resolve.

But perhaps the most difficult emotion she faced at that moment concerned Jet and her decision about the bounty on his head. Yes, she had known about it, and had chosen to let him remain unfettered. It was yet another decision that she questioned.

She had originally struggled with what to do about the bounty; should she place a curfew on him, order additional protection, or even lock him up at headquarters? That treatment would've shaken his already low self-esteem. If she wanted to lead, she had to show trust and have faith in her fellow Lucem. Coddling Jet would not help him grow—she had to let him go and allow fate to take over. If that meant he was destined to die, then it would happen no matter what she did to intervene. But was her sister's life the payment for allowing Jet to live freely?

She gripped the console tighter and tried to remain focused.

She had to remain focused.

She calmed her anger, but it still simmered in the back of her mind and threatened to explode. There would be a time to find who was responsible for her sister's death. She stored it away and nailed a lid on it, at least for now.

Skylight City had private hangers for the Agency at one of the outskirt industrial quadrants. Both Solan and

DiJinn donned their aliases as they left the hanger. Solan's political senator guise was perfect for being out of touch as often as she was. Her tall athletic frame was about the same, but with dark brown eyes and lighter color hair. DiJinn tapped the hologram on her ring, brought up the menu and selected her alias, Detective Marsh—a high-ranking agent on the police force, which allowed her access to nearly unlimited resources. Her red hair changed to a dark chestnut, pinned into a ponytail with pale skin and piercing blue eyes.

DiJinn took the upper half of the quadrant's suburb while Solan took the underground portions. These were the dodgier areas of the city, according to DiJinn, and where most of the crime took place. It might be a long shot, but it's where she would choose to hide out if she were Albright.

There weren't any public avenues to get below since it wasn't considered publicly accessible space. But it was so vast that policing it was nearly impossible. At times, there were raids, but vagrants and underground gangs always made their way back after being cleared out. Solan stayed in the shadows, her cloak drawn. She had the place in mind she wanted to go, but it could be dangerous if she wasn't cautious.

Makeshift homes, shops and thoroughfares lined the bowels of the hull some twenty meters down. It was hot and steamy in the interior of the belt, due to its environmental heating system, which helped regulate the belt's surface temperature. Large high-rise foundations from above tied directly into the structural members of the belt's hull for support, and the thoroughfares wove between them. At thirty meters down, she hit the main thoroughfare and fell in with a group of traveling traders. She pulled her hood down and blended in with the group, who didn't notice.

She took in her surroundings. It was a spat of dingy colors—browns, grays, and mottled purples. Artificial lighting lit the space and shone through the road surface, which was made of strengthened graphene. Several layers of the paper-thin material allowed her to see beneath her and into the depths of the massive hull. Below was a chasm of pipes, conduits and valves, then darkness beyond like an abyss. Large pipes and city utilities intersected the road and made the way ahead look like an obstacle course. The throughfare widened to about one hundred meters and a haphazard bazaar appeared to have sprung up from disused materials, trash, and space debris. The loud roar of trading drowned out everything. Once through the gates, Solan moved in and around the vast market, looking for any potential breadcrumbs left behind by her father.

One of the shops caught her attention, and she moved into the store. The storekeeper sat behind a counter with an assortment of goods for sale, mostly tech gear, weapons and armor, all of it likely stolen.

Solan made her way toward the counter and browsed the bulletin board next to it. Holographic postings showed advertising for flight lessons to more exotic services. She located the lost and found area and searched it.

"What can I do for you?"

Solan turned to see the shopkeeper staring at her. His eyes lingered a second too long. "I'm searching for someone," Solan said, "An older man, probably wearing custodial clothing, and a government employee badge. He's about six foot tall and sixty years of age."

The man scratched three-day old stubble around his chin, and one of his eyes oozed some watery substance. On his shoulder was a tattoo that she hadn't noticed till now—golden weavings interlaced with red gems in the shape of a tetrahedron.

He shook his head. "Honey, people disappear all the time around here. You'll have to be more specific."

She smiled and nodded. "I imagine they do, but any help you can offer would be appreciated."

"What's it worth to you?" he replied. He propped his chin in his hands and stared openly at her. "I'm sure I can dig up some information for the right price, or favor."

"He was a good friend of mine and may need my help," Solan said.

The man looked at her again. "Your help, huh?" he whistled. "I'm sure he would."

She ignored him and placed a few credits on the counter. "How about now?"

He slid the credits into a drawer. "Come to think of it, there was a man like that some time back."

"How long ago?"

"Let's see…I'd say it was about two or three months. He was down here buying supplies, food… some other essentials, like clothes and soap."

"Did you talk to him?"

"I sold him the goods, so yeah."

"Did he say anything else that you recall?"

"Nothing. He was wearing a cloak like yours, though."

Two men stepped in behind Solan. They held a few items and waited for her to finish. The voice in Solan's head began to whisper.

"Anything else, sweetheart?" the storekeeper asked.

Solan turned and left without a word. She walked out of the store and waited to make sure the two men got a good look at her. Then she walked down one of the dark alleys, dim and quiet. A few dumpsters lined the sides of the buildings, and a shack with holographic graffiti covering it sat at the opposite end of the alley.

She crouched next to it and waited.

A few seconds passed before the two men appeared. Both were dressed like the storekeeper and had matching tattoos on their shoulders. The shorter one dropped his items. "Bad place to be, someone like you."

She cracked a smile. "This should be interesting," she said. "I thought you two might follow me. This seems like a perfect place for a casual conversation, doesn't it?"

"I don't think you understand the situation, lass."

Solan stood with her hands folded behind her back as they encircled her, but she quietly gritted her teeth. Apparently, a bait and tackle ploy the storeowner ran on unsuspecting customers. She was well aware of these tactics, though. The store owner would identify the target and send a signal to the henchmen, then split the loot… and whatever else they could get. A single female with plenty of credits made a good target. She wondered if Tyberius had fallen into the same trap, but if he had, these two men wouldn't be standing here now.

"All I want is some information," Solan said. "I think it would be better if you two answered a few questions and forgot about any other plans you might have."

Both men looked at each other and laughed. "It's too late for that. You should've stayed inside the shop."

"Last chance," she warned. She slid her hands forward and moved her cloak to the side, preparing herself.

Both men hesitated slightly at that. Solan smiled. She didn't want to injure these men…permanently. But teaching them a lesson seemed in order, plus, she had some frustration to take out.

The entire fight lasted about fifteen seconds. The first man's nose met with the back of her hand, and he went down, unconscious. The second man managed to get close enough to grab her arm. She flipped him up into the air with her leg. On his way back down, Solan spun and landed a roundhouse kick in the small of his back. He shot sideways several feet and hit the wall. With the wind knocked out of him, she placed one hand on his neck and squeezed gently, which was enough to make his eyes bulge. He tapped her arm, and she let up.

"Are we ready to talk now?" she asked.

К

Solan met DiJinn near the hangers.

"Any luck?" Solan asked.

"Nothing," DiJinn said and shook her head. "Even in my detective alias, no one really seemed to want to talk. Most of the citizens up there are middle class people, just in a hurry to get home from work. This is primarily a commercial district, hardly any amenities nearby. It just doesn't make any sense that Tyberius would have been looking in this area."

"Well, I had an interesting adventure."

"You get a lead?"

"Yes, at one of the markets. The shop owner had sold some goods to a person matching my father's description."

"Did the timeline match up?" DiJinn asked.

"Yes. I also got jumped. Two men with tattoos that match the one Harok shared with us. A tetrahedron."

"You got jumped? Lucky you."

Solan smirked. "Neither of them knew anything about Tyberius, though. But at least we're in the right vicinity. The tetrahedron marauders are a group of mercenaries, more specifically, hitmen for hire. A syndicate network that takes a percent off the top."

"Do we know where they're located?"

Solan nodded and showed DiJinn a map on her holopad. "Time to go deep undercover."

CHAPTER 14
Goliath's Gate

ΑΒΓΔΕΖΗΘΙΚΛ**Μ**
ΝΞΟΠΡΣΤΥΦΧΨΩ

A LADY WITH short hair and a muscular frame trotted toward Jet and Cord as they stood looking around the massive port. Her jaw continually clenched, and her faded fatigues matched the other local troops walking around.

"Lucem, yes?" she asked.

"I'm Jet, and this is Cord."

"I'm so excited you're here," she said and shook their hands. She seemed genuinely interested and kept staring at their glowing eyes. "I've heard the rumors, but never thought I'd meet a Heliographi. I'm head science officer Blankenship and in charge of sector six. We're nearing completion on this stage. I take it you're here to keep these marauders off our back?"

"We're primarily here to observe, so we'll keep out of the way, unless we're needed," Jet said. He didn't want to give away anything about their real purpose, since the tracking device was still considered a covert operation.

"Would you like a tour of the facility?" Blankenship asked.

Cord perked up at that. "Yes, I believe that would be enjoyable."

Blankenship showed Jet and Cord to their sleeping quarters first, then led them to an observation tower about fifty meters above the surface of the belt. The tower was part of a large complex of buildings and outposts, which was surrounded by a wall. It separated the port from the surrounding forest and prevented any views into the internal operations of the collider.

"Beyond these walls are undeveloped land and wilderness. There are some denser cities out there, but this belt is primarily used for livestock and other resources. When the system planners designed this belt, a portion of the interior hull was left vacant in hopes this massive particle accelerator would eventually become a reality. Goliath's Gate gets its name because of its size. It's been about a century now, and we're almost there."

It was hard not to notice her excitement. Jet wondered if Blankenship got out much from the project, but it looked like she spent very little time doing anything else but focusing on it.

"Is there any part of the accelerator visible from above ground?" Jet asked.

"Just these observation towers; there are eight total. They help preserve the secret underground project. We've managed to keep this development hidden so far."

"Seems like citizens would've figured it out by now," Jet said. "It's amazing that word hasn't gotten out."

"There may be some rumors floating around, but the idea of someone actually building a particle collider of this size probably sounds like a myth."

"And the rare-earth being brought in is primarily to power it?" Jet asked.

"For part of it, yes. There are eight ARC fusion reactors, one at each of the eight main detectors, with hundreds of minor detectors in between. Because of the size of the belt, we require an immense amount of power to operate the collider. The size of each ARC reactor is large enough to supply that demand. Each detector is named in order—Alpha, Bravo, Charlie, Delta, Echo, Foxtrot, Golf, and Hotel. We're at the Foxtrot detector facility now."

"Forgive me for asking, but what exactly do the detectors do again?" Jet asked.

"They will eventually monitor and track each collision. Subatomic particles are shot around the loop in opposite directions at tremendous speeds where they smash into each other. The detectors record the collisions. This way, we can recreate rare particles, test theories and even answer questions about how our universe was created."

"Jet," Cord said. "I can explain all of this to you later—"

"No…it's okay," Blankenship interrupted. "I quite enjoy the opportunity to explain it. The rare-earth is used in the high-temperature superconductors for both the ARC reactors and the particle accelerator. These elements are a family of chemical compounds that exhibit a high temperature superconductivity and allow us to operate the accelerator by keeping the particles on the curved track. In short, we can create much stronger magnetic fields with rare-earth. Follow me, I'll show you around below."

A vector accelerator took them down perhaps two hundred meters. Hundreds of laborers milled about the space, working frantically on the detector. The tunnel was perhaps twenty meters wide, where several transports unloaded supplies. A massive concrete tub about five meters thick surrounded two metallic tubes that extended out miles beyond and out of view. Clusters of conduits and other gadgets filled the area. In the middle of the chamber was a large eight-sided dish perhaps thirty meters tall with thousands of mirror-like devices covering every inch of it. The long tubes crisscrossed just below the detector.

"This is where the magic will happen, assuming we have enough rare-earth to finish the project," Blankenship said. "We're running about two weeks ahead of our supply chain of rare-earth. If we lose any more of it to the marauders, we'll be off schedule. The future of this project depends on stopping those raids."

M

Cord shook Jet awake.

He arose, eyes still bleary from his late night of training and meditation; his promise to Sylvant had started last night, and he'd barely slept. He had felt a spark, like a tiny flash in a dark room. Small at first but growing in intensity with the promise of greater things to come. He was gaining his confidence back, now that he had an approach he could handle.

They hurried to the main command post. Blankenship was there, pacing about and tapping her legs. Her hands were shaking as she fidgeted with something in her pocket. "We got the crooks this time." She pointed at the radar and a blip on the holographic field. It split into three blips. "Take the transport to Echo detector. They'll be after that last shipment."

With hoods drawn, Jet and Cord boarded the transport with about a dozen recon troops, led by Dane. It shot down the wide tunnel at a speed that left his stomach in the back of the seat. In minutes, they were slowing. He hopped out, followed by Cord. It was dim in this sector, since it was still under construction. They could see the supplies ahead, strewn out across the tunnel. Crates of refined rare-earth minerals sat unattended.

He didn't know if the ploy would work. To him, it was obviously a trap, but the allure of rare-earth just sitting there would be appealing to the right person, regardless. The recon troops lined the corridor, hiding in the shadows on both sides of the tunnel with a spotlight shining on the crates. The silvery metallic metal shone dully in the light as a few staged workers went about their business. The large Echo detector dominated the concrete chamber. Jet could hear some testing being done and muffled noises echoed in the background and funneled down the hardened tunnel. He and Cord remained crouched near the troops with hoods drawn and invisible. Dane waited, some sweat on his forehead as he peered up through the observation tower at the moonlight.

Seconds turned to minutes.

Then the sound of low thrumming could be heard in the distance, and it grew louder. Suddenly, several zip lines hit the floor and dust puffed out. Recon locked and loaded their rail guns, but Dane held them in formation, waiting for the first marauder to hit the floor. Several recon troops at the front readied their strengthened graphene shields and faced forward, prepared to take the brunt of the assault. Without warning, two recon troops were lifted and thrown through the air. They hit the concrete wall with a crushing blow.

Jet let his thoughts reach out to Cord to warn him. *Atrum!*

I got it…you get the tracking device planted, Cord replied and grappled with the Atrum.

Jet could only sense one Atrum, though, and grabbed one of the zip lines as multiple marauders hit the ground around him. He scaled up the side of the concrete observation tower and toward the hovering skiffs above. He jumped between multiple zip lines as he climbed, knocking marauders off as they slid down. At the top, he climbed aboard the skiff through the open cargo bay. There were still several marauders on board, preparing to drop. Jet stayed cloaked until the last one dropped. Seconds later, the skiff began to rise slightly. Several large cables lowered, which Jet assumed would hoist the crates into the cargo hold of the skiff.

He took hold of one large cable, closed his eyes, and focused some energy on it. He pulled, feeling his shoulder and back muscles strain, then the cable sheered in half and dropped out of the cargo bay. He reached for the second of the three cables, grasped it and was about to rip it in half when something hit him in the back with enough force to topple him.

He rolled and hopped to his feet, scanning the cargo hold. The skiff yawed in the gusty wind as it corrected and stabilized. His footing slipped a bit, searching for balance as a blur across the cargo bay darted at him. He saw it and lowered to a knee, then quickly brought both arms up as the Atrum hammered down. He swept his foot out and took the Atrum down. But the Atrum was instantly back on its feet and turned to face him as it slowly lowered its hood.

Vail stood in front of Jet and pointed a finger at him. "I warned you, Stroud. What did I say would happen the next time we met?"

He didn't respond at first. Vail looked almost unrecognizable, as if her physical form was shifting in and out of reality. She was different, even since their last meeting, in both appearance and thought. *Hatred, anger…deceit.* Her voice intertwined into multiple tones, as if there was more than one person speaking.

One of the cables suddenly went taught. He gazed down at it to see the first crate being hoisted up.

"Stay out of my way, Vail!" Jet grabbed the cable and tried to rend it, but Vail kicked him before he could focus enough energy on it. She circled him across the open cargo bay door.

Marauders were starting to climb up the zip lines, and Jet quickly went through his options. The rare-earth minerals weren't important at the moment, but getting the tracking device on the skiff was imperative. But he couldn't accomplish that with Vail looking on. He had to make it look like he was interested in the minerals, then somehow get the device planted without anyone noticing.

Jet hit the deck, rolled, and dropped out of the skiff's cargo hold. He fell about ten meters and landed on top of the crate that was being hoisted into the skiff. From underneath his cloak, he discreetly flung the tracking device up toward the back tail fin of the skiff, where it stuck. Then he grasped one of the cables in both hands, focused his energy, and tore it in half. The crate hung from the last cable, swaying in the breeze as Jet climbed to its top side. Then the weight of the crate sheared the final cable free, causing the marauder's skiff to dip momentarily from the sudden release of weight.

Jet gripped the top of the crate as it plummeted toward the observation tower's opening. As he fell, someone grabbed him and shoved a knife into his back. Fortunately, the graphene fibers in his cloak prevented the knife from puncturing his flesh. He spun, ripping the knife free, and stared at a person dressed in black. The would-be assassin kicked Jet off the falling crate, then it leapt off in the opposite direction.

Jet fell but managed to maneuver toward the tower's thin parapet and landed on it, dropping to a knee to absorb the impact. Above, the marauder skiffs rocketed off as the falling crate hit the ground below with a loud crash.

He stood to search for the mysterious figure when he noticed it on the opposite side of the tower, staring directly at him. The dark figure moved quickly and pulled out a pistol. It managed to fire several rounds at him as he leapt across the tower's opening and landed right in front of it.

As they sparred, Jet began to understand what he was facing; this was another assassination attempt, sent by the Backer. But Jet wanted this assassin alive for questioning.

Solan or Cord would have dispatched the assassin quickly, but Jet struggled. The assassin was quick, but thanks to his cloak, many of its blows did little harm. Jet finally had the upper hand and bent the assassin's elbow back, hearing bones snap. It swiftly brought a knee up and freed its arm, then did something that shocked him. It jumped over the wall and to its death.

Jet watched as the assassin crashed down on top of the wrecked crate of rare-earth below. The impact sent chunks of shiny rare-earth flying into the concrete walls. It sounded like an explosion, followed by wind chimes, that echoed down the hardened tunnel and then into silence.

Jet found a metal ladder bolted to the side of the tower and slid down it. He stood next to the large detector below, surveying the damage and bloodshed from the fight as Dane and several recon troops examined the assassin.

"This doesn't look like a typical marauder," Dane said.

"It isn't," Jet replied. "This one was sent specifically to murder me. It appears that the marauders have their own elite troops as well."

He walked over and looked at the body of the mangled assassin, its limbs bent at awkward angles. He knelt and pulled the assassin's face mask down. It was a young female and on the side of her neck was a tetrahedron tattoo.

Jet let his thoughts reach out for Cord.

"I'm right here," Cord replied. He helped an injured recon troop over to Dane. Both marauders and recon lay sprawled out in the dim light, dead or injured. More troops walked through the carnage, checking the bodies around the chamber.

"Was it worth it?" Dane asked.

Jet pulled out a modified holopad and held it out for Dane. "They got some of what they were after, but so did we. Let's just hope no one noticed the tracking device."

Dane's grin turned into a hearty laugh, and he clapped Jet on the back.

CHAPTER 15
Inside Knowledge

ΑΒΓΔΕΖΗΘΙΚΛ**Μ**
ΝΞΟΠΡΣΤΥΦΧΨΩ

WITH THE TRACKING device in place, Jet sent Solan an encrypted message. Then he and Cord headed back to the first belt to resume their normal assignments, at least until the next calamity happened. During the flight, Jet decided to check in on Cutter again.

"You doing okay?" Jet asked.

In the hologram, Cutter sat on his couch, watching the blaze playoffs. He had a piece of toast in his hand and a drink in the other. Jet could sense that he was in a grumpy mood and didn't really want to talk. "You having second thoughts?" Jet asked.

"What do you think, Jet?" Cutter said as he kicked his feet up on the coffee table. "I'm not really lookin' forward to any of this."

Jet already felt bad about it and listening to Cutter made it worse. "Look, it's not what I wanted either. But we have no choice now."

Cutter ignored him and stared at the game.

Then Jet had an idea. He knew Cutter had a soft spot for helping others. Jet could use that to his advantage. "Hey, you know this is going to be an opportunity for you, right?"

"What are you talkin about?" Cutter asked. "How the hell is *this* remotely an opportunity?"

"Even though the Lucem aren't on great terms with the Agency right now, they still do good things… well, mostly. They protect the system, which in turn protects citizens. They don't just let anyone in, only people they deem an asset. You have what it takes to be a part of this, Cutter."

Cutter was looking at him now and sat up. "In what way?"

"You're charismatic, you're a leader. You have great physical ability. This is an opportunity to help others who need help. You wouldn't want to walk away from that, would you?"

Cutter smirked. "You're trying to butter me up. I know you better than you think, Jet."

"Okay, yeah," Jet said. "You're right. But I'm also telling the truth. This is what you live for, Cutter. You get to help others. Right now, I get the sense that's the part missing in your life."

Jet noticed a slight grin on Cutters broad face. He could see that Cutter was starting to finally buy into the idea.

"I mean, if you had to sacrifice your old life, isn't this how you'd want it? In service to the Skylight System and its citizens… to help the less fortunate?"

Cutter stood and threw his toast and dropped his mug to the ground. "Why didn't you just say it like that the first time?"

"I knew you wouldn't disappoint me, Cutter," Jet said.

Cutter walked around his living room hopping up and down and clapping. Jet could see he was fired up, like he was getting ready for a game of blaze. "I need to go work out," Cutter said and switched off the hologram before Jet could say anything else.

Jet smiled and sat back, relieved. That had worked out better than he'd hoped.

Now, on to the next issue, he thought. It was time to tell Cord about the person called, the Backer. He opened a channel to Cord's skiff.

"Cord, you awake?" Jet said, hailing him over the intercom. Cord's skiff was cloaked somewhere behind his.

"Yes," Cord replied. "And you should be cloaked with radio silence."

Jet ignored him as their skiff's cruised along one of the lesser used system lanes. "I need to share something with you, probably should've already told you."

"Are you ready to discuss Sylvant?"

"It has something to do with that," Jet said then paused. He tried to think where to begin as Cord remained silent on the other end. "I spied on Solan the day of the summit."

"Why does that not surprise me?" Cord said.

"Just following my intuition, and I'm glad I did. Solan met with Harok and his generals that day, if you recall. The fireworks didn't start till after she left, though."

"How so?"

"Harok left his office and took a secure call, but it was in an area I didn't know existed. The caller, who he referred to as 'the Backer,' was some wealthy drug lord from the ninth belt who offered him a bribe."

"I'm sure that happens all the time," Cord said. "Out of curiosity, what was the bribe?"

"The Backer wanted Albright's easter egg. But that's not all. This person made a threat that if they didn't get it, then no one would. It sounded like sabotage during the eclipse. The Backer claims that if the Skylight Fallout dies before the eclipse, then the duty would pass to the next Heliographi in line, which is an Atrum. Do you know anything about this?"

"Sounds like rubbish to me. I've seen no indication about that in my work. Which Atrum did they claim it to be?"

"None other than Vail," Jet said.

"That's fascinating. The two of you are right next to each other on the spectrum."

"Well, anyway, Harok needs more funding for Goliath's Gate. Apparently, the project is about out of money, and the marauders have stolen too much rare-earth. So, the Backer is offering to fund the project and also offered mercenaries."

Cord didn't say anything. Jet assumed he was processing the information.

"Oh, yeah. One more thing," Jet continued. "The Backer demanded that Harok help murder me. I have a bounty on my head."

"Now, that is also intriguing," Cord said, sounding truly fascinated.

"Wow, really?" Jet asked and chuckled. "That's your response?"

Cord ignored him. "Why haven't you shared this with the entire group?"

"Because Solan would put me on a leash. There's no way I'm going to let that happen."

"It's a risk, Jet. If you die, we lose a considerable asset."

"You're too kind," Jet said. "Look, I understand the risk, but that's never stopped me before. I thought you'd be more excited about my decision *because* of the risk."

"As always, I respect your bravado. It's exactly what I would do as well. But what if someone else gets hurt? If you die, will the Atrum end up with the key? Who will look over Kamber and Cutter? There's a lot you need to consider."

"Well, I can't help the Lucem if I'm bottled up. I need to be free to figure this out. You know that Solan won't let me out of her sight if she finds out. So, what do you think? Should I bring it to the others?"

"It is your decision. Of course, I'll help you with whatever you decide. It appears you've made up—"

But Cord never finished his sentence.

A missile-shaped skiff uncloaked and dropped in behind Jet's skiff. Jet cloaked immediately and maneuvered down through a cloud bank, then hammered his thrusters. The jammer skiff followed in tight behind him as he flew low over the unpopulated terrain of the sixth belt. He wove between the tree line at supersonic speeds but couldn't shake the jammer. It spit out rounds from its forward mounted cannon, all the while Jet wondered how it was able to follow his cloaked skiff. Apparently, the jammer had some sort of device that allowed it to see in a different light spectrum.

The **Skylight Fallout**

The jammer was making up ground on him. Even in his recon-issued skiff, he was being overtaken, outmaneuvered and outgunned. Jet's console lit up, and the jammer had a lock on him, which he couldn't break free of. At any minute, his skiff would explode, and he was about to eject when the lights on his console went silent.

Jet looked over his shoulder to see Cord's skiff uncloak just as the jammer exploded into a brilliant ball of flame.

Cord cleared his throat. "You're welcome," he said.

Jet wiped his brow and eased back in his seat, slowing his speed.

Cord continued as if nothing had happened, his voice still calm. "By the way, the legend says that the Skylight Fallout must die to set the second phase of the Prism Effect into motion. Just thought you might want to know that."

Jet sat silent for a few seconds, letting it sink in. "Thanks. This day just keeps getting better."

"For the record, I'm still not entirely convinced you're the Skylight Fallout. However, I was wrong once before, I think."

"You're killing me, Cord," Jet said.

"Perhaps it's wisest if you stay home during the Century Eclipse," Cord said.

"What, and miss out on all the fun? Not a chance. Besides, you know me. I never back out, and I've got some payback to take care of. I'll be there, and hopefully this 'Backer' will be too."

M

Since Cutter's week was now up, Jet had scheduled a visit. Cutter had his items packed and ready. A news release about Cutter's death had been prerecorded by Detective Marsh, a.k.a. DiJinn, earlier that week. Jet approved the order to have the press release sent to the media that evening.

He met Cutter in the forest near the Clipton portal and helped with his gear as they walked into Lyrinthum.

"You'll have an apartment on campus, of course, but you're welcome down here any time," Jet whispered. "Just be careful as you come and go from here. We would prefer you stay up top in your apartment, and I think you'll find it much nicer than this place, anyway."

"Hey, Jet, hold on a minute," Cutter said and grabbed him by the shoulder, bringing him to a halt. "I heard about Sylvant."

Jet turned to face him in the tunnel, the light from his eyes illuminating the rusted metal bulkheads. He wasn't sure what to say at first. "Does that affect your decision now?"

"Why would it?"

"She died because of me," Jet said. "I need to be honest with you, someone is trying to assassinate me, Cutter. Just tell me if you want out because we can fix this, at least to some degree. I understand if you're having second thoughts because of Sylvant."

"Just wanted to say I was sorry, that's all. I agreed to do this and I'm not backing out now. Besides, I'm a walking dead person anyway, right? Cutter Jade no longer exists. And, after your pep talk, how *could* I back out? This is what I want."

Jet left Cutter at the control room with Booker, who would give him some background and his new alias. Jet took the passages back toward the forest's edge. The haunting whispers emanated from the steel walls and infiltrated his thoughts, sending him to places he didn't care to be. Those tormented voices of pain and agony begged for mercy and made his skin crawl. Whatever dimension they came from, he knew he never wanted to go there, and he pushed them from his thoughts.

During the last mission, he had used his free time to do some heavy meditating and training. Once again, he'd had an epiphany. This time it was about Kamber and what he felt should be done to keep her safe. Although Solan would not allow her into the Lucem just yet, he saw no reason why he couldn't give her a little inside knowledge. He recalled his final days at Skylight University and the near-death experience he'd had with Sybold—the Atrum's leader. During the triclipse, Solan and DiJinn had arrived just in time and rescued him. Thankfully, Solan had given him the Book of Vishmu ahead of time, which had probably saved his life. Jet saw no reason he couldn't do the same for Kamber, except this time, he didn't plan on hiding behind a cloak when he did it.

Now that the Agency was out of the picture, he felt little remorse in bending a few more rules. If there was to be an encounter, at least Kamber would have fair warning about it. She would have access to the Book of Vishmu, and what she did with that knowledge was up to her. He would tell her tonight; he wouldn't risk waiting any longer. The timing felt right, and his intuition pressed him forward.

He popped up through one of the Clipton Forest portals, leaving the voices behind. Mist clung to the cool ground as crickets chirped contentedly. A lone runner flitted through the woods, followed closely by another. Two points of light glowing from their eyes, puffs of steam flowing from their lips. Jet rose and followed effortlessly in the woods beyond, cloaked and silent.

He kept both Kamber and Tetra in his sights. The university pins he'd gifted them were working nicely. He could keep tabs on Kamber's whereabouts, just as Solan had done to him with the Book of Vishmu during his first year. Those gifted items magnified the mental connection, but also took a lot of effort to establish.

Opposite him, another shape glided through the mist.

It was Hurse.

Fine, Jet thought. *Hurse could stay on his own side.*

As long as their paths didn't cross, all would be well.

Except…all wasn't well.

Hurse had made his threat. If Jet went too close to Tetra, all bets were off. And considering that Tetra had come along on the field trip to Lybra's estate, Jet was betting Hurse was out for revenge. He'd known Hurse would keep a close eye on Tetra, just like he did with Kamber.

Tetra and Kamber were sprinting now, both neck-and-neck. He and Hurse ignored each other for the moment as the two girls raced down the winding trail. Their glowing eyes lit the way in front of them in the deepening dusk. With less than thirty meters to the next bend, Tetra fell in behind Kamber and kicked out at one of her legs. Kamber went down and hit the dirt hard. She knocked her head on the ground and lay unconscious. Tetra leapt over her and disappeared down the trail without looking back.

Jet waited. He stared at Hurse from across the woods and wondered if Hurse would make a move on Kamber while she lay on the trail unconscious. He felt his muscles quivering, ready to spring from the underbrush if Hurse made a move toward her. Hurse knew Jet was there, and even though Jet wasn't yet strong enough to best him, he would fight till the end.

Kamber began to stir.

Jet tensed, readying himself. But Hurse turned and sped off in Tetra's direction. Jet sat silently waiting for Kamber. She sat up and ran a hand through her hair. A bit of blood dripped from a cut on her forehead. Her track suit was ripped just under her arm to her hip. She looked at it and cursed.

She stood and started to walk down the path. Jet followed behind her in the underbrush, silent as a whisp of smoke. The area was growing dark, and crickets hummed louder around them. Above, the sky was changing over from a fiery reddish orange to a velvet purple tone. Stars were starting to twinkle, and he could see several outer belts in the far distance, engulfed in the eerie greenish light of the aurora borealis.

Kamber walked through the brush and past the ravine and stopped at the edge of the glen of Firefly Falls. She walked toward the edge of the lake and knelt to splash some water on her face. She used her arm to wipe away the blood and sat on a rock, pulled her legs up to her chest and stared at the waterfall. Jet could see her begin to shake as she wiped away a tear with the back of her hand. The fireflies surrounded her, as if they were trying to comfort her.

Jet felt his heart ache as he watched her. He knew what emotions she was experiencing. It was a feeling he was all too familiar with and one he had faced for so long… like all the rest of them.

Now was the moment, he thought, and he didn't wait a second longer.

Jet stood and walked toward her. He lowered his hood and materialized in front of her as he approached.

Kamber looked up, her cheeks wet with tears, her glowing eyes bright in the moonlight. The fireflies parted for him as he approached and solidified in front of her.

Kamber's reaction shocked him, though.

She didn't faint, or curse. She simply looked up at him and smiled. They both faced each other silently before Kamber finally spoke.

"I've been waiting for this moment, Jet Stroud."

Jet continued to stare at her, still in shock and not sure what to say. Of all the reactions he had expected, he never would have guessed at this one. She continued to smile at him, and he finally sat down next to her on the boulder and waited for her to continue.

"I've dreamt of this very moment," Kamber said. "I've been having reoccurring dreams about you, Jet. I knew this time would come. I don't know how to explain it, but I always assumed it had something to do with my condition."

Jet finally found his voice. "You knew this would happen…exactly like this?"

She nodded. "Vaguely, in my dreams…I don't know what will happen next, of course, but I saw this coming."

It was the first time he'd heard of a Heliographi being able to see into the future this way. He cleared his throat. "Well, I'm not sure I'm the one to explain why you knew this would happen. That's not the reason I'm here."

"Okay, I believe you. Then why are you here?"

"To warn you, and to let you in on a little secret. But you must swear to keep it a secret."

"Of course," she said.

Jet crossed his arms. "I was planning to introduce myself first, but I see there's no need for that."

Kamber gazed at him and tilted her head, then she looked away. "I've done some prying, and I know you were a student here four years ago. You were a fantastic blaze player and scored high marks on your entry exams. Then you allegedly died in that horrible skiff accident. But what were you like before all that? I really want to know more about who you are."

Jet smiled. "No one's ever taken an interest in me like that before. I'm afraid my story isn't all that exciting."

She waited; her legs pulled up to her chest.

"How's your head, by the way?" Jet asked, changing the topic back to her. "You took quite a tumble."

She rubbed at it. The welp had gone down, and the small cut had already clotted. "It's fine, just a small bump. So, I guess you saw all of that?"

"Yes," Jet nodded. "You hit your head pretty hard."

"Tetra hates to lose. That's just who she is."

"Well, one of the reasons I'm here tonight is because of that. What you didn't see was the shadow in the woods, a person who is sworn to protect Tetra. His name is Hanley Hurse, and he's part of a group known as the Atrum."

She shook her head. "Don't think I know them."

"That's because they're a secret order. They are a group of people who've been around for thousands of years… just like the group we're both a part of called the Lucem."

Kamber narrowed her eyes at Jet. "We?" she asked.

"That's right. You won't die when you turn twenty-four, at least not the way you've been told."

She smiled at him and blinked. "What? Is this a joke?"

"I reacted the same way when I learned about all of this. Look at me. I'm still alive, aren't I? Those rumors you've heard throughout your life are just rumors, fabricated by an organization called the Agency. When people like us are ready, we're brought into the group. We go through a process, a conversion ritual. Once that happens, we're full members of an elite order called the Lucem."

"Is that your plan tonight? To bring me into this group? Because I don't think I'm ready for any of this."

"No, I'm not here to bring you into the Lucem, not tonight. When you were doing research on me, did you run across a girl named Solan Alexander?"

"Yes, she was the track star, a student with E.M. about fourteen years ago, right? Somewhat of a legend around campus, like you. Why?"

"Solan is a Lucem, and she's still alive, like me and all the other students with E.M. She's the leader of our group right now, and we have rules we have to follow, or at least, we used to."

"What kind of rules?" Kamber asked. "Because I'm guessing we're breaking quite a few tonight."

Jet smiled at that. Kamber was sharp. "Well, yeah, a few, to say the least. But things have changed recently, and we have a little more leeway than we used to. Solan won't allow you into the Lucem until she thinks you're ready."

"So, if you're not here to bring me in, then what?"

"I'm here to warn you."

She gripped her legs tighter. "Am I in danger?"

"I'm known as your warden, someone sworn to defend you until you're brought into the Lucem. That Atrum who was following you and Tetra tonight is a powerful person. He wants to harm you. When I was a student, Solan was my protector. But she waited to tell me about all of this. I've decided not to wait any longer to tell you, though. I believe you should know the danger you're in."

Kamber furrowed her brow. "What do I need to know?"

"That you're special, and you're not an outcast," Jet continued. "This all started with something we call the Prism Effect."

"The prism effect? Like the ones we see on Skylight University all the time?"

"No, this was something that happened over a century ago. It involved several others like us, and it affected the way we look today."

"Do you mean our eyes?" she asked. "So, that's why they glow?"

"A long time ago, we were one group, working together. Over time, the Atrum splintered off from the Lucem. Then, something strange happened that changed us. We call this the Prism Effect, because of the influence it had over us. This further split us into twenty-four individual entities, and it showed each of us our true color. That color is the special light known as a Heliographi, and it resides in each of our souls. Some of this was prophesied by the artist named Shiloe Van Saint and is rumored to be hidden in her paintings."

"Does that include the one we saw at Lybra's estate?"

"Yeah, that one was called *The Plan*. It holds holographic messages in its brush strokes, which you and

Tetra apparently noticed. But there are two other paintings that go with it. Together, we think they tell the whole story. We have someone working on that now."

"Your friend who was with us that night?"

"Yes. His name is Cord Ledbetter."

"Right," Kamber said. "Of course. He's the math savant who died the same year you did… well, not really, I guess."

"Well…all that being said, Solan did do me a favor when I was a student. She gave me this." Jet slid the Book of Vishmu from his cloak and handed it to her.

Kamber took the book and held it. She leafed through the pages, looking at the text with genuine interest.

"This is called the Book of Vishmu," Jet said, nodding to the worn book. "It's an ancient practice that only people like us can use. In here, you will begin to learn how to protect yourself. Some of this is advanced, and you won't understand it yet. But some of it you will. The time may come when you need this."

Kamber looked back at him and set the book down next to her. "Thank you, Jet."

"I hope you won't need it, but better safe than sorry."

"Is there more to all of this?"

"Yeah, a lot more," Jet said with a smile. "We could spend the whole night out here talking about it, but I wanted to share just a few of the more important things for now. I promise I'll tell you more when the time is right."

"It's good to know I'm not going to die after all."

"Kamber, I don't want to paint a rosy picture about all of this. You are still in danger. The truth about E.M. isn't what you think it is, but you still have to join the Lucem before your twenty-fourth birthday, or you will eventually die. What we call a Heliographi lives in your soul. That light will extinguish and leave if you don't accept it."

"I don't think that will be a problem. I get to leave all this behind, and I can still run when I want."

"Well, once you do join, I have a few items that belong to you. I wish I could give them to you now, but that has to wait."

"I assume one of them is the cloak?" she asked. "How does that thing work?"

"It's an invention by Christian Albright. By bending light, it shrouds our form, making us practically invisible. It's not the most comfortable thing, because of the reinforced graphene fibers." Jet slid the hood over his head and vanished. Then reappeared.

"So cool," she said with a smile. "I really want one."

Jet laughed. "Just wait, there's more." He stood, then leapt to a tree branch about ten meters above. He did a backflip and landed softly on the ground next to her.

"That was incredible!"

Jet bowed, somewhat embarrassed, and sat down. "With training and meditation, you'll become a dangerous adversary, and we need all the Lucem right now. We are facing an ever-growing threat from the Atrum. But that's another story for a different day." Jet stood and held out a hand. "Let's get you back to your dorm, it's getting late."

Kamber took his hand and stood. "When do you think Solan will allow me to join?"

Jet sighed. "I don't know. It's hard to guess her approach at times. But I think it's safe to say this will be your last semester at Skylight University, so you might want to prepare for that. There's no going back once it's done. Since you're already twenty-three, my guess is that it will happen soon. And, with the Atrum being so aggressive lately, Solan won't want to push her luck too far."

Kamber walked beside him as they made their way to the edge of the glen. "You never finished telling me about yourself," Kamber said.

Jet chuckled. "After all I just told you, and you still want to hear about me?"

"Of course I do."

"Alright," Jet said and shook his head. "I was born in a place known as the ARC district, a cave system below the great plains of North America. It was mostly a mining site, dirty and gritty; we called it the pit. Not a pretty place. My parents dumped me at a halfway home when I was a toddler because of my condition. It's a tough existence in the ARC, and having a child like me would've made life on them very difficult. There was a lot of abuse in the halfway home; I sometimes wonder how I even survived. Luck, I guess. Well, when I was a little older, I fell in love with the sport of blaze. In a lot of ways, that sport took the place of parents and family. I learned to fend for myself, how to overcome challenges and the value of hard work because of blaze."

"Running filled that same void for me," Kamber said. "Maybe that's why we're so good at sports?"

"You've got a point there. Blaze never talked down to me, hit me or took advantage of me." He looked at her as they walked. "Kamber, a few more things I need to share with you. I have a friend named Cutter who just joined our group. I've asked him to look after you, in case you need something and I'm not around. He has an alias as one of the blaze coaches named Harper Jade, here's his contact information." Jet handed her a small holopad. "Promise me you'll do your best to stay in large groups and indoors at night."

She nodded.

"And…try your best to practice Vishmu. It'll give you—and me—some peace of mind. Plus, it's pretty interesting stuff."

Kamber looked out across the glen, gazing at the fireflies and holding her hand out to let them land on it. "Jet, do you believe in destiny?"

He thought for a moment, a bit thrown off by the question, and he wasn't really sure how to answer it. "Well, I'm not sure. I suppose everything happens for a reason."

"Do you think you were destined to be here, tonight?"

"Maybe. I usually listen to my intuition, and it guided me here."

"If everything is predestined, that means our future is set. I'm not sure I like the sound of that."

Jet looked at her thoughtfully. "Maybe it is, but we don't know what the future holds. So, in that regard, it doesn't matter if the future is set or if it isn't. Why do you ask?"

"Because I knew all of this would happen before it did. What I can tell you is that the future is set, as is our destiny."

CHAPTER 16
The Pit

ΑΒΓΔΕΖΗΘΙΚΛ**Μ**
ΝΞΟΠΡΣΤΥΦΧΨΩ

AFTER JET FINISHED his training that day, he caught up with Cord at his lab on Skylight University. His approach of using blaze to mentally prepare for his training sessions was working well, so far. He had made greater progress in the last several days than he had in the last six months but knew he still had a long way to go. He felt a primal stirring in his mind and soul. The voice was louder, quicker to speak to him. At times, he sensed there were others there with him, a strange presence looking over his shoulder.

He could also feel a mysterious energy flowing through him at times, like a vibrating string ready to snap.

Cord was perusing his three-dimensional map of the system when Jet arrived. He sat cross legged, tugging thoughtfully at his goatee, bifocals pushed to the top of his forehead.

Jet dropped his backpack, hoping to break Cord's concentration. "What are you caught up in now?"

Cord finally looked up. "Van Saint's paintings, the Century Eclipse… this pesky splinter code." Cord pushed back and rubbed his temple.

"Something about the eclipse still bothering you?"

"Seems like a fitting end to something, does it not?" Cord replied. "Exactly the sort of prank Albright would enjoy heaping onto someone. It's supposed to be a celebration, but I'm not so certain."

"What would it be the end of?"

"Kind of depends on the Atrum and this Backer you mentioned." Cord stood and walked across his lab. On the opposite side, beneath a clerestory window, sat a wooden stool with a small red ball on it. "I need to show you something."

Jet followed him and looked at the ball. "You taking up sports now?"

Cord sat down about three meters in front of the stool. He closed his eyes and held his hands on the floor, palms flat. He slowed his breathing.

Jet waited silently next to him.

"Watch the ball," Cord said, his eyes still shut.

The ball rolled slightly, then moved around the top edge of the stool in faster circular patterns.

"Heads up!" Cord snapped. "The ball lifted from the chair, hovered for a second then shot straight at Jet's face. He snagged it out of the air and held it, staring at Cord in disbelief. "How in Skylight did you do that?"

"Loads of practice."

"A bit more than practice, I think. But how?"

"I can't quite formulate the right words," Cord said. "I understand how I do it, though I can't explain it. The best explanation I can offer is to think in terms of energy and vibration. Everything surrounding us is a wave. It's manipulating those waves at a molecular level. I suppose that doesn't make much sense."

"Does Solan know about this?"

"Negative. I'm working my way up to larger objects."

"So, energy and vibration?" Jet asked, thinking about the strange energy he had recently felt.

"Quantum fields. They're all around us. Somehow, Vishmu has unlocked ideas I still don't comprehend and haven't dared to try yet. It was known as telekinesis in the past. Four years ago, I would have strongly disagreed with any of these beliefs. It should not be possible in our world. I used to require factual proof, backed by scientific studies. But now…these mind-over-matter theories are no longer just theories. Telekinesis, quantum entanglement, astral projection…it's a new reality. Very fascinating to my mind."

Jet looked at the ball in his hand. "Do you think the Atrum know anything about these techniques?"

"I'm sure they know about them, but I have not heard of anyone else with the ability to actually pull them off. Perhaps Albright could, which means Sybold probably could too."

Jet tossed the ball back to Cord and sat down on the stool. "Well, I just did something that might land me in deep trouble with Solan."

"You approached Kamber, didn't you?" Cord said with a grin.

"I couldn't help it. I just felt like it was the right time for her to know. What's wrong with that, especially considering that we're no longer under the Agency's rules?"

"For the record, I believe it was the right decision, regardless of what Solan may say," Cord said. "I'll support you on your decision, if it comes to that."

"Let's hope it doesn't. I just wish we could bring her into the Lucem now."

"When did you tell her?"

"Last night," Jet said. "She was out running with Tetra in the Clipton Forest. Hurse was tracking them both. I think he might have tried to kill her if I hadn't been there. He could've easily overwhelmed me, too. I'm no match for him."

"You are no match for him…*yet*," Cord emphasized.

"Last night was a perfect opportunity for him."

"They still aren't ready to make their move. Hurse takes orders, and he won't jump over the chain of command, no matter how much he might want to. Furthermore, last night proves that the Atrum aren't behind the assassination attempts on you. Consider this; they wouldn't have missed and accidently killed Sylvant, and they certainly wouldn't have used a sniper rifle—that's simply not their style. That assassin wanted you both dead and killed Sylvant on purpose but tried to make it appear as an accident."

"Who would want to murder Sylvant? She had no stake in this."

"Let's think about that," Cord said. "The first assassination attempt got the Lucem expelled from the Agency. Suddenly, we're not as interested in investigating the rare-earth raids. The second attempt killed Sylvant, the leader of the Lucem's sister. We automatically suspected the Atrum."

Jet finally grasped what Cord was hinting at. "Someone's trying to provoke us into battle with the Atrum," Jet said.

"The Atrum aren't blind, they know about the assassination attempts, but there's no reason for them to interfere. But they probably aren't aware that they're being framed."

Jet thought for a moment. If Solan thought the Atrum were responsible for her sister's death, she would want revenge, and if the Lucem went to war, that would certainly make someone's job a lot easier. *But who was responsible?*

"The Backer, right?" Jet asked.

"It's the only person I can think of who would benefit from the Heliographi killing each other off."

K

Solan and DiJinn were already headed toward Earth in separate skiffs when they received the encrypted message from Jet. It matched the coordinates Solan had lifted from the marauders at the underground market. The tracking beacon was coming from an area below the great plains of North America.

"Payback time," DiJinn said.

"Easy, Jinn. We have to keep a low profile, which is why it's just the two of us. We're looking for info on the stolen rare-earth, then Tyberius, not payback." But in truth, Solan was also hoping for a little action.

"The tracking beacon is coming from a place called the ARC district," Solan continued.

"Isn't that the cave system where Jet's from?"

"The same," Solan answered.

"I didn't realize that was a rare-earth mine."

"That's because it isn't, at least, not one that's public knowledge. I'd have known about it."

"Loads of dark outfits there. Not a pleasant place to vacation," DiJinn said. "The black markets there make the ones on Skylight look like an amusement park. But no matter, let's just get this show on the road."

About thirty minutes later, two unmarked skiffs entered the lower atmosphere of earth. Turbulence knocked Solan's skiff around as she sliced through the thunderheads from the massive storm blanketing the planet. Lightning clashed outside her cockpit with DiJinn's skiff close enough behind to indicate a single blip on radar in case they were being tracked.

She checked her channels and dropped closer to ground level, hugging the rugged terrain of what used to be the Great Plains of North America. The storm known as the Unbalance had rearranged the topography into an unrecognizable landscape of dunes and debris. Any built structure above ground had been wiped away long ago. No man-made building had survived the past few centuries of the storm's relentless aggression. All civilization left on the desolate planet had moved below ground into the vast man-made caverns like the ARC district. Mining had become the main source of living to those unlucky souls left on earth. Specifically, rare-earth elements, like the kind required for Goliath's Gate, were in high demand. Up until that point, Solan had been unaware the ARC district even had rare-earth deposits.

Solan's console lit up, and she provided an Agency clearance code and was granted access to land. Ahead, an enormous bunkerlike dome lit up with a stasis field covering it. There were thousands of frigates entering and leaving through numerous portal-like airlocks in the dome. They were directed toward a large airlock that spiraled open. Their skiffs entered it and descended through its gaping maw.

Solan glanced over at DiJinn as their skiffs dropped several hundred meters. DiJinn had already switched back into her alias, Detective Marsh. Solan slipped into her own alias and settled back. The main port for the ARC district was called Tuxson Burrough, or Tux. Their skiffs went into autopilot mode and moved along a major throughfare with other mining skiffs and frigates.

Once they docked at a private hanger, she paid and turned to DiJinn. "The marauder's frigate was traced back to the fifth level mining complex some four kilometers away."

"You sound anxious," DiJinn said. "Take it easy."

"There are Atrum around. We can't afford to take it easy. Stay sharp and keep your thoughts closed. If we get separated, meet me back here. I'm leaving a mental signature as we go, just in case we need backup."

Outside the private hanger, a large, cavernous thoroughfare stretched for kilometers in front of them. The massive tubular void was a sunset of red and brown striations of earth strata and vaulted up to a height of about forty meters in diameter. The roof was scraped smooth from whatever drilling machine had been used to hollow out the cave system, and thousands of plants, known as shale ferns, grew right through the rock walls to provide a dim greenish glow throughout the cave system. There were hundreds of offshoots branching from the main highway with even smaller arteries filled with shops and markets. Thousands of halfmoon-shaped pods that looked to be housing were cut into the sides of the large vault. Below them were several more decks that stretched in the same direction with foot traffic and vehicles. It was like a series of thin highways suspended in the middle of the vast tunnel network.

They had gotten a good look at the standard worker attire and used their rings to match the garb; drab colored overalls caked with grime and dirt. A large group of miners walked past, and Solan and DiJinn fell in without notice.

The group moved down from the dusty paths and along a large rock formation that eventually changed over to a mining pit, filled with soot and loud chiseling noises that vibrated the ground. They entered a large metal building with the group, who appeared to be returning from lunch. Inside were racks of hard hats, safety goggles and headsets for noise protection. They put the gear on, along with a respirator. Inside the headset was a mic and communication device like a holopad. Solan listened to the chatter, nudging DiJinn as she reached out with her mind.

Inside the mining caverns were huge transports. They began to notice some of the workers wore the tetrahedron insignia on their overalls. It was standing room only on the transport as it ferried them over the rough terrain. Along with the shale ferns, artificial lighting was strung haphazardly along the top of the tunnels. The sound of hammering, explosions and chiseling soon filled the air. A fine mist of dust and particulates created a haze around the light, one that would surely clog a person's lungs in short order, she thought.

The miners stood silently till they reached the first drop point. Solan decided to hop off and fell in line with another group of miners as DiJinn continued on. The workers appeared to be simple miners, probably locals who knew the area and didn't care who they worked for.

She stopped as the line paused. Several miners passed their hands in front of a holopad that appeared to chart their employee number and time. She passed through without scanning her hand and followed the line deeper into the caverns. When the color of earth strata changed, they stopped again.

A group of tetrahedron ahead, who appeared to be higher ranking officers, barked orders to the miners. Some sort of sonic chisel was handed to her, which had an X-ray device on it—to help locate specific minerals, she assumed. She followed the miners and mimicked their movements by scanning the rock wall next to her with the chisel. She probed their thoughts as she worked, trying to gain any information she could. Doing so was tedious work, and she had to be careful not to probe too deeply or risk impairing their psyches. She was after answers and wished no harm to these locals.

After a few brief probes of the miners nearby, her suspicion had been correct; the majority of them were simply local residents who knew very little about the group they worked for. However, the group leader did shed some light. He had seen a shadow wraith recently, at least, that's how his mind had perceived it. The color Solan sensed from him was one she knew... fear. It passed into her thoughts, and she knew instantly this man had witnessed an Atrum. *But what would the Atrum be doing down here?* Most likely, the Atrum would look down on such people in the ARC district. They despised the simple-minded.

Solan could decipher no more information, though, without risk of harming the man. She waited for an opportunity and slipped off silently. She decided to reach out with her mind to locate Jinn. It was risky with Atrum nearby, and those thoughts could be picked up by other Heliographi, if she wasn't careful. She sensed that Jinn was up another level and closer to the surface. She made her way up until she could see the translucent domelike stasis field covering the vast pit. It soared up about one hundred meters, topped by the clear stasis dome. It reflected the continuous lightning strikes outside but prevented the rain and other elements from entering the pit. Lightning strobed through the cavern as thunder shook the ground. The cavern had several crane towers with snipers watching the activity below, alert for any theft. These people meant business. The pit was circular with the large crane structures rising to the top of the dome and braced with steel trusses. A stair wound up and around each of the crane towers.

Many of the frigates were being loaded with precious metals and gems, some including rare-earth minerals. The containers were stacked ten high and waited to be tagged before being loaded. The amount of rare-earth was staggering. It seemed there was enough to finish the Goliath's Gate project right here, except that none of it appeared to be refined. That was the most important step in the process. Something wasn't clicking about this operation, she just couldn't put her finger on it, yet.

Solan noticed DiJinn kneeling behind a crate and nudged up next to her. They moved away to a quiet area, dodging between forklifts and cranes that hoisted the large containers around the space.

"What are you thinkin'?" DiJinn asked.

Solan shook her head. "Not sure yet. I still have questions. Did you get any intel?"

"Not much," DiJinn whispered. "All of these people are wearin' the red insignia, though. This outfit looks bigger than we thought."

"I agree. We're going to find out how this is tied to the Atrum before we leave."

They shed their uniforms and changed back into their cloaks.

Solan worked her way up one of the crane towers while Jinn did the same on the opposite side. About halfway up, she paused. Crouched on the metal stair, she saw the blurry outline of an Atrum, lightning distorting its shape and revealing it to her.

They had finally found the Atrum. *But how many were there?*

She gave DiJinn a quick warning, then found a quiet corner, hunkered down, and waited.

CHAPTER 17
Distress Call

ΑΒΓΔΕΖΗΘΙ**Κ**ΛΜ
ΝΞΟΠΡΣΤΥΦΧΨΩ

SOLAN HAD WAITED longer than she cared to. But now she couldn't detect Jinn's presence as she remained hidden in the shadows. She assumed Jinn had simply closed off her thoughts out of caution and shielded her location. Lightning strikes strobed through the chamber, and the marauders continued with their mining operations as if things were normal.

But things weren't normal, and she knew it.

With all the activity in the pit and the noise of the sonic drills, she could barely hear herself think. If there was an altercation, she wouldn't have noticed, and she grew concerned.

Fifteen minutes had passed when several Atrum sped by her location. Solan remained stationary and cloaked, but now she knew something had happened to Jinn.

She leapt from the tower platform and landed on the gravel path below. She paused at the base of the opposite crane tower where Jinn had last been. She considered reaching out with her thoughts but resisted the urge for now, knowing it could possibly give her position away. But the flurry of activity above concerned her, and she sprinted up the tower stairs.

When she reached the top, she saw three Atrum, still cloaked, dragging Jinn's unconscious body along the metal platform. A large cut over Jinn's forehead dribbled a bit of blood onto her cloak. Solan cursed under her breath and decided to follow but not engage the Atrum. Three on one was a stretch, even for her. She was anxious, but she still had the element of surprise and had to calm her emotions and wait for the right moment.

The Atrum moved quickly along a path that spiraled downward. There were fewer shale ferns lighting the area at this depth, which allowed her to get a bit closer. The spiraling path turned to dirt and gravel once they reached the bottom, with walls roughly chiseled from the stone and rock. Downward they marched until entering a large cavern with high ceilings. Solan noticed prison cells carved from the walls with cages piled on top of each other in the center. The cages here were filled with local miners and some children.

The marauders were using children for slave labor.

Solan felt outrage rise inside her, a quick anger that burned from her soul she hadn't known was there, and it surprised her. The children ranged in age from eight to probably early teens. Most of them didn't have shoes, and what little clothing they had was ripped and stained. A few were coughing or sleeping from exhaustion. It made her think of Jet and what he must have gone through growing up. She'd actually had no idea, and honestly had never bothered to ask about his upbringing. And if she did, would he even want to talk about it?

She tore her gaze from the cages.

She had to focus on Jinn *first.* Then she would return for the children. She only hoped she could contain her emotions when she did, for the marauders' sake.

The cages were all reinforced with graphene screens that even a Heliographi would struggle to break free of. Two Atrum dragged Jinn out of sight and returned minutes later. Solan would have trouble locating Jinn amongst the maze of cages unless she reached out to her using Vishmu—a risky option. But she might be forced to, whether she liked it or not.

Now that she knew Jinn's location, she left the prison block and found a dark side tunnel to consider her next move. Multiple Atrum walked past her, barely visible, with their hoods lowered and cloaked. She recognized them all: Brit, Hurse, Quark and Vail. Vail, one of the newest Atrum, already looked different. Anger and hate seemed to ooze from her soul in a color that looked black to Solan's eyes. The four Atrum stood in front of the prison entry, speaking softly to each other. She dared not make a move now, knowing she would be hopelessly outnumbered against four Atrum, no matter who they were.

She needed backup.

A distress signal would bring reinforcements even though she hated to do it. But she wasn't leaving Jinn in a cage any longer than she had to. Solan hurried back up the spiraling trail and got as close as she could to the surface—the higher, the better. The distance she was attempting was tremendous. Any Heliographi would hear the signal she was about to send, but if she coded it the right way, she was willing to bet Cord could figure it out.

Once the distress call was sent, Solan stole back down to the prison block. The group of Atrum were still standing there but began to move down another passage. Hurse and Vail stayed behind. Solan briefly considered ambushing the two, but there would be reinforcements on her before she could find and free Jinn. So, she continued to wait and scan the hundreds of cages lining the walls. Eventually Hurse and Vail left, and Solan reached out with her thoughts, searching the area for signs of Jinn.

A faint hiccup, like a ripple on a pond, landed in her thoughts. It was Jinn, and she followed the trace. The ripple grew stronger in her mind as she scaled up the stacks of rusty cages. Prisoners inside the cages were oblivious to her as she climbed silently. Most of them were malnourished, weak and emaciated. The ones that were awake cried softly or stared off in silence, and their squalid living conditions enraged her even more.

It was clear to her now that these marauders were in league with the Atrum, and they were using the locals for slave labor and who knew what else. How this had gone on without the Agency knowing was disturbing…and concerning. She was willing to bet this was just the tip of it, too. Based on the size of this operation, there were bound to be more disturbing things going on. She didn't think the Atrum would do such a thing, but they apparently didn't mind turning a blind eye to it.

She could feel Jinn's presence growing stronger until she finally saw her.

They'd locked her in a cage that was suspended high above from the cavern's ceiling. Jinn had a device around her neck, which Solan recognized immediately. It was a mental signature collar, a device that immobilized the prisoner and could only be released by the captor. Jinn was despondent; awake but unaware of her surroundings. Solan risked a quick mental connection, hoping no Atrum would hear it.

Jinn!

But there was no response.

Solan sat atop the highest cage and had to refrain from trying to spring Jinn now. She knew she must wait for backup and hoped the signal she'd sent made it. She would give it no more than an hour, then she had to make a tough decision; risk freeing Jinn or wait longer for the others. But something else swirled in the back of her mind…

The Atrum had set this as a trap, it was obvious to her now.

Even though she could see no Atrum there now, she knew they were nearby and watching. This was all too easy, placing Jinn here in a highly visible location like this. She could have her freed in just a few seconds. But the Atrum knew there were more Lucem around—they knew Jinn hadn't come alone and now, she was the bait. But what would they do with Jinn when no one came for her? That was the caveat she had to contend with; wait too long, and Jinn might pay the price. The Atrum would eventually dispose of her, but how long would they dangle her as bait?

The longer Solan sat there, the greater the chance of being discovered, too. Even as she hid, the Atrum were searching the area for her, and it was only a matter of time till they found her. It was the first time in a long time she'd felt so vulnerable. But Jinn meant more to her than anyone else, especially now that her sister was gone, and she would not leave her behind, no matter what. All she could do now was wait and hope the other Lucem had received her distress call.

She settled into the shadows, huddled up, and waited while studying Jinn's cage for a weak point.

CHAPTER 18
Halfway Home

ΑΒΓΔΕΖΗΘΙΚΛ**Μ**
ΝΞΟΠΡΣΤΥΦΧΨΩ

JET WAS MEDITATING when he got a call just after 2 AM from Cord. He was steadily getting better now, he felt it. His training sessions were coming together, and day by day he was getting stronger, but he remained cautiously optimistic.

He dressed in his cloak and quickly made his way to the control suite. Ti-Leer, Harriet, and Cord were already there, talking urgently.

"What's wrong?" Jet asked.

Cord had a three-dimensional map pulled up and pointed at it. "We received a distress call from Solan. Ten minutes ago."

"Where did the call come from?"

"It came from earth," Harriet said. "Jinn and Solan must have followed the tracking device on the marauder's skiff…alone."

"What's more interesting is the location," Ti-Leer said. "Recognize those coordinates?"

Jet looked at the blip on the map and shook his head. "No. Should I?"

"Your old stomping grounds, the ARC district," Ti-Leer said.

"You're kidding," Jet said and looked closer at the coordinates.

"We need to get down there," Harriet said. "If Solan is sending a distress call, that can only mean the Atrum are involved. There's not much else that can get in her way."

"I know that area like the back of my hand," Jet said. "I can take Cord, but someone needs to cover Kamber."

"I'll keep an eye on her," Harriet said. "Are you sure the two of you can handle it?"

"We'll find out what's going on," Jet said. "If we need help, I'll let you know."

It was a bumpy ride in Cord's skiff as they punched through the earth's atmosphere. Jet never thought he would set foot in the ARC district again. He hated the smell of the place and the mining soot that seemed to cover everything. A thousand bad memories came roaring back to him as the storm clouds parted to reveal the hellhole called the pit, an appropriate nickname for the ARC district. Cord sent an access code to the control tower, cloaked the skiff, and maneuvered into a private hanger.

"Lead the way," Cord said.

Jet probed the area, looking for signatures of Solan or DiJinn, and found one. Solan was no fool, she had left some breadcrumbs behind; tiny psychic fingerprints imbedded in the walls. They followed the trail and walked silently along until they hit the main thoroughfare. Several groups of miners passed by, a few wearing the red insignia on their work clothes, and Jet and Cord followed the group.

About halfway down the thoroughfare, Jet paused, and Cord had to backtrack. Jet walked off in a different direction and toward the middle of what looked to be a central business district. A series of markets and shops stretched along the town square.

Cord followed silently, not asking any questions as if he knew where Jet was headed.

They left the sounds of the busy market behind and moved further down a deserted alleyway. Old rock structures lined the street, many abandoned. Jet finally stopped in front of a narrow building. Its windows were shattered, and the front door hung open. A few vagrants sat inside, sleeping on the floor. The front porch was covered in soot, and a sign on the front of the building read *ARC halfway house for youths.*

Jet stood there in the middle of the alley, looking at the derelict building with his hands clenching into fists. Cord stood silently next to him and waited. They were near the end of the district where there was hardly any traffic, and it appeared to have been vacated long ago.

"This is where I grew up. It's the halfway home where I was raised."

"Halfway between purgatory and nowhere," Cord said. "Forgive me, but it looks awful."

Jet looked at him. "That's what I love about you, Cord… straight to the heart."

"No offense," Cord followed up.

"None taken. It was a horrible place to live. I hated every minute." Jet walked up to the front door and stepped inside. He knelt to the vagrants and gave them each a handful of credits.

"Thank you," one of the ladies said. She was too weak to stand, and Jet bent to help her up.

"Do you mind? I'd like a moment alone here," Jet asked.

The two vagrants left.

Cord waited in the street as if he knew what Jet was there to do. "I fear we don't have the time for this stroll down memory lane. We must hurry."

Jet paused at that, realizing Cord had a point. He knew they had a mission and lives could be at stake; time was of the essence. But he *had* to do this, he couldn't ignore this loose end that had been festering in him for so many years.

He turned to Cord. "I'll be quick," he said and walked inside.

"Jet," Cord persisted. "We really need to be on our way."

But Jet ignored him and paused in the hallway. His glowing eyes lit the interior of the darkened house. At first, he only wanted to stop for a quick visit, maybe to put some old issues to bed. He remembered the dirty hallways, the splintered doors, and creaky worn-out floors. But then he recalled the screams, the nightmares, the fights. Kids sneaking into his room at night to wake him, beat him bloody and leave. The adults had been no better, and he wondered to himself again how in Skylight he had ever survived his youth. Something seemed to snap then, and his heart raced as he stared at an old picture on the wall. A sunlit beach from an era long gone, a picture meant for solace and reflection, but in reality, an awful lie.

He hurled his fist through the portrait and the wall and screamed. He pulled back on the wall, and a large section ripped free. He hurled it down the hallway, then launched himself into the opposite wall with his shoulder and slammed through it and into the next room.

Jet felt rage build inside him as he ransacked the old house. He lost all awareness as he punched, kicked, and released a lifetime of anger on his childhood home. Finally, the entire structure groaned and collapsed down around him.

When the dust settled, Jet stood in the middle of the debris and what was left of the house. He simply stood there for several minutes with Cord watching from the street. Jet eventually pushed his way through the rubble to the front porch and cleared off an area and sat down, resting his elbows on his knees in thought.

Cord walked over and sat down next to him. "Sometimes there aren't enough walls to knock down…right?"

"Do me a favor, Cord. Don't mention this to anyone."

Cord smiled his crooked smile and clapped him on the shoulder. "Let's move on, we've got work to do."

They backtracked and started probing the area again until Jet picked up Solan's signature. They followed the trail, eventually drawing their hoods and cloaking themselves. Jet stayed on the opposite side of the tunnel until they entered a vast mining pit. Frigates were being loaded with precious gems and metals. Multiple guard towers, topped with cranes and snipers, were sprinkled around the pit.

He reached out with his thoughts to Cord. *I think she was there…*he nodded to one guard tower.

They crept up some metal stairs, pausing occasionally. At the top, a catwalk led them into the tower. They waited for a guard to open a door and then slid inside unnoticed. Three guards stood inside while several operators manned computer terminals. All wore the red tetrahedron on their fatigues. Jet walked around one side, again using his thoughts to probe for signs as Cord flanked the opposite side. On one of the screens, Jet noticed a holding area filled with detainees. One monitor showed a redheaded lady with ponytails and glowing eyes. They had somehow captured DiJinn.

K

It had been over an hour now.

Solan's self-imposed deadline had come and gone, and she assumed her call for help never made it to the other Lucem. It appeared she would have to rescue Jinn alone, even though she knew it was a trap. As soon as she made her move, several Atrum would be on her.

Despite all of that, her first move needed to be getting Jinn freed from her cage. After analyzing it, she had determined its weakest point was the bottom panel, primarily because of the connections. Even though the bars were fitted with graphene screens, the bolts holding the bottom were made of steel. She didn't have to get through the panel, she just needed to pry it free. She'd have to catch Jinn as soon as the bottom fell out, but she could manage that. The more difficult part was getting her free from the neck device. If it utilized a mental signature, which she was betting it did, then removing it without the proper code could possibly hurt Jinn. She guessed Hurse was the one with the code, and she had to subdue him first or all of this would be pointless.

She waited a bit longer and saw several Atrum return to the chamber. It was the same four she had seen earlier, and Hurse was amongst them. She prepared herself for the leap, making sure she was cloaked. It would buy her a few more seconds at least.

Just as she was about to jump, a voice called out to her.

It was Cord telling her to wait.

Solan settled back, and a sigh of relief escaped her lips.

Several minutes went by as she waited for Cord to send her a signal. As soon as she heard it, she leapt up to Jinn's cage. She dug her fingers into the edge of the bottom panel. From her peripheral vision, she saw two of the Atrum rushing off in the opposite direction and assumed Cord had created a diversion.

She focused energy on the panel bolts as she heaved, and two of them sheared in half, opening the bottom of the cage and releasing Jinn's limp form. Solan slid her fingers through the graphene cage holes and dropped her lower body, swinging her legs out with the momentum and locking her feet around Jinn's waist. But suddenly the panel let loose, and they both fell.

M

Jet and Cord slid out of the control tower unnoticed. Jet led the way down a long spiraling ramp that eventually turned to a gravel path. They followed it deeper as the mining noises died off and the lighting dimmed. They crouched before the edge of the cell block and paused.

"Solan is in there," Cord said. "She's planning to free Jinn on her own."

Jet considered. "Ask her to wait."

Cord reached out to her and nodded to Jet. "She'll wait. There are four Atrum in there with her. It's obviously a trap, and they know we're here now, I'm afraid."

Jet took a knee to think. "There's a network of passages back there. I think I can draw at least a few of them with me and circle back. Solan will need your help as soon as she springs Jinn free. Give me a few seconds, then send her the signal."

Cord nodded and stayed cloaked in the shadows as Jet stood and walked into the chamber. Jet waited until he was in the middle and in clear view, then lowered his hood. He saw the four Atrum but wasn't entirely sure who they were. Suspended from the ceiling above was a cage with DiJinn. As he watched, he saw a blur leap to it and knew that Cord had sent the signal. Two of the Atrum charged at him. He turned and sped from the chamber.

He knew the two following him wouldn't go far before returning. He made it about fifty meters before they did, and he turned and followed them back to the chamber.

When Jet returned, the place was alive with shouts and yelling from the prisoners that echoed around the stone chamber. Solan had managed to free DiJinn, who lay on the ground behind her. One of the two Atrum who had stayed behind sparred with Solan while another Atrum lay at her feet, unconscious. The other two Atrum had just arrived, and Solan was outnumbered. Jet sprinted straight at them, wondering where Cord had gone. He slid in the dirt and rolled under the two Atrum, taking them down in a cloud of dust. Jet managed to pin one of them and noticed it was Brit. He wrapped his hands around Brit's neck, trying to choke him unconscious. Cord suddenly appeared behind Vail and lifted her over his head, then threw her to the ground. Solan had finally managed to gain the upper hand against Sojahn, and it looked like they had things under control when Jet noticed the fourth Atrum was gone.

Hurse stood behind them with one arm wrapped around DiJinn's waist, supporting her upright. He held her left arm behind her back.

"That's it, Hurse," Solan said. "Let her go, and we leave these three unharmed."

Jet stood and hoisted Brit up by his arm, still applying pressure to it. Cord had Vail in a similar position, and he could see the hatred in her eyes—Cord had bested her yet again. Sojahn remained calm as they all looked at Hurse, waiting to see what he would do next.

But Hurse stood there silently, and Jet started to think he was stalling for backup.

"All you Lucem are the same," Hurse said. He gave each of them a long stare, perhaps considering his next move. "Sympathy…it's such a weakness in you all. You'll never win like this."

"Spare the lecture," Solan said. "Let Jinn go and move on."

Hurse waited a few seconds longer. What Jet assumed was an expression of resignation flitted across Hurse's face, then it was gone. Hurse closed his eyes and the collar around DiJinn's neck clattered to the ground. The prisoners finally quieted down, waiting to see what would happen next.

"I did that for you, my sweet Jinn," Hurse said with a smile, his mouth close to her ear. DiJinn was able to stand now, and Jet saw the look on her face turn to anger and disgust. Hurse let his mouth linger near her ear for a moment. "You know my love for you will never fade…I release you now so you can feel this."

Then Hurse did something that shocked them all. He yanked on DiJinn's arm, and it snapped backwards with a loud crack. DiJinn grimaced in pain as Hurse released her, pulled his hood over his head, and disappeared.

Solan roared in anger and brought an elbow down on Sojahn's head, knocking her out cold. She grabbed Vail and Brit and hurled them into one of the cages as Cord lifted Sojahn's body and threw her in behind them.

"Get Jinn back to headquarters," Solan instructed. "Have Harriet check her out."

DiJinn was still dazed, and Jet could see her arm was bent at an awkward angle.

"Where are you going?" he asked.

"Just do what I say!" Solan said and sprinted from the chamber.

Jet and Cord helped Jinn up the spiral trail and loaded her aboard his skiff. Cord boarded DiJinn's skiff and followed them out of the hanger. Jet cloaked the skiff and flew out of the ARC district in a different route, making sure they weren't being followed. Eventually, they entered the ninth belt's air space, and he used the debris to throw off any pursuers. The rest of the way back to Skylight University, he couldn't stop wondering what Solan was up to.

К

Solan bolted from the chamber before Jet could ask any more questions. She knew the three Atrum wouldn't be locked up for long. And Hurse was still lurking about somewhere, but she wasn't concerned about him. If he knew what was best, he would avoid her.

She searched frantically for the cell block with the children. As she ran, she twisted the locks off from the other cages and freed as many prisoners as possible. Many of them were simply too weak to move. More guards would eventually come, but the stampeding prisoners would provide good cover for her. Inside, her soul wanted to save all of these people, and perhaps soon, she might return with enough Lucem to shut the whole operation down. But for now, her inner voice was telling her to find the caged children she'd seen earlier.

She finally located the cage she was looking for. There were three girls and two boys. One of the smallest girls, perhaps eight years old, was coughing and had no shoes. Solan ripped the lock off and flung the gate open. She picked the tiny girl up and folded her into her cloak.

"Hurry," she said, speaking softly to the children. "Follow me."

She led the way, blending in with the other prisoners. The commotion soon gathered attention from other guards, and reinforcements were starting to arrive. She hurried up the spiraling path, speaking encouragement to the children as they ran. They had to stop a few times, the children weak from lack of food, but eventually made it to the private hanger.

Solan hit the cloaking button on the console as they left the hanger. She set a course for the third belt and Skylight City. Then turned her attention to the children.

They all stared at her, too afraid to speak. The oldest girl sat in front of the others, shielding them from Solan. She looked to be about fifteen with piercing hazel eyes. The girl had an air of determination about her, and Solan could see that she had taken in the younger children as their protector. Solan didn't have to ask where their parents were…she was certain they were dead or had abandoned the children. All five of them had shaved heads and a tattoo on their shoulder in the shape of a red tetrahedron. A red number 6A was tattooed below the tetrahedron.

"It's okay," Solan said, and sat down cross legged across from them. They stared back at her, dirt and grime covering their faces and hands. "I won't hurt you. I'm here to help. What are your names?"

"They call me Six," the girl said. "We don't really have names, just the block we're from."

"Where is your real home? Where are you from?"

The girl looked at her, confused. "We are from block 6A. Is that what you mean?"

"I'm asking what town or city you're from."

"What is a town?"

Solan suddenly realized these children had not been taken from anywhere. They had been born into slavery. It took her a second before she could control her emotions, and she looked away. The children waited silently for her.

"It's okay, I think I understand now. I'm going to take you to a special place, one where you can stay and not worry about others hurting you. Is that alright?"

Six looked at the others as if trying to get a majority vote. One of the older boys, who appeared to be her second in command, nodded and smiled. "That would be great," Six said.

Solan let her skiff drift close to the outer skirts of the third belt. They were near a remote location of Skylight City and what some considered a slum area. It looked dirty and gritty from her vantage, but hidden below was a halfway home that was well funded by a group of people that owed her a favor. The group was friendly to the Lucem, who had helped the children there on many occasions. Solan was finally calling in a favor today.

Her console blipped, and Solan maneuvered the cloaked skiff in toward a hanger. It was pay by the hour, and anonymous…for the right amount. Expensive, but not for her. The Lucem had amassed a staggering amount of wealth over the centuries.

She docked her skiff and then spoke to Six. "I need you all to come with me."

"Where are you taking us?" Six asked, remaining seated between Solan and the others.

Solan knelt to one knee and took the girl's hand. "I have a really close friend who lives here, and she helps children like you. I'm taking you to her…can you trust me?"

Six looked over at the boy again, and he nodded. "Okay," she said.

Solan led the children down one of the busy streets. They all held hands to avoid getting separated. She stopped at a tall, narrow building with boarded up windows and a reinforced pair of steel doors. Solan banged on it three times, waited, and hammered on it twice more. Seconds later, the door cracked open, and Solan smiled at an elderly lady with gray hair pinned in a bun. She wore an old knit sweater with holes in the sleeves. The door swung open, and Solan ushered the children quickly inside.

The front area of the living room contained two couches and a round table with four chairs. A galley style kitchen lined the back wall with a large center island. Solan turned to the lady, smiled, and gave her a hug.

"It's good to see you, Stell."

"And it's good to see you too, Solan," the lady replied.

Solan gave the lady a long look. "Tyberius is missing. We think he was following up on a lead for

Albright. It's been a while now, and we've heard nothing from him."

The lady named Stell frowned. "Where were you looking?"

"The Galleon Quarter of Skylight. We could use some help. The Lucem's relationship with the Agency is on shaky ground right now, and with the Century Eclipse coming up, we're stretched pretty thin. I can't devote the time I need to track him, unfortunately."

Stell had a massive network of informants at her command. Her syndicate was an underground web of ordinary citizens comprised of just about every imaginable profession. They were the eyes and ears of her group known as Vine and provided a wealth of information for the Lucem. At first, Solan had resisted the urge to approach Stell. She wanted to find her father on her own, but she was desperate now.

Stell remained silent, considering. "I have other dire news that you need to hear."

Solan took a seat on one of the sofas. "What news?"

"The Atrum will be part of something at the Century Eclipse. You probably already assumed that much, but now we have concrete evidence."

Solan sat silently for a moment. "You obviously know we've been tracking the raids by a group of marauders known as the Tetrahedron, and they're backed by the Atrum. They've been stealing the Agency's refined rare-earth supplies. The Agency can't finish

Goliath's Gate without it. We managed to track the stolen shipments to a mining colony on earth but found no sign of it."

"You weren't looking in the right place," Six spoke up.

Solan and Stell looked at her.

Six sat with her knees pulled up, the other children behind her. "The holding cell, where we were kept. There's a secret passage cut into the rock below."

Solan looked at her. "Are you positive that's where the rare-earth is?"

"I don't know what rare-earth is, but they put a bunch of shiny rocks down there."

Solan chuckled. "Well, that would explain it. No one would think to look in there. That must be why we kept seeing Atrum, too. I didn't understand why Atrum would be guarding captives."

"We'll keep our ears to the ground. If we hear anything about what they are using it for, we'll contact you, Solan." Then Stell turned to the children. "And who are these lovely people?"

Solan knelt in front of Six. "These brave beauties are from Earth. They need a new home, and I told them you were one of the nicest people I know."

Solan watched Stell's reaction. The elderly lady knew immediately what the children's situation was without Solan saying a word. Stell had been around long enough to witness every imaginable situation involving homeless children. She took one look at the tattoo on their shoulders and gave Solan a meaningful look full of understanding and heartache.

Stell stood and walked over to the kitchen. She opened a cabinet door. Inside was a digital keypad, and she punched in a code. The kitchen island slid sideways to reveal some stairs. Stell walked over to Six and put a hand on her shoulder as she faced the other children. "Welcome home, all of you." Then Stell looked at Solan. "You're going to want to come with me now."

CHAPTER 19
An Unscheduled Meeting

ΑΒΓΔΕΖ**Η**ΘΙΚΛΜ
ΝΞΟΠΡΣΤΥΦΧΨΩ

DIJINN KICKED HER desk hard enough to send it sliding across the floor of her quarters. It had so many dents now that it didn't resemble a desk anymore. She was still upset at herself for letting her guard down with Hurse. It had always been personal between them, going all the way back to their days at Skylight University. At first, she had protected him, then fallen in love with him, which was something she'd managed to keep a secret. She had a thing for rebels, she supposed, and maybe there was still a spark with Hurse. But she loved Sol too much to let

Hurse get in the way. Besides, Hurse had been on a power trip since joining the Atrum, which she detested. He was no longer the sniveling little kid in the back of the classroom. As an Atrum, he had immense power, and there were no rules or principles to restrain him like there were with the Lucem. The Atrum were a chaotic group intent on power and destruction, and Hurse was out for payback on Skylight's citizens.

She was already in a foul mood because of Hurse, but there was something else nagging at her since she'd left the ARC district.

Why had Sol stayed behind?

DiJinn thought she knew why—*she was hiding something.*

Her main goal had always been to protect Sol, and if she was taking on missions alone… DiJinn couldn't bear to think of it. She'd never forgive herself if something were to happen to her beloved Sol.

Her temper flared again, and she kicked her desk hard enough to send it through a wall. She sat down and rubbed her arm. It had already healed, and she ripped Harriet's cloth sling off and threw it. The voice in her head whispered to her, accompanied by a vision of their old ninth belt headquarters, Flotsam. Something was happening there…*but did it involve Sol?*

Thirty minutes later, DiJinn cloaked her skiff as she entered the debris field of the ninth belt. She landed her skiff near a private hanger at Memorial Park. Hooded and cloaked, she walked into the vast bunkerlike museum. Its domed transparent roof gave visitors a commanding panoramic view of the Earth. Being this close to the edge of the synthetic atmosphere generated by the system's Core left the air thin, cold, and difficult to breathe. The azure blue sky was tinged a dark purple with the aurora borealis dancing like green sprites in the background. Inside the bunker, thousands of visitors milled about, perusing artwork, educational learning venues, and movies. DiJinn slid past a few school tours unnoticed and found the back of house area. The maze of corridors wound around, and she located one of the hidden passages. Her credentials were still valid, and she moved toward the Agency headquarters. The built-in counter measures in her cloak scrambled the security and surveillance systems automatically. Being cloaked allowed her unfettered access into the inner sanctum of the Agency.

She finally found familiar areas and slowed her pace. In the back of her mind, the voice started whispering again, and she began to wonder why she was really there. At first, she assumed she'd catch Sol in the act of something. But that perception was changing the closer she got to the Agency's inner sanctum. Sometimes, her inner voice guided her in ways she didn't understand. But when it spoke to her, she always heeded it. So far, it had never led her astray.

Eventually, she stood in front of the main Agency board room. Here, the most secretive meetings took place. Very few in the Agency even knew this room existed. Around the perimeter, guards were posted, along with motion sensors and heat detectors. The security provisions that were in place would've prevented any normal intrusions. But the Agency's technology was no match for the Lucem. DiJinn could break into practically any space she desired; it was one of her specialties. But even this place would require the utmost care. Her attention had to be laser focused.

She waited for an official to enter and slid silently through the doorway. She stood motionless near a back wall of the posh board room. The wood trim and plush carpet made her want to puke. In the access ceiling above, she noticed several cameras and other equipment for surveillance. Harok was no idiot and took every precaution.

At the head of the long conference table sat President Harok. Next to him was General Dane and General Yune, followed by other department heads. They were in the middle of a heated disagreement.

"She told me herself," Yune said. "The Lucem are out of the question for the immediate future."

"What does that even mean?" one of the higher-ranking officers asked. "Are you saying the Lucem have abandoned their posts?"

"Yes," Yune said. "It would appear that way. I don't believe they plan to return."

"Then they are derelict of duty and should all be hunted down and court-martialed!"

"Good luck with that," Dane scoffed. "You'll not win that battle. Your best bet is to let things run their course and hope the Lucem accomplish their goal and return on their own. Hopefully sooner rather than later."

"And what is their goal?" Yune asked. "Do we even know where they are now?"

"That, I have no idea," Harok said and leaned forward, steepling his fingers in front of his nose.

"They've not said a word about any of this, and it's absolute insanity," Yune continued. "The Lucem have been a part of this Agency since it was founded by Albright!"

"And yet, you were the one who wanted them gone," Dane shot back. "How many troops have we lost now? Do you still stand by your demand, Yune?"

Yune stared at Dane but remained silent.

"Regardless," Harok said. "Whatever mission the Lucem are pursuing, they are no longer around, and we can't count on them at this point. We need more firepower."

"So," Yune said. "We sit and watch as these marauders, led by the Atrum, plunder all of our rare-earth stockpile? We are hopelessly outmatched, no matter how many troops we throw at them."

"So, what do you propose?" Dane asked. "That we team with another group of mercenaries?"

"And if we did, how would we afford it?" Yune asked. "Nearly all of our resources are being poured into the Goliath's Gate project. Any more and people will begin to notice. I'm shocked they haven't thus far."

The council began to murmur, and a department head stood. "The amount we require is staggering, who could possibly fund this?"

Harok held up his hands for silence. "Please. We require help if we want to see Goliath's Gate completed. We need funding, manpower, troops. We need an army. The Agency will have to make some sacrifices if we want to accomplish our goals. It is evident we cannot defeat the Atrum-backed marauders with our elite troops."

The council began to murmur again. Dane looked at Harok dubiously.

"Hear me out," Harok continued. "In exchange for a few gifts, art, paintings, and some confidential information, a backer has stepped forward and agreed to fund Goliath's Gate. This Backer prefers to remain anonymous but will provide the additional troops needed for the rare-earth shipments."

"Why would anyone do this?" one of the council members asked. "What information are you planning to disclose?"

"The Backer has an interest in our project," Harok said. "For their generous donation, we have disclosed everything."

"Sir," Dane said. "I'm guessing these troops are mercenaries. If we aren't careful, this could spiral out of control. We might be risking a system wide war."

"We have the weapons, and the ships," Harok said. "But we don't have the troops. We need these mercenaries, Dane. If there is another option available, let it be known."

"Do you trust them?" Dane asked. "What training do these mercs have? Most of them are not very disciplined from what I've seen. They are reckless and unruly. All it takes is one bad decision."

"And that will be your responsibility, Dane," Harok pointed out. "Along with General Yune. You will train them."

"What if the secrets you've shared with this Backer get out?" Dane asked.

"At this point, I no longer care about shielding the Lucem," Harok said. "But outing them does us no good. If people find out, fine. Right now, our focus needs to be on the Goliath's Gate project. We will simply deny any rumors if they arise."

Dane took a deep breath. "I don't know if I agree with this direction, Harok. It's a doomsday scenario, in my opinion, and I'm not sure we're at that point just yet."

"You have no idea what a doomsday scenario is, Dane," Yune said. "But these Lucem…these Atrum…they will bring doomsday to our doorstep, if we do nothing."

DiJinn had heard enough of the council's rubbish and slid out of the chamber. What she had just heard resonated like an explosion inside her head. DiJinn needed to find Sol and deliver the news. Things were about to get downright nasty. It appeared that the Lucem had just been kicked to the curb. They hadn't abandoned the Agency, but apparently someone had Harok's ear and had convinced him the Lucem were traitors. If the Lucem were on their own now, they needed to regroup quickly.

К

Solan and the children followed Stell down the stone stairs and into a tiny vestibule as the sliding door above closed. Before them was another set of heavy steel doors, and Stell placed her hand over a palm reader and waited. Then she spoke into a mic.

The doors opened, and they were greeted by a pair of guards with heavy rail guns. They looked at Solan and saluted. Stell led them into the underground complex.

"This is our halfway home, children. You are safe here."

The children stayed close to Six as they looked around the cavernous space in awe. The upper ceiling was supported by steel columns some fifteen meters high with several levels above that, which appeared to be apartments. Around them, dividers separated the massive open cavern into individual classrooms. Groups of children of all ages sat on the ground listening to instructors. A chow hall occupied the back of the space, large enough to support the entire operation. Below them were openings in the ground that stretched down another fifteen or twenty meters where Solan could see construction crews and scaffolding.

"We are expanding our facility," Stell said. "It's unfortunate that we have to. I love what I do, and helping these children is so rewarding. But there are so many out there; we receive more every day. We are running out of room quickly."

"You are in good hands," Solan said. "We will supply the funds necessary, as will the other backers, I'm sure."

They followed Stell as she led them to the far end of the cavern. She stopped at a door and turned to face them. "Would you children mind waiting here for a moment?"

Stell led Solan inside the room, shutting the door behind her. She turned and looked at Solan and held her hands.

Solan stood there, not sure what was happening until a tall gray-haired man walked into the tiny room.

Solan sprang from Stell and threw her arms around the tall man. She hugged him, refusing to let go. The man chuckled and hugged her back.

"It's good to see you too, Solan," Tyberius said.

CHAPTER 20
Loose Ends

ΑΒΓΔΕΖΗΘΙ**Κ**ΛΜ
ΝΞΟΠΡΣΤΥΦΧΨΩ

SOLAN COULDN'T STOP smiling. "Father, what do you think you're doing? You can't just leave like that."

Tyberius stared at Solan for a moment. His typical cropped gray hair had grown long, and he sported a gray beard. Otherwise, he was the same man, confident and direct, but gentle.

He sat her down in a chair and looked at Stell. "Thank you, Stell."

"I'll leave you two to catch up." Stell smiled and left the room.

Solan faced Tyberius and crossed her arms. "Care to explain?"

"Let me apologize, Solan," Tyberius said and knelt. "I know that I've placed you in a difficult position, and I wouldn't have done so if I thought you couldn't handle it."

She shook her head. "You knew I wouldn't have agreed to this."

"Precisely. Which is why I didn't tell you. I had to leave the way I did. I couldn't let anyone know what I had found, even you."

"I'm here now. Let me hear it."

"I believe you already know why I'm here."

"You've located Albright, I take it?"

"He's nearby. But you know he's still too young. He can't go through the conversion ritual at his age and bringing him in now is too risky. I don't trust anyone, not right now. He stays with me until he's ready."

"I understand," Solan said. "But I can't continue to lead the Lucem, father. That's not what I'm cut out for."

"I'm not sure I believe that," he said. "From what Stell has told me, it sounds like you're handling the situation."

"Is that a fact? On my watch, we've been kicked out of the Agency, we're currently holed up in an old, abandoned control center, and we have no idea what these marauders are up to. I'm not sure how that sounds remotely successful."

"These are trying times, no matter who leads the Lucem," Tyberius said. "Do you know why I trust you?"

"Please don't tell me it's because I'm your daughter."

"Absolutely not. It's because you didn't want the role. I believe the best leaders are those who don't let ambition make their decisions. When ambition is a primary goal, a leader isn't looking out for the ones they serve. Great leaders serve, Solan. It's a trait I can always trust."

"I don't want to be responsible for the others, father."

"I'm aware," he said and gripped her shoulder. "But you absolutely must remain strong. They need you. Like it or not, this is your duty now."

Solan furrowed her brow. "You intend to stay? We need you now more than ever. We're down four Lucem without you. We are outnumbered by the Atrum, and they're planning something during the Century Eclipse."

"We both know that Albright is more important. He *must* survive until he can go through the ritual. I trust you, Solan, and you will trust the others. You have some talented individuals to lean on."

She stood and leaned against the wall. "Can you at least tell me what you would do right now?"

Tyberius shook his head. "No. You are the leader of the Lucem. You'll know what to do when the time comes."

"Can I at least come see you?"

He stood next to her. "I think you know that would be unwise. We cannot risk giving away Albright's location, and you must not discuss our meeting with anyone. There is a spy very close, somewhere in our midst. Somehow, the Atrum have guessed our moves."

Solan kicked at the ground with her worn boots but couldn't look into her father's eyes. "I sense that you already know about Sterllar? I can feel your grief, though you don't show it."

Tyberius remained silent for a moment before he spoke. "I know what happened. Stell gave me the unfortunate news."

"Aren't you upset that I brought her into the Agency?" Solan asked. "She's dead because of my decision to do so. I wish you were more upset about it…*more upset with me!*"

"Had you not brought her in, things might have been even worse for her," Tyberius said calmly.

"My sister is *dead!* Your daughter is *dead!*" Solan choked back tears, long overdue tears that she had fought back since her sister's death. She hadn't wanted the other Lucem to see her like this, not as a leader—she couldn't afford that. But standing there in front of her father, under his glowing gaze, she finally let go and dropped to her knees. She hammered the stone wall with her fists over and over until it fractured and crumbled to dust. She let her tears fall for her sister, for her failures, for her loneliness…for the family she always hoped to bring together, and now, never would. Her dream of reuniting her family had been within reach, but now her sister was dead, and her father wasn't coming home after all, maybe never.

Tyberius watched Solan closely and didn't say anything, letting her grieve, but remained silent until she had finished. Then he reached out and grasped her shoulder. Solan could sense the sorrow in his touch, knew he wanted to reach out to her and embrace her. But then she knew why he wouldn't…*why he couldn't*. He was letting her resolve this on her own. She knew he had to take a hard line on this so she could overcome her grief without his help. She had relied on him for so long, and this was his way of passing leadership to her. This was her trial to pass through, and she knew how difficult it must be for him to stand by as she fought through it.

"I've done my grieving for Sterllar," Tyberius finally said. "She is beyond us now, though we may see her again someday. Regarding whether I'm upset about the decision to bring her in doesn't matter. You are in charge, and you did what you thought was best. I can't argue with that. Being a leader is difficult and can be lonely. I have placed a great responsibility on you, my daughter."

Solan eventually stood to her feet and stared at the ceiling. The grief she felt for her sister only added to her stress. She'd never had to worry about much; her father had born the weight of the Lucem. She had hoped locating him would alleviate that weight and she could return to what she liked the best—seeing after her own affairs. But it was apparent that wasn't going to happen now. There were so many things going on, it felt like a huge weight was anchored about her shoulders. But surprisingly, that weight seemed to lighten as she stood there. She felt more confident just knowing that her father had placed his trust in her.

"I don't know what else to say," she said and gave him a weak smile. "I only wish Sterllar could've met you. She was so excited about that."

"I wish that too," Tyberius said. He placed his hands on her shoulders and faced her. "Solan. I need you to promise me one thing."

Solan looked up at her father, noticing the strained look in his glowing orange eyes, and waited for him to continue.

"Promise me that you won't seek out vengeance for your sister, it's not what she would want. We don't work that way, and you must set this example for the others, especially the younger Lucem. There may come a time when they face a similar situation, and they will look to you. No matter how much you want it, you mustn't. Can you do that?"

"I don't know, father. I will try."

"You must! The essence within your soul depends on it. There will be justice for your sister, but let it come by its own path, do not seek it out. And most of all, do *not* blame yourself for this."

Solan didn't speak, not knowing what to say at that moment. She had mixed feelings tugging at her: *vengeance, anger, guilt…indecision.* If she ever came face to face with her sister's killer, she would be hard pressed to stay her hand. It appeared that her battle with her inner demons was only just beginning.

Solan hugged her father and said goodbye to the children before she left. Solan trusted Stell and knew she would care for the children as her own, just like she had done for thousands of other homeless children.

K

Less than thirty minutes later, Solan's skiff entered the ARC district's air space, and she docked at the same private hanger. She knew returning so soon was risky. Then again, who would be crazy enough to do such a thing? Even though she had several pressing issues that required her attention, she had to be sure the rare-earth was where Six claimed it was. She needed to see it with her own eyes before reporting back to Harok.

It seemed that all the commotion from the freed detainees had set off a full-blown riot. The markets and shops were in total chaos, and citizens had taken to the streets. Freed detainees had taken up arms and were ransacking nearby guard posts. Marauder troops with the red insignia patrolled the streets, and she witnessed numerous clashes around the district. All the commotion helped provide cover as she moved quickly. But Solan saw no sign of the Atrum. They appeared to have left the area.

When she reached the cell block, there was no one to be seen. She stayed in the shadows and searched for signs of this secret passage Six had mentioned. She noticed that several of the cages were actually bolted together, and on further inspection could see metal tracks imbedded into the ground. It appeared the whole section of cages slid on the track.

There was indeed something below.

Still, she needed to see the rare-earth with her own eyes, not that she could do anything about it at the moment. She just had to verify it before reporting back to the Agency. A crew of miners entered the chamber amongst the shouts and fighting. They transported several large crates on a floating slab and looked around anxiously. She watched as they entered a cage, then seemed to disappear. They reappeared just as the group of cages slid open to reveal a long sloping ramp leading down below. Solan crept closer to see the dull shine of refined rare-earth twinkling from the dark holding area.

CHAPTER 21
Hostages

ΑΒΓΔΕΖΗΘΙΚΛ**Μ**
ΝΞΟΠΡΣΤΥΦΧΨΩ

JET SAT WITH Cutter and Cord in the bleachers, waiting for the track meet to begin. Jet talked quietly to Cutter, going over some of the finer details of his alias and assignments. Cutter had already been given his first assignment as one of the coaches on the blaze squad and seemed to be pleased, now that he had settled in. He had also been given a secondary job as night security around the campus and directed to provide surveillance. He was excited about his new duties but was already pushing for more. Jet had been right; Cutter sank into a depressive state when he had no one to care for. Having a purpose fueled Cutter and protecting others gave him that drive he needed.

There was a lively atmosphere around the track stadium that day and plenty of activity on and off the field. Announcers bellowed from the speaker system, acknowledging the athletes and their race times. Student athletes from across the system stretched and prepared for their heat. Citizens and family members wore face paint and cheered on their university. It reminded Jet of game days as a college athlete during the blaze season, and how much he missed that feeling.

They watched the runners as they stretched and prepared for the day's track meet. Jet felt relieved to be back on Skylight watching over Kamber. He trusted the other Lucem, but he wanted to be the one watching over her personally. Being away from Kamber made him feel anxious, which surprised him since he had never felt that way about anyone before.

Solan called Jet, and he sat forward, Cord and Cutter huddled in close to hear her. "We need to talk," she said. "When can you get down here?"

"We're in the middle of Kamber's track meet," Jet said. "Is this something that can wait?"

"It's important. Just try to get here as soon as possible."

When the track meet ended, the three of them worked their way down to the field. Jet wanted to check on Kamber before they left to meet Solan. He assumed he had missed her event, since he hadn't seen her since warmups. Solan's call had been the only distraction during that time, but when he saw Tetra, he knew something was wrong.

Jet stopped her. "Nice work today, Tetra. You took all-system honors. I didn't see Kamber, though."

"Thanks," she replied. "I wanted to let you know that Kamber missed her start. I don't know what happened to her, but I'm a little shocked. She never misses. Coach Minette is looking for her now."

Jet gave Cord and Cutter a concerned look. "Stay with Tetra, won't you?"

Coach Minette was in her office under the stands.

"Where is Kamber?"

"I know," Minette said, holding up her hands. "We're trying to locate her now. No one has seen her."

Jet tried to remain calm, but inside, he wanted to strangle Minette. "She was your responsibility, was she not?"

"Yes, but I have a host of athletes to watch over on track meet days. I can't watch all of them at once."

Jet left before his frustration with the coach boiled over. He decided to reach out with his thoughts to locate her. Thankfully, Kamber's lapel pin left a small trace. He slipped into his cloak and found a portal near the track stadium. He raced along an underground passage, running at top speed once he understood what was going on. If anything happened to her, he was responsible. He wanted to kick himself for letting his guard down—she was his most important assignment, and he was failing her already.

He arrived at the hangers through a portal, having taken a few shortcuts to get there. A lone skiff hovered in the hanger bay. To his left, something blurry emerged through another portal. An Atrum cradled Kamber in its arms.

For a split second, neither of them moved, both surprised by each other's appearance. Then they both raced for the skiff.

Carrying Kamber slowed the Atrum enough to allow Jet the advantage. He stopped in front of the skiff, blocking its path. He waited as Hurse lowered his hood. Below the folds of his cloak, Jet could see an unconscious, but unharmed, Kamber.

"Looking for someone?" Hurse asked.

"Found someone, it seems. You've crossed a line this time, Hurse."

"I see no lines from where I stand, Stroud. But you've already crossed a line by breaking our agreement."

"This is your last chance. Release her now and leave."

"You were fortunate last time," Hurse said. "You know you can't best me in a fight."

Jet crouched into a defensive stance. "You're not getting on this skiff with her."

"Watch me." Hurse lashed out at Jet with a psychic attack meant to stun him. Jet easily swatted it down.

"You're going to need both hands to fight me, Hurse. What's it going to be?"

Hurse dropped Kamber, and she hit the ground and lay there between them. "Come get her then," he said and stood over her body.

Jet took a step forward, then stopped when he looked at Kamber. Her skin was pale and her breathing shallow. She seemed to be in a comatose state. "What have you done?"

Without warning, Hurse lunged and tackled him. They grappled in the hanger bay, and Jet felt the surprising strength in Hurse's attack, belying his slight frame. He cleared his mind from Kamber, knowing if he didn't focus on Hurse, he would pay the price. Hurse was cunning, and it took all of Jet's skill to maintain his balance.

After several minutes, Jet began to tire. But he sensed that Hurse was too, and it seemed to be a stalemate. Jet needed to get to Kamber and check on her condition—he needed to end this. He gambled on a risky maneuver, hoping to catch Hurse off guard, but instantly regretted it.

The uppercut meant for Hurse's chin missed and left him off balance. Hurse used Jet's momentum and placed him in a headlock. Jet was able to get just enough of his arm between the chokehold to prevent Hurse from rendering him unconscious. A flurry of thoughts raced through his head of what Hurse might do to Kamber if Jet couldn't protect her now. He couldn't afford to let Hurse beat him yet again.

The portal at the far end opened, and a cloak stepped through. Cord let his hood drop and revealed the limp form of Tetra. She was unconscious. Cord laid her on the floor in front of him. Hurse paused but maintained his grip on Jet.

"Step away, Hurse," Cord said.

"You wouldn't hurt her," Hurse said. "I know you Lucem too well. Weak, even to a fault."

Cord gripped a handful of Tetra's hair and lifted her entire body from the floor. Her limp form dangled, swaying gently. "You don't know me that well, Hurse. You might think you do, but you have no idea what I'm capable of."

Hurse released Jet and hurtled toward Cord, his jaw set in anger. Jet noticed the discrete grin on Cord's face as he released Tetra at the last second. Jet hurried over to Kamber as Hurse and Cord sparred.

But Cord was simply too quick for Hurse, and it didn't take long for Hurse to realize he was outmatched. Hurse tried to grab Tetra in one swift motion and dart away, but Cord caught him by the ankle and slammed him to the concrete floor. Hurse let out a cry of pain. Cord lifted him and gripped his arm, twisting it behind Hurse's back.

"Do you have information about Sterllar Sylvant?" Cord asked.

"That had nothing to do with us!" Hurse said.

Cord considered for a moment. "I suppose I should kill you, Hurse. But I won't…*this time*. But I *will* have payback for Jinn," Cord whispered in Hurse's ear and wrenched up on his elbow. The snap echoed through the empty hanger, and Hurse gritted his teeth in pain. He dropped to his knees, head bowed and his left arm hanging at an awkward angle. Jet saw the surprise on his face when he looked up at Cord.

"I suggest you leave," Cord said to Hurse and gave him a shove toward the skiff.

Hurse stood and looked at them, holding his broken arm. "Don't even think about doing anything to Tetra. We have one of yours, and they would pay dearly." Hurse looked at Tetra one last time before boarding his skiff, then turned and left.

CHAPTER 22
Bartering Peace

ΑΒΓΔΕΖΗΘΙΚΛ**Μ**
ΝΞΟΠΡΣΤΥΦΧΨΩ

JET AND CORD watched as Hurse's skiff shot skyward.

"We need to figure out what Hurse did to Kamber!" Jet said and lifted her. "But what do we do with Tetra?"

Cord looked at her. "She's coming with us."

"What?" Jet said. "We can't do that. That's—"

"Exactly what they were planning to do with your warden," Cord interrupted him. There is no telling what they had intended for her either."

"We can't stoop to that level, Cord."

"We won't. She'll be safe. Regardless, we are going to send them a message."

"I think you just did that with Hurse."

"Wrong. That was simply payback for Jinn."

Tetra began to stir, and Cord knelt. He focused, forcing her back into a deep sleep. He lifted her and drew his cloak around her unconscious form, then leapt down through the portal.

"Great!" Jet muttered under his breath and followed him with Kamber in his arms.

They wandered silently down the hallways of Lyrinthum and past vacant chambers. The smell of earthly mildew filled Jet's nostrils, mixed with battery acid from the defunct equipment. Once again, the haunting voices infiltrated his thoughts as they moved quickly. He closed his mind as best he could and ignored their anguished screams. Before long they were near the old particle collider and the lower depths of Lyrinthum.

"Are you familiar with this area?" Jet whispered.

"Somewhat," Cord said in a low voice and crouched. "We're close."

Jet knelt beside him. Across the large chamber he noticed two pairs of glowing eyes staring at them. Jet remained silent, then he breathed a sigh of relief and lowered his hood. Booker and Harriet stood and approached them.

"You two okay?" Booker asked. It sounded like a low growl in the steel corridor.

"What took so long?" Harriet asked. "We've been waiting."

Jet revealed Kamber. "Something's wrong with her."

Harriet placed a hand on Kamber's forehead and closed her eyes as she probed her thoughts. "Let's get her to the control room."

Once they made it to the control room, Jet lowered Kamber onto a table. Solan and DiJinn hurried over.

"What happened?" DiJinn asked.

"Hurse," Jet said. "He tried to kidnap her."

"She's in some sort of catatonic state," Solan said, "This is a technique I've seen before. Hurse has placed a mental signature on her, and she won't awake until he releases it. It's the same method he used on Jinn in the ARC, but without the collar. I think he may have been trying to convert her to an Atrum."

"Interesting," Cord said. "I'm not sure it works that way, though."

"Experimenting on her, it seems," DiJinn said. "Must've failed, and he was tryin' to get her back to their base to finish the deed."

"I can't believe they'd attempt something like that," Jet said. "Even for the Atrum."

"Better believe it," DiJinn said. "Cause you have no idea what they're capable of. If you ever get a glimpse inside one of their heads, you'll understand."

Jet thought about his recent encounter with Vail. Her thoughts were distorted, morbid and desperate. "But they must know that trying to convert a Lucem this way isn't possible, right? Am I missing something?"

"The Atrum might be on to something we're not aware of," Harriet said.

"Can you get through to her?" Jet asked. Kamber's skin color was even paler now, and her breathing was so shallow he could barely see her draw in breath.

"Maybe," Harriet said. "I've never seen this before."

"If she dies, we go to war," DiJinn said.

"If she dies, then we have something as collateral." Cord opened his cloak and revealed Tetra's unconscious body.

"What are you doing with her?" Harriet said, shocked. "Are you insane?"

"Probably," Cord replied. "But we already knew that."

"We can't keep her here," Booker said. "She's still a student."

"Wasn't planning on it," Cord said. "Just until we get Kamber back to normal…and the other Lucem they mentioned."

"What other Lucem?" Solan asked.

"Hurse told us they had a Lucem captive, but didn't say who," Jet said.

"Albright?" DiJinn said. "They've found Albright."

"Or Tyberius," Booker said.

Jet watched Solan. She seemed to hesitate and didn't respond at first. They all sat around the dimly lit control room and waited for her. "We need to reach out to the Atrum, let them know we have Tetra and we're ready to bargain."

"How do we manage that?" Booker asked.

"I have a back channel with Hurse," Jet said. "We met a while back to discuss a few things."

"You did what?" Solan said, raising her voice and glaring at him. "You did that without our knowledge? You know that's a huge risk; you could've put us all in danger."

"I know. And I apologize," Jet said, holding up his hands. "But I did what I thought was best for Kamber."

"You don't know how devious Hurse is, Jet," Harriet reminded him.

"Anyway," Solan said. "That's in the past. Okay, Jet. Your call then."

"I'll send the message," Jet said. "Just tell me when and where."

"You realize they'll have all the Atrum there, Solan," Cord reminded her. "We're outnumbered if anything goes wrong. And they have Sybold."

"I'm well aware," Solan said. "But we will not hold a student. I will handle Sybold, if it comes to that."

M

About an hour later, Jet focused a message to Hurse. He was sure that Hurse was waiting for it, probably too proud to reach out to Jet first. The demands were simple; release Kamber, then an Atrum for a Lucem. Despite Cord's strong disapproval, they would give Tetra back to the Atrum, regardless. Solan ordered Tetra to be kept under the same catatonic state as Kamber. Cord used the same mental signature that Hurse had; a bond that couldn't be broken until the psychic release was given.

The meeting was set for midnight at a remote location on the sixth belt, which was primarily used for logging and replanting trees for the system. The barter would take place at an old lumber factory, which had long since been abandoned. Solan had demanded the location primarily because it was mostly devoid of citizens, except a few random resorts sprinkled about. If things did get out of control, no one would be injured or witness the gathering. It marked the first time in over a thousand years that their clans had met in full like this. Jet only hoped things didn't get out of control.

K

They split Tetra and Kamber up. Jet and Cord rode together with Tetra, followed by Ti-Leer and Annaka, Booker and Harriet, with Solan, DiJinn and Kamber bringing up the rear of the procession of skiffs. DiJinn took the opportunity to brief the group about the secret meeting she had witnessed. Jet listened in, but he and Cord remained silent about the additional information they knew.

"So, you're telling us that Harok believes the Lucem have abandoned the Agency?" Booker grumbled. "They're the ones who wanted us out."

"Sounded like someone's in Harok's ear, a person he called the Backer. Whoever it is will fund Goliath's Gate and give 'em mercenaries," DiJinn said. "I guess this person is feeding him lies. A few in the council even called us traitors."

"Whatever Harok said, he wouldn't come after us by spreading rumors," Solan replied. "It's beneath him, and all he cares about is Goliath's Gate. His entire political career hinges on the success of that project, and he'll focus everything on that."

"At the rate they're going, they'll never get enough rare-earth," Ti-Leer said.

"Actually, I have something to say about that," Solan said. "I went back to the mining pit—"

"You did what?" DiJinn interrupted her.

"I had to," Solan said. "I'd been given a tip to the location of the rare-earth. The stolen shipments were hidden beneath the cell block."

"Sol," DiJinn said. "We travel in groups. You're puttin' yourself at too much risk."

"I know, Jinn," Solan said. "But I had to see it with my own eyes."

"She's right, Solan," Harriet said. "We need you. We can't afford any losses at this point, especially you."

"Well?" Booker asked. "What did you see?"

"It's there, all of it," Solan replied. "The stockpile of purified rare-earth was enormous. It's easily enough to complete Goliath's Gate."

"But… you're havin' second thoughts 'bout telling Harok now, I take it?" DiJinn asked.

Solan paused for a moment. "I feel like we should hold on to that information, especially after what Jinn just told us. We may need that as leverage later."

"I agree," Cord said. "I also believe it wise to start reworking our aliases…all of us, Solan. That's Annaka's specialty."

"Annaka, can you hack into the Agency database?" Solan asked.

"Sure. I can even reset our credentials without changing our aliases," Annaka said. "It'll take some time, though. It'll probably be after the Century Eclipse. I've got a few savvy tech assistants on staff at the university who moonlight on the black market. For the right amount, they're tightlipped."

"Let's get to work on it then," Solan said. "We're better off being unplugged from the Agency at this point."

CHAPTER 23
Standoff

ΑΒΓΔΕΖΗΘΙΚΛ**Μ**
ΝΞΟΠΡΣΤΥΦΧΨΩ

SOLAN WENT OVER everything again as a precaution.

They were outnumbered, assuming all the Atrum showed up. Solan was gambling on the fact that the Atrum wouldn't risk a confrontation with Tetra in their possession, at least that's what Jet assumed. The mental signature placed on Tetra had elicited several grumbles from the others. Jet didn't like the idea of holding a student hostage, even an Atrum, though the Atrum had just attempted the same thing with Kamber.

And if Hurse was to be believed, they had another Lucem captive.

The mental signature Cord utilized could only be released through him, which he would perform after the exchange was made. Till then, Tetra was placed on a floating slab and strapped to it. Jet thought it was somewhat barbaric, though he understood the precaution. The Atrum couldn't be trusted, that much he'd learned already.

"I sense your anxiety," Cord said. "Why the concern?"

"Just a bit nervous. It's been a long time since our groups have met like this, anything could go haywire. Aren't you worried?"

"No," Cord said. "The Atrum won't push a conflict over this. They are still waiting for the right moment, and this is not it."

"I hope you're right. It's just difficult thinking of Bo and Vail like that now."

"You are aware they cannot be helped. It's best to let them go."

"I just wonder how far they will sink. I felt some hesitation in Vail when she warned me about Cutter."

"I am unaware of how the Atrum mind works," Cord said. "But attempting to comprehend their thought process is a dangerous quest. I would recommend avoiding it. They were once our friends, but those people are gone. Accept that and move on."

"If you had to guess, what do you think is happening to them?"

Cord stared straight ahead and gripped the console a bit tighter. "Are you familiar with the term possession?"

Jet remained silent.

Cord looked over at him. "An entity resides within all Heliographi, you know this, of course. But what *type* of entity?"

Jet remembered hearing multiple voices when Vail last spoke to him. What Cord was suggesting suddenly hit him.

"Not a very cheerful picture, is it? I believe the Atrum are a conglomerate of spiritual entities, and not the happy ones. They've managed to comingle with each other over time, perhaps from other dimensions. Whereas the Lucem work independently, or with a single entity. Now you know why you shouldn't stray too far into their thoughts. Move past the fact that Vail and Bo are still with us…they are a shell of who they used to be."

"You sound like Solan."

"Perhaps in this instance…I suppose that's a good thing."

Cord was right, of course, and Jet knew better than to even consider mixing up with Vail or Bo now. If it were somehow possible to convince them to come back to reality, it might end up destroying their souls anyway.

But even still, there was a glimmer of hope buried in his heart for Vail.

"I have a theory on that, by the way," Jet said.

Cord looked at him with genuine interest. "Intriguing. Let's hear it."

"I think the voice I hear—that intuitive, inner voice—is the previous Lucem who bore my symbol. He died on a mission just before I was born. Though it speaks to me in a single voice, I think there are other Lucem with it. They are trying to help us, Cord. They warn us, keep us safe, let us know when something doesn't feel right. I guess, based on what you said about the Atrum, maybe their system is different, and they hear *all* of their past Atrum at once. That would drive me mad, too. I suppose I would call them demons as well. But what if those ancient voices from past Heliographi come to us through another dimension?"

Cord stared at him, a bit shocked, then smiled. "Perhaps you are on to an intriguing theory. I had not thought of it quite like that, but it does make sense, actually—"

"Here we go," Solan interrupted him over the intercom. "Stay focused, everyone."

Cord uncloaked the skiff and followed as Solan took the lead.

The distant lights from the outer belts combined with the moon and lit the ground around them. A thick fog clung to the vegetation and reflected the greenish glow from the aurora borealis above, adding a sinister ambiance. The heavy ground cover made finding a clear spot to land difficult. The convoy of skiffs continued on until he saw a clearing where several black skiffs emerged. Solan settled her skiff across the field from the black skiffs, and the other Lucem did the same.

Jet and Cord clambered out of the cockpit. Crickets murmured as they all approached. Standing across the moonlit field were the Atrum. Jet and the other Lucem approached with Tetra trailing behind, strapped to the floating slab. They stopped about five meters from the Atrum. Jet waited to see what Solan would do, but she simply stood next to DiJinn with arms crossed.

The glow from the Atrum's eyes ranged from turquoise to blue, purple and red. Vail glowered at Cord as she stood next to Brit. Bo looked completely different than what Jet remembered. His blonde beard had grown long and shaggy, his shoulder length hair covered most of his face, and his skin was ashen. Bo didn't move or show any emotion, and if Jet hadn't seen the purple glow from his eyes, he would've assumed Bo was a walking corpse. Hurse stood next to Sojahn and Myranda, his arm already healed from the break issued by Cord. There were four Atrum that Jet knew only from what he'd read or heard through the others; Bofisto, Renzie, Joshia, and Mosstrom. A lady with a runner's build stepped forward and stood just inches in front of Solan. Her blonde hair was shot through with a streak of silver down the middle.

She was tall, like Solan, and had a similar physique with long legs and tapered shoulders.

Solan clenched her jaw and crossed her arms. "Joshia. You're looking lovely," she said in a voice thick with sarcasm.

"Solan," Joshia responded. "How pleasant of you to join us. Beautiful night, wouldn't you say?"

Jet had heard Solan talk about Joshia in the past. They'd been classmates, best friends, and heralded track stars at Skylight. But their friendship had suffered that same fate as Jet and Vail's.

"You have someone that belongs to us, Solan."

"And we're happy to return her as soon as you do the same. You know how this works."

"Careful, Solan," Joshia said and lowered her voice. "We might just take what's ours. It appears we have the upper hand."

Solan motioned to Cord. "I don't think that would work out very well for Tetra. We have a mental signature on her."

Joshia sneered, her lip curving upward. "You always were so thoughtful, Solan."

"Only Cord knows the signature. He'll release her when we have Albright," DiJinn said.

Joshia glanced at DiJinn and smirked. "Albright? Who said anything about that fool?" Joshia looked at the man to her left. "Bofisto. I don't think they understand."

Bofisto, who was as tall as Booker and maybe broader, placed his hands behind his back. Jet noticed some sort of steel devices in his mouth when he spoke, like tiny daggers fixed to his teeth. "You're such an embarrassment to our race, DiJinn," he said.

Solan tensed as DiJinn stepped forward. Her ponytails fluttered in the breeze and emerald-green eyes flared bright. Her cheeks flushed red to match her hair as she clenched her fists. Booker and Ti-Leer stepped up beside her, and Cord took a knee, as if preparing to leap at Vail. Annaka and Harriet shuffled calmly around to the opposite side and waited. Hurse moved forward, along with Vail and the other Atrum. The tense standoff was on a knife's edge, and Jet knew that one false move would cause all hell to break loose. Solan was ready to fight, and he sensed she wasn't herself at that moment.

Jet slowly brought up his hands. "Joshia, wait."

She continued to stare at Solan and didn't acknowledge him.

"This isn't what you're here for," Jet continued. "Think about Tetra. Let's just make the swap. Then we can finish this business later."

Joshia continued to stare at Solan, and Jet thought for an instant she would back out of the entire deal. They were outnumbered, even with Cord and Solan, and Jet didn't feel like testing their luck tonight. After a few tense seconds, Joshia straightened and Solan finally relaxed.

"Let's get on with it," Solan said.

"Fine," Joshia said and snapped her fingers.

Jet breathed a sigh of relief.

Brit pushed a slab out of one of their skiffs. Lying on it was the form of a person covered by a blanket. Brit shoved the slab over the rough terrain. It bumped along, and Jet stopped it with his hands. "That's far enough," he said.

Cord returned with Tetra and stopped just in front of the line of Atrum.

Joshia looked at Solan. "Well, what are you waiting for?"

Solan pulled back the blanket and stared in disbelief.

Lying unconscious on the floating slab was a girl about fourteen or fifteen years old.

"Is this a joke?" DiJinn said.

"I don't think so," Joshia said calmly.

"It's okay, Jinn," Solan said.

"How's this okay?" DiJinn replied. "Shouldn't we be lookin' at Albright or Tyberius?"

"The barter was one Atrum for one Lucem," Joshia said. "Figure it out!"

"We accept," Solan said.

DiJinn started to object again, but Solan glared at her, and she clamped her mouth shut.

"Jet," Solan said. "Bring Kamber out."

Jet walked to Solan's skiff and carried Kamber over. She was still pallid and her breathing shallow.

"I don't remember discussing this," Joshia said.

"Maybe Hurse will," Jet replied.

"Do you wish to have Tetra back?" Cord said. "I don't believe Hurse will want to test me again." Cord stared at Hurse, who rubbed his arm but didn't look at him.

"Fine," Hurse said and closed his eyes. Kamber stirred and took a deep breath. Jet watched as her color started to return. He probed her thoughts to confirm she was okay. Once he was convinced, he placed her into a deep sleep and nodded to Solan.

"One more thing, Joshia," Solan said.

Joshia stopped and turned to face her.

"When I find out which one of you is responsible for my sister's death, I'll come after you myself."

Joshia held Solan's gaze. "We tried to help her…I'm sorry things didn't work out. That wasn't our mark, you know me better than that."

"Then help me understand, Joshia," Solan said. Jet caught the slightest hint of anguish in her tone and knew it was a slip she hadn't meant to show. Joshia heard it too.

"All I can say is that she wasn't our mark." Joshia bowed her head and headed back to her skiff.

Cord tapped his forehead. "We release the mental signatures once we're airborne."

Bofisto bared his teeth, the tiny steel daggers glinting in the moonlight. Cord smiled his crooked smile back at him.

The Lucem boarded their skiffs, and Solan loaded the girl in hers.

Jet contacted Solan once he settled in. "What just happened?"

"If you can believe the Atrum, they weren't the ones who assassinated my sister."

"And what do you believe?" Cord asked.

"I can sense that Joshia is telling the truth," Solan said.

"Me too," Cord agreed.

"What do you make of her saying they tried to help her?" Jet asked.

Everyone remained silent until Cord spoke up. "They tried to kidnap Sylvant. Maybe it was meant to protect her instead?"

Solan considered. "I don't know. That seems awfully compassionate for the Atrum."

"And what do you propose we do with this girl?" DiJinn asked. "We just lost our best bartering piece. I know you want to save *all* the children, Sol, but I don't agree with this trade."

"I don't think this is just any girl," Cord chimed in as he focused his thoughts on Tetra, releasing her from his mental signature. "Something tells me this is Shiloe Van Saint."

CHAPTER 24
The Lost Lucem

ΑΒΓΔΕΖΗΘΙΚΛ**Μ**
ΝΞΟΠΡΣΤΥΦΧΨΩ

THE REST OF the trip back, Jet couldn't stop thinking about their encounter with the Atrum. So many things could have gone wrong and almost did. And now they had even more proof that the Atrum weren't behind Sylvant's assassination. On top of that, they had offloaded Tetra, which he was grateful for. And—perhaps the most interesting news of it all—they had finally found Shiloe Van Saint. The Lucem who had been declared a prophet, the most famous painter ever known, who had been missing for over a century, had returned home.

But in what state of mind?

If the Atrum had held her hostage that entire time, what tortures had Shiloe been subjected to? What horrors had she endured? It was apparent she had passed away at least once during that time, and hopefully not at the hands of the Atrum a second time. Jet only hoped she was of sound mind, but they wouldn't know until she awoke.

"Did anyone notice something odd?" Jet asked over the intercom.

There was no answer at first, just radio silence.

"Sybold was missing," Solan finally said.

"Wonder what that means?" Harriet asked. "I thought for certain she would be there tonight."

"I'm not sure what to make of it," Solan answered. "I admit, I was surprised too."

Back at Lyrinthum, Jet kept Kamber in a deep sleep and tucked her into his bed. Then he met the other Lucem to strategize what their next step should be. They sat around the table in the old control room, waiting for Solan to return.

As if on cue, the door to the control room opened and Solan walked in, followed by the young teenager who had once been Shiloe Van Saint. Everyone grew silent as the two paused and looked around. Shiloe touched the back of her chair timidly. "I know this table," she said. "I've seen it before, only…I've never seen it before. How is that possible?"

Solan placed a hand on her shoulder. "I've explained some of this to you already. This is the table I mentioned. That is your chair. Let me apologize for the squalid conditions. We are currently without a permanent home, so this will have to do for now. We had hoped to find you sooner, but you've been missing for over one hundred years."

Shiloe pulled the wooden chair out and sat down. She seemed to have another glimpse as she did. Her blonde hair was pulled back into a long ponytail, and Solan had given her some clean clothes. Shiloe sat patiently, her feet dangling.

"Shiloe," Solan said. "Can we call you that?"

The teenage girl nodded. "I don't have a name, so that one will do. I know you said it's my old name, anyway. I like it."

Solan smiled. "That's good. Can you tell us what you remember?"

Shiloe propped her elbows on the table and rested her chin on her hands. "I've already tried to remember, a lot of times, but things are fuzzy."

"It appears they've scrubbed her memory," Harriet said. "We should've known they'd do that."

"Cord," Solan said. "Do you think you might be able to probe her thoughts?"

"I can make an attempt," Cord said. He had been sitting in his chair meditating and stood. "Shiloe, you will need to grant permission first. It's not something that comes freely."

"Shiloe?" Solan asked. "Are you okay with that?"

The young girl blinked a few times. "Can you remind me again who all of you are? I know we look alike, but so did the others, and they didn't treat me very well."

"Think of us as your family, Shiloe. We have a long history with each other…we're here to help you. You're part of our group, which is known as the Lucem, or the Light. You've been held captive by the other group known as the Atrum, or the Dark."

"Shiloe," DiJinn said. "This is Cord Ledbetter. He's a friend you can trust."

"I'm still confused," Shiloe said. "But if it will help, then okay."

Solan nodded to Cord.

He approached Shiloe and smiled at her. "Try to relax," he said and placed his fingertips to her forehead. He closed his eyes, and Shiloe did the same.

Shiloe slumped in her chair as Cord stood in front of her. After several minutes, he opened his eyes and removed his hands from her forehead. Jet noticed ten impressions on her skin from his fingers. Shiloe remained quiet, her eyes closed.

Cord walked back to his chair and sat down, not saying anything. The others remained silent, and Jet assumed he needed time to gather his thoughts.

DiJinn finally spoke up. "Well?" she asked. "Let's hear it, Cord."

Cord crossed his arms. "She's been utilized as a test subject."

"But, how were they able to relocate her after she died?" Harriet asked. "Seems like we would have heard about it and found her first, at least on a few occasions."

"They had a system for tracking her," Cord said. "Unfortunately, I couldn't glean enough information on how it operated."

"Did you see where they were headquartered?" Booker asked. "Any background information or anything about the paintings?"

Cord shook his head. "Nothing. And probing further might cause harm."

"No hints about Albright or Tyberius?" Annaka asked. "Hopefully they don't have either of them."

"I could detect no knowledge of their whereabouts, but I did witness some of the experiments on her. We should be thankful they scrubbed her memory. I lost track of how many times Shiloe has died at their hands."

Jet didn't think there was much that could rattle Cord, but he was clearly shaken by what he'd seen.

"What is it, Cord," Solan asked. "What experiments? What were they trying to do?"

Shiloe suddenly sat up, her eyes opened wide, and she began to scream.

Solan and DiJinn were next to her instantly. Solan placed a hand on Shiloe's forehead and spoke calmly under her breath. Shiloe went limp and slumped in her chair. Solan looked around the room at them and grimaced. DiJinn's eyes flashed momentarily with anger.

"She's starting to remember," Solan said. "I'm afraid she will begin to remember more as time goes on. I need to spend time meditating with her in Vishmu. That may heal some of the wounds."

"Let me do it, Solan," Annaka said. "She is my warden. I can take care of her. Besides, you have other things to focus on, like the eclipse, which is two weeks away now. We know the Atrum will be there, and if tonight was any indication, things should be interesting."

"What about taking Shiloe through the conversion ritual now?" Jet asked. "Maybe that will help her."

Solan shook her head. "She's still too young. We wait till she's closer to twenty-four, and if our situation gets worse, we'll consider it. Till then, she'll stay close to Annaka."

"Does that mean Shiloe's coming with us to the Century Eclipse?" Jet asked. "You sure that's safe?"

"I'm not letting her out of my sight, especially now," Annaka said.

"We can manage it," Solan said. "Now, let's talk about assignments, posts and strategy. We're going to have our hands full."

Solan stood and walked over to the large window. Next to it was an old holopad built into the wall. She plugged in the coordinates for Revelations Plaza, and a three-dimensional hologram enlarged over their table, fizzled, and then shut down. She kicked the wall with her foot, and the holopad sputtered back to life.

"We're spread thin. There are eight of us compared to the eleven Atrum, unless Sybold doesn't make an appearance again. Should we split up to cover more ground, or go with the safer option like we usually do and pair up?" She pointed at the hologram of Revelations Plaza and the nine stars spaced equally around the perimeter with the massive statue of Albright atop a large dais at the center.

"It's a large area to cover in pairs," Harriet said. "Then again, it's risky to go solo."

Solan considered. "I think there's just too much area to cover in pairs. Ti-Leer can take the portside star, then we place a Lucem at every other star. Booker, Harriet, DiJinn and me. Annaka can take the center with Shiloe."

"What about Cord and me?" Jet asked.

"You two are up above," Solan said. "We have one advantage; we'll be able to see the entire plaza from the underbelly of Chroma. The rest of us are boots on the ground."

"You want us on Chroma?" Jet asked.

"That's right."

"But there's not going to be anyone up there. All the spectators and the Atrum will be on the ground. Chroma isn't even open to the public. It'll be an invite only event. I thought you just said we need all of us to patrol the plaza?"

"I agree with Jet," Cord said. "If there is a disturbance, it'll be down in the plaza. We're short-handed; it might be a miscalculation to place us too far away."

"We need someone to survey from above," Solan said. "You two will relate all information and let us know what's going on below."

"They have a point, Solan," Booker said. "If the Atrum are looking for the greatest area of damage, the plaza will be the obvious target. We need all the help we can get."

"That's why we will have a command center set up," Solan said. "We have to have observation, and I don't trust anyone else. Cord, Jet. You'll have a few trusted aides to help with the equipment."

"Should we even trust aides at this point?" Harriet asked.

"They'll be pre-screened," Solan said. "Annaka can handle that through the university. We can probably trust them more than the Agency at this point."

"Seems like a really safe place to put someone," Jet said. "Are you trying to put me out of harm's way because you think I'm the Skylight Fallout, or are you just upset about Sylvant?"

Solan gave Jet a meaningful glare. "Have I yet held you accountable for that?"

Jet took a moment, then bowed his head. "I'm…sorry, Solan. That was uncalled for. I just hate to think about all of you facing the Atrum while I'm caged up on Chroma. We're outnumbered already."

"You two are the junior members," Solan said. "I know you're more than capable of taking care of yourselves, but this is the assignment. Can I count on you?"

Cord didn't say anything, and Jet could tell he was fuming inside.

"If you think that's our best use, then who am I to argue?" Jet said and held up his hands. "But is our mission to collect Albright's easter egg, or not?"

"Our mission is to protect citizens first, and always has been," Solan said. "Then the key."

"Can't we do both?" Jet said. "If the Atrum get to it first—"

Solan held up a hand. "We don't even know what is going to happen. Right now, we focus on the safety of the citizens first, then the key."

"So, where is Kamber in all of this?" Jet asked.

"She'll be up top with you. I've arranged for a field trip of students to tour Chroma during the eclipse.

Cutter will be there as a guide; I've already talked to him about it."

Jet saw the logic behind Solan's plan. She was putting him as far from danger as possible. And though he still had an assignment to observe and alert the other Lucem in the plaza below, it was menial and somewhat embarrassing. Cord was *only* there to protect him; otherwise, he would've certainly been on the ground with the others. Cord was missing out on all the action because of him.

"Are we all in agreement?" Solan asked.

Everyone nodded, except Cord and Jet.

Shiloe began to stir, and Annaka took her by the arm and helped her to her feet.

"Why don't you get her to a bed," Solan said. "We can start some Vishmu therapy in a bit."

Jet watched as the others left. He wasn't happy about his assignment for the Century Eclipse, even though it made some sense. Stuck on Chroma with the possibility of the others being outnumbered in the plaza below worried him. Solan seemed to be listening to her instincts. Of course, the Atrum were a part of something that would happen during the eclipse, and they all knew it. But Jet felt they were missing something obvious. He was reminded of the time when Solan had rescued him from Sybold. During their trip to Flotsam, she had told him something, and he'd never forgotten it.

The Skylight Fallout

Most people are so preoccupied with their surroundings they can't see what's right in front of them.

CHAPTER 25
Ground Zero: Part 1

ΑΒΓΔΕΖΗΘΙΚΛ**Μ**
ΝΞΟΠΡΣΤΥΦΧΨΩ

OVER THE NEXT month, Solan spent much of her time working with Shiloe and Annaka, meditating with Vishmu to deal with Shiloe's ever-increasing episodes of anxiety. Jet could hear Shiloe in the room next to his, talking in her sleep and occasionally screaming out in anguish at night. She mumbled to herself and stayed in her room most of the time. Solan spent as much time with her as possible, and Annaka rarely left her side. Jet found himself wondering if Shiloe would ever find her way back to the light.

During that time, Jet had also survived several assassination attempts. In fact, the last one had come that week during a mission to Skylight City. A bomb had detonated just a block ahead of him, and only his intuitive voice had guided him in the opposite direction. That voice was something he heard with greater clarity now. He had no doubt that it was the result of his improved training.

Jet also tried to cram in as much training and meditation as possible. He sensed that a great challenge lay before him, and if he wasn't prepared, more people might pay the price. In the evenings, he would hang his cloak on the wall as he practiced. Sylvant's bloodstains glared at him, whispering and taunting him as weak and feeble—her dying thoughts driving him to the brink of his endurance during each training exercise. The dreams persisted too, the ones he'd had so frequently—visions of serpents and prisms. The crushing, suffocating feeling haunted his dreams and at times he would wake in a sweat. He thought about what Solan had told him—the legend of *The Serpent and the Prism* represented a great war, at least that's what Tyberius seemed to believe. Solan felt that was a war somewhere in the near future, though, which meant that Jet needed to remain focused on what was immediately in front of him—the Century Eclipse.

He knew he might die at the Century Eclipse, but he was determined to face this challenge head-on. If he was the true Skylight Fallout, and this was his final chapter, then he would leave nothing behind. He would either find Sylvant's killer or die trying.

However, the week leading up to the Century Eclipse remained oddly calm.

The Lucem kept a close ear on all their channels through Stell, who monitored the chatter around the system. Stell was able to obtain all of the Agency's codes, which allowed them to pry into some additional intel. But they heard very little from the Atrum, and there were no raids from the marauders, other than the assassination attempts on him. Down in the control room of Lyrinthum, most of the Lucem seemed to retreat into themselves, as if in preparation. It all felt eerily reminiscent of his final days at Skylight University and the triclipse. It was the calm before the storm, and the other Lucem felt it too.

By contrast, the rest of the Skylight System was lively and in full party mode. Everywhere Jet went, banners heralded the upcoming Century Eclipse. Businesses granted their employees the day off, and billboards advertised after-glow parties around the system. News stations ran ads nonstop and concerts were planned to celebrate one hundred years of Skylight.

Shops, stores, and companies seemed to be in full holiday mode as well. Families and tourists booked their tickets and hotel rooms in preparation of the big day. The event promised not to disappoint, and Jet felt a nervous anxiety in his stomach, but it wasn't from excitement.

On the eve of the event, Solan asked all the Lucem to scour the site again individually. Even though she had been over and under the site multiple times, she wanted to run one last check. *Search for possible gaps, missed sight lines, oversights where security might be relaxed…anything you can think of,* she had told them.

Jet and Cord waited till midnight, and under cover of dark, they cloaked and made their way to Revelations Plaza through Lyrinthum. They decided to take the nearest tunnel that ran below the plaza, checking it for devices, charges, or traps of any sort. Then up to the plaza, where they split up. Jet checked the edge of the plaza where the authorities had already set up a perimeter. Guards patrolled the area, though he had no issues bypassing their checkpoints.

He scanned the entire area and spent nearly half an hour combing through the center portion. The dais, with the massive statue of Albright, looked to be fine.

Once he was convinced the plaza felt secure, Jet decided to inspect the massive floating time dial above. Normally, ferries were the primary way to access Chroma, but the three large cables that prevented it from floating off had large staircases circling around the outside of them.

Once inside the large spherical structure, a vast series of interconnected decks ringed the globe. Each deck was perhaps fifteen meters wide and was sandwiched between the clear, chrome like outer shell and an assortment of gears and cogs on the inner side. The interior bowels of the intricate clock system spun and chugged, ticking and clicking in unison. A guardrail prevented people from getting too close to the gears but wouldn't have kept someone out if they were determined to hop over. One feature he hadn't noticed before was a clear observation shaft that punched all the way through the entire orb from the top deck to the underside.

It was mesmerizing to stand there and watch the wheels churn. The spinning gears apparently powered some sort of anti-gravitational mechanism that kept Chroma afloat. The amount of thought and expertise that had gone into the planning of the clock was astonishing. Cord had once explained how a simple holographic timer would have sufficed just fine, and the gears of the clock were more or less for show, though they were indeed functional. Either way, it was an impressive array of craftsmanship that harkened back to an era long past where clock makers relied on spring loaded cogs and perpetual motion. There was no electricity or power used to run the clock, which still fascinated Jet. The large tungsten carbide gears with their teeth looked like some ancient torture device, and he felt sorry for anyone who ventured too far beyond the railings.

M

On the day of the eclipse, Jet rose early and met Cord in the control room. The Century Eclipse was set to begin at exactly 12:12 PM that day and would last approximately twenty-four minutes. Solan wanted everyone at their posts early, and with all the crowds flooding into the first belt, it was going to be a chaotic day.

The mood around the system that morning was thick with anticipation. Tourists from all over the system were starting to pile into the plaza to get to their seats nearly five hours in advance. The Parks and Recreation department was there setting up for the festivities, including additional stadium seating, artificial lighting, food venues, music and other forms of entertainment.

The enormous plaza was full of activity already. Above, banners swayed from the underside of Chroma commemorating the historic event. The gigantic floating orb displayed a countdown timer that scrolled around its midsection, and news crews broadcast live from around the plaza.

With just a few hours left, Jet and Cord decided to explore the festivities. Several news stations were already interviewing famous celebrities, and the center of the plaza had tents set up for food and other fun activities. Music mingled with the buzz of excited citizens, and children ran around with balloons. Jet recognized several staff members from the university blaze team and spent some time talking with them. Likewise, Cord chatted with several colleagues from the math department. It felt good to take a break from his worries for just a while and forget about the possible consequences the day might bring. But he had to refocus when he noticed a platoon of recon troops patrolling the plaza. He remembered the threat he'd heard in Harok's secret meeting and knew today could end up in disaster if he didn't stay sharp.

On their way to a ferry, they bumped into Cutter. He and another faculty member were leading a group of about twenty students up to Chroma. Kamber was among them, but Tetra was missing, which didn't surprise him. He had assumed the Atrum wouldn't bring Tetra back, which was why she had gone missing. They were being cautious with her by pulling her out early, whereas the Lucem were trying to do the right thing by leaving Kamber in as long as possible; it was the difference between the two clans. Jet only hoped that waiting for Kamber wouldn't come back and bite them in the end.

The ferry skiff ascended slowly, due to the weight of all the spectators. Chroma was open for tours until the eclipse began, then it was a V.I.P. event only. He found Kamber and leaned against the ferry's railing next to her as she watched tiny prisms of mist dance between the cloud cover. She looked tired, and the purple-green highlights in her hair were tangled. She had added a few more beads, all of them purple in color, in support of Tetra.

"You excited about the eclipse?" he asked. "It's a once in a lifetime experience."

He caught the split second of hesitation on her face when she didn't answer.

"What's on your mind?" Jet asked.

Kamber crossed her arms. "I woke up early this morning with a strange feeling in my head…I don't know why."

"Is it about the eclipse?"

"I'm not sure. I had this awful dream last night… I think it was about death. And now Tetra's been missing for a while. No one's heard anything about her. I went to the police, but they don't seem to be concerned. It's like no one cares that she's missing."

Jet thought about telling her the truth but didn't think it was the right time or place. "Well, I can explain that, but not right now. After the eclipse, alright?"

She nodded. "I just have this strange feeling inside, like something bad is going to happen. Can't you feel it?"

"Yes, I feel it. But we'll be fine up here. Have you been practicing from the book I gave you?"

"Yes. It's interesting, but most of it I don't understand."

"It's okay. Just stay close to Cutter—I mean, Harper. Cord and I will be nearby too."

Cutter clapped his hands as the ferry neared the docking station of Chroma, which was near the bottom of the globe. "We have about an hour 'till show time, folks. Let's make our way up top and get seated."

Jet and Cord walked with Cutter as the group of students talked excitedly.

"You get a good feeling about all this?" Cutter asked.

Jet looked at him. "What do you mean?"

"I overheard you and Kamber. She's nervous. You used to get those feelings a lot, I remember. And when you did, it was usually for good reason. Hell, you haven't talked to me in a while. You concerned?"

"Just keep an eye on the students, especially Kamber. Something tells me we're going to need you before this is all said and done."

"I can manage the students with the help of the other professor," Cutter said and turned to catch up to the students. "Hopefully, this will all go smoothly."

"Hey… Cutter," Jet said and grabbed his arm. "You be careful too."

Cutter looked at Jet for a long second and gave him a playful shove. "Don't worry about me, you've got plenty on your plate."

The group moved slowly, stopping to take pictures as they climbed the decks upward toward the top. The students murmured in amazement at the intricate workings of cogs and gears. The ticking, churning sound filled the space in a whimsical lullaby. Much of the interior was made from all sorts of metals ranging from bronze to platinum, brass and copper, though the gears and cogs themselves were constructed of tungsten carbide for strength.

"Chroma got its nickname from the students some ninety years ago," the other professor said and stopped to point a few things out. "This amazing structure was a gift to the university by the system government. The core of the clock houses a glass tube that punches all the way through the globe. From the top observation deck, you get a perfect view of Albright's statue in Revelations Plaza below."

The group eventually made it to the top observation deck of Chroma. It was a bit breezy, and Jet could see the outer system loops starting to align miles above them in an ominous sort of way. There was a low roar from the audience below, and the sunlight was already beginning to dim from the belts above as they closed in on each other. The aurora borealis around them glowed in an unnatural way, green and turquoise blending together in a way he hadn't seen before. It danced and shimmered like waves of water crashing around the Skylight System's protective atmosphere.

"Thirty minutes," Cutter bellowed over the chatter.

The students milled about, barely able to contain their anticipation. Several clusters of people Jet didn't recognize perused the deck, but they all wore the required access badge like the rest of them, which meant they'd been screened and cleared. Jet didn't like the idea, but it wasn't up to him who was invited to the event.

"It's time to go," Cord said. "We need to be at the control deck soon."

They left the chatter behind and headed down to the lowest deck where the observation equipment had been set up. They would stay there throughout the eclipse and relay activity to the other Lucem below. Jet had gone over the controls and was familiar with it, but the aides the university had brought on board would handle most of the work.

Tourists were beginning to leave Chroma, a mass exodus of citizens trying to get down to Revelations Plaza below before the eclipse began. The wide decks were crowded as Jet and Cord walked. Jet scanned the people around him, searching for anything out of place when someone bumped into him. The girl brushed his arm just enough to cause his skin to prickle. She was heading in the opposite direction as everyone else and at first, it didn't seem out of place. Perhaps she was just hurrying to the restroom or back up to the observation deck for something she'd left behind.

Jet stopped and grabbed Cord's arm, pulling him back. "That person," he said, nodding after the retreating girl.

Cord turned and looked. "Someone you know?"

"I'm not sure. Maybe. I just brushed against her arm and…" he didn't finish his thought and turned to follow her with Cord right behind him.

The girl continued up several decks, then turned and looked casually over her shoulder at them and smiled.

Then suddenly, she vanished.

Jet looked at Cord in shock. "You thinking what I'm thinking?" Jet asked.

"It would appear that we've made an error," Cord said. "The Atrum have plans up here, it seems."

Jet faced Cord amidst the crowded deck with Solan's words suddenly coming to mind.

They had been so preoccupied with their surroundings they hadn't seen what was so obvious to them now. How had they all missed it?

Chroma was meant to be ground zero.

They stepped off to the side and slipped into their cloaks.

Jet reached out to Cord with his thoughts. *You go after the girl. I'll search the inner gears…*

Jet watched Cord move up the stairs and toward the top after the girl. Jet leapt over the rail and landed amongst the spinning gears, careful not to get caught in one. He worked his way inward, following his intuitive voice as he searched.

Eventually he stopped at an area near the very center of the clock. Several large gears convened into this one spot and transitioned down to smaller cogs until it was just one tiny gear. He stood at the linchpin that connected the entire clock system. This one tiny cog looked to be the brain system behind the entire clock mechanism. Some of the nearby gears whirled so fast that he felt nervous standing there.

If these gears were to suddenly let loose…

That was when something clicked inside his head.

There were probably thousands of moving gears inside Chroma. If the clock were to suddenly come apart, anyone caught in the path of the flying shrapnel would be shredded, and there were millions of citizens below. It didn't take a genius to figure it out now. The Atrum were going to use Chroma as a bomb. But did they really want to kill thousands of people? The Atrum were ruthless, but killing people for sport seemed beneath them. It was too petty. No…the Atrum were simply carrying out orders, and it was just as the Backer had said during the secret meeting with Harok…*if I don't get the egg, no one will.*

Jet had to relay the message to Cord immediately. Then, Solan had to be notified.

Jet lengthened out his thoughts, preparing to send a message. But the nearby gears seemed to cause too much interference and scrambled his mental distress call. He needed to get clear of the mechanisms if he wanted to send the signal, and millions of citizens could be in danger if he didn't act fast.

Jet hurled up the decks, leaping from platform to platform. He saw the blur of a cloak; Cord sat atop a gear, scanning the area for movement. Jet tried to contact him again, but the whirring mechanisms still prevented any thought waves from reaching him. With the decks devoid of citizens now, he uncloaked and waved at Cord to gain his attention.

Cord appeared next to him so quickly that Jet almost thought he'd teleported. "I know what they're planning!" Jet had to practically yell to be heard over the droning gears. "Sabotage…at the inner most cog. They're going to use Chroma as a bomb."

"I'm not sure that's even possible," Cord yelled back. "That would require a massive magnetic field of some sort—" Cord trailed off and clapped a hand to his head. "The rare-earth! The Atrum must have built a device to reverse the direction of the gears. Did you notice anything?"

"No, but I didn't stick around long enough to investigate. We have to notify the other Lucem. How long till the eclipse starts?"

"Approximately twelve minutes and twenty seconds now."

"What's the best way to send a signal? These internal gears are causing too much interference."

"The control room, where we're expected to be right now anyway," Cord said. "The second you send it, every Atrum will hear it."

Jet thought about the best approach. One mistake now could be disastrous. "I don't see that we have a choice. We *have* to get a message out and alert the others. Any idea what this device might look like?"

"I have no clue, except that it will be disguised. I assume it will be near the central cog for maximum effect. I can steal more information off an Atrum; that shouldn't be problematic on some of the novices."

"I'm betting there'll be plenty of them up top right now. Five minutes and I can have the distress signal sent."

"You must hurry then," Cord said. "I won't be able to hold them for long."

Jet grabbed Cord by the shoulders. "Look after Kamber first, alright?"

Cord cloaked and vanished.

Jet didn't bother with the stairs, he simply lept over the side rail and dropped three story distances at a time, trying to dodge gears as he fell. In just a few minutes, he had made it to the bottom deck and sprinted over to the control room door. Through the translucent mesh of Chroma's membrane, he could see the shadows of the belts covering the ground in black, approaching slowly and eating up the surroundings. The greenish glow from the borealis lights shifted in the background.

He kicked the door open, and it flew off its hinges.

Inside, all four aides sat slumped in their chairs, and the equipment was smashed and smoking.

To one side of the control suite, something blurry shot from the doorway, trying to flee. Jet reached for it and grasped just enough of its cloak to bring it back into the room. He pulled hard and felt the Atrum tumble backwards, knowing now that it was Hurse.

Hurse swung a fist at him but missed and smashed into the ruined control panel. Jet hooked his arm around Hurse's outstretched hand and hoisted up, bringing Hurse with him. They rolled on the ground of the control room. Jet kicked and missed as Hurse thrust an elbow at his head but broke out a window instead. Jet finally had Hurse by the neck with the crook of his elbow.

Hurse tried to twist around and back out of the hold Jet had him in. He shoved hard, and Jet was barely able to maintain his grasp. Hurse had tremendous strength and nearly managed to break the hold, which would have meant the end for Jet. But he held on with all his strength, squeezing as hard as he could to maintain his hold until Hurse slipped out of consciousness. Jet finally released him and rolled over to catch his breath. He felt a tiny burst of triumph as he lay there, having bested Hurse for the first time; his training had finally paid off. But he didn't celebrate for too long and stood to his feet.

Near the broken window, he could see one of the massive steel couplings that tethered Chroma in place. Jet crawled through the opening, using his cloak to clear the debris. He leapt down the large cable until he was about five meters outside and clear of Chroma. He steadied himself in the rush of wind as he clung to the coupling. The eclipse's shadow overtook him at the same moment he sent his message, willing it toward Solan.

He didn't wait for a response, knowing he'd just alerted every Heliographi in the vicinity. But that was the least of his concerns. He had to get to Cord and Kamber now.

He left the control room and leapt up the same way he'd come down. He jumped and hoisted himself over the spinning cogs in one fluid motion, slowing when he approached the top deck's entry vestibule. When Jet stepped through the airlock, he was completely unprepared for the chaos he witnessed.

He counted three Atrum and hundreds of citizens running in all directions. Fireworks shot up from the deck and exploded overhead, providing intermittent flashes of colored light mixed in with the aurora borealis in a green backdrop. The ruckus around him flashed like freezeframe images in a strobe light. Cutter stood protectively in front of the students as they huddled under the bleachers. Cord was engaged in an intense hand-to-hand battle with Vail, Bo, and Brit. Jet rushed over and slammed into Vail and toppled her. He swept Bo's legs out and took him down to the deck. They rolled around, wrestling each other for the upper hand. Jet relied on his training now, utilizing everything that Solan had taught him. Cord countered Vail and Brit as Jet tried to gain leverage on Bo. He watched as Cord managed to knock Vail to the deck again with a backhand, then grabbed Brit by the neck and spun him around. Then Cord placed his hand on Brit's forehead, causing him to slump momentarily.

Bo stood and Jet backflipped to his feet. Bo's long arms outranged Jet, forcing him in close to get inside his reach. Jet managed to land a few heavy blows on Bo's ribcage, forcing him backwards. Jet worked his way over next to Cord as they faced Bo and Brit.

"I have what I need," Cord said. He was breathing heavily and had a deep gash along his brow and claw marks along his neck.

Cord and Jet turned to face the Atrum when Vail stepped forward. She pushed Kamber in front of her as she glared at them.

CHAPTER 26
Ground Zero: Part 2

ΑΒΓΔΕΖΗΘΙ<u>Κ</u>ΛΜ
ΝΞΟΠΡΣΤΥΦΧΨΩ

SOLAN STOOD AT her post as thousands of Skylight citizens hurried past her. Everyone was rushing to get settled into their reserved spots as the Century Eclipse quickly approached.

She checked her wristband and shook her head. There were less than five minutes till the eclipse, and she hadn't heard a peep from Jet or Cord. She glanced up at the translucent ball floating in the sky. The aurora borealis lit Chroma's clear skin with a ghoulish green that reflected back onto Revelations Plaza. Scrolling across its mid-section was the countdown timer.

The countdown timer, she mused to herself. What was she missing?

Had she made the right decision this time by sending Cord and Jet up to Chroma? Was she being overly cautious, or had her intuition been correct? She tried to put herself in her father's shoes and think what he'd have done. But it was pointless speculating now.

She cleared her head and searched the crowds for the other Lucem. Somewhere far to her left was Booker mixed amongst the throng of citizens. Then DiJinn, Ti-Leer, and Harriet, all spread out around the perimeter of the enormous plaza. Annaka and Shiloe were somewhere in the center, near the statue of Albright. The massive metal monument towered over the crowd like a god gazing up at the heavens. Its right hand grasped a rolled-up set of blueprints, and its left hand faced palm upwards in a gesture of peace.

It had been too long since she'd heard from Jet or Cord. Something was wrong.

It was time to gather the other Lucem and decide what to do.

She was about to move when a gasp went up from the crowd. Miles above Revelations Plaza, the outer belts began to align. She watched as they came together from different angles; the spectacle was breathtaking and silenced the crowd.

The long-awaited Century Eclipse was unfolding.

The combined shadows from the outer belts unified into one black shadow that crept slowly across the campus and toward the plaza. The crowd began to murmur in anticipation as the shadow reached the edge of the plaza and the countdown timer from Chroma neared zero.

Then all hell broke loose.

Solan looked up to see a person clinging from one of Chroma's coupling cables. In her thoughts, she heard a message pass to her, and she knew instantly it was Jet. He had just sent a distress signal, and any Atrum nearby would have heard it, too.

Then the eclipse's shadow plunged everything into darkness.

The countdown timer hit zero with a loud bang, and Chroma's wheels and gears sped up rapidly as fireworks shot out from its top observation deck.

The citizens cheered at first, but then began to run from the center of the plaza in panic. Thousands of Tetrahedron marauders were flooding into the plaza, armed with rail guns and light armor. They kicked and shoved people out of the way while some of the marauders held citizens hostage. The skirmish grew larger near the foot of the statue as groups of elite recon troops and mercenaries raced in that direction. Solan fell in behind them.

When Solan got to the statue, the skirmish had morphed into a full-on riot. Recon troops fought alongside mercenaries as pockets of Tetrahedron marauders slammed into them and forced them back toward the statue's base. Solan looked but saw no signs of the Atrum. Near the statue, Harriet and Ti-Leer stood back-to-back and fought off marauders, trying to clear the way for fleeing citizens. Solan pushed and shoved her way toward the statue and the others.

"What's this about?" Booker roared, holding an injured child in his arms. The lighting from the fireworks added to the chaos surrounding them. Like pulsing strobe lights in every imaginable color, the exploding fireworks echoed around the plaza. The melee continued to spread as more troops joined the fray. Ti-Leer and Harriet disappeared in a crowd of marauders and recon. Booker was forced to set the child down as another group of marauders barreled into them. Soon, they were all fighting off attackers. The Lucem were getting separated and swept away by the surging battle.

"I heard Jet's distress call!" Annaka yelled. Shiloe stood behind her with her hands over her ears. "We need to regroup and get to Chroma!"

"What about all these citizens?" Booker said. "They need our help down here!"

Solan cursed under her breath. Throwing elite recon, mercenaries, and marauders together was an explosive combination. This would result in civilian casualties, no doubt. But there were no Atrum, and now she finally understood why. The Tetrahedron were meant to be a *diversion*. The real battle was up above on Chroma.

How had she not seen this scenario?

Now she was forced to make a difficult decision; help save citizens down here or come to Jet's aid above.

|

Cord left Jet and didn't look back. He jumped from spinning gear to spinning gear, working his way closer to the center of Chroma. He hopped deftly, avoiding the cog's teeth as they came together. The grinding metal would rend flesh and crush bone if he made a mistake. Cord hated to leave Jet alone, he only hoped Jet could buy enough time for himself and the others until he could return.

Cord had the information he needed now…and more. He had easily lifted it off that poor sap, Brit. Hacking past his defenses was child's play, and Brit hadn't even realized it. Cord knew about the rare-earth device and what it looked like. He also knew there were three of them. He had to locate them before they detonated and destabilized Chroma.

Cord stood on the surface of a large, flat gear that churned slowly. He matched its pace as he searched for the rare-earth devices. From what Brit knew, they had been fashioned to appear as part of the clock's mechanism to help camouflage them. The device was simple; its magnetic fields would slowly reverse the motion of the gears and push the inner cog out of place, as if the lynchpin had simply slipped, making the whole event look like an accident.

The inner most cog was small, compared to the other gears, but it was still three meters in diameter. Like the other gears, it was constructed of tungsten carbide to ensure it could withstand all the compression it received; the clock makers had understood that much. What they had failed to see was how easy it would be to sabotage. One little slip would send parts and pieces flying across the entire university with enough force to rip through buildings and hull alike.

Cord finally saw one device and moved closer. It sat next to the spine of the central cog and was about a meter wide with a dull metallic sheen to it. The eclipse had already begun and would end in about twenty minutes. He had until then to disable the devices and prevent Chroma from dropping to the university below.

M

Jet turned to Cord, but he had suddenly vanished. It was now three on one, and he was hopelessly outnumbered. Above him, the last belt aligned with the others; the eclipse was starting, and Cord had twenty-four minutes to find the device and disable it, which meant Jet would have to stall for as long as possible.

Jet gave Kamber a quick glance and could see her trembling. He wished he could reach out and comfort her, tell her everything would be okay. But he would be lying to her if he did.

"Let her go, Vail. I'll give you whatever it is you want."

"Just tell us where Albright's key is," Vail said. "Do it before the others show up, you can save your friends if you do it now."

"What makes you think I know the location?" Jet asked. "Why would I lie? If I knew where it was or how to get it, don't you think I would've already done it? Besides, what makes you think I'm the Skylight Fallout anyway?"

"We have our sources," Brit said.

"Oh, you must be referring to this so-called Backer?" Jet said. "Is that who is feeding this misinformation to you?"

Vail looked at Brit and Bo. "How did you know about this person?"

"I have my sources too," Jet said. "Killing Kamber isn't going to make information magically appear in my mind, no matter what this Backer tells you. I don't know where Albright's key is, and I don't know what it does. But I do have some information that you don't."

"You're lying, Stroud," Vail said and grabbed hold of Kamber by the neck. "I might just kill her right now if you don't tell me what you know."

"Why not just take me and let Kamber go? You wanted to kill me anyway, you said it yourself the last time we met. If it's me you want, here I am."

"Oh, we want you both," Brit said. "And once the other Atrum arrive, we'll take care of those loose ends."

"Why wait for the others? Show me how brave you really are, Brit."

"I think killing Kamber first will be more satisfying," Vail interjected. "You'll witness that first, then we'll see about you."

"The Agency will track you all down," Jet said.

"The Agency?" Vail scoffed. "They're so incompetent they can't even protect their own frigates from those blundering marauders!"

Jet narrowed his eyes. "Did the Atrum fund the raids with the Tetrahedron?"

"No, we only provided the muscle. The Backer funded them and has paid us quite a bit as well. We don't care about the Tetrahedron."

"I thought the Backer was providing mercenaries to fight *against* the Tetrahedron?"

"I don't ask questions, Stroud," Vail said.

"Well, maybe you should, because I think the Atrum are getting played against us."

"Why don't you tell me that information—"

Vail was interrupted by a group of skiffs that materialized from thin air and hovered just over the edge of the deck's platform. Several shadows leapt onto the deck and materialized behind Vail. The rest of the Atrum had arrived.

Jet counted nine, the only three missing were Tetra, Hurse and Sybold; it was nearly the full assortment. His time for stalling was about to end.

"Why, Jet…you're all alone and nowhere to go," Joshia mocked and walked over to stand in front of Kamber.

Jet tried to think what else to do now. He could take a shot at Joshia and maybe land a few good hits on another Atrum before they all got to him. But that would be the end of it. His only hope now was to continue to stall and wait for Cord to return.

"What do you want?" Jet asked.

"The Skylight Fallout, of course," Joshia said. "And here you are. Thank you for showing up, I halfway thought you wouldn't have the courage to do so."

"Jet…what's going to happen?" Kamber asked.

Joshia smiled, and a few Atrum laughed at her.

Joshia's presence seemed darker than before, like a cloud of malice surrounded her thoughts now. Her look of indifference was unsettling. He knew Joshia was a dangerous Atrum, based on what Solan had told him; he probably didn't stand much of a chance against her in a physical fight. Nevertheless, he prepared himself mentally for battle.

Joshia took a step forward just as the entire platform shuddered with a massive shock wave.

|

Cord crept in for a closer look at the device when someone grabbed him. Caught off guard, he spun to see Hurse and shifted just enough to keep him from getting a good grip on his arm. Cord brought his knee up and drove it into Hurse's stomach, then followed with an uppercut.

They rolled across the surface of the large gear as it spun, causing them to slide outward toward the grinding teeth. They both rolled in sequence to avoid being crushed by another gear feeding into it. Cord bent two of Hurse's fingers back and watched his face twist in pain. While he was distracted, Cord headbutted him in his face and his lip split open, spilling blood across the gear. Hurse recovered quickly and pulled Cord by the wrist and flung him across the gear. Cord tumbled and rolled, stopping himself just before sliding over the edge. Below were hundreds of layers of gears, churning away with loud clicking. Cord stood just as Hurse barreled into him, and they both tumbled over the edge to the next tier of cogs below.

"Time's ticking, Cord," Hurse laughed.

Cord smiled his crooked smile. He hated to admit he kind of enjoyed his encounters with Hurse and might have found an equal counterpoint in him. Hurse was devious, which Cord respected, even if the other Lucem didn't. Hurse's strength was his ability to distract. Even now, he was simply trying to slow Cord down and let the clock run out. Cord had no time to waste—he had to disable the device and get back to Jet.

One of the gears suddenly slipped and caused Chroma to shudder violently.

"That was the first of three devices, my friend," Hurse said.

M

Jet steadied himself as the platform stabilized. Everyone waited to see if there were more shockwaves to follow. Bofisto launched himself at Jet, and he braced for the onslaught. But then something huge barreled into Bofisto and knocked him to the deck. Jet turned to see Cutter roll and back toward him and Kamber.

"What are you doing!" Jet yelled. "Stay back, Cutter."

"You told me to keep an eye on Kamber. Well, here I am."

"Cutter. They'll kill you," he said. "Stand back!"

"No way. We fight beside each other this time," Cutter said and raised his fists.

Kamber stepped up beside them. "I can distract them a little, maybe use some of that reading material you gave me."

As Jet, Cutter, and Kamber stood facing the Atrum, another large skiff with the presidential seal on the front of it rose just above the edge of the platform and hovered there. President Harok stepped onto the deck, followed by a platoon of elite recon troops. Behind them stood the hunched figure of an elderly lady and a platoon of mercenary soldiers. The lady hobbled forward with the help of a metal cane, and Jet recognized her immediately. She wore a pair of solar shades and a bright shimmering blouse that glinted in multiple colors.

Fireworks continued to explode above them as everyone waited apprehensively. The Atrum moved to the side as Harok and Lybra stepped to the front.

"Lybra," Jet acknowledged. "Why am I not surprised that you're the Backer?"

"Mister Stroud," she replied. "Ah… we meet again. I believe the last thing I told you was not to play coy with me, it might be the last thing you do. And, well, here we are. It appears that I spoke the truth after all."

"Why are you involved in this?" Jet asked.

"Oh, one might say I'm just a concerned citizen," she replied.

"Right. I'm sure that's why you're lending funds to Harok," Jet said. "You tried to kill me, and you murdered Professor Sylvant. Why, to frame the Atrum?"

"Oh, come now. Why would I do such a thing?" she replied with a wave of her hand. "But now that you mention it…you, and those like you, are a nuisance. Your kind should be eradicated, and I will hunt you all down if it's the last thing I do. The Heliographi are a danger to the entire system. Wouldn't you agree, President Harok?"

Jet turned to face Harok, who stood next to her in his expensive suit and tie and ran his hand through his hair. "Yes, of course, Madam Howling. I couldn't agree more," Harok said and shot Jet a grin.

Jet stared from Harok to Lybra. "How could you do it, Harok?" Jet asked. "We've saved countless lives and have always stood behind the Agency. You've betrayed your office by joining with her. She's playing you on both sides. Don't you see that she's the one paying off the Tetrahedron?"

Suddenly, a second shockwave rocked Chroma. This one was violent enough to send everyone tumbling to the deck.

"Enough talk!" Lybra crowed. She motioned for her troops to move in, and the mercenaries engaged Jet, Kamber and Cutter as the recon troops and the Atrum stood by and watched.

Jet easily fought off the first wave of mercenaries. They surrounded him on all sides and kicked, punched, and barreled into him. Eventually, he was overwhelmed by their sheer number, and he lay pinned to the deck. He glanced at Cutter, who had managed to fight off about half a dozen mercenaries, but he too was soon immobilized. Kamber also struggled but was held by three mercenaries.

"The eclipse is nearing an end. I need that key, Mister Stroud," Lybra hissed. "Tell me where it is, or your friends will die."

Jet looked at Vail, who hadn't moved, but he saw the concerned look on her face as she stared at Cutter. "Vail, tell them!" Jet yelled. "I don't know where the key is. You know that I'm telling the truth!"

Vail remained silent. Even though she held a look of indifference on her face, Jet could sense her concern turning to fear. She was afraid for Cutter.

"I don't believe you," Lybra said. She stepped closer and looked down at him as he lay on the deck. She took her metal cane and held it under his chin. "The legend says that the Skylight Fallout possesses the power to reveal Albright's key. Your symbol is unique! This is your duty. Last chance, Mister Stroud."

Cord had never faced a more slippery opponent than Hurse. He was quick and cunning, somehow able to slide out of the holds Cord placed on him. But Cord finally had him pinned.

Hurse laughed. "It's too bad we're on different sides, Cord. I quite like you. You're clever…but clever never outwits devious."

There was always something more when it came to Hurse, and Cord contemplated probing his mind until Hurse broke down. Cord almost relished that thought. But he had neither the time nor the patience, and Jet was foremost on his mind. He needed to hurry.

Cord brought his elbow down on the crown of Hurse's head, knocking him unconscious, then took a knee to catch his breath. He was tired from all the fighting, yet another ploy by Hurse to slow him down. Hurse couldn't beat Cord and knew it, so he was using the clock to win. But Hurse was also gambling that Cord wouldn't kill him once he'd been bested.

Cord grew angry at that thought, rage overtaking his calm composure.

Why did the Lucem always have to play by the rules when the Atrum didn't?

He lifted Hurse and held him over the edge of the gear.

Why not throw him over? Who would ever know?

No doubt Hurse would have done the same to him, had he lost this fight. Even though Cord was in a hurry, he lingered at the precipice, indecision gnawing at him. If he didn't rid the world of Hurse now, he would certainly regret it later. This Atrum had a habit of sowing chaos, and he would continue to do so.

There was a second shockwave, and this time, Chroma tilted to the portside and didn't correct itself. Cord held on to Hurse and leapt away from the edge. He propped Hurse up against a gear—if he happened to slide over the edge, so be it—and sprinted over to the central cog. Two adjacent gears had frozen now. It appeared there was just one gear left, and when it locked up, the central cog would too; then it was game over.

Cord studied the third device. He had never defused a bomb before, but he had studied schematics. Even though this wasn't a bomb, it was constructed in a similar fashion. He felt confident in his abilities and knew he could do this. In the back of his mind, he heard Jet whispering to him—*remember humility…remember.*

Cord took a deep breath and began.

M

The entire top deck of Chroma listed to the portside now. Jet waited to see if it would correct, but it remained at an awkward angle. He strained with everything he had to break free of the mercenaries holding him down, but there were simply too many of them.

Jet looked up at Lybra, then Harok. "I'm telling you the truth. I don't know where the key is, or how to get it!"

For a brief second, he thought Lybra would listen to reason and release them. But then she nodded to the mercenaries holding Kamber, and they lifted her and carried her to the edge of the platform.

"Wait!" Cutter said. "Lybra, you remember me, don't you? It's been a few years, but I remember you. You're a coward, always hiding behind your guards… a bit of a hag as well."

"Cutter," Jet hissed. "Shut up!"

Lybra walked over and stood in front of Cutter and glared up at him. "Oh, I do remember you, young sir. And I think I warned that you were in over your head. I wasn't wrong about that."

Without warning, she reached over and pulled a long knife from a mercenary's belt and shoved it into Cutter's midsection. Cutter groaned as the mercenaries held him up. Lybra grinned and leaned into the knife until the hilt touched the front of Cutter's T-shirt. She held it there as she stared into his eyes, a slight curl at the corner of her lip, then ripped the blade free and spilled his blood across the deck. Cutter held her gaze as he slumped forward and fell to his knees.

"NO!" Jet screamed as he watched in horror. He struggled to free himself again; he strained to lift the mercenaries as tears flowed down his cheeks. When he glanced at Vail, her expression was vacant, but her eyes brimmed with tears.

The mercenaries held Cutter by the shoulders for a second longer, then they let go, and he fell face first to the deck and lay there.

"It's a shame, Mister Stroud," Lybra said. "You could have saved him. Oh well, on to the next, shall we?" Lybra seemed to hop joyfully over to stand in front of Kamber, the bloody knife held in her hand. "Now, this would truly be a shame. Such an incredible specimen, Kamber Caster…"

"Leave her, please," Jet pleaded. His voice trembled now, but he didn't care. "She has no idea what any of this means."

"Are you starting to remember now, Mister Stroud?" Lybra asked. "Funny how this works, isn't it? Loved ones die, and we suddenly recall things that might have been forgotten? Now, tell me what it is I desire—" Lybra paused mid-sentence and looked toward the entry vestibule. "I don't believe it," she whispered.

Cord stepped onto the deck holding an unconscious Hurse. "Tell them to let go," Cord said. "I'm talking to you, Joshia, if you want Hurse back in one piece."

"You're a brave one, Ledbetter." Joshia took several steps toward Cord. "Are you here to take us all on?"

"If that's what it takes," Cord replied. "I assume you know that Lybra is double crossing you, at least, I hope you're sensible enough to realize that. Why do you bow to her? I assumed no less of Harok, but I am disappointed in how far the Atrum have fallen."

Joshia remained silent, as if trying to probe his thoughts. Then she leapt forward. Cord tossed Hurse at her, and she caught him, which allowed Cord to land the first kick on her cheek.

As Cord and Joshia sparred, Jet took advantage of the distraction and focused all his strength and energy on the mercenaries holding him down. Like Cord had done with the small red ball, Jet concentrated, letting subatomic vibrations move outward from his fists and then explode. With a surge, he lifted himself from the deck, and the mercenaries flew off him and into the air. But almost immediately, more of them pressed in on him, and he backed toward Kamber. He reached out and just missed her outstretched hand as dozens of mercenaries fought between them. Kamber was swept away in the crowd, closer to the edge of the platform. No matter how many mercenaries Jet heaved out of his way, the void was refilled with more.

With just a few minutes left in the eclipse and the sun's corona becoming more visible, a mercenary grabbed Kamber by the arm and threw her over the edge of the platform.

CHAPTER 27
Ground Zero: Part 3

ΑΒΓΔΕΖΗΘΙΚΛ**Μ**
ΝΞΟΠΡΣΤΥΦΧΨΩ

KAMBER GRAPPLED FOR a handhold as she landed on the outside of Chroma's clear shell. But the smooth surface had nothing to grab on to, and she slowly slid down and out of sight before Jet could reach her. Jet heard the crowd let out a collective gasp as she fell to Revelations Plaza below. During the confusion, Joshia had backed away from Cord and stood staring uncertainly after Kamber in what appeared to be shock. Jet managed to move closer to Cord and leaned against him for support. Near the edge of the platform, he stared at Cutter's lifeless body lying in a pool of blood and nearly lost control of his emotions again. He had failed to keep the two most important people in his life safe. The emptiness he felt at that moment was crushing. He was weary from the day's events, and there was little fire left to muster in his soul now. He was nearly spent.

Cord gasped for breath as he leaned on Jet, their backs to the center observation tube's railing as mercenaries surrounded them. Cord's face shone like a sunset of bruises and scrapes, he cradled his left arm, and he could barely stand.

"If it's any consolation, I defused the third rare-earth device."

But Jet barely heard him and felt tears sting his eyes. He took an unsteady breath. "Let's make them pay, Cord… make them pay for Sylvant and Kamber. For Cutter."

"It's impossible odds, Jet. I'm too weak, I'm nearly useless, and there are too many of them."

"This isn't over," Jet said. "Don't quit, I need you to fight with me."

Cord took in a sharp breath and spit some blood onto the deck. "I keep underestimating you…forgive me."

Side by side, they fought and held the mercenaries off for a brief minute until Cord stumbled. Jet moved to steady him from falling backwards and down the observation tube. He let his guard down for just an instant, and the mercenaries piled on top of him. When he glanced at Cord, he had slipped again and was in a fight for his life.

The mercenaries pummeled Jet. He fought, kicked and shielded Cord as he lay on the deck. Jet yelled at him to stand. But before long, he too was on his knees and straining to protect himself. His vision started to fade as he continued to fight. He felt like he was having an out-of-body experience and looked down on himself. There seemed to be another Lucem standing at his side, like a ghost warrior from the past, or perhaps another dimension, Jet wasn't sure. He looked thin, ethereal and was dressed in a Lucem cloak.

Jet and the other ghost Lucem stood over Cord, protecting him and fighting off mercenary after mercenary. The ones that made it past Jet were immediately engaged by the ghost Lucem that stood next to him. He wondered if he were dreaming, or maybe even dead and just didn't realize it yet. He felt no pain or fatigue.

It seemed to go on for hours when Jet was suddenly brought back to the present by someone with glowing yellow eyes whispering to him.

It was Solan.

Jet woke from his trance to see all of the remaining Lucem charging the deck, led by Solan. The mercenaries were forced to turn and face them, and chaos ensued. The recon troops and Atrum stood to the side and watched the fighting until one of the mercenaries inadvertently elbowed Bofisto in the mouth. Bofisto picked the mercenary up and tossed him over the edge of the platform. He was immediately swarmed by more mercenaries, and two of the nearest Atrum engaged them. One of the mercenaries unintentionally kicked a recon troop in the groin, and it wasn't long before everyone on the deck was fighting, wrestling and cursing.

Jet was swept toward Brit and Vail, and together, they fought off the first wave of troops near the center observation tube. Cord and Booker joined Bofisto near the edge of the platform. Sojahn, Myranda and Bo fought off mercenaries alongside Ti-Leer and Harriet. Two Atrum Jet didn't recognize joined Annaka while DiJinn and Hurse stood back-to-back, her red ponytails flailing, and her emerald-green eyes burning in the dim light. She bellowed as she ripped through ranks of troops, casting them to the side and off the platform. Joshia and Solan stood near the bleachers and battled troops together. During the mayhem, the students, who had hidden beneath the bleachers, used the cover provided by the Lucem and Atrum to board one of the ferries and flew off.

The combined ferocity of the Atrum and the Lucem was a sight to behold. But Chroma continued to list to the port side until another massive shockwave ripped through the platform and sent everyone tumbling. A few mercenaries near the center had a hold of Hurse and shoved him when the shockwave hit. The momentum caused him to tumble into the observation tube. Jet tore himself from several troops and managed to grab Hurse's hand. Hurse looked up at him, and there was a look of fear on his face for the first time. Hurse reached out to Jet with his thoughts and sent him a single message.

I know this duty was meant for me now. I deserve this… Tell Tetra I'll see her again someday.

Hurse relaxed his grip and let go.

Jet stared down the observation tube as Hurse plummeted toward Revelations Plaza. The fighting around him continued as he watched Hurse fall. Everything seemed to unfold in slow motion, as if time stood still.

The fighting suddenly stopped just as the eclipse ended. The outer belts broke apart and went their separate directions like clouds dispersing after an intense storm. Sunlight flooded through in blinding God rays and poured down the observation tube, highlighting Hurse's falling form. The light shone down in a perfect axis through the observation tube of Chroma and lit Hurse's body like the tail of a fiery comet. He finally crashed down on the outstretched palm of Albright's statue.

The impact was violent, and Hurse's body lay motionless… lifeless. The statue's hand seemed to be molded perfectly, as if it were intentionally designed for that very moment; the true Skylight Fallout had finally come home to rest.

A vibrant velvet-burgundy light shot from Hurse's body and danced around the plaza, then shot straight up the observation tube and into the heavens above. Then the drawings in the statue's right hand lit up, and something dropped to the plaza below.

"That's it...Albright's easter egg!" Jet whispered. "It's the second phase!"

The nine stars embedded in the paving around Revelations Plaza lit up and began to glow. Each star projected a point of light into Chroma, matching the three-dimensional map of Skylight Cord had created over the last year. But it quickly faded and disappeared.

Then Chroma quivered, groaned, and fell from the sky.

CHAPTER 28
The Skylight Fallout

ΑΒΓΔΕΖΗΘΙΚΛ**Μ**
ΝΞΟΠΡΣΤΥΦΧΨΩ

AS THE CENTURY Eclipse ended, the true Skylight Fallout had been revealed and was now dead, his body motionless in the plaza below.

Phase two of the Prism Effect had been set into motion, the Heliographi Memoirs' location had been revealed, and Chroma was plummeting toward Skylight University.

"To the skiffs!" Joshia roared with a last glance at Solan. The Atrum raced to the edge and leapt to the skiffs hovering nearby.

"Let's move!" Solan yelled to the other Lucem and returned Joshia's gaze. The two remaining ferries hovered in close and stasis ropes lashed out for them to grab on to. Jet helped Cord to his feet and then sprinted over, grabbed Cutter's lifeless body, and hoisted him onto his shoulder.

Vail screamed as Bo dragged her away, tears streaming down her face as she stared after Jet carrying Cutter's body.

The remaining recon troops and mercenaries helped President Harok and Lybra onto the large skiff, and it rocketed away.

Chroma's internal mechanism finally let go. There was an ear-splitting bang, and the globe seemed to disintegrate into a shower of metallic bits and pieces. It took only a few seconds as large gears, wheels and cogs flew in all directions, a few barely missing their ferry. When Chroma hit the ground, it created a huge impact crater in the belt. Shockwaves rocked the ferries and shook them violently for several seconds before they finally stabilized. The buildings around Revelations Plaza swayed, and glass facades were blown out.

"Cord!" Jet had to yell over the rushing wind from the ferry's open bay door. "I thought you disabled the third device?"

"I did!" he shouted back. "Hurse lied to me. He must have planted a fourth one as a backup! It's exactly what I would have done, and I didn't even think to check!"

Jet sat back in his seat and looked down at his friend's lifeless body, and realization finally crashed down on him. The adrenaline surging through his veins during all the fighting had occupied his thoughts. But now, seeing Cutter dead shocked him into a sudden resignation. The wound in Cutter's stomach was so jarring that his mind reeled to catch up. He wiped his eyes with the back of his hand and hunched forward, then buried his face on Cutter's still chest and screamed. He gripped his friend's arms, willing him to move, to take a breath, wanting to see his chest rise for air.

Not again! Please, not this time!

He felt similar emotions racing through him again as with Sylvant. That had been a devastating loss, but this…*this!* Cutter shouldn't have even been there today. Such an irony, as Jet couldn't protect Sylvant, Cutter had been present only because of Solan's request. Cutter's protective spirit would have given his life a thousand times over to save Kamber, but his sacrifice hadn't mattered in the end. Kamber had died anyway. Still, Jet knew that Cutter would do it all again. That thought made Jet's heart ache even more. Cutter had died doing what he believed in the most: protecting those who were weaker. It was his payment in full for the one life he *could've* saved but had always regretted that he didn't: his younger brother, Kedrick.

Jet wondered how long this would go on.

Was he destined to always be in a state of suffering?

Would he ever break free of his dismal existence?

He had lost everyone dear to him. Sylvant, Kamber, and now Cutter.

Jet felt someone sit next to him and wrap their arms around him. When he finally looked up, a pair of bright glowing eyes stared back at him.

It was Kamber.

Jet couldn't speak. His relief at seeing her alive filled him with a happiness that seemed strange, as he struggled with his feelings of grief over Cutter.

M

The two ferries flew in single file over the remains of Revelations Plaza. Even though the diameter of the plaza was nearly a kilometer across, the extent of the damage stretched past it and into the surrounding buildings of the university's campus; a few had even toppled over. A light mist had formed, causing the surroundings to soak up the rain, which darkened the pavement, giving off a musty smell mixed with the acrid scent of burning materials.

The statue and most of the plaza were covered by what was left of Chroma. It sat crookedly on top of the plaza, the lower half of it buried below the ground. Citizens ran around the debris in confusion as the authorities began to arrive. Though most of the citizens had been cleared before Chroma fell, the shockwave had caused some fatalities, it appeared. The Lucem looked on at the destruction and death below. It was a sobering scene as families ran through the wreckage, looking for loved ones. Wails could be heard as the ferries settled down.

"Aliases on, everyone," Solan shouted. "Let's move!"

The Lucem leapt to action, searching for survivors and moving debris. Thousands of wounded citizens lay around the plaza, some more critical than others. Jet couldn't count the dead but guessed it would be in the thousands. First responders were already showing up, and he lent a hand where he could. But it wasn't long before Solan recalled them to the ferries.

They were bruised and battered, but every Lucem was accounted for. DiJinn leaned on Ti-Leer, favoring one leg. Booker had taken a beating, and his forearm looked to be broken. Harriet leaned against the skiff, and Annaka held Shiloe in her arms. Cord had fashioned a temporary sling for his arm out of cloth and stared off into the sky. The look on his face was grim, his eyes seemed to glow a little brighter in the falling mist. Jet knew he was angry with himself for missing the last device, but he wondered if Cord was more upset about Hurse outsmarting him. Cord had finally failed, and people were dead because of it, at least, he assumed that's how Cord would view it. Cord was getting a crash course in humility at that instant. He had never witnessed Cord in this state and wondered how he would respond in the upcoming days. Could he learn a lesson here, or would he fail to take note? Would he reengage? Jet was betting that he would.

Solan stood looking at him with her arms crossed. Everyone remained silent, lost in their own thoughts, waiting for her decision. He guessed that she was fighting her own internal battles at that moment. He'd known she struggled with her choices, trying to live up to her father's high expectations. She had been forced to make difficult decisions and was perhaps learning something Jet had learned a long time ago while leading a blaze squad: making a wrong decision was, on occasion, part of the job. Accept it and move on.

"Jet, you were the only one who saw what happened when Hurse died," Solan finally said. "What can you tell us?"

"The nine stars around the plaza lit up and projected points of light into Chroma. It matched the spherical three-dimensional map of the Skylight System that Cord constructed. Personally, I don't understand why Albright would want to advertise it to the entire system. He went to a lot of trouble to keep it a secret for so long. Anyone who was paying attention now knows the location of Albright's memoirs."

"So, it's bloody information we already had?" DiJinn asked.

"Except… the clue was to be revealed," Annaka said. "Jet, did you see anything else?"

"Yeah, something fell from the statue's roll of drawings when Hurse landed on the palm."

"Must be the easter egg, which is currently buried in the rubble below us," Annaka said. "That's gonna be nearly impossible to locate."

"Doubt it survived," Booker said. "That impact crater destroyed everything around it."

"I suspect Albright went to great lengths to protect whatever it was," Solan said. "Jet, are you sure you were the only one who saw it? No Atrum?"

"I think so," Jet said. "Everyone else was fighting."

"So, it's pretty obvious that Hurse was the Skylight Fallout, I assume?" Kamber asked.

Cord pulled his gaze from the wreckage and looked at Kamber, seemingly trying to focus his thoughts. "It was Hurse."

"Didn't you mention the possibility of two outcomes?" Jet asked.

"There were two Fallouts," Cord said. "I admit, I made a mistake."

"Well?" DiJinn asked. "For crying out loud, Cord. Who was the other Fallout?"

"It was me. I was simply too daft to realize it," Cord said. "I cracked Albright's code, but Hurse paid the sacrifice to set it all in motion. It's very similar to how the first phase played out, except a Lucem had to die for that one while an Atrum was the harbinger. It took the full force of Hurse to trigger the clue. Albright timed it perfectly. A century of planning to align the belts, mixed with the angle of the sun…genius, really—"

"We should be helping with search and rescue," Harriet interrupted. "Skylight citizens need us. We can discuss the rest of this later."

"I hear you, Harriet," Annaka said. "But we shouldn't underestimate the Atrum; Jet's not certain who saw it. They may be out there now, looking for the egg. Perhaps that's why they were so willing to destroy Chroma. They knew Albright's key would survive when everyone else would assume it was lost."

Solan bowed her head as she considered. "We continue with the rescue efforts for thirty minutes, that's all we can afford. Annaka is right, we must find the key. Everyone prepare yourselves; this is a crucial moment for the Lucem."

Solan turned to Jet and gave him a long look. Then she did something that surprised him and the rest of the Lucem. She pulled him into an embrace.

Surprised, Jet didn't know what to do. He simply stood there, realizing that such a gesture was probably difficult for her. But she held on, and he hugged her back, sensing that it was something they both needed. Sylvant, then Cutter…perhaps it was an unnecessary apology from each of them for what had happened to their loved ones.

He felt the other Lucem gather around and place their arms around him and Solan. Jinn was there, then Ti-Leer, Cord, Harriet, Booker, Annaka, and Kamber last, even Shiloe managed to squeeze in between them all.

It was an act that finally brought everything home, not just for him, but for Solan and the other Lucem too. The events of that day, the loss of life, the damage and destruction, and the death of their loved ones. Feeling their combined embrace helped ease his loss, allowing it to slip away for just a moment as he basked in that feeling of love.

Solan eventually let go and spoke softly to him. "We'll talk more later. But right now, you know what needs to be done," she said and handed him a cylinder-like device. "After you're finished, meet us below Revelations Plaza as quickly as you can. We're going to need everyone, including Kamber."

"Where did the other Lucem go?" Jet asked. "The one on the deck before you arrived."

She looked at him in confusion. "There were no other Lucem, Jet. Just you and Cord, until we arrived."

Jet looked at her and blinked. "No, there were several others, they were fighting alongside me. Didn't you see them?"

Solan slowly shook her head. "We don't have time to discuss. Just take Kamber and—"

"Solan, wait," Jet interrupted. "Lybra was the one who ordered the hit on me. She's responsible for Sylvant's death."

"I know, Jet," Solan said with a steady face. He could see her stoic resolve was back for now, but there would be hell to pay soon, and he wondered if Lybra was aware of the fire that would rain down on her.

CHAPTER 29
Lighting of the Soul

ΑΒΓΔΕΖΗΘΙΚΛ**Μ**
ΝΞΟΠΡΣ ΥΦΧΨΩ

JET TOOK KAMBER and guided the ferry into the Clipton Forest and settled it under cover of the trees. Then he lifted Cutter's body in his arms and led Kamber quickly through the woods. It was growing late, and the sun settled on the horizon just as they arrived at Firefly Falls. The roaring of the water in the background was a welcome sound and set his soul at ease as they strolled into the covered glen.

Jet cleared an area and dug out what he could in the rocky shore, then he laid Cutter in the hole and began piling stones on his body. Kamber joined in without a word, and fifteen minutes later, Cutter's body lay beneath the pyramid-shaped tomb.

They stood next to each other, staring silently at the stony grave. Jet was still in a state of shock, not ready to accept what had just happened. His first real friend, *his best friend*, was dead because of Lybra. A feeling he wasn't familiar with stirred inside of him.

Hatred.

He wanted revenge, but that feeling made him uneasy, as if his soul's essence rejected it. The voice whispered to him to be careful. *Avoid that one*, it warned.

Dusk crept forward, causing purple pastel shadows to lengthen out. Green and yellow fireflies buzzed overhead, dousing the canopy above them in a wash of color. Jet noticed how the reflected light seemed to match the color of Kamber's eyes, which glowed brighter than he remembered, and he suddenly knew why. Her impending conversion ritual was near.

"How did you survive?" Jet asked. "I saw you fall; I heard the crowd."

"Solan grabbed me," Kamber said, hugging her arms as she continued to stare at Cutter's grave. "The ferries were coming up at the same time. I was so scared…I've never felt that afraid before. First, all of those Atrum. Then, the fall from Chroma…"

Kamber waited expectantly for him to say something. Jet started to speak but didn't trust his voice when he looked at her. His anger and sadness still lingered, like an open wound trying to scab over—he doubted it ever would.

"Why did you bring me back to this place?" she finally asked.

Jet took a deep breath and managed to steady his voice. "This just seemed like a better place to talk about your next step."

"Next step? Does this have something to do with the conversion ritual you mentioned?"

Kamber looked exhausted, and he was sure he looked worse. It had been a day full of surprises for her, and it was about to get even more interesting.

"Yes, it's time for you to make a decision. I know you're tired, and it's been a tough day for all of us," Jet said.

She returned his gaze. "I'm just trying to keep up. So much has happened today. I understand why we're here, but I don't know if I'm ready, especially after what I just saw. I thought I would jump at the chance to join you, but after seeing those Atrum and all that we faced…I don't know if I can do that again."

Jet held her hands and faced her. "I'm sorry you had to go through that. I felt the same way when it happened to me—I was afraid like you. This is scary; we could die at any time. But you have a family now. The Lucem will protect you. We're in this together, and I'm here for you, always."

"I don't know, everything is still sinking in. I saw people die today. And Cutter…" she trailed off, her eyes brimming with tears as she looked over at Cutter's grave. "He died to save me…he barely even knew me."

Jet took another long moment before he spoke, trying to get his emotions under control again. "Kamber, you have to make this decision tonight. We can't afford to wait any longer. I think you're ready."

Kamber took a deep breath and steadied herself. "What is this next step?"

"It's called the *lighting of the soul*. It was somewhat unpleasant for me when I made the decision. This ritual is what frees your inner light, your Heliographi. Once that happens, you become a full Lucem, and we can start your training. There is no going back after this."

"I understand. Is this training similar to the stuff I've already been practicing?"

"Yes, that's called Vishmu. But now, you'll have full access to dive into it and learn things you never thought possible. You'll need to work hard to protect yourself and others who need our help."

Kamber still looked hesitant. "After what I saw today, I think I'd prefer just to go back to school. But…I know I can't."

"Every Heliographi that has gone through this has faced the same challenges. You're not alone."

"I feel like I need to know more. I'd like to hear the full story before I make this decision, is that possible?"

"Okay. If you can try to relax and trust me, I'll guide you."

She took another deep breath and nodded. "Alright, I'm ready."

"Just have an open mind…literally. Close your eyes and focus on me standing at the end of a tunnel. Lengthen out your thoughts."

Her hands trembled as he held them. He closed his eyes and projected his thoughts to her. She stood at the end of a long tunnel, confused and vulnerable. He let everything he knew about the Heliographi and their history flow to her, and her thoughts began to flow into him as well. He knew in that instant he could share his soul with her and be happy. She seemed to be the missing key, someone who could heal his wounds—his lifelong scars and pain. He could see her soul, too. She lit up like a bright sun, her color was kind and happy…hopeful and forgiving. Her inner light stole his breath away and nearly brought him to tears.

He would die for her, if it ever came to that.

Then, he was back. Standing in front of her and holding her hands. She blushed and looked away.

"I saw you!" she said. "I could see into your soul, Jet! I saw you as you are, who you are. Your…essence? Does that make sense?"

"Perfect sense," he said with a smile.

"You… you've suffered so much. Your parents, your childhood…Sylvant and now Cutter. I felt your pain. It hurts me, here," she said and held his hand to her heart. She wiped tears from her eyes and reached out to hug him.

Jet held her for a long moment.

"We've all been hurt," Jet said. "Sometimes I wonder if it was meant to be. It's like someone chose for us to go through this suffering before we can truly become a Lucem. I know the Atrum go through the same struggles; we're like them in many ways, it's just too bad we're on different paths."

Kamber nodded. "I understand the Heliographi now, thank you."

"Are you ready to do this?"

"Of course, let's don't drag this out any longer."

Jet slipped the cylinder out of his cloak that Solan had given him. "This will sting a bit."

"Can't be much more painful than running a forty-two-kilometer race, right?"

"I don't know, never ran that far. Don't care to either," he said and smiled. "Hold out your right hand."

Kamber did and Jet slid the nail-like device through her outstretched palm. She slumped forward, and he caught her and held her until she awoke.

EPILOGUE 1
The Spy in Plain Sight

ΑΒΓΔΕΖΗΘΙΚΛΜ
<u>Ν</u>ΞΟΠΡΣ ΥΦΧΨΩ

VAIL COULD BARELY contain her rage.

She sat in the skiff, her fingernails digging half-moons into the back of her arms as she rocked back and forth. She couldn't believe what Lybra had done!

Her heart ached for Cutter. But why? She shouldn't have feelings like this, not anymore.

She tried to move past her sadness and turn it into rage. She burned that last image of Cutter into her mind. She would use it for fuel against Lybra.

She had felt brief glimpses of confusion, ever since that night at the university when she'd been converted. At times, the rage inside of her flared so violently it felt like she was seeing the world through a small red window, laden with hate and torment. At other times, she felt as if she'd been reprogramed. A tangle of wiring, crisscrossed and short-circuited, representing her memory and making reality seem distant and hard to access. But when she tried to remember her old self, the rage of a thousand voices would rise up and remind her how weak she had once been…reminded her she was an outcast, an unclean person.

She still wanted revenge on all of them.

And one way or another, she would have it. The people who had once mocked her and looked down on her would pay with their lives.

She wiped tears from her eyes, looked out the window and thought about her broken friendship with Stroud. She'd known, just like all the Atrum, that Lybra had placed a bounty on him. Lybra had even asked the Atrum to do it, but they'd declined. Certainly, they could have, but hunting other Heliographi at the behest of that old hag was not in their interest. They would eliminate the Lucem on their own terms. But when Lybra had approached them about raiding the rare-earth, that was something they *could* get behind. They had built the rare-earth devices to sabotage Chroma, but what were her plans with the massive stockpile of the rest of the stolen rare-earth? That was still a mystery, but the money Lybra had offered was too good to walk away from. It would fund their operations for the next decade. And though the Tetrahedron were loyal to the Atrum, Lybra had the money, and Vail was worried that she might eventually pull the marauder army away from the Atrum.

Had they been played by Lybra? Had she tried to purposely frame them by pitting them against the Lucem? The ambush on recon troops, the accidental death of Professor Sylvant… those had been conducted to *look* like the Atrum. The Atrum had even tried to kidnap Sylvant to protect her, but that had backfired. So much for their 'good deed.' Stroud was probably correct, Lybra was behind those, just like she seemed to be behind everything else right now.

"Did you see it?" Bofisto asked.

Vail turned to look at him. Bofisto had blood on his lips and chin, the razor-sharp steel teeth glinted as he spoke. She assumed the blood was from one of the unfortunate mercenaries he'd fought.

Vail knew everything the Lucem knew. Ledbetter had cracked Albright's code in the paintings. *Brainiac was smart, she granted him that much.* She had been using her old locket to spy on Stroud, that physical connection allowed her to see the Lucem's plans. Though Stroud had only worn her locket on a few occasions, he'd had it on when it counted the most. It was taxing to make that connection, but it was worth the effort.

Now, she knew all of the Heliographi Memoirs' locations, and when they would be revealed. And, thankfully, Stroud had also worn her locket to the Century Eclipse; she knew that Albright's easter egg lie buried beneath the rubble at Revelations Plaza.

"Well?" Bofisto asked.

"I know everything," Vail said.

"Then Hurse did not die in vain," Bofisto said in a low growl. "We'll get our revenge."

"We need to turn back, immediately," Vail said. "The clue is buried in the rubble, and the Lucem will be looking for it soon."

Bofisto radioed Joshia and the other Atrum. Then he maneuvered the skiff into a steep bank and accelerated toward the Clipton Forest. The Atrum hopped out and cloaked just outside the forest's edge. Soon they were in the underground passages and headed toward Revelations Plaza.

"Prepare yourselves," Joshia said as she led the way through the dark corridors. "Our existence depends on finding Albright's key first."

EPILOGUE 2
An Assassin
Two Years Prior

ΑΒΓ**Δ**ΕΖΗΘΙΚΛΜ
ΝΞΟΠΡΣΤΥΦΧΨΩ

TYBERIUS HAD KNOWN Albright's location since the beginning, but he had been so consumed with keeping it a secret that, at times, he questioned if it were fiction or reality. One mental slip and someone might read his thoughts. Even the Lucem he surrounded himself with could catch a stray thought and figure it out.

Would they share that information with others if he asked them not to?

Obviously, they wouldn't. He could trust the Lucem with his life.

But that wasn't the issue. The real danger was if a Lucem were captured or kidnapped by the Atrum. Then the secret was out, and the teenage Albright would be murdered again, or worse. The Lucem would be in a difficult position if that happened. So, he had chosen to keep it all a secret, even from Solan. He had, in fact, lied to her a few times to maintain that secret, and he hated having to do it. He might eventually be forced to leave the Lucem behind in order to protect them.

Since Albright's assassination, the Lucem had been considerably outnumbered. The Atrum were nearly at full strength with just one Atrum left to join them; Tetra Wride. And once they were at full strength, they would begin implementing their plan. Tyberius still didn't know what that entailed, but he assumed it wouldn't be pleasant. He knew what needed to be done…he needed to reset the table. He just hoped he could muster the courage to do it.

Remember, we do this for balance, not retribution, Albright had said.

Sybold was the problem. She alone tipped the balance so far toward the Atrum that it was a mismatch they couldn't overcome. Albright was still too young to convert to a Lucem. But with his help, Tyberius might be able to give the other Lucem a fighting chance.

He had been communicating with Albright for the last several years. The young Albright had been located by Stell. She'd had her full network of informants out in force the very day Albright had been assassinated, and they quickly located him. Albright had secretly been raised in her halfway home. Tyberius had managed to fashion a ring for him—one similar to those issued to citizens on the witness protection plan—by hacking into the program to modify the alias. The young Albright could move around, off the grid.

Tyberius also knew that Sybold had personally been looking for Albright. She would find him without help this time. If the Atrum could bring Albright in and try their conversions on him, they'd have all the Lucem secrets laid bare. That would be the end of the Lucem.

But he and Albright had been planning this for years, and today their effort would succeed or fail. Albright was young, but he was still a genius, and had access to all of his former knowledge throughout the millennia. He was a master, able to see into the future and guess outcomes before they happened, it seemed. Tyberius often wondered if Albright's psyche lived in another dimension while his physical form walked this plane of existence. Regardless, Tyberius was putting all his faith in Albright. They would either both die today, or Sybold would. The events of today would change the course of their feud with the Atrum, at least for the foreseeable future.

Tyberius settled in, his long frame wrapped tight in his cloak as he sat alone at the edge of the main market square of the subterranean bazaar. Shops littered the streets as the crowds bellowed, bartering goods and illegal contraband. He had spent the last several weeks down in this colorful place, leaving traces of himself behind. He wanted to be noticed here. He and Albright had chosen this spot specifically for one reason. Decades ago, Albright had designed the belts and knew things about them that no one else did, and this area was special. He had planned it long ago for one thing in particular—to ambush a killer.

News of his appearance eventually found its way back to the Atrum through their informants, the Tetrahedron marauders. They were the eyes and ears for the Atrum, and their network was vast…and devious. How they had slipped under the Agency's radar for so long was concerning, but Tyberius knew why. The Tetrahedron had infiltrated the Agency and had spies imbedded in high positions.

Tyberius was certain of one thing at that moment. Sybold would come for him tonight. Of course, she would know this was all a trap, but her ego blinded her.

He smiled at that. *Oh, Sybold was beyond dangerous.*

But if the Lucem were to have a chance without him and Albright around—since Albright was still too young to go through conversion—Sybold had to be taken out of the equation. Otherwise, the Lucem were doomed.

She was the source of evil, and she drove the spirit of the Atrum. The serpent, or *wyrm*, within her was a being of legend, and would destroy them all, one by one. She had already tried to do it so many times over the years while Albright had been missing. Thankfully, Tyberius and the other Lucem had managed to keep her at bay, just barely. But Sybold was growing stronger it seemed, and soon they wouldn't be able to hold her off. The legend of the Serpent and the Prism was approaching, but now wasn't the time. It was too soon, and it was up to him and Albright to reset the table, until the time was right.

He waited for hours, until the shops had closed and the bartering had died down to silence. He grew nervous, sweat ran freely down his dark-skinned face, something he hadn't felt in eons. So much depended on this outcome. He could not defeat Sybold, and she knew it too. He was trusting in Albright.

At half past midnight, a wisp of smoke darted through the empty streets and stopped near the edge of the square.

Sybold had arrived.

Tyberius walked out to meet her. She uncloaked, and he did the same. They stared at each other for several minutes before she spoke to him through her thoughts. Tyberius had only conversed with her a few times, but Sybold preferred to communicate this way. Her psychic speech intermingled in multiple voices, each one a different octave and pitch layered on top of each other.

Tyberius imagined this was how a demon sounded and wondered how many possessed her now. Her essence was old, perhaps millennia in age. Her thoughts were chaotic and left him feeling cold and empty. He had to take care that she didn't overwhelm him.

Tyberius. Where is Albright?

Straight to the point, Sybold, he replied. *No time to waste?*

I will torture you and take the information…SHALL I ruin your mind FIRST, Tyberius?…or you can TELL me what I…DESIRE.

If you can get that information from me, then you deserve it, Tyberius said and crouched, ready to fight.

Sybold lifted the sleeve of her cloak and disappeared.

Tyberius wasn't fooled and spun, lifting his arm to block her elbow aimed at his temple. She was quick, and he felt a split second of panic. He had never faced a more dangerous foe. But he recalled Albright's words of encouragement; *Sybold will use brute force against you, but she will not see what a more observant attacker would. She knows this is a trap but will refuse to believe she can be harmed by it; she will ignore it.*

Tyberius had to maneuver her into the right spot before the trap could be sprung. She possessed tremendous physical ability, and he had to get her near the center of the square. If she caught on to his ploy, he was as good as dead. He had to make his movements look natural.

Sybold's attack was relentless, and Tyberius was soon struggling to fend her off. The dusty square crumbled around them, paving cratered and stone structures shook as the two titans fought. Sybold pressed Tyberius, and he began to tire. Tyberius stumbled and fell to a knee. His breathing was heavy, and blood and dirt caked his gray beard. Sybold let out a shriek and hammered down on him with both fists. Tyberius felt his arm give as his shoulder shattered. He let out a groan when his arm twisted, and he fell to the pavement and lay on his back. Sybold stood over him, glaring with her red glowing eyes. Her face morphed and elongated as she seemed to consider her options. The lust in her thoughts made his heart quell.

Tyberius looked across the square and breathed a sigh of relief.

Sybold hesitated.

A teenage boy stood at the edge of the large square. He held a small rail gun. His eyes glowed a bright red, and he smiled at them with a boyish grin, full of mischief, and gave Sybold a wink.

At that instant, Sybold knew she had been outwitted.

She sprinted toward the young Albright, but he was too quick. He pointed the pistol at the stone fountain in the center of the square and pulled the trigger. His aim was true, and the bullet split the top of the stone fountain.

A light sprang from the fountain followed by a loud bang. Then the bottom of the entire square fell out, and the fountain crashed down. Sybold leapt, but too soon, and she had nothing beneath her to gain leverage from. In her excitement at seeing the young Albright, she had miscalculated.

The young Albright tossed a stasis rope out, and Tyberius grabbed it with his good arm. He slammed against the side of the metal wall and hung there, looking down the old, abandoned skylight well as Sybold fell. Her red glowing eyes stared back at him, but there was no emotion on her face as she plunged downward, gravity pulling her toward the system's core like a falling angel. She simply smiled at him and stared, as if memorializing the moment for revenge later. He reached out to her and opened his mind; *a peace offering*, he thought. Not the wisest thing to do, but he needed to understand her feelings as she fell. Her thoughts lashed out at him like a serpent's tongue, babbling and screaming in different languages, some long forgotten. There were undercurrents of ancient memories, some going back to the very beginning of time. Sin and hatred; emotions he could not comprehend, colors he had never witnessed. Death, murder, torture…whispers from other dimensions, clawing and gnashing to get loose. It was enough to drive one mad, and Tyberius quickly snapped their psychic connection closed.

Sybold plunged downward toward the core's red-hot surface, and it slowly blotted her out. Her cloak began to burn, an intense red flame engulfing her, flaring brighter as she fell…

Fell…

Fell…

And disappeared in a brief flash of light.

Thank you for reading The Skylight Fallout. I truly hope you enjoyed it. If you don't mind doing me a small favor, please consider leaving a review on Amazon or your favorite website. Reviews are critically important to a writer's work and help get the word out. Additionally, please consider heading over to the website www.theskylightseries.com and sign up for updates, information and special offers. I'd love to connect with you and talk about this series and hear your thoughts and ideas. Once again, thank you. This would not be possible without your support.

J. Wint

Reviews can be left here:

9 781736 302934